JAZZ ETC.

JAZZ ETC.

John Murray

FLAMBARD

First published in the UK in 2003 by Flambard Press
Stable Cottage, East Fourstones, Hexham NE47 5DX
Reprinted 2003

Typeset by Gainford Design Associates
Printed in the UK by Cromwell Press, Trowbridge, Wiltshire

A CIP catalogue record for this book
is available from the British Library.

ISBN 1 873226 62 4

The author wishes to thank New Writing North
for financial help during the writing of this novel.

Flambard Press wishes to thank Northern Arts
for its financial support.

For Caminha Town Council, North Portugal,
for providing me with my first taste of live Portuguese jazz
(Maja Makaric and her excellent Brazilian sound
at the Largo Turismo, 13 August 2001).

Also for Sue, Di and Katie.
Love and thanks.

THE AUTHOR

John Murray was born in West Cumbria in 1950 and now lives with his wife and daughter in Brampton, near Carlisle. In 1984 he founded the highly acclaimed fiction magazine *Panurge*, which he and David Almond edited until 1996. He has published a collection of stories, *Pleasure*, for which he received the Dylan Thomas Award in 1988, and five novels: *Samarkind, Kin, Radio Activity, Reiver Blues* and *John Dory*. Two of these have been nominated as Books of the Year in *The Spectator*, *The Independent* and *The Observer*, and *John Dory* won a Lakeland Book of the Year Award in 2002, the first novel to be so honoured in this way. He likes jazz and foreign films.

'Jazz is an ocean. Rock 'n' roll is a swimming pool.
I hang out on a lake.'
>   Carlos Santana, interviewed in *The Guardian*,
>   February 2000

'The name of that song was *Spring Song* and it was
written for one of my cats.'
>   John Abercrombie, jazz guitarist, during a
>   Radio 3 concert broadcast in October 1999

'There's an inner force in us, he said. It has to wake
up. Sex, he said, and character. How do you like
that? A genius he was – but I'm pretty well pissed.'
>   Boris Pasternak, *Doctor Zhivago*

'Aw fick, fick, fick, fick –'
>   Vince Mori, drunk at his seventieth birthday
>   party, Chase Hotel, Whitehaven, Cumbria,
>   1990

1

♪♪♫♬

It was a person with an unfortunate surname, Mr Tuatta, who introduced me to jazz, and it happened in that warm and fertile September of 1967. Tom Tuatta started up a regular lunchtime jazz club which undoubtedly revolutionised my life. Yet before very long I was to leave the club in disgrace, after a humiliating scene in which I displayed my dismal ignorance of what this thing 'jazz' was all about. To my amazement Tom Tuatta himself was sneering at me more gloatingly than anyone else. I wasn't at all sure why I felt so painfully shocked but I guessed there was a sound historical reason, if only I could remember what it was. More than a month went by before I eventually recalled how I had doggedly stood by him, my hero Tuatta, when he had suffered his own public shaming five years earlier.

Tuatta was a nervous sardonic young teacher of English whose ancestry was rumoured to be Estonian or Latvian, perhaps even Finnish. Tom himself, though he had an unusual short-tongued lisp, had not a trace of an accent as he had been raised in South London and spoke as well as looked remarkably like the television satirist David Frost. Like that sarcastic young celebrity his hair was expensively gelled and sprung like a mattress a couple of inches at the front. Later, after Frost went out of fashion, he would comb it in a stern and scowling imitation of the composer Igor Stravinsky, of whose ballets and operas he was an enthusiastic fan. In 1961 he had migrated up here with his young wife and three boys to take up a junior post at Solway Grammar School.

A year later he found himself the form master as well as the English teacher of a remarkably unprepossessing outfit known as 1B2. In his class of thirty skinny twitching eleven-year-old West Cumbrian boys and girls he found someone else with an interesting surname, Mori. Mori's first name was Enzo and perhaps that also touched a sympathetic cosmopolitan chord. At any rate he seemed to take to me at once and treated me with an uncondescending playfulness that can still warm my heart as I think of it. Tuatta, as well as relishing the sparring with his brainy sixth formers, was very happy teaching the little ones, the effervescent midgets of the first and second forms who responded to his tolerant lenience and gentle teasing quips by assuring each other that Tom Tuatta really was bloody *great*.

Though even they, even I, his favourite, could not resist the obvious puerile gags about his impossible handle. Most popular and hackneyed of which was the imaginary roll call of his family, as we pictured them gathered together around the Tuatta breakfast table in their rented farmhouse somewhere down the Santon Bridge end of Wasdale.

"Mr Tuatta, Mrs Tuatta… and all the little Tuatts."

How we roared and chortled, and with me, Enzo Gianmaria Mori, cackling louder than anyone else. Because if it wasn't old Tuatta was being mocked, it was that other entertaining foreigner, the diminutive Eyetie with the scraggy haircut and the skew-if tie. I might have been Italian but my nickname was Maori, and I was the constant butt of jokes about spears, war paint, grunts and grass skirts. This raucous fantasy was aggravated all the more by the fact that I showed an improbable brilliance at junior rugby. Five stones wet through explained why I could run like a hare, but it was still a mystery why I was such an expert if reckless tackler. I could bring down wingers and forwards three times my size, I feared nothing as I moved straight in with shoulder muscles taut and powerful as the outspread diggers of a JCB. Despite which, the PE teacher Mr Tovis always laughed as much as the uproarious boys as I tore off down the pitch for an obvious try, and my exhausted opponents, instead of wasting their energy in pursuit, chose to do their hysterical version of a Maori chant.

"Heegaa! Hoooph! Heegaa! Woooph! Eeyaa!"

One drizzly Friday afternoon, I noted with some bitterness, as I sped towards the line, my *own* bloody side was joining in the offputting chorus.

"Maori's done it again," sneered overweight vindictive Bellowes. "What an arrogant little twat he is, sir! I know he's on our side, Mr Tovis, but I'm sick of him hogging the bloody ball. There's no point in us being here if he won't pass it. Why did no one tap his ankles? What, Sissy? Of course you can't get sent off for fouling your own side! Buggerit, he's taking the bloody conversion as well, he's doing a drop kick instead of an ordinary kick, the poncy poncy ponce. Wahee, heegaa, heegaa, splice it, neegaa! Splice it, you miserable Eyetalian get, Tom Tuatta's bloody pet!"

Bellowes was second from bottom in English, which perhaps explained his inordinate hatred for Mr Tuatta. Parsing, précising, parts of speech, clause analysis and grammatical cases made as much sense to Benny Bellowes as Old Persian rock cuneiform or particle physics. Also, whenever we went round the class reading aloud in turn from our set book of *Great Expectations*, Bellowes not only read without any expression but frequently without any sense…

For example when the adult Pip, the London profligate, balefully remarks, *'So now as an infallible way of making little ease great ease, I began to contract a great quantity of debt'*, Bellowes read it:

'So now as… as in falling away and making little easy great easy, I began to contact. I began to contact a great quality of de… of… debbut.'

The original non-Bellowesian text is infinitely rhythmical and sonorous. Like a beautiful phrase in virtuoso jazz, it is poetic, balanced, delicately nuanced, perfect. Which is not to make the false anachronistic extrapolation that Charles Dickens would have liked anything as uncompromising as jazz. As with that shocking contemporary movement, the pre-Raphaelites, he would have probably wanted its exponents jailed. No, Charles Dickens would not have liked jazz at all, but he would certainly have understood it, for in his own way he was indefatigably his own improviser, interpreter and performer. By contrast Bellowes's nonsensical rendition was as hamfisted, discordant and unrhythmical as the uncomprehending listener will confidently tell you contemporary jazz sounds.

Benny Bellowes did not enjoy appearing so incorrigibly stupid at English. As soon as the opportunity presented itself, he got his own back very cruelly on Tuatta. Our gentle and hypersensitive form master ended up being brutally humiliated through the good offices of Benny's older brother Wally, a pitiless bully and petty extortionist who flourished on the back row of 5R. The R apparently stood for Remove, though forty years on I still have no idea what that verb-derived noun properly stood for. At the intuitive level it surely signified that Wally Bellowes should have been swiftly 'removed' from society and banged up into a punitive borstal. Regardless of which, and apropos the younger brother's sense of injustice, Benny was smarting not just because of his inability to distinguish direct and indirect objects or possessive and personal pronouns. He was smarting very painfully from an appalling trick that I, Enzo Mori, had played on him on the very first day at school. As this trick involved the peculiar surname of that same 1B2 form teacher, Tom Tuatta, it inevitably increased the indignation Benny felt towards what he precociously termed 'that lisping Lunnon puff'.

Benny and I both sat right at the back of Tuatta's class, but while I had perfect eyesight Bellowes wore strong lenses and had to strain and squint as he copied off the board. At the start of our very first English lesson, Tuatta told us to write on our exercise books *English Language, Mr Tuatta*, and beneath that *Name, 1B2*. Bellowes had dreamt all the way through this morning's induction given jointly by form master Tuatta and form mistress Wilma Burlap. He had forgotten already what David Frost's double was called, and had no idea how such an idiotic name was spelt. He turned to me and brusquely ordered me to dictate it. Irritated by his piggy boorishness but never imagining he would fall for it, I whispered a ludicrous phonetic version which Bellowes absently inscribed in huge, messy capitals. Meanwhile Wilma Burlap, a volatile and monstrously rouged apparition of about forty, who ought to have gone on to her free period, was shuffling round the aisles making amiable if bullying repartee with the new bugs. At the end of our row she turned to me and said that my funny name Enzo sounded like a kind of washing powder or washing-up liquid. I smiled back sweetly and as she turned towards Bellowes bared my teeth as if about to bite a big lump out of her immense, unattractive backside. She squatted her podgy elbow on Bellowes's desk and amusedly inspected the first ever feat of composition by this ugly little scholar with the oversize glasses.

"What's this?"

Wilma's rouge seemed to go pale or possibly her blood turned so heated it calcined her face mask. She gave an appalled shriek, grabbed the mystified criminal by the ear, and with her other hand flourished the incriminating book. Her outraged haunches thrust out in righteous reproof, she hauled him all the way up to the front and whispered something to Tuatta. Tuatta usually had a pallid, tired complexion but as he examined the exercise book he blushed a fierce purple. Burlap slammed the door behind her as she pushed Bellowes out into the corridor. He was dragged all the way by the ear to the headmaster's office where he broke all records by being caned across the arse before even finishing his very first lesson...

Who but a fool like Bellowes would have doggedly transcribed MR TWATHEAD/1B2? Predictably enough, he tearfully tried to defend himself by blaming the outrage on me, Enzo Gianmaria Mori. But Boss Pendry scoffed his loud disbelief, and said that even if it was true he deserved an extra couple of strokes for such imbecile credulity.

♪♫

Bellowes's horrible revenge against Tuatta came during a lethargic dinner hour. It was a rainy unhappy spring day in those last few weeks before the school finally went with the times and instituted a cafeteria-style lunch. Until then the pupils went to their fixed tables and sat at their appointed seats. Two first formers, Bellowes and Mori, were sat opposite two sullen fourth form girls, both called Agnes, who gloatingly entertained themselves by squinting and grimacing at us and trying to make us cry. A burly sixth former sat at the head of table and dealt out all the helpings. He and the girl prefect at the opposite end gave themselves enough to feed an entire council estate in Whitehaven, while Bellowes and Mori were presented with portions suitable for someone nursing a duodenal ulcer. Before tucking in, we had to wait for the solitary teacher in charge to say grace. Before that could happen, silence had to be called for of course.

That day I was pleased to see it was nervous Tom Tuatta was up at top table. Alone he was supervising approximately four hundred pupils, an ordeal he faced perhaps once every six weeks. Always hesitant and tentative, today he looked exceptionally brittle, more unsure of himself than ever. I felt unpleasantly embarrassed and compromised on his behalf. His facial pallor seemed theatrical, peculiar, unwholesome. Wally Bellowes at the adjacent table had just rabbit-chopped a weeping second former and was loudly scraping his chair. Twitching oddly, Tuatta at his elevated table called for silence with as much light assurance as he could muster.

"Quiet!" he cried.

Unfortunately his voice cracked as he shouted, and it came out as a catlike squeak. Tuatta blushed and struggled to feign a calm insouciance. Half the four hundred pupils laughed in sympathy and the other half cackled their derision. Among the latter, Wally Bellowes managed to look both vacant and calculating as he spontaneously decided to create a more refined and ingenious entertainment. Stealthily and invisibly, by subtle masonic signals to chosen allies at other tables, he succeeded in keeping the guffaws alive and vibrant in the air. He raised his finger like a conductor minus a baton, and held the mockery on a level sonic pitch, a deathless chortle that refused to die. It was as if he was Vaughan Williams or Barbirolli practising a difficult air or round. Tuatta flushed angrily at the nightmarish chorus and snapped:

"*Quiet! Be quiet all of you, will you!*"

With astonishing timing his full-blooded shout produced an after-echo, a shrill repetition of the first soprano squeak. It was Wally Bellowes who had impudently ventriloquised that eunuch's squawk. Tuatta hesitated, glanced at him warily, and considered a public confrontation. He opened his lips for half a second, as he surveyed that five-foot thug. It was half a second too long. His craven fear stood out a mile. Benny Bellowes smirked at the humiliating sight and hissed across to his brother:

"Do it again! He's frightened stiff of you, man. He's scared bloody shitless."

It was true. Tuatta presented the pitiful and unforgivable spectacle of a diffident, sensitive thirty-year-old afraid of confronting a child of fifteen.

"Do it again," urged Benny.

Wally didn't. He had a better idea. He chose the safest mode of vocal retaliation, a vengeful music if ever there was. He started humming. He hummed with penetration, expertise and great intensity. He hummed with his lips shut tight, and no one except perhaps an anatomist, a physiologist, or an ear, nose and throat specialist could have proved that the sound was coming from his invisible vocal chords. As he did so he raised his left hand, the one Tuatta couldn't see, and indicated to his cohorts and janizaries in 5R that they were to follow suit. Within a few seconds the whole of the dining room was alive with a hideously loud and penetrating din. It rose to a great height, to a lofty vertiginous plateau, and stayed there buzzing and droning its nauseating sound. It was a very malign sort of mantra, a rebarbative kind of jazz, an insane imitation of a forest full of monotonal hornets.

"Mmmmmmmm. MMMMMMMM. Mhmhmhmhmh. MHMHMHMHMH."

Four hundred throats were busy assaulting Mr Tuatta, or

rather 399 as I refused to join in the destruction of my favourite teacher. My lip trembled as I felt his blushing shame and I felt my own jot of contempt for the weakness of the man before me. Tuatta by then was pure beetroot, a mass of molten lava, a terrible sight. The whole of Solway Grammar School was mocking him, the whole of the world, the whole of the bloody universe was on the attack. And for what? Even the puniest squirts, even the skinny little midgets of 1B1 and 1B2 were busy humming away, leering and despising his lack of manliness, his putrid inability to wield power. Tuatta paced around his table, his eyes going in all directions, the cowardly sweat on his temples now visible in great drops. He looked like a hunted beast, a bear or a badger, being mercilessly baited. I felt his persecution as if it was my own. Such undiluted, unremitting cruelty. Give them another inch, 5R, and they would tear him to pieces like a pack of wolves. Put Wally Bellowes in a torturer's uniform or a hangman's garb, and he would do precisely anything you ordered him to do.

How long did it go on for? Tuatta went beyond the chromatic spectrum and entered areas of shame normally reserved for murderers and perverts. For a while the purple reverted to white as if in the aftermath of vomiting. Then with renewed vigour, as the humming rose to a new intoxication, the white transformed to a lush magenta. Tuatta stayed quite motionless, hanging his head by his table like some egregious medical exhibit. Benny Bellowes was openly heehawing at the voluptuous sight. Enraged, I began to kick at his podgy ankle and call him insulting names.

"Stop it you ugly, wall-eyed bastard," I shouted. "You four-eyed, squinty-eyed fat get. You bloody brainless little Milky Bar Kid. Did you know that you're as ugly as Torchy, Torchy the Battery Boy?"

"Watch your neck," Bellowes growled in some amazement, kicking me back twice as hard. Then he pointed contemptuously at Tom Tuatta. "Look what your hero's really like, Maori! There's your bloody London pin-up, for what he's worth. If he was a real man he'd come down here and knock one or two of us flying off our chairs. That's what he should do. He should fist Wally in the face and ask his questions later. Why doesn't he do it, the white faced sickly-looking bint? He's not a real man, he's a puff, a nancy, a charlie, a piece of bloody fluff."

"No he's not," I said in a hoarse and feeble voice. "He's just a decent man and you lot... you lot are all just bloody stinking savages."

When, five years later I joined Tom Tuatta's Jazz Club, Benny Bellowes was obviously the first to scoff. Though at seventeen, astoundingly, Bellowes had metamorphosed into a very confident and fashion-conscious young man. His spectacles now were rimless and gracefully hexagonal, and his hair, which he had expensively styled at a lady hairdresser's, danced up and down on his slouching shoulders. He was perhaps no Renaissance prince, but he was certainly no longer plug-ugly. Leaning indolently against a radiator in the corridor, with a dry unbending expression, he derided me roundly. In his limited but eloquent vocabulary he criticised me for my unintelligible, effete, deliberately decadent musical taste. For admiring this spurious and bastardised stuff called 'jazz', that patently went nowhere. This repulsively obscurantist rubbish that made no sense, had no rhythm nor intelligible structure, was incapable of being sung, hummed, whistled, much less enjoyed.

"For me," he finished scathingly, "listening to jazz is like listening to a burst tap running. The sound keeps changing a bit, it whistles and sings and splutters from time to time. But it's of no bloody interest to anyone but a physicist or an audio-engineer."

I answered him stiffly, trying to stun him with words. "What a septentrional philistine you are, Bellowes. The irony is that you know just enough about music to know what you're saying is utter bloody crap."

He looked at me matter-of-fact, flounced his dancing hair, then conceded, "OK, I'll be kind and say it's like listening to something not really musical although technically very complex. It's a bit like listening to the song patterns of a skylark down at Drigg near Sellafield. The sound is all over the place, it's running in ten directions at once, and the pattern is well-nigh impossible to duplicate. But no one in their right bloody mind would want to buy a whole record of something like *that*."

"I would," I said stung. "I would sooner listen to a record of a skylark improvising in 13/4, than the bloody Tremeloes or the Troggs strangling themselves over a 12-bar blues."

Bellowes surveyed me diagnostically. He was aware that I had a girlfriend called Elizabeth, but perhaps there was a crucial element missing from my physiological make-up.

"You should grow up, Mori. You should get yourself into some decent cock-rock."

I flushed if only because I was shocked. "Into *what?*"

"Cock-rock. Hard-on rock. There's no bloody sex as such in jazz, is there? It's more like drizzle or fog or a chronic bloody migraine in my opinion. But heavy rock is another matter, Enzo Mori. The way that the musicians literally ride and hump their guitars, it's the only music that speaks its pure intentions. It's orgasmic bloody sweat that comes streaming off them, not just ordinary perspiration. Jody Grind, Deep Purple, Spooky Tooth, King Crimson, they're all the same in that respect. Cock-rock, Mori, it's a proper musical definition."

By 1967 Bellowes was playing a very proficient bass in a Whitehaven rock band and thus spoke as one who knew. The Jazz Club that he hated consisted of an old Dynatron record player and a rotating dozen LPs from the two thousand strong collection that filled up Tuatta's Wasdale farmhouse. The Club met every Thursday in the lunch hour and was open to sixth formers only. The venue was an upstairs physics lab where a reliable half dozen students lounged against the benches with their hands in their pockets and either tapped their feet or chattered on regardless. Which is to say half of the group were attractive science sixth girls who had no interest whatever in jazz but were keen to have somewhere different to lounge. More to the point, they were lured there not by the bohemian ambience of easy-going Tuatta, but by the magnetic presence of one of the English teacher's favourite drinking mates. Tom Tuatta's closest friend in the school was the junior lab technician, the also alliterative Bertie Batey. Every Thursday handsome, smirking Batey liked to wander along to Tuatta's club from the biology room, after he had consumed his staple lunch of four salami sandwiches. There he would pay scant if any attention to the jazz on the Dynatron, but would enjoy a chinwag with Tuatta and a sly wink and an ambiguous sally with Christine Horsfall, Maggie Endifer or Janette di Palma.

Batey was twenty-five and single and had long sideburns, vivid blue eyes and an obsessively seductive manner. He was great friends with the sixth form science boys such as Bellowes and Mori and genially referred to his employer, their alma mater, Solway Grammar School, as 'The Brothel on the Hill'. He was the living proof of this reputation, for he had recently for a fee of five bob posted me as look out while he copulated and noisily exploded like a pulsar in the physics dark room with the other lab technician, a Mrs Biggie Lancaster. Technically I believe, by the age of seventeen, I must have been guilty of procurement, poncing or pandering.

Everyone has heard the apocryphal story that jazz originally meant 'sex' or less decorously 'fuck'. There was certainly an erotic suggestion rather than an erotic elaboration to those Thursday lunchtimes in 1967. There was a subtle hint, a teasing nuance, of where this thing called jazz might take you, if you were only willing to bend and tease life's sober and complacent rhythms. Bertie Batey, while principally entertaining Tuatta with extravagant anecdotes, would lazily permit the three women his sporadic attentions. The three women would vie with each other to banter with Batey. Baz Storey, one of Tuatta's best English students, would turn up there so that he could be in the mute devotional presence of capricious Christine Horsfall. Naively he assumed she had a serious interest in modern jazz and made painful efforts to emulate the same passion. He also tried to wink and smirk like Bertie Batey but in his case it looked as if he was suffering shell-shock or had damaged frontal lobes. At the end of one meeting he shyly presented Christine with an LP by Dizzy Gillespie and, with a deferential nod to the astonished lab technician, an entire Hungarian salami. Presumably the logical sequence must have been: Bertie Batey likes salami; Christine Horsfall likes Bertie Batey; ergo if I give Christine a catering quantity of salami she will fancy me more than Bertie Batey. Any fool could see the speciousness of that particular syllogism. His face fell as she stared at him aghast. At £4/2/11 it had cost Baz almost an entire month's pocket money. Bertie Batey slapped the thigh of his very tight trouser leg, cupped his mobile mouth and commented on the singular shape of the 'whole' salami. Tuatta hesitated, then made a jocular reference to lingas and Carl Gustav Jung. He assumed only he and Bertie would know what he meant, but I had recently finished reading the complete works of Aldous Huxley and understood both references immediately. I gave Tuatta a calculating smirk and he blushed bright puce for the first time in years.

"I made Tuatta blush," I thought wonderingly, as I walked off down to double physics. "A schoolboy making him blush must stir up painful memories even now. It must remind him of psychopathic Wally Bellowes and the Cosmic Hum. But I still think a lot of Tuatta, and I owe him a great deal for his musical influence. If it hadn't been for him, I might never have learnt anything about jazz. I might never have known my West Cumbrian arse from my West Cumbrian elbow."

I soon realised that the only ones in the Club with a genuine interest in jazz were Tuatta, Enzo Mori, and a dull eighteen-year-old recluse called Dixon Dimmock. Dimmock's three passions in life were canal navigation, radiophysics and Charlie Parker. The Jazz Club attracted a pitiful three out of eighty possible sixth formers, one out of thirty possible staff. Clearly it was esoteric, connoisseur's stuff, and I preened myself complacently as

I realised this music demanded a special type of person with a penchant for the wilfully recondite. Plus of course an unquenchable interest in sex. Plus a seasoned taste for all things exotic or profound, *per esempio* literature, oriental philosophy, Afro-American culture, Islam. And sex, yes, with a steady rhythm and emphatic insistence on the one thing that no one could put a lid on. Whether it be Boss Pendry trying to stop school courtships developing during O or A level years, or Christine Horsfall disdainfully taking the salami from Baz and passing it across titteringly but meaningfully to Bertie Batey. A pledge, an amulet, no less, this great weight of aromatic continental sausage. Spice, flavour, peppercorns, garlic, power and... *sex...* and all stirred up by the anarchic sounds of Forties and Fifties jazz.

What did Tom Tuatta include in that first selection from his farmhouse sitting-room collection? Miles Davis's 1958 *Milestones* was one of the first jazz records I ever heard. With absolute facility it demonstrated how the depths of tender melancholy offered the infallible emotional foil to the frantic world of raging, ranting improvisation. It indicated the complementary and respectful opposite to that squawking, ejaculatory madness. Alliteration was never far away with Tom Tuatta and there was also Sonny Stitt's LP, *Sittin In With Stitt*. Stitt was a massively energetic saxman who risked potential pantomime as well as anarchy, because he employed a jazz *bagpiper* called Rufus Harley on one of its braying tracks. However instead of sounding like shortbread Jimmie Shand music, Harley's piping was groaningly bitterly Balkan and beautiful. There was also Thelonious Monk's *Live at the Five Spot* in that first two-foot pile that Tuatta brought along. One of its tunes was called *Crepuscule with Nellie*. That astonishing title first alerted me to the fact that jazz musicians are not afraid of the oxymoronic limits of the English language. There was also Dizzy Gillespie's *Ooh-Shoo-Be-Doo!* of 1953, as well as *Diz and Getz* from '54. Until now I had never even heard of any of these jazz giants, yet already I wished I had a curt but allusive monosyllabic nickname like Getz or Monk or Bird or Dook.

"Thelonious Mori," I said to myself one drizzly evening as I paraded in front of our bathroom mirror. I blew a cloud of Capstan smoke at my reflection and pretended I was consuming a joint of New York grass. "Enzo Ellington. Dizzy Mori…"

Enzo Mori sounded far too much like an Eyetie ice-cream salesman. This unfortunately was exactly what my father did for a living, and to make matters worse he had made sure that he and I shared the same Christian name. As for music, Vincenzo (Enzo) Mori (aka Mr Softy and later Mr Whippy) was the proud possessor of every single LP made by Miki and Griff, The King Brothers, Ronnie Carroll, Ronnie Hilton and 'the glamorous' Anne Shelton. My father despised my passion for jazz even more than Benny Bellowes, but he despised it as it were selectively. Vince knew perfectly well what real jazz was, and it bore no relation to his son's ludicrous definition. What I classed as jazz he classed as howling wolves, clanking dustbins, screams in the dark, farts in a bucket, and (*pace* the Light Programme's *Music While You Work*) *Music To Slit Your Throat To*. Mori Senior confidently rewrote all musical definitions, defining Dixieland and Trad as the original corpus, *das Ding an sich*, and everything else pretending to be jazz as an infamous abortion. As well as cherishing all the Fifties crooners, Vince Mori bought every foot-tapping record he could find by George Chisholm, George Melly and Chris Barber. Father versus son, traditional versus modern, the quaintest and yet the harshest and most damning of antitheses. You might call it Turgenev, Whitehaven-style. And Vincenzo Mori did not stop at mere theory. In his weekend leisure hours he was a founder member, the clarinettist and occasional tumultuous vocalist, of a Whitehaven traditional jazz band which called itself The Chompin Stompers…

At this point I beg leave to fulminate against the irreparable unfairness of contingency and chance. Holed up here in a remote northern province, before 1967 I might have accelerated my musical education through the handy didactic media of radio and television. For example I might have sat up late and watched Thelonious Monk performing a studio concert on BBC2, had not '625-lines' TV been completely unobtainable in this wind-swept backwater in 1967. Alternatively I might have chanced upon some occasional Gillespie or Miles recordings in among the classical music broadcasts of Radio 3. My transistor radio was a pristine, gleaming pocketsize affair, yet the pitiful bloody thing possessed no VHF band and Radio 3 medium wave reception was quite impossible along the Solway Firth. My father had flung out his old valve radio years ago, and refused to purchase another just so that I could sicken him every night with Bach, Scarlatti and Dave 'grinlikeabagochips' Brubeck. In the local record shops, if you were rash enough to ask for jazz, they assumed you were the son of your father, the Chompin Stomper, and responded accordingly. They proffered you either Kenny Ball, Monty Sunshine, Alex Walsh or Acker Bilk. Once a beaming sixty-year-old Whitehaven sales assistant called Totson seriously hazarded to me that Miles Davis must be snooker-playing Fred's younger cousin, and that Dizzy Gillespie was surely that elderly Blackpool comedian who had been awfully big in the Thirties.

Between the ages of twelve and seventeen, hampered and thwarted by the available technology, I used to lie awake listen-ing to Radio Luxembourg, making do with its top twenty rock. Genetically endowed by Vince with an insatiable appetite for music, I felt painfully starved of important vitamins, but had no idea of how to remedy the loss. I did not know what I was missing, but it was not true to say that I was as happy as a pig swilling in shit. I was sick of the slop I wallowed in but I knew of no alternative. True, I half-admired Cream and Chicago and John Mayall, and all the rest of those white rock bands who humbly plagiarised the elaborations of the great blues guitarists. But having no technical knowledge of music, I could not con-vincingly articulate to Benny Bellowes why I disliked the majority of what I heard. Vaguely I sensed it was because my musical dissatisfaction mimicked the dissatisfactions of daily life itself. Daily life meant the sweathouse of a provincial grammar school whose rhythms were the epitome of a facile spurious harmony.

As in real life I was thoroughly fed up with predictability, hackneyed structures, timeworn routines, lazinesses of ambition and imagination. With most of these Radio Luxembourg records I knew precisely what was coming after the first beat. It was not necessary to be a clairvoyant to anticipate the template of the pattern and to realise that that pattern was banal. Clearly the template needed chucking away and the musician needed to start again from scratch. As a last resort the only thing that could mitigate and thus transform a banal melodic pattern was the sheer intensity of feeling with which it was expressed. Hence a very simple tune when sung by a genius like Stevie Wonder became a real work of art, because of the intense emotional passion of that very gifted and blind singer. The unsung pattern remained sterile and artless, as witness a thousand hellish cover versions, but the spiritual power of the original singer had miraculously infused that simple little pattern with enduring life.

♪♪♪

Just as shame and humiliation inevitably united Tom Tuatta and Benny Bellowes, so shame and humiliation eventually united Tom Tuatta and me. Once upon a time, an eleven-year-old bully had been unjustly caned because he couldn't spell the lisping quasi-foreigner's ridiculous bloody surname. The eleven-year-old bully had also writhed and stammered and gone through purgatory when forced to read out difficult sentences in *The History of Mr Polly*. He would have preferred to have shoved H.G. Wells's hilarious comic euphuism right up H.G. Wells's and/or T. Tuatta's terylened arse. Ditto when required to stand up and define the predicate, the copula, redundance and tautology. Tuatta had never openly mocked one of his very dullest students, but had perhaps let the corners of his mouth indicate a hint of gentle amusement. A year later Benny had lost all sense of proportion and instigated the public ridiculing of Tuatta, while the teacher's cottage pie and chips had turned stone cold in front of him. It was Benny, invisible to all but me, who had egged brother Wally on to destroy the teacher in front of the whole school. If Benny had kept quiet, easily led, semi-moronic Wally would probably have been too indolent to go to such extremes. Ironically, now that he was a grown man and not a member of his Jazz Club, Benny no longer had any need to take Tom Tuatta seriously at all. To my amazement last week I had seen the two of them, Tom and Bellowes, chuckling together over Benny's out-spread copy of *Private Eye*. Tuatta was on lunchtime corridor duty and was cheekily lip-reading it over long-haired Benny's shaking shoulders. Oddly, I felt half-disappointed by the time-bound fickleness of human antagonisms. Nothing ever stood still, I suddenly realised. Clearly yesterday's enmities could be as meaningless as yesterday's news.

My own humiliation came on that last Thursday before the Christmas holidays. It was the only time I had ventured to bring along one of my own records to the Club, partly because I wasn't at all confident of my taste, partly because to date I only possessed two jazz albums. The thirty or so Beach Boys, Beatles, Rolling Stones and Geno Washington Ram Jam Band LPs of my youth now lay gathering dust underneath my mother's antique sewing machine. Of necessity both jazz records had been purchased for me outside the county by one of our lodgers, a flamboyant, sardonic pharmacist called Watson Holland who visited his sister in Newcastle most weekends. LP1 was a *Best Of Dave Brubeck* compilation and LP2 entitled *Bravo Brubeck!* had the same musician playing jazz improvisations of Mexican and Brazilian music. On the cover of the latter there was a buf-foonish photograph of Brubeck wearing an outsize sombrero and an outsize grin. Although the picture looked unarguably ridiculous, it was accepted wisdom that Brubeck was a technical genius and therefore the music inside this absurd cover must be likewise. Because it represented fifty per cent of my jazz collec-tion, I had played it at least fifty times in the last week, just to get to know it thoroughly. As it happened, all but one track on the first side seemed wholly admirable to me. These days I would sooner listen to my bath emptying than listen to the majority of Dave Brubeck, but at seventeen I was an indiscriminate tyro who had yet to develop a connoisseurial musical ear. That one uncomfortable track left me in a considerable quandary. It was a kind of amiable peaches and cream tune, rather reminiscent of the *chili con carne* melodies that had been wont to pulse from the Light Programme ten years earlier. Back in 1957 Mr Edmundo Ros's Latin Band had been all the rage and Vince Mori in particular was an ardent admirer both of Señor Ros and of all Brazilian, Mexican, Cuban dance music... just as long as the timing didn't get too treacherously complex and the lyrics could be sung when in the bath and/or drunk.

"Ay ay ay ay!" we often heard him, when, back from work, he would be booming away lustily in the tub, an open bottle of Guinness or Barley Wine in his soapy hands. *"They all go togezzer like pishish and krim. Ayayayay."*

My specific dilemma was this. Vince Mori had flatly declared to both his son and Watson Holland that twenty out of the twenty-one tracks on those two 'jazz' LPs were absolutely bloody hellish. Only one, he averred, and lordly Holland nodded his muted acquiescence, that tumtytum peaches and cream tune of Brubeck's, was what Vince Mori would categorise as *real* music.

"The rest is blurry caca, son. Like Maestro Semprini fumpin six pianos at once an takin a blurry electric fit. But yes, this one is nice cashy number, Enzo. *Tum, tum, tum, uwah, tum, tum, titty, titty. Ti-tee!* It remind me of a real good old-fashiont professional bandman sound. *Per esempio."* His eyes began to mist up in a fog of near agonising nostalgia. "Good old Desi Arnaz. *I Luff Lussy. Dio*, wasn't she a damn beautiful women goddess as well as a blurry comic sheenyus, really? I Luff... *I Luff Lussy Bowl."*

"Lucille Ball," I corrected scornfully. *"I Love Lucy.* Her husband Desi Arnaz, the bandman who loved her, hence the title of the show, had just run off and deserted the Cuban revolution."

I spoke very pejoratively of the famous émigré bandleader.

At the time, 1967, I happened to be an ardent theoretical communist and believed that Fidel Castro was semi-divine.

Vince stared incredulous at tutting Watson Holland before exploding at my righteous tone.

"Of coss Desi buggert off outer blurry Cubber! Wif damn good reason for a blurry band lidder! Desi knew there be no appy singin an dancin in Huffanna night club if Fiddle Caster was in blurry charge!"

I shook my shoulder-length hair and sniffed at him dismissively. Watson Holland musingly tweaked his luxurious moustache.

"Nobody is allowt to be cheerful an enjoyin imself in front of them misbel communishtas! Go and spen a blurry week in damn Moshcoo, boy, if you don belief me. Bressniff! Krussniff! Micky Yarn! Of coss, *sesso*, sex, is what it's all about, in my opinion. *Sesso, capisci*, Watson? They is all ugly, blurry sulky old men *wif no blurry sex drive left*. That's why they is allus scowlin, frownin an sneerin like Borish Karlop wit a bellyache."

"You're talking completely irrational rubbish," I told him loftily.

The Chompin Stomper narrowed his Calabrian eyes and snapped, "So why, Enzo, all them guffment Rushies wear orrible foonral offercoat an orrible blurry trilby ats? Ever seen Leonardo Bressniff in a jazzy shut?"

"No, but – "

"*Per che* Fiddle Caster allus look like scruffy old tramp in a bush jacket?"

"Hear, hear," agreed Holland in his jaunty officer's mess drawl. "Why indeed, Enzo?"

The cultured pharmacist had grown visibly animated, obviously hopeful of some heated two-generations dialectic. Perhaps we would start some angry father-and-son fisticuffs and that would be a real diversion for an overeducated and understimulated paying guest. However I decided, just for once, to resist a full-scale row. I pointed at my LP on the turntable and said:

"That one track of Brubeck's that you like sounds a bit of a dud to me. A little too bloody singsong tumty-tum, isn't it? It has too much bloody obvious tune for my liking."

But Vince Alfredo Mori wasn't listening. He was still thinking about his succulent little American pin-up, the greatest comic actress in all recorded history. His restless eyes glazed over as his mind rolled back a decade, to the twelve-inch TV he had bought on H.P. out of his first Whitehaven pit wage. He was remembering that scarcely credible pre-Cambrian period before 1961 when Border TV didn't exist, and we had to tune in to the distant Glasgow transmitter of Scottish ITV. Half the programmes regularly disappeared in snowclouds of interference, and you swore your bloody head off as you tried to guess the ending of *Dragnet* or *Mark Sabre* or *Tugboat Annie*, or tried to fantasise the final hilarious folly of madcap Lucille Ball.

"That was real kwalty entertainmen, Watshon. It was real blurry funny, Enzo boy. 'Ree-kee, ree-kee! *Aiuto!* What you done now, honey? Ooh, I just accidental wallpapert myself inside this cubbud! Sob, sob, ugh, ugh. Honey, how many time I tell you to leave men's chops to me? You too fether-braint to do difficult wallpepperin! And where's my blurry tea, as well, bebe? I have to go out with Bub and Chuck to play a portant gig for Thansgiffin Party and how you press my shut when you stuck inside blurry wallpaper?'" He glanced round hastily to check there were no sensitive female lodgers in sight. "I laff till I blurry pisht myself."

"Mm," replied Watson Holland in a guardedly neutral manner.

It worried me considerably and for very good reason that my father enjoyed that peaches and cream track on *Bravo, Brubeck!* By definition, anything this Chompin Stomper enjoyed must have serious structural not to say grave aesthetic faults. Vincenzo Mori from dirt poorest Reggio di Calabria only ever liked the obvious bones, the crude exoskeleton of a thing. By thing I mean *qualunque cosa*, anything and everything under the sun, whether it be music, books, television programmes, the feelings of his wife, the sensitivities of his son, or of human psychology in its entirety.

I should have followed my instincts, hearkened to my doubts, and left the South American medley at home. Instead of which

I chided myself for such cowardice and took *Bravo, Brubeck!* along for that final Thursday meeting. Nonetheless it was important, I felt, to wait until there was an appropriate interlude preceded by a suitably sympathetic, perhaps equally controversial record. It came after Tom Tuatta had finished playing something very advanced for 1967, a track from Stan Getz's symphonic poem based on Lewis Carroll's *Alice in Wonderland*. Getz's sax playing was of course impeccably delicate and plangent, but the accompanying string orchestration sounded wonderfully like Mantovani to me. I didn't dare blurt out my philistine novice's judgement, so instead I strutted across and slapped *Bravo, Brubeck!* on the ancient Dynatron. I hesitated, then thought, buggerit, if he can have his Alice-cum-Mantovani, I can have Edmundo bloody Ros! After that there was no going back, of course. My reckless precocity was to be my brutal undoing. The peaches and cream instantly went into full regalia. I turned apprehensively to face my fellow cognoscenti, to expose myself to their stringent critical scrutinies...

I blanched, then blushed, then blanched again. No one in the room had started to sing *aye, aye, aye, aye* yet, but it was clearly just a matter of time. I glanced round the circle of faces and saw Tuatta and Batey caught in startled, by which I mean frozen, mid-anecdote. Only Baz Storey was nodding his head in sagacious appreciation, as if we were savouring late Hindemith or Dallapiccolla, rather than Herb Alpert's sombreroed cousin. Christine Horsfall was staring at me incredulous, with a finely-tuned derision. I heard her guffaw to Janette di Palma the words 'Alma Cogan', at which Janette tittered back, No, Chris, Dorita y bloody Pepe! Then Maggie Endifer erupted into open laughter and said loudly, Bloody hell, that ice-cream rumpus is even worse than Workers bloody Playtime...

Whispering loudly with Tom Tuatta, the leering lab technician began to whack his leg hilariously. Then, before anyone could stop him, he began to sing the very cruellest Latin American parody possible.

Aye aye aye, the beat is crazy!
Sucu sucu is everywhere!
Aye aye I feel so hazy
Sucu sucu is everywhere!
Aye aye aye, I feel so crazy
Ah, sucu sucu, oh I doan care!

Why did Bertie Batey bother to stop there? Why didn't he carry on and sing, *Fuck you, fuck you, oh I don't care*? In 1965, my drunken father sang that precise bawdy version at a collier friend's silver wedding in the roughest pub in dockland Whitehaven. At once he was ejected by a nineteen-year-old bouncer who treated him relatively gently because of a tasty strawberry cornet he'd bought from Vince Mori in 1959. Personally, I would have loved to have been lifted up by some Jazz Club bouncer and ejected on the spot from this bloody physics lab. Oh, just to run, flee, and escape from their mad hilarity. Meanwhile, the peaches and cream went cascading on and on, way up to the classroom ceiling, and I felt my mortification rise to at least twice the height of Scafell Pike.

I began to blush like a Workington Bessemer furnace. I began to do a Tom Tuatta. I became an impressive incendiary magenta, and beads of sweat started to gather on my temples. Am I perhaps too colourfully exaggerating the severity of my paralysis? Surely all I had to do to extricate myself was walk across and rip the stylus off the record? But I was frozen rigid with shame. My tenuous aficionado's reputation was ruined. I was now a prize laughing-stock and deservedly so. I pretended to be aesthetically at one with the most sophisticated jazz, yet clearly I'd failed to distinguish shite from sugar. Even cloth-eared Christine and tone-deaf Bertie Batey realised as much. Of course I hated and despised myself for blushing so fiercely and for being unable to move my limbs. Why couldn't I just pretend I was off to the toilets, then hide myself away in the school library? With my blessing they could keep my bloody *Bravo Brubeck!* or they could donate it to the nearest charity shop as soon as they liked. In the meantime, they must be wondering what fatuous easy listening pearls I was going to bring along for their delectation next term. Theoretically, I might decide to avail myself of two or three of Vince Mori's timeworn favourites: Marty Robbins, Pat Boone, Frank Ifield, Mrs Mills's Party Medley, The Best of Matt Monro, Andy Stewart's Hogmanay? (Re which succulent roll call, Vince's boozed-up rendition of one of the latter's tartan tracks performed on New Year's Eve 1964 was *Donaldo, Donaldo, poverino, dove your blurry truzzers?*)

In the end it was Tom Tuatta's, not the general derision, that undid me. After Bertie Batey had carolled the last refrains of *Sucu Sucu*, I looked to my sympathetic old teacher for some friendly consolation. I was still crimson with my adolescent humiliation and I must have looked a most pathetic sight. I must have been the very double of Tom Tuatta on the Day of the Terrible Hum. That day, defending Tuatta, I had sworn tearfully at Benny Bellowes and been booted on the shin for my pains. I had risked myself then for the sake of my favourite teacher, so Tom Tuatta should now be repaying me in kind...

I looked to my old hero imploringly. When no one else in 1B2 had known what an interjection was (Fuck! Balls! Arseholes! What ho!) Enzo Mori had. Enzo who always wrote lively and amusing stories that got him an A+ and once even an A++. Twelve-year-old Mori could spell the difficult Wellsian variant of Methusaleh as in Kipps's Old Methusaleh, the whisky that gave him and Chitterlow 'an 'ead and a mouth'. Once upon a time – a mere half a decade ago – Enzo Mori had been Tuatta's affectionate little pet, and Mori the man now sought his needful paternal protection.

Tuatta seemed to hesitate as he concentrated severely on the farcical carnival of the peaches and cream. Then he sighed and pursed his mouth. Then he looked very carefully at me. Then he sniffed.

After what seemed about a century he curled his lip at Enzo Gianmaria Mori with a profound and absolute disdain...

It was the derision that one saves for the condemnation of an absolute fool. It could not be construed in any other light, there was no doubt at all what it meant. Trembling all too visibly in my puny dismay, I stood rejected and abandoned while that paralysingly awful music finally died its unglamorous death.

I blushed yet again, turning redder and uglier than the colour of the creaky old Dynatron...

Tuatta's bottom lip remained curled in an ecstasy of scorn. He might be sneering at me but he was also busily sneering at *tutto e qualunque cosa*. I sensed myself to be the whipping boy for anything and everything that had ever mocked at this diffident and far too sensitive man. I was the youthful scapegoat for all his private and his public humiliations. I was his handy young sacrificial foil, and I burned and writhed at the ugly injustice. From that day onwards, I played my jazz only at home.

2

♪♪♪♫

The door to the back parlour was ajar and from there, just audible, came the dark, delinquent music of the organist Jimmy Smith…

Watson Holland lifted up the tails of his handwoven tweed suit and warmed himself luxuriously against the kitchen coal fire. My mother Angelica Mori was preparing his supper as well as evening meals for eight other lodgers. Watson Holland called this meal his dinner but she being West Cumbrian always called it his tea. I was sat at a cramped corner of the table laboriously doing my biology homework, the illustrated, tabulated differences between symbiosis and parasitism. Suddenly Holland cleared his throat like a restless sheep, always a prelude to some whimsical delivery.

"I am engaged in toasting my *bow-hind*, Mrs Mori," he boomed, like an old Edwardian gentleman actor. And he touched and tweaked his meticulous moustache as he ruminated further.

"Ah," said Angelica distractedly. Grilling nine lamb chops and nine pieces of Cumberland sausage and dividing thirty-six roast potatoes and twenty-seven baked carrots nine ways was no simple matter. "It's cold to the marrow today, Mr Holland."

"Mm?" he smiled politely. "Talking of the old bow-hind, has this thought ever occurred to you Mrs Mori? Half the people that you come across in everyday life say the word *back*side, the stress being on the back, while the other half say back*side*, with the stress being on the side?"

By chance his landlady was bending over her tray of chops and Holland was actually addressing her backside. She was about to turn round blushing but Holland went on stanchlessly.

"The working classes, army instructors, no-nonsense policemen and the like invariably say *back*side. But the middle classes, the anally retentive and the socially ambitious usually go for the final syllable stress. That's only the start of the anomaly however. Apropos the rear end, if you travel abroad as I've done for the last few years, you find that Americans and Australians invariably say the ludicrous bee-hind, while all Britons regardless of class say be-*hind*."

I looked up from my drawing of the tapeworm and gave him a baleful glance.

"Why does no one say bo-*ttom* or bu-*ttocks*?" he challenged us stoutly. "Regardless of class or nationality it's always *bot*tom and *but*tocks. That's why I always say bow-hind, just to show that I regard the whole business of stress and pronunciation as absolutely relative and variable, a matter of individual preference. All this damn silly nonsense in *The Telegraph* letters page about contro*versy* and *contro*versy. Pure dictatorial fascism. It's all as blasted damn relative as Einstein's Relativity."

Mention of physics and Einstein brought him round to me and my zoological drawings. Holland stood over my shoulder and stared at my A level homework.

"Good God," he said disgustedly. "What execrable execution. Is that supposed to be a horse or a duck?"

"Ha, ha. It's a tapeworm."

"You could have fooled me. It's a drawing of my old school tie I believe."

"We're doing parasitism for the next few weeks."

"An apt subject in your case, Enzo Mori. I'm sure your dear father would be the first to concur."

"I'll bet he would," I said.

"Here you are doodling away listlessly at seventeen years old, when arguably you could be doing a useful job and turning an honest penny. Half-heartedly sketching a bloody tapeworm that looks more like a crumpled bandanna. All this money that your conscientious parents have so selflessly sacrificed, one day you realise will need to be repaid to society in full. The first obvious step in your maturation from youthful parasite to independent organism would be to do your biology drawings with some scientific accuracy." He picked up my exercise book and began flicking through it with a stern judicial frown. "Ahah. Cell division. Mitosis and meiosis. First-class stuff. Or is it? All written down to the teacher's dictation I've no doubt. Lists and more lists and scores more of your hideous inky illustrations. I'll bet my life you've forgotten anything he dictated to you three weeks ago. Here, let me ask you a simple question, just to see if any of this pathetic rote learning has had any effect."

"Give it back," I said irritably. "This criticism is very entertaining but – "

"Name me the five stages of meiosis!"

I paused as if stumped. Then slyly rattled off, "Leptotene, zygotene, pachytene, diplotene, diakinesis."

Holland stared at me wide-eyed. "Well. Fancy that. Fancy that, Mrs Mori. Your long-haired pre-Raphaelite son here shows a certain application."

"Good boy," said Angelica, patting my head.

"Nothing to do with me," I said drily. "It was Willy Bollocks and his patent mnemonic aid. London Zoo Pays Double Dividends. Leptotene, Zyg– "

"Who on earth is Willy Boll– ?"

"His biology teacher, Mrs Mori. Such tender, flattering respect the Sixties generation have for their selfless pedagogues. His real name is probably Barlick or Bullock and they couldn't resist the puerile corruption. This Bollocks… this Bullock fellow gave them a memory formula which in technical parlance is called a mnemonic. The variety and efficacy of these peculiar *aide-memoires* is almost as fascinating as syllabic stress and the dear old backside, don't you think? Believe it or not, for my pharmacology final exams in 1949 I devised an exhausting total of 418 mnemonics. Counterproductive in the last analysis because

I needed a subset of twenty-four others to remember all the original bloody categories. You see a good mnemonic, Mrs Mori, has to be as memorably absurd as possible otherwise you would never…"

That was Watson Holland's jazz. That was the way he established a theme, improvised, returned to the original, set off again and stayed out on a branch line of a branch line for the next ten minutes. His two principal compositional modes were monologue narration and the duet of virtuoso two-hander banter. Thirty-five years on I can see how some of our jousts were as lunatically intense as say those demented early Seventies battles between the Czech pianist Jan Hammer and the Yorkshire jazz guitarist John McLaughlin. The fifty-year-old pharmacist and I liked to bombard each other with playfully barbed insults, a standard means of intimacy between all sorts of males of all generations and cultures. Holland was the only son of two Halifax doctors but he had had to do National Service alongside rough Geordie and Lancastrian factory workers which was where he had learnt how to spar so ferociously. My mother had not thrown up her hands in protective outrage when he called me an idler and a parasite because she knew it was just our harmless manner. Watson had been divorced in ugly circumstances ten years earlier and had no children. Though both of us would have hotly denied it, I sometimes functioned as the son he'd never had, and he regularly took me off for a spin in his car to do some birdwatching along the Solway Firth.

My mother disappeared into the dining room, and he stood for some moments in restless silence. Suddenly, amazingly, he began twitching his fleshy lips in exaggerated confusion. He raised his palm frantically in the air as if in melodramatic amateur rep. Astonished, I put down my pencil and waited for him to say, Hark! Finally he cupped his hirsute left ear and his face became a picture of incredulous horror.

"There's something absolutely dreadful running loose in your parlour!"

"There's *what*!"

"I believe it might be an escaped psychopathic lunatic on the run from his doctors! Alternatively a rattlesnake hissing in the grate or a hyena escaped from that little Lake District zoo. You run through pronto, Enzo, and save your dear mother and I'll pop into the lobby and ring for 999."

It took a full ten seconds for the penny to drop. Resentfully I put down my pen and jibbed at him:

"Holland, why mock what you can't understand?"

"Come again?"

"My jazz."

He peered over his shoulder suspiciously. "Jazz? Jazz you say? You mean to say we're talking of some species of music as opposed to amplified cardiography?"

"It sounds nothing like a bloody cardiac machine!"

"You're referring to that piteous wailing sound of someone being broken on the wheel in seventeenth-century London? Is... tell me what particular torture instrument is it we're supposed to be listening to?"

"The organ of course."

"The organ? The organ! *Mein beliebtes Orgel?* Good God, you don't say... the same heavenly instrument that the divine Bach, Pachelbel, Fux and Ritter and Sweelinck and..."

"Jimmy Smith would not despise any of those musicians," I said swiftly. "I don't underestimate any of them either."

"Mighty big of him and you, old son. Jan Pieterszoon Sweelinck can relax and whistle in his grave after your fulsome testimonials. This Smith chap, I assume he is in his mid-fifties and empties dustbins for the Whitehaven and District Corporation? Is that an autographed record of him conscientiously going about his job, commissioned by the Northern branch of the Workers' Educational Association as a documentary testament for the twenty-first century?"

"Bugger off," I said exasperated. "You simply *refuse* to understand."

"Precisely," he said smartly. "Refuse is the accurate verb. I should be a bloody fool to do otherwise. I know in advance that the effort involved is in direct inverse proportion to the probable, by which I mean the bloody certain outcome. Just as I know that, *inter alia*, turning to the visual arts, and I believe I might have mentioned this to you before, that that buffoon Piet Mondrian, the so-called Dutch painter, was not a proper painter but a retarded infant who enjoyed drawing bloody rectangles. I know, Enzo Mori, that I could vainly spend the rest of my life struggling to see art in his monstrous infantilism. Instead I nip over to Amsterdam as often as time permits to look at the works of Mijnheer Rembrandt van Rijn. I don't need, you see, to furrow my eyes or stand upside down to convince myself that old feller-me-lad Rembrandt could bloody well paint. Ergo – "

I passed across the record sleeve and told him, "Jimmy Smith is a black American who is regarded as probably the greatest jazz organist in the world."

"Neither fact cuts any ice with me," he said, handing it back after cursory scrutiny. "He ought to be singing piquant negro spirituals rather than debasing himself and his race on a sacred Baroque instrument. As for his international standing, I'm reliably told that *both* the Nijmegen *and* the s'Hertogenbosch Rectangle Painting Societies regard Piet Mondrian as indisputably the greatest rectangle painter alive or dead. But how can I put it, I'm not categorically convinced by their unanimous judgement."

In the end the left half of my personality, my irritable South Italian half, asserted itself against his provocation. The pharmacist had a richer vocabulary and subtler eloquence than I would ever have, and he was just sufficiently patronising in his sarcasm to make me feel a juvenile fool.

"I refuse to discuss it," I said pompously.

"Oh come come!" he mocked. "A chap of your learning, a young man of your intellectual promise. Joking aside, Signor Mori, you have to cut your teeth on intelligent opposition. Shake all those effeminate cavalier curls out of your eyes and argue your damn case. Stand your ground, man. Debate and die for your cause if need be."

"Jazz isn't some bloody game," I said sulkily. "It's – "

"Of course it is!" he snapped impatiently. "Of course it bloody is. What are two intelligent people supposed to do, fight a duel over this Johnny Smith organ grinder? We were all put on this earth to play as much as to work. Wit and argument and cut and thrust are the spice of bloody life. Lack those and you might as well be dead and buried, as indeed half the current British population apparently are. As a pharmacist do you know what I dispense more than anything? Sleeping pills and tranquillisers. Mogadon and librium and lithium and bloody valium. It's a sad fact that people scarcely know how to play any more, my boy. Look to Shakespeare, if you want any proper guidance in that respect. He loved to play, he was the biggest player ever. Even his tragic plays he leavens with the idiots, the rude mechanicals and the punning artisans. Only a humourless teenage buffoon such as yourself would take himself so seriously as to spurn the challenge."

In this one particular context I did not like being called a teenage buffoon.

"Just let me get on with my bloody homework," I said gruffly.

"Oh diddums," sighed Watson, raising his eyes at such a sullen baby.

That was a grave mistake. I sounded exactly like an enraged Vince Mori hissing *'va' fan culo'*, as I shouted back: "Fuck off will you, Captain Hornblower! Just bloody well leave me alone!"

I regretted this eruption immediately. Watson Holland flinched at the horrible roughness in my voice and he fought off a tiny blush. He blinked at me mournfully, bowed his head at my lamentably hereditary nature, and sat down in dismal silence.

I had broken my promise of course. I had called him that insulting forbidden nickname. It was the spring of 1968 and I hadn't called him Hornblower for at least three years. I was old enough now at seventeen to know what I hadn't known as a mere boy. Then I had had to be brought to heel by deliberate blackmail, no less. Watson Holland had blackmailed me for almost a year, before handing me it back, that murky little secret treasure. I simply hadn't realised that grown adults could be so upset by insulting names. I just hadn't understood that childish taunts could hurt them as much as they could hurt someone like myself.

♪♪♪

Captain Hornblower arrived in this West Cumbrian coastal town from his hometown of Newcastle on a red-hot July afternoon. It was Whitehaven Carnival that day and the endless noisy parade seemed to have been specially instituted to coincide with the arrival of the magnificent swashbuckler. As well as a dozen sumptuously decorated floats there were five or six local brass and 'jazz' bands, including the nationally renowned Flimby Saxhorn Band and the wildly-attired and raucous Ellenborough Jolly Boys.

Looking out of the front window and admiring the waving Rose Queen, Holland said:

"Permit me to park my little bow-hind on your splendid leather sofa, Mrs Mori. No, *signora, per piacere*, please do have one of my own cigarettes instead. Kingsize Dunhills, yes. Though 'Dunghills' would be an altogether apter name for 'em, I suppose. I'm a trained pharmacist, you see, I know altogether too much when it comes to the business of sickness and health. I'm not at all certain these seductive blighters'll lengthen either of our lives. But…"

The bold moustache and the booming address were responsible for the obvious soubriquet. The whole of the household called him Hornblower behind his back, including Angelica Mori who heard it first from Kelsie Mullins, the prim and plump Northern Irish schoolteacher who had been our very first lodger. Equally well they could have called him Ronnie the Air Ace or Archibald Roylance or a dozen other nicknames redolent of the jovial, the seigneurial, the adamant. He had taken over a run-down pharmacy in a little town lying ten miles away and before long had turned it into an impressive upmarket off-license as well as a busy chemist's. He sold expensive alcoholic fruit wines produced in a Highland factory, bottles of peaches in brandy, rare single malts, together with quaint accessories like hip flasks, stirrup cups and pewter tankards. Notwithstanding alimony to Mrs Penelope Holland, he could easily have afforded a decent house of his own. Instead he chose the company and the comforts of a respectable Whitehaven boarding house. As well as teasing the landlord's lad he liked to bamboozle Kelsie Mullins who was also in her late forties. Despite having a fiancé of ten years standing, a bank manager called Hipsley Petty, Kelsie was stiffly prudish and reddened very easily. Even the most tangential mention of the sexual and she coughed her indignation before blushing like an Ulster rose. Captain Hornblower gauged this modesty very finely and liked to embarrass her by reading out carefully-edited snippets from his *Daily Telegraph*. About such blandly innocuous matters as contraception in the Third World, or the sociological consequences of the recent liberalisation of the British homosexuality laws.

It was after one of these confrontations with Miss Mullins that the pharmacist began his outrageous blackmail.

One eight o'clock breakfast, as I was bringing them a pot of tea.

"I wonder what Petty Hipsley would say about this article here, Miss Mullins. Do Cumbrian bank managers knowingly employ homosexuals these days I wonder?"

Kelsie Mullins froze in mid-bite, barely a quarter way through her Cooperative muffin. Inhaling sharply and hastily wiping her lips, she snorted:

"I'm certain he certainly doesn't. I'm sure he'd be the very last manager in the whole world to take on any per... to take on an..."

Holland smirked at her prim tautologies. "But how would he ever know, Miss Mullins? Unless the invert in question were to flaunt himself as an unrepentant nancy, perhaps drop a spot of his talc or rouge on one of the bank's pink withdrawal slips. Wouldn't Petty Hipsley – "

"It's Hipsley Petty!" she growled.

"Is it really, Kelsie? Matrilineal nomenclature no doubt?"

The teacher flushed crimson, evidently assuming he was talking more smut.

"Hipsley must be your fiancé's mother's maiden name?"

"I must be dashing, I must be off. Thank you for the tea, Enzo. My, but your hair is getting terribly long and tangled and altogether scruffy these days. Are you trying to be like another Beatle?"

"Not at all. He aims to be a bluebottle or an aphid, does this chap. Thank you young soldier for my chay chay, chay-wallah. Here's ten bob for the weekend and don't go blowing it all on strumpets and beer. Use it to get yourself a decent bloody haircut instead." Then slyly addressing the back of the teacher's quivering neck. "But how about that interesting word 'withdrawal', Kelsie?"

"Honestly, I really haven't the time to chat now."

"Withdrawal as in 'withdrawal slip'. As in Pettsley's bank, where he may or may not employ a duplicitous blue-rinser. Funny word 'withdrawal', ain't it?"

"I'm sure I wouldn't know," she said, her cheek muscles twitching furiously.

"Old English 'dragan', to draw, and the prepositional prefix 'with'. Why the two should coalesce to mean what they mean is anyone's guess. 'With how contrarious thoughts am I withdrawne', said the poet. Did you know that a common regional use of 'withdrawal' used to be in the sense of 'a place where one withdraws'. Meaning out the back to park the frozen bow-hind on the dear old privy or jakes. However on the same page I've been reading you in *The Telegraph* I see that the dear Pope..."

Kelsie Mullins who came from six generations of Bangor Protestants and was a leading light on the Whitehaven Orange Parade turned white with anger.

"The dear old Pope refuses to sanction even the withdrawal method as a Third World contraceptive means. What do you think of that piece of episcopal folly, young Enzo?"

"For heaven's sake, Mr Holland! I'm sure that a child of his years couldn't possibly have any – "

"Chastity alone, abstinence and damn all else will sort it all out in India, Brazil and China. I should cocoa eh, Miss Mullins? A mature affianced woman of the world like yourself might also cocoa likewise."

"Bfah," spat the horrified teacher, and I didn't know if it was the Pope or Captain Hornblower she was damning.

She flounced out, clumsily knocking the breakfast table so that the teacups rattled wildly. Soon we heard her disputing censoriously with her landlady in the kitchen. My mother laughed disarmingly and said that Mr Holland was just a harmless bit of a tease. There was a stiff silence, then Kelsie's stumbling, prudish attempts to convey a piously concerned indignation. To be sure she could hardly find the vocabulary to avoid certain painfully offensive terms of reference. To describe, as vehemently as she could, this unabashed corruption of Mrs Mori's impressionable young son.

"He doesn't need any corrupting," said my mother drily, after listening to the evidence. "Mr Holland can't be blamed for that, I'm afraid. In any case, they have to do all about methods of contraception for their O level General Studies."

There was an intake of Northern Irish breath and an expression of disbelief at the anarchic sociology, not to say fallen morals, of the English university examining boards.

"They might as well call it O level General Depravity. Why would a fourteen-year-old boy need to dabble in any matters like that?"

Watson Holland tapped my arm and whispered at me in a meaningful way. "Why indeed, Enzo Gianmaria Mori?"

Irritated by his knowing, enigmatic air, I said roughly, "You've made yourself a dangerous enemy there, Watson. You've really put the cat among the pigeons, Captain Hornblower."

The pharmacist winced as he always did at my impertinent honorific. "Please don't call me that name. As I've told you numerous times, it offends me."

"Captain Hornblower," I answered him by way of apology. I was fourteen years old, bursting with adolescent glandular hormones, wired with electricity, and had no control over a great many things.

"Don't!"

"Cap– " I repeated, then stopped dead.

Holland looked at me imploringly. "Don't!"

"Tain Hornblower. There! Everyone has a nickname, so why shouldn't you? You can't really stop me, Captain. You can't stop the rest of the house either. They all call you that behind your back, you know."

"Of course I know," he answered with a quivering mouth. "But not to my face they don't. I don't give a tinker's damn what people say about me behind my back. If you had an ounce of intelligence you'd know there is a universe of difference between third-party gossipping and this face-to-face ridicule."

"They call me 'Maori' at school," I answered coolly, "and they do bare-arse savage dances while they're at it. If I can put up with that day in day out, you can put up with me calling you Captain Hornblower." I paused for sadistic effect. "Captain Hornblower."

"Very well," the pharmacist replied with a weary air. "In that case, I shall have to stoop to your abysmal level. By stooping into the depths of my briefcase, that is."

He bent, unzipped his case, and shuffled through two or three copies of the *New Scientist* and *Scientific American*. I watched him mystified, wondering perhaps if he was going to bribe me with substantial amounts of cash. Which was exactly the reverse of what took place. At length he fished out a battered-looking exercise book with a familiar faded orange cover. A whole second elapsed as my outraged disbelief battled with a mortified horror.

"Give me that!" I said lunging.

He held it aloft and pushed me away none too gently.

"My, my. You seem extraordinarily keen to get hold of this unremarkable object."

"Give it me! It's bloody mine."

"Are you sure that you wish to claim the ownership? If I were you I might be urging an anxious disclaimer. That this old exercise book does not after all belong to Enzo Mori of Solway Grammar School, 2B2. That rather it must belong to some other Enzo Mori of ditto ditto. Pity that you weren't called Johnny Mitchell or Tommy Thompson or Walter Walker or you might have stood a chance. Though your pa's called Enzo Mori as well isn't he? Should we ask him if it belongs to him?"

"Like bloody hell."

"Quite. And the things in question glued into your Religious Education exercise book of all places. Why that one specifically, I ask myself? Personally I think Sigmund Freud and all the rest of them were twopence-halfpence gobbledeygook charlatans. But they would certainly have had a royal field day with the likes of you. And with *this*."

He opened the R.E. exercise book and displayed its centre pages. On the left-hand side a huge pair of naked female breasts were visible sellotaped across my twelve-year-old's handwriting concerning the patriarch Abraham. The words Ur of the Chaldees, Sarah, Isaac and Esau were all inscribed on the page opposite. Odd, truncated versions (Chal, aac, Esa), like some bizarre morse code, decorated the amazing periphery of the mammoth cleavage of nineteen-year-old Amanda Sarandon of Paignton.

"Must-be-loved is what her name means literally in the Latin," said Holland as he scrutinised Miss Sarandon's modest biographic note. "Quite, quite. I see that pin-up Amanda is keen on local history, gardening and chess. As well as sprawling naked and pugnacious on a batiked Indonesian rug. She also apparently goes in for fertilising her bosoms with vast quantities of Baby Bio until they are so enormous they would do justice to a Friesian heifer. Chess, specialist horticulture and the history of bygone Devon. A polymathic Renaissance woman all resplendent in the fetching buff. No wonder you had to put her in your connoisseur's collection."

He thumbed through a few more outrageous pages. "Would you describe yourself as a breast man or a buttock man, Enzo? There seem to be more or less equal numbers of each. Two succulent pairs of provocative bottoms opposite the stories of Samson and Saul. I see that bum the first belongs to Trudy from Droitwich who likes pasta and pressing flowers, and bum the second to Babette from Driffield who goes in for disco dancing to the music of Tom Jones. You have Nina's and Tina's breasts opposite the tale of Ruth and an account of the Babylonian captivity respectively. Nothing at all opposite Daniel and the Lion's Den. Perhaps that would have been too great a sacrilege. I am pleased it's all Old Testament material, for your sake that is. At least these hoary old patriarchs knew what it was to be sexual sinners themselves. David's adultery with Bathesheba almost undid him, but not quite. But what," surveying me gravely, "Mr Mori, what exactly is this unusual theological treasure trove of yours trying to *tell* us?"

I lunged in vain for my exercise book. "It's not trying to tell you anything. It's my private bloody property. It's for my eyes and no one else's. How on earth did you – "

That was the real mystery, much more mysterious than why he was offended by his harmless maritime nickname. For months I had been racking my brains to think of some foolproof hide-away for my explosive pin-up collection, well aware that Angelica Mori was one of the nosiest landladies in the whole of Cumberland. At long last I had lit upon the perfect place. No one on earth, I chuckled to myself, absolutely no one would ever come poking and prying in this unusual eagle's nest. That same evening I had hidden it in the folding recess of the old-fashioned window shutter halfway up the bottom staircase. In mild weather like this all the cumbersome wooden shutters stayed folded away for months at a time. The only possible alternative, I'd decided, was to bury it in the herbaceous border behind the back lawn. But our dog Ricky (named by Vince after the Desi Arnaz TV character) was likely to dig it up five minutes later, in which event all those beautiful female backsides would be covered in weeds and worms. Naturally I'd believed myself entirely unobserved as I'd fiddled with the creaking shutters, but evidently Hornblower had been skulking on the upper landing and had caught me in the enigmatic act.

"What are you going to do with it?" I said sternly. "Nobody admires a blackmailer like you, you know."

"No doubt," concurred the pharmacist drily. "But as you know, I've reluctantly been driven to it by your continued impertinence. In any case, I doubt whether anyone would *admire* the juxtaposition of this torrid little *ars erotica* with the exemplary biographies of the Hebrew patriarchs. They might think I was performing a public service by exposing this photo album to the public gaze."

"But I'm only fourteen," I said defiantly. "If I'm mixed up and confused, it's all perfectly understandable."

"Tell that to your father, Casanova."

"It's half his bloody fault," I said righteously. "If not more than half his fault."

"Giacomo Casanova's? Have you really read his *Memoirs?*"

"No, my father's fault. Vincenzo Mori is South Italian which means I'm half South Italian and that obviously explains a hell of a lot." I held out my hand in a tolerant, accommodating gesture. "Come on. You might at least tell me what you intend to do with it."

"Nothing for the moment," said Watson Holland, after a tantalising pause. "Provided, that is, you stop calling me that insulting nickname. I hate it, I loathe it, I really detest it, and I've told you often enough to stop. Because you won't cease your idiotic taunting, I'm having to force you to do so. I'm obliged to keep hold of your onanist's encyclopaedia as my necessary insurance policy. Now let's say if, after six months – "

"Six months!" I gasped, almost in tears. "But I'll never last without it for all that time!"

The pharmacist guffawed. "You'll need to sublimate your salacious fantasies by some other means. Try writing poetry or learning Russian or playing the flute. It might work, you never know. If after six months you have ceased to call me what you call me, I shall give you back your seedy little notebook."

That night I lay in my bed without my orange exercise book. It was the first time in a month it hadn't been my chosen bedside companion, my literary bedfellow, and I ached and pined for its comforting pages. Where others might have been moderately depressed without their copy of *Argosy*, *The Saturday Book*, or *Constable's Winter Tales*, separated from my old R.E. notebook I felt deprived of life itself. In the bedroom adjacent Vince Mori could be heard playing one of his 45s on one of his three mono record players. In my time I have met several people who love their radios so much they have one in every room of the house, but in 1964 I knew of no one else who had a Dansette gramophone in his parlour, his bedroom and his outside workshop. Vince was lying fully dressed on his bed playing Acker Bilk's *Stranger On The Shore* and loudly humming – or was it softly groaning? – the sweetly melancholy tune. Not so long ago, to my father's crowing delight, Bilk's tune had been Number One in the British charts. I was only fourteen and knew nothing of jazz or of musical notation, and yet I sensed, ever so impalpably, that the bowler-hatted genius left something deep inside me unexplored. I preferred the lachrymose falsetto harmonies of the Rocking Berries, the Ivy League, the Bee Gees and the Beach Boys, though even they, I also dimly realised, all left something in me unexplored.

Suddenly I recollected something that had me leaping out of bed with excitement. I remembered the obvious fact that although I lacked my orange exercise book, I did not lack what might reasonably be called my primary sources. True, I'd almost thrown them away after I'd extracted the best of their contents, but eventually I'd decided to conserve, for a rainy day, my 'denuded' materials. Racing feverishly to the big bedroom wardrobe, I fished underneath a heap of winter blankets and unearthed my two precious copies of… *Parade*. Incredible as it might seem now, those 1964 photographs were all in black and white, the nudity was never more than partial, and there were no such things as genitals or pubic hair. I skimmed expertly through these two specialist periodicals, both of them well and truly edited, not to say laid waste, by my mother's darning scissors. All that was left was, as it were, the bottom of the barrel. A girl called Liz from Bradford-on-Avon, Wilts, was lying on her stomach wearing nothing but some see-through fishnet tights. Her back was bare but her breasts were concealed from view and she had turned round to the camera with an artlessly teasing wink. The heavy contours of her Bradford-on-Avon backside were vividly heightened by the black tights, and I felt a mighty urge to tear off the tights and avail myself of what lay beneath the contours. But of course Liz of B-on-A was not a real naked woman, she was only a piece of bloody paper. How then to straddle the philosophical chasm, to dispel the infuriating mirage that was the difference between the thing-in-itself and the representation-of-the-thing? Someone, almost certainly Watson Holland, had told me that Bertrand Russell could only ever begin his philosophic lucubrations on epistemological matters such as this after an initial masturbation. I looked at Liz's tanta-lising buttocks and had to restrain myself from tearing at the bit of paper that was not, shall we say at bottom, a real backside? I fumed and swore at that point. Sometimes I found myself yearn-ing with such phenomenal intensity for a pictorial woman to metamorphose into a woman of flesh, I was flabbergasted that the wish did not incite the miracle.

"Come alive," I whispered passionately to leering Liz of the West Country. "Be my Pygmalion. Just once will do, I promise. It can't be right in anybody's book that you stay just a piece of bloody paper."

Would I have had a heart attack if she had arrived at my side wearing her impudent smile and nothing else, whooshing down my chimney like a betighted, befishnetted Father Christmas? Hardly. Deplorably, I would have swapped my birthright just like unfortunate Esau. I would have emptied my savings account just to have had two minutes, no, just a minute, no, just half a second, with the B-on-A teenager. Meanwhile I read with glazed, uncomprehending eyes about her impressively versatile hobbies. Liz, it transpired, enjoyed wine-making, philately, upholstering, and listening to short wave radio…

I heard Vince Mori shuffling about noisily next door. After a long day on the ice-cream van he usually helped Angelica with the lodgers' dinners before retiring for an hour with his records. I could hear him changing the 45 and opening his second bottle of beer. I listened to the cap being prised off and his throat being hawked the way he had learned to do it down the Whitehaven pit. Before long he would stop the records and start playing his own clarinet at moderately muted volume. I had grown so used to his impromptu music practice that it scarcely ever kept me awake. Instead, those poetic, Bilkesque lullabies he invariably favoured these days acted as highly efficient sedatives.

Suddenly a mellifluous trumpet pierced the tranquil West Cumbrian night. I immediately recognised it as 'the golden trumpet' of Mr Eddie Calvert, a middle-aged musical celebrity who like Russ Conway was a regular star on the Billy Cotton Band Show. Calvert, just like Acker Bilk, was a potent master of the melancholy and the plangent and the pregnant. Next door I could hear my father hoarsely, possibly tearfully, muttering away at one of his favourite records:

"Eddie Calf Foot! *Che squisito!*"

Meanwhile my earnest wrestlings with Liz the philatelist's fishnet tights were getting more and more desperate, not to say sweatily deranged. As I twisted and panted and groaned with the herculean effort, I seemed to hear Captain Hornblower muttering something very important in my left ear.

*"A delicious, most delectable bow-hind that Paignton lass possesses. Easy does it, m'boy. Piano, if not pia*bloody*nissimo will do it. Just start up at the top and work your way patiently down to… the bottom."*

As the piquant golden trumpet and my remorseless one-act drama reached their parallel poignant climaxes, I realised two things: 1) Eddie 'Mr Trumpet' Calvert was self-evidently a horn-blower, a literal blower of horns, and 2) Captain Hornblower, aka Watson Holland from Newcastle-upon-Tyne, was always blowing his own bloody trumpet.

"Ya-goof!" I squawked, not unlike a baritone sax gone mad. "Ug-ug-ug-ug-ug-guh…"

At this point I could have sworn that Liz the Bradford-on-Avon short-wave buff, who was of course just a piece of bloody paper, that she actually winked and smiled at me…

"Eddie Calf Foot!" repeated Vince Mori next door. "*Putana, che bellezza. Che* blurry *squisito,* ee is."

The rest of his eulogy was in a dense Calabrese dialect that I hadn't a hope of understanding.

3

♪♪♪♫

More concerning shamelessly revelatory lingerie. This time instead of fishnet tights we have a very rudimentary Nineteen Sixties 'thong' and the town in question is not Bradford-on-Avon, Wiltshire, but Santa Monica, California. Instead of Enzo Mori it involves a young Portuguese whose surname literally means 'onion' and who crossed the seas to seek fame and fortune and rapidly succeeded. I have in front of me a colour photograph of a very good looking Toto Cebola aged perhaps twenty-three. It is one of the oddest photographs I have ever seen and fittingly enough it reminds me of the old orange notebook that Watson Holland stole from me all those years ago. That notebook belonged to a very naive north-country teenager and it guilelessly mixed up the sacred and the profane, the Old Testament and the Newly Permissive. This equally incongruous picture, shot at roughly the same time as those ones in *Parade*, was a publicity photograph taken to promote the Portuguese 'gypsy' on his victorious tour of the United States. It has him awkwardly clutching by his side, as if it were a cumbersome hunting rifle, his unusual instrument, the jazz violin. The violin even has its back to us as if in an agony of shyness. The bow in his other hand is held as stiffly as if it is a switch he uses for swatting flies. All the recognised experts (*Downbeat* jazz magazine; Sy Knopf of the Santa Monica jazz station, to name only two) are loudly assuring Cebola that he is already a jazz virtuoso, and yet he clutches the tools of his genius as if they are embarrassing and unmanly impediments. He looks in fact the exact picture of the legend he has become, the ungainly and unworldly musical gypsy. He is by promotional sleight-of-hand a Portuguese Django, if not one of the numerous bastard offspring of the notoriously womanising and peripatetic Reinhardt.

It is important we take note of Cebola's bright purple sweater which is of an uncompromising if thoroughly commonplace turtleneck design. Throughout the Sixties turtleneck sweaters gave a mock-clerical, almost priestly aura to the expressionless pop stars who wore them. These numinous vestments might seem all too apposite on angelic crooners like Peter and Gordon and even upon the Fab Four, but in Cebola's case he looks as if he has been poured unwillingly into a plastic mould and re-emerged as a resentful plaster cast. Away from the cameras or the recording studios, Toto actually prefers to wear checked, old-fashioned, brightly-coloured lumberjack shirts. These solid, no-nonsense garments not only suit his tawny and brawny physique, they also, as a biographer's bonus, confirm his 'gypsy' preference for vivid and childlike colours.

But hold on. What's this? Who can this be sitting at the Portuguese's feet? This is certainly a photograph of its time, of a period when the most daring photographers opted for the trenchant power of stark aesthetic contrast. As if to throw Toto Cebola's overdressed turtleneck awkwardness into high relief, they have plonked down a half-naked young woman at his nervous feet. Perhaps eighteen years old, she has a moderately revealing bright pink bikini bra, which in three-quarters profile allows an anomalous perspective on her taut, very heavy breasts. She is obediently kneeling at his feet in a parody of a devotional pose, squatting on her solid thighs with hands half raised in dazed supplication to the embarrassed Lusitanian idol. The other half of the swimsuit is not a bikini bottom, but a thong of the thickness of a slim-jim tie as sported circa 1961. She might be in a humble supplicant's pose but she also wears a jadedly sultry expression well beyond her eighteen years. She stares sulkily and inscrutably as well as submissively and soporifically up at Toto Cebola. Obviously the Californian photographer has coached and choreographed her into doing all of this. As a final intoxicating touch, Cebola's electric violin cable is clasped in her hands in a poetic suggestion of willing bondage. She is held in thrall by the Portuguese's mesmerising electrifying instrument, should we be unable to guess the polymorphous symbolism. It is all so subliminally stated, it induces breathlessness, or at least it makes Cebola look petrified at the implications. The three-quarters view of the Californian girl's thong reveals most of her eighteen year old's sinuous and serpentine buttocks. Even Cebola's irresolute, faintly unhappy expression touchingly confirms his *cigano* credentials. Because everyone, even a twenty-five-year-old radio DJ called Sy, knows that gypsies are old-fashioned monogamists who frown upon open sexual display.

Let's listen to Sy Knopf's pre-studio session preamble heard 8 p.m. eastern time, March 25th, 1969, SMJAZ station, Santa Monica. Of Toto Cebola, he is 'incomprehensibly yet utterly fantastic', 'the Portuguese prodigy who is a veritable violin virtuoso of the same impregnable stature as Stuff Smith, Stéphane Grappelli and Cebola's near-contemporary, the equally astonishing Frenchman, Jean-Luc Ponty'. Furthermore he is 'an unarguable genius, if by genius we mean having a technique so refined, so innovative, so breathlessly fast if it chooses to be, that it is beyond the ready analysis of any mortal man'. The ecstatic Knopf had also interviewed Fuzz Fenster, distinguished veteran producer of Cebola's recent album *Energetic Eels*. On the same programme a very gravel-voiced Fuzz told Knopf in a threatening tone that this was the most dazzling jazz debut album he had produced in at least twenty-five years. Lest his listeners assume both he and Fenster were proffering par for the course 'sycophantic hyperbole of a facile nature', Knopf stresses that this is 'no anodyne panegyric, no vacuous eulogy'. Both of them were reacting to the Portuguese's genius with the feelings in their hearts as well as with the brains inside their heads.

The biographical information that follows is culled from an

extremely lengthy interview which Cebola gave to the British jazz magazine *Cahoots* in its October 1985 issue. The great violinist had just turned forty and was touring the UK with a brand-new line-up and a brand-new album, so there was good reason to make the interview more than half the length of the magazine. The photo accompanying it shows an instructive metamorphosis from the portrait that promoted *Energetic Eels*. Sixteen years after that turtleneck and thong picture, Cebola had acquired some impressive degree of mature dress sense. He wore a beautiful white shirt tailored after the Italian Renaissance manner, so that he looked like a discreet young noble in a Mantegna painting. The blushing awkward gypsy had transformed into a sober, relaxed, intensely spiritual-looking man. The inner Cebola had evidently ripened as his life and music had taken ever more philosophical trajectories. His latest LP, which had been issued to coincide with his European tour, rejoiced in the name *Craving Infinity Always*. I was almost too embarrassed to repeat the ridiculous title when I rang up the Whitehaven Our Price.

Tomás Manoel Rui Cebola was born in Coimbra, Portugal on the 17th July, 1945, in a cluttered, narrow and desperate little alley off the Rua da Sota. In fact Toto is not a recognised diminutive of Tomás, but it happened to be his baby pronunciation that stuck, added to which it had a quaint and exotic Brazilian sound which appealed to both his parents. Toto was the only child of an unmarried laundrywoman called Leonor, and his father was a lanky circus hand called Luís Miguel de Carvalho. Luís Miguel, who was six foot six and a mild stammerer, might have worked in a scruffy circus but he was neither musically gifted nor on either side of his family a *cigano*. Nor would he ever have claimed to be for any conceivable reason, given that the Portuguese noun for swindle or trickery is *ciganice*. He would call in to see his son on average once every three years, whenever the circus visited Coimbra, and to soften his massive absences Leonor Cebola always referred to him as Toto's 'uncle'. '*Tiozinho*', as Toto addressed Luís Miguel, reluctantly approved this very businesslike, pragmatic accommodation to reality. Once every three years he salved an amnesic conscience by taking his son to the circus every single night for a week.

I would like to offer a significant if subjective opinion at this point. As I hope to amplify later, a young child's tender vision of the circus (or equally, a motley and sparse little Portuguese fairground) is the repetitive pictorial suggestion in Toto Cebola's music. Which is to say that his electric and electrifying effusions owe their peculiarly haunting flavour to the exotic if homely flavour of his father's occupation. No one has ever suggested as much in the jazz books or the specialist journals, nor has the musician himself ever said anything to that effect. What I want to stress is that when I first listened to *Energetic Eels*, the lasting mental images that came to me unheralded were of touching small-town circuses holding impoverished and melancholy children in a trance of reverent expectation. This spontaneous imaginative response to his music first occurred in 1970, meaning a full fifteen years before I knew anything at all about Cebola's personal history. I am not clairvoyant, needless to add, but I know for a visceral certainty that my singular response was completely consistent with the musician's own source of inspiration.

Well into the 1980s the poorest women of Coimbra did their washing on the wide sandy banks of the Mondego. It was by the edges of this *praia fluvial* that resilient and pugnacious Leonor laundered for a weekly total of twenty rich and stingy customers. The infant Toto would play beside her and sometimes help to spread out all the sopping shirts and linens. Occasionally, especially in the hot spring afternoons, he would spend eternal moments watching the blazing and impossible colours of the hovering dragonflies. Let me interpret again and say it seems to me after thirty years of pondering this question that the creative content (as opposed to the notational form) of an improviser's music originates from the subtlest historical crenellations of his or her – forgive the terminology – 'soul'. This soul, or 'self' in Toto's adult case, has its abiding core, its exquisite notation, in the form of its very earliest, tenderest years. Thus for example when Miles Davis's trumpet scores the depths of haunted sadness in a number like *Sanctuary*, it is surely because the sensitive infant form of the grown musician knew those same sad excavations. This is scarcely speculative psychological gobbledeygook, so much as a naively self-evident truth. In Cebola's case, on more than one of his albums we can hear, by which I mean see, the vividly suggested presence of exquisitely fragile insects. A perfect entomological example is the tune *Gossamer Love* which is Track 2, Side 1 of Cebola's *Infinite Resonance* (CBS 1977). It might sound fanciful if not a downright lie, but I swear that I, Enzo Mori, saw those same hovering dragonfly insects when I played that tune in 1978, a good seven years before I knew anything about the violinist's childhood.

Infinite Resonance is a characteristically ponderous mouthful, of course. As with all Cebola's later albums and consistent with much in the way of jazz language, it is po-faced and poetically sententious. Though nothing could have been less like poetry than Cebola's ragged riverside upbringing and the hollow, unrelieved poverty of fascist mid-century Portugal. There was nothing at all dignified about those seasonal occasions of obligatory mendicancy. If Leonor in the height of summer came down with some noxious Mondego germ, she made him stand by the Ponte Santa Clara and beg. By the time he was nine he was never in school but was touting Coimbra's finest cafés as a cut-price shoeshine. Because he was a kid he was given less than a quarter of what a man might ask. A few wretched *tostões* and in one case an off-duty policeman offered him either a broken cigarette or a kick up the arse, take it or leave it. To start with all he had were black and brown polishes, a couple of mangy brushes, and a disgustingly battered biscuit tin to carry it all around. After about two years he was able to afford a modest range of coloured polishes and a proper ornamented wooden case. It was not as humiliating as begging but it felt like a pariah occupation and especially in a town full of pampered, swaggering students. The pride he had inherited from Leonor had to be frozen and set aside as he learnt to make himself invisible like some evolutionarily adapted moth. More than once this ghost of a shoeshine would be frequenting a sumptuous art deco coffee house along the Rua Ferreira Borges, obliged to kneel in adoration at the immaculately shod feet of some indolent, obese boy his own age. Nine times out of ten the same boy in his ornate suit would be wheezingly stuffing himself with a succession of the sickliest egg bolos and wouldn't even notice the ghost's noiseless ferretings at his feet.

Once Cebola took courage and stole a nervous glance at one of these pampered brats. Bizarrely the boy's bloated face was masked by not one but a pair of little painted wooden barrels. The boy who was aptly called Narciso was holding up the trophies that his young aunt had just purchased from the café cabinet. Two *ovos moles*, luxurious candied egg yolks manufactured in Aveiro. Cebola briskly calculated that it would have taken him a whole month of shining, two hundred hours, to purchase those two beautiful things. The uneasy-looking aunt had just ordered herself a plateful of Aveiro eels and a glass of *bairrada* wine. How could Cebola possibly guess that when he was this stiff lady's age, in his early twenties, he would be almost as rich as her, just as good looking, and would call his first money spinning enterprise *Energetic Eels*? Her Portuguese eels were dead, as were her anaemic blue desolate eyes, as were her nephew's petulant lazy shufflings and neurasthenic facial tics. Her eyes perhaps became a little more animated with the Aveiro *bairrada*, one of those *especialidades regionais* so potent that *Tiozinho* Luís Miguel could drink no more than two bottles of it at any one sitting.

University students were more likely, out of pure whimsy, to pay him generously. But they were often puerile and boastful, endlessly jabbering absurd melodramatic claims about their adventures with cheap women. Some of those women lived in Cebola's street, where there was a famous fado café that catered for these boyish Don Juans. Coimbra fado was even more melancholy and regretful than Lisbon fado, and these pampered young men liked to cultivate a kind of vaunting morose desperation. On one occasion in that legendary café he cleaned the shoes of a thin unhandsome student of about twenty who had put down a beautifully carved cane sporting three odd looking notches. Seeing him staring at it, the student moved it well away from his unappetising paws. He turned and guffawed to his overweight friend:

"This little gypsy's gawping at my cane. I guess I should be flattered by such curiosity. Have you ever seen one like this before, kid?"

Cebola blushed like a brainless infant and murmured something meaningless.

"Can't you understand me, you dopey bloody *cigano*? I mean have you ever seen a stick like this one with three notches?"

"Never," he whispered with a pounding heart. "Never at all."

"Of course you've never seen such a rarity. Previously you've seen them with only one notch. Or two notches at most. On the sticks of other students that is."

"I don't know," Cebola gabbled. "To be honest…"

"Yes? Go on!"

"I've never noticed any notches before."

"Really?" the ugly student scoffed. "Well you must be bloody blind as well as stupid. Listen kid, if ever you do manage to observe one of these again you'll need to know what it signifies." He beckoned histrionically then confided very loudly. "A notch for a university man means a woman that he's *had*, d'you understand? One notch means that he's had only one conquest, meaning been to bed with her and done it all. Three notches means three women he's had and done everything with. Absolutely everything. D'you understand?"

"Yes," said Cebola very hoarsely. "Yes, I see."

"How many have you had?" his fat friend asked the blushing kid and then burst into extravagant laughter. It was only then he realised there was a table of four young women nearby, seemingly very disdainful yet smirking nonetheless. Toto understood that he was being used as a comic vehicle for these two ugly men to make a public declaration of their rampant virilities. And these men were from the same vaunted, dignified university where Prime Minister Dr Salazar had studied, where indeed in the

Twenties he had been an eminent Professor of Economics. Had there been one, two or two dozen notches, the kid wondered, on the youthful Salazar's stick, given that these days he looked like a lifeless and sullen pork butcher?

One rainy evening he was wandering past a noisy café in the narrow little Rua dos Gatos, when he heard something absolutely extraordinary. He stopped stock-still as if he had been shot or put under arrest. There was some frighteningly unearthly music coming from inside it. Or was it even music? Cebola remained motionless and rigid and listened to a sound as alien yet magical as the turning of the planets on their axes. Instead of the café resounding to fado or dolorous Spanish and Portuguese ballads from a juke box, it was something altogether foreign and indescribable. It was a raw, energetic, seemingly formless music, a type he sometimes heard in a more accessible but far less mesmerising version if he lurked outside the back door of the Centro cinema. Most of the films shown there were Thirties and Forties American musicals, and if he pressed his ear hard enough to the fire door he could make out the barked unintelligible English dialogue and the frequent clamorous bursts of Negro dance band music. Naive, extravagant, sometimes openly clowning, it was the very opposite of the formalised grieving of fado. What he could hear tonight standing outside of the Fim do Mundo café was in an altogether tighter, more restrained and eloquent language. Like fado it was highly formalised and extremely solemn but that was where the similarity ended. This stuff was horn, saxophone, drums and bass, and they were following each other in grave solo sequence instead of all blurting and blaring simultaneously. It seemed impossible that this kind of music could ever pursue the spirit of clowning. It was slow, hieratic, processional, almost a graveyard saunter at times. Every once in a while a patter of thin hand clapping would applaud a solo performance. Cebola felt his head throbbing with frightening excitement at a thing which, against all the odds, spoke an immediately intelligible language. Surely a spectral shoeshine, a pitiful down-and-out like Toto, had no right at all to understand anything as foreign as this? Of course he had never heard a single modern jazz record in his life. Even assuming Leonor Cebola had been able to afford a wireless, such a phenomenon on the Portuguese state radio of the Fifties was as unknown as documentaries on urban poverty or Marxist atheism.

It was his unique profession as a shoeshine, Cebola always maintained, which had allowed his salvationary ticket to the world of jazz. If he hadn't been a shoeblack specifically he might still have been holding his hand out every summer on the Ponte Santa Clara. Though an obvious manifestation of beggarly status, it permitted him a licensed entry to the world of the rich. Because fashionable toffs above all had to have their shoes shined on a regular basis, you did not need to knock nervously on the door of the café nor go up and humbly beg the proprietor if you could solicit business. The only grounds for turning you away were if more than two competitors had got there in the first place. Also, even if you were filthy and unpleasant-looking no one seemed to mind, you had the impregnable invisibility of a floor servant, a nameless skivvy who only functioned properly and invisibly on subservient knees.

The jazz quartet playing inside the Fim do Mundo were a freak appearance, by rights they shouldn't have been there. They had been contacted in Lisbon and booked to perform in a café patronised almost exclusively by foreign expatriates. They were playing there, rather than say Porto or Setúbal, because the band's trumpeter, Red Conto, was the brother of the owner of a Coimbra English school. Joey Conto had invited the band to come and stay for a weekend in his exquisitely marbled mansion just outside Conímbriga. There, in response to his spendthrift hospitality, they gave him his own private concert. Prompted by a jazz-loving Portuguese, the Dean of his English school, Joey also arranged this one-off performance in one of Coimbra's most beautiful cafés. Cebola learnt of this later from the lips of Joey himself, who remarkably exchanged a few friendly words with him that first night in the Fim do Mundo.

Cebola wove his way awkwardly through the tables. They

were candlelit, but the stage was illumined by subdued electric lights. Up there on the spotlit dais were the four Americans, two of them crew-cut and two of them with marine neckshaves. All of them had gel on their hair. It was cosy and comforting inside here and the food smelt wonderful. A young couple nearby were tucking voraciously into trout and *rojões* respectively. The remains of their previous course, a big plate of shellfish, had not been cleared away. There was plenty of flesh left on the shrimps, and Cebola had a great urge to shovel it, bones and all, down his famished gullet. They looked a nice reasonably sympathetic couple, they probably wouldn't mind at all. Yet if he obeyed his animal instincts and made himself visible in all his obnoxious poverty, he'd be turfed out immediately and would miss this extraordinary music. The four men playing were all in dapper black suits, like funeral attendants. One of them, the sax player, was a negro, and it was remarkable to see a black man in a beautiful suit. They were all playing as quietly and undemonstratively as if they were at a graveside. But of course the tightly controlled music wasn't at all without passion, nor was it about anything as ugly as death. It was about... God knows what it was about.

Passion with the lid on it? Passion and desire with the lid on them?

Vincenzo Mori emigrated to the north of England in 1948. The initial leg of the bus journey to Naples took place on Good Friday, the same day that three-year-old Cebola almost drowned while chasing dragonflies in the Mondego. Terrified Leonor hauled him out by his ringwormed legs, walloped him cruelly, and taught him how to swim in about twenty minutes. Meanwhile Vince and all the other young unemployed males in a tiny hamlet near Roccella moved en masse to a very remote part of a rich foreign country. Amazed at what they found, they settled in the grimy western coastal strip of a curious area in the far north west. It was called 'Koomberlent'. Twelve of them took lodgings in the biggest harbour town, Whitehaven, and exchanged the olive groves and molten sunsets of Reggio di Calabria for the subterranean galleries of Haig Pit. Vince was so claustrophobic he passed urine on that first descent in the pit cage, yet he stayed on five years as a Haig collier. West Cumberland was conspicuously deprived by English standards, as well as being dirty, cold, wet and melancholy. Yet they all felt extraordinarily pampered. Miners were better paid than all other manual workers, and they ate copiously four times a day, and could smoke and drink nearly half as much as they wanted. The food though was extraordinary. It was as if these friendly but sun-hungry North English hated anything suggestive of colour, taste, aroma, music, passion. Stringy meat and potato confections predominated, and pasta and rice were entirely unknown. As indeed was wine, which could only be obtained at exorbitant cost from a single quality grocer in a complacent little village with an enormous public school called St Bees.

Vince spent two whole days getting his naturalisation papers sorted out in the county seat of Carlisle, and lost two days' pay as a result. This was a remarkable not to say mystifyingly enigmatic achievement, given that he only spent a brisk half hour in the county offices and afterwards caught the first bus back to Whitehaven. What on earth could have happened in that anomalous intervening period to keep my father from his work for an extra day and a half? Was it conceivable that Vince had gone missing in a curious paranormal time gap? Did he, more prosaically, visit a lurid North Cumbrian brothel, then get monumentally drunk and pass out for the next thirty-six hours?

He had no car, of course, in 1948, so he stood at the handiest request stop on Lonsdale Terrace, and waited for the bus to Carlisle. He had learnt that it took an hour and a half to the big city, and that the buses went once every hour. They were astonishing vehicles these 'Lodekka' Cumberland buses, double decker juggernauts, about the only thing in the county showing any evidence of swaggering majesty. Twenty-eight-year-old Vince had about twelve words of English at his disposal, of which half were obscenities and the rest were in rasping Cumbrian dialect, nice and brutally modulated by his own anomalous Calabrese vowels. 'Fooka' and 'coonta' and 'bassarda' were the tripartite sovereigns of his new lexicon; partly because coal mining was an angry, frustrating business, partly because it was a proven demographic fact that West Cumbrians swear more than anyone else in the British Isles.

Vince stood and waited and a roaring Lodekka went whistling past. He knew that it would only stop on request but as it didn't say Carlisle on the front, the miner let it sail on wherever it was bound. The bus he was after apparently stopped at Workington, Maryport, Aspatria and Wigton, meaning about half the county's principal towns. Having glimpsed Workington on a night out with a miners' darts team, Vince was not anticipating a spectacularly scenic journey. All steelworks, scrapyards and pits, 'Vukkytown', as he invariably called it, looked like the grimiest, slummiest parts of Naples, though instead of dingy tenements it had these dismal little two-up two-down terraces.

An hour passed and a second bus approached. Vince twitched his hand hopefully but it didn't say Carlisle. What it said was preposterous, but he had already been warned that Cumbrian words weren't like any other. He'd been stood here an hour and a half and he was getting painfully bored. He glanced across the road to some smart-looking villas and noticed an attractive woman of about thirty. She had a tight red headscarf and was energetically flogging a rug on a washing line with a carpet beater. A romantic single man, he liked the look of her sturdy arms and the unbridled fury with which she belaboured the rug. Gaping a little too intently, he then noted her stringy husband upstairs in the bedroom staring back at him. Vince blushed and looked away, but not before the Englishman, with a critical, quizzical stare at the little foreigner, put a large and bizarre object in his mouth. At first Vince imagined it was something mystifyingly analogous to a Whitehaven hookah, but then as the unexpected sound percolated across the quiet 1948 West Cumbrian highway, he understood that it was a *musical instrument*…

It was a clarinet. The man, with a dismissive expression in his eyes, as if wholly indifferent to what the unmusical world, including Mori, might think, began playing at careless volume. The only clarinet music Vince had heard previously was in old carnivals and festivals way up in the Sicilian hills. It was queerly Arab-sounding stuff that seemed to have come down from the birth of time. In contrast to that dirging and groaning which always got the goats infectiously tinkling their bells and the shepherds squinting their dubious approval, this music was lilting, cheerful, hypnotic… and clean and healthy sounding. Not a suggestion of anything moaningly Arab or squawkingly Oriental… or crazy gypsyish… anywhere in any of this.

A few months later Vince discovered that he had been listening to a composition by one Alphonse Picou. The composer was an early New Orleans player, the daddy of them all, Bechet included, and the tune was a jazz standard called *High Society*. Try as an imaginative exercise to picture Alphonse Picou wafting from an open window in Whitehaven in 1948, an effusion being ever so raptly overheard by a rustic South Italian waiting in vain for an elusive Cumberland bus. Vincenzo listened wholly enchanted for the best part of an hour. The clarinettist was an assiduous amateur performer who worked back-shifts at the Workington steelworks, and had until one o'clock to perfect his latest number. Six weeks later Vince recognised him on the stage at Whitehaven British Legion, walked across and shyly introduced himself. The steelworker who was called Geoff seemed suspicious at first but eventually was impressed by the Italian's bashful enthusiasm. Vince spoke doubtfully about possibly taking lessons himself, so Geoff generously referred him to an expert clarinet tutor down in Gosforth. To get to distant Gosforth Vince boldly acquired his own Ford Popular, took three driving tests, and all the rest was fabled history. Ten years later my father had assembled his own Chompin Stompers trad band, with Geoff's son-in-law, Wilfred Phizacklea, as its dogged and doleful trombonist.

Yet another Lodekka approached the hopeful collier. He twitched his paw in readiness, but dropped it despondently when he saw the unsatisfactory wording on the front. It sounds quite impossible, but like an endlessly patient Hindu waiting for his never arriving train, my father stood at that bus stop until late afternoon. By then the clarinettist had driven off to the Bessemer plant, glaring at the odd little man whose hobby seemed to be staring witlessly though irritatingly into space. He opened his mouth to quiz him about his bizarre sentinel behaviour but decided not to bother. Later his wife gingerly inspected the loiterer who struck her as probably harmless but possibly a little simple or, as the West Cumbrians say, 'daft'. When a sixth bus sped past at three o'clock, Vince, who'd had no lunch and was feeling miserable, not to say murderously irritable, decided to risk his hopeless English. He walked across reluctantly to this sturdy foreign woman who was stooping to weed the cracks in her crazy paving.

Coughing, blushing, pulling at the left leg of his new flannel trousers. *"Per piacere."*

She turned and started slightly. Yet noting his anxious and very humble expression, she attempted a tolerant smile.

He hurtled three sense units into a single sentence: *"Ciao,* missis, wanner booze Karlail, nora cummin."

"Nora Cumming?"

Vince uneasily repeated his Italo-Cumbrian pidgin and did a massive feverish arm sweep to indicate the ironically named Lodekka.

"The bus-to-Carlisle?" she enunciated musically, as if addressing a mute retarded imbecile. "What are you? Polish? No? You're one of those displaced Germans staying on after the war? No? Eyetalian. Working at Haig Pit. Fancy. They are scheduled ONCE AN HOUR. Understand? ONE-BUS-ON-THE-HOUR. There've been at least five gone by since you arrived there.

DON'T YOU REALISE THAT AT LEAST FIVE CARLISLE
BUSES HAVE GONE PAST YOU?"

My father gaped, then shuddered very violently. He glared at
this attractive woman with outraged disbelief. *"Putana! Non ha
potuto capire."*

"You what?" she said, startled by his salivating foreigner's
vehemence. "Look! Look there! There's another one coming at
the bottom of the road. Race across. Look sharp."

"Rice?" echoed Vincenzo suspiciously.

"Race across! Sharp!"

"Rice chap? *Che?* Rice chip?"

"That bus there is headed for *Carlisle.* Don't dally. Hurry up!"

Vince Mori scowled impatiently at this obviously gratuitous
liar. He squared his squat shoulders and waved his hands
aggressively at her too bright headscarf.

"Basta! He is non Karlail. Yon booze he nod Karlail. *Basta!
Che ridicolo…"*

More than the foul language, those two 'bastards', she was
amazed by his insolent certitude. Of course, all this linguistic
misunderstanding happened almost fifty years ago, yet even today
Vincenzo Alfredo Mori is equally notorious for his belligerent
rebuttals of the self-evident.

"It bloody well is!" she insisted with her hands on her jutting
hips.

"It is blurry *nod*!"

She bawled incensed, "But I'm bloody local. I should bloody
well know, shouldn't I? It says bloody Carlisle on the bloody
front of it, man!"

Vince flung at her venomously. *"Fosse vero!* Ee sez Kar-liz-lee."

"Carliz–?"

"THEE BOOZE SEZ KARLIZLEE!"

The headscarved young Whitehaven housewife collapsed with
lunatic hilarity on her crazy paving and went into extremely
painful hysterics. Reasonably enough she was to tell the same
ludicrous story at least once a month for the rest of her life.
About the silly little monoglot Eyetie who stood at the top of

her road for five hours because he thought that the name of our county capital was pronounced *phonetically*...

Without a word of thanks, Vince leapt on the bus and reached Karlizlee at half past four. It took him nearly half an hour to find the council offices, the clock said one minute past five, and the doorman cheerfully slammed the door in his beseeching face. Vince pounded his fists on the glass and threatened to cut the Karlizlee bastard in two, but the vindictive old North Cumbrian was unimpressed. The next day my father enterprisingly whiled away the same journey with a Hotspur comic and a library picture book about the history of the clarinet.

By the autumn of 1969 Toto Cebola had completed his victorious American tour and had returned temporarily to Portugal. With a single album he had already established himself as the Frenchman Jean-Luc Ponty's only possible world rival on the jazz violin. In October of that year I went up to Oxford University to begin a BA degree in animal physiology. When Kelsie Mullins learned I'd gained entrance to Oxford she looked very worried and suggested I get a haircut as a suitable act of deference now that I was mixing with the elevated classes. Watson Holland pooh-poohed that and opined that Gay Cavalier Enzo could do what he bloody well liked, now that he had shown his real intellectual mettle. Why he could even join the Balliol-affiliated branch of the Knights of St Columba, Miss Mullins, should he so choose. Kelsie turned apoplectic and watched in horror as Holland presented me with a congratulatory ten pound note. It was the first tenner I had ever seen in my life. It was almost as much as Vince Mori made in a week of selling ice-cream cornets. As for cavaliers, in 1969 the adjective 'gay' signified nothing more contentious than affable. Watson Holland, more than either of my parents, was deeply moved by my imminent departure. Not only was his favourite sparring partner deserting the place, he was going up to read a biological science at the most distinguished university in the universe. Writing which I notice that those two words are virtual homonyms, and it was certainly true that the pharmacist equated a good tertiary education with the romantic conquest of things cosmic, universal and ultimate…

"Oxford," he echoed wonderingly, the day that I got the results. "Good Lord. Oxford University. Animal physiology, forsooth. Well bless my Islets of Langerhans. Well blow my old *vasa deferentia*. After a manner of speaking. Good Lord. Dark horse has nothing in it. Did you bribe them at Balliol or what?"

"It was the interview that did it," I said, almost as stunned as he was. "I started telling them about an ethology book I'd read called *The Love Life of Animals*. After that it was all in the bag."

Holland raised his heavy eyebrows. "The cheesecake merchant strikes again. Did you show 'em your old scripture exercise book as well? No, suppose not. They're all notorious pederasts at Oxford in any case. Bachelor dons and those arid single-sex colleges. High Anglicanism, Lewis Carroll, paedophilia and port-induced gout. A great pity that intellectual prowess and sexual degeneracy have to be such disgusting bedfellows."

I lit up a Perfectos cigarette and said, "It was written by a chap called Buddenbrocks and I got it off the stack in the town library. One of the physiology dons had met this Buddenbrocks at a conference on animal sex in Utrecht in 1952, and so he joked about that for the next thirty minutes. He was very brilliant and witty but for some reason he thought it was me who'd been brilliant and witty. All I did was grin obsequiously throughout, yet he seemed to think me a precocious genius."

"Mm. Did he proposition you before making you the offer of the schol? No? Well beware of Oxbridge bumboys be they e'er so insidiously fawning and profligate with the Bristol Cream. Take care of the old bow-hind, and I'm not being flippant, young Rimbaud. You stick to rotund young women though don't adhere too doggedly even to those. What I mean is sow your oats as if you were using one of those old-fashioned fiddle-drills to spread your youthful seed. And, well, I know you have a girlfriend up here in Cumberland, aka Britain's own Novya Zemlaya. But that sort of Laurie Lee calf love isn't going to last you know. Get in with some of those Roedean fillies at the Ox and Cow secretarial college and milk their pendulous udders for everything they've got, boy."

So much for Captain Hornblower's deliberations on advanced pastoral care. The same night Holland produced a bottle of malt whisky and informed my mother that he was going to get the pair of us drunk. It would be good practice for the Balliol Commem Balls in '70, '71 and '72, and now that I was eighteen it was time I learnt to hold my booze like a man. Angelica looked dubious at this hazardous rite of passage, but graciously granted us the back parlour. At ten o'clock she came in with two plates of Hungarian salami, connoisseur sausage that Vince had ordered last week from a Carlisle delicatessen. By that stage I had drunk four whiskies and thought the world as I knew it was the funniest, most joyous playground possible, and that God above was among other things the Divine and Brilliant Comedian. Watson Holland was holding his drink much steadier and was certainly very sober in his didactic ruminations.

"Thing about bloody women – thank you so much, my dear Mrs Mori – bloody women overall is they are so appallingly inflexible. Give or take the odd exception, they seem to special- ise in thwarting, controlling, manipulating, wheedling, cajoling, adulating, but never, and I mean never, communicating with a man in an honest and unambiguous manner. I used to think all that misogynistic stuff in the Restoration dramas, Farquhar and the rest of 'em, was anachronistic nonsense until I met my own hideous wife. This salami is absolutely delicious, Mrs Mori. Gosh, black peppercorns and flecks of ground red capsicum. You know, I believe those goulash merchants, the Magyars, classify over three hundred different types of paprika. Twenty-five vari- eties just in Szekesfehervar alone. When I was there in 19 – "

"I don't agree," I said stoutly. I felt so euphoric with the whisky I couldn't possibly criticise anyone or anything, least of all the whole of womankind.

"I think I know rather more about Szekesfehervar than you do, Rimbaud."

"Elizabeth doesn't manipulate me. She speaks her mind and I speak my mind and we get on like a house on fire."

"Enzo, your little girl Elizabeth is only sixteen as far as I know. At sixteen she still trails clouds of glory as Wordsworth has it. Still a child, still in possession of a soul and a flexible sensitivity. Every young girl is like that at her age. But give her five or six years, give her engagement and marriage and perhaps a child and then note the poisonous transmogrification."

I pooh-poohed such theatrical denigration and tried to change the subject, but Holland was not to be sidestepped. His wife might be a particularly rank apple in the pile, he maintained, but all adult women were capable of the same pointless animosities and provocative hostilities.

"I think you're making a false extrapolation," I said, and I had problems with the last word as my cheeks seemed to be made of whiskified putty. "Point A, I don't believe all women are like your wife. Point B, I don't seriously believe she was anywhere near as bad as you make out."

Holland gave a strange little nervous start. Then he threw me a sour, old-fashioned look, as if belatedly realising he had been wasting good malt on a callow and fatuous stripling.

"Enzo, you've only just graduated from cheesecake photographs of tits and female bow-hinds to the living breathing thing. Sorry to disappoint you but you know nothing, old son, about the real state of things, absolutely nothing. If I told you exactly what my ex-wife was like, in minute and uncensored detail, it would put you off the entire bloody gender for life."

"Try me," I challenged him brazenly.

He snorted at my boozy bravado and feigned chucking the dimpled whisky bottle at me. "Be it on your own head then," he snorted.

Hornblower took a deep breath and contemplated a distant point which just happened to coincide with my parents' framed wedding photograph. Visibly blanching at the sight of a brilliantined little South Italian in a hideous top hat, he shuffled uncomfortably and said:

"But where to commence with this vile Sheridan Le Fanu saga? Let's begin at any random point, shall we. Let's start with an appropriate thematic prelude, the musical motif being humiliation pure and simple. Suffice to say, Enzo Mori, that after less than a year of marriage, Penelope Holland had achieved an extremely terrifying virtuoso talent at belittling me in front of all our friends."

"Making you small," I translated witlessly, as I helped myself to more of his malt.

"Belittling me, I must stress, not in any minor pedestrian sense. I've seen plenty of that pantomime business where you have a pintsize, under-earning puppet being mocked in public by a shrewish Gorgon's head. Underneath the fearful Medusa visage is the familiar carnivorous harpy-hag who once tremulously pledged her fealty at the altar. No, that kind of domestic nagging and persistent jibing was an elementary warm-up exercise, *Easy Pieces for Little Fingers*, in the case of my Penelope. Instead of simple bullying, my wife worked very hard at developing the talent of precise imitation, of theatrical mimicry. Give her her due she was a budding genius, if she had pushed it professionally she might well have made a handsome living on the stage or as a television entertainer. However she confined her powers of parody to her luckless bloody husband and him alone.

"On numerous social occasions, dinner parties and the like, behind my back she would mime whatever I was saying in complete grotesque silence. She would do the same crazy business with regard to my gestures, my pauses, my moustache tweaking, my facial expressions. Of course children frequently do the same sort of thing in schoolyards, but not with the intention of psychologically destroying their playmate as a rule. Penelope did this mimicry with such delicately poised finesse, it was possible to believe it was borderline playfulness of a boisterous, possibly artistic sort. Theoretically it was akin to Parisian theatre or the avant-garde Fifties dramas of Ionesco or Samuel Beckett. Our friends, who, like us, read novels and went to see plays and subtitled films in Newcastle and Durham, chose to take it in that neutral spirit. Both the ones who enjoyed my shaking discomfiture and the ones who felt deeply embarrassed on my behalf. Once Penelope had tired of this silent phantasmagoric mime, she would practise her various other refinements. If she'd had a lot to drink she would go in for the brutal staccato repetition of my sentences. Can you imagine what I'm talking about? It was really quite uncanny, as well as being infinitely distressing. She became my instant ghostly echo, and the imitation was of an absolute and quite miraculous fidelity. She would take on my base tones, my booming resonance, my idiosyncratic speech rhythms…

"For example, at some pleasant little dinner do or drinks party, I might be saying to George, my chemistry lecturer friend at the university, 'As I was saying, George…', … and then as the 'rge' of George was uttered, its revolting doppelganger twin would shoot out as if in some bloody awful catch or musical round. *As I was saying, GeorGeorge, as I was saying Georgeas I was saying.'* Can you imagine the effect that that kind of overlaying and dubbing has on one's powers of conversation? Poor old George would laugh weakly and I would laugh weakly, and then Penelope, the beautiful woman with the name of a handsome Greek heroine, she would ferociously imitate my weak grin. So that I would grin even more desperately at poor old George, whereupon Penny would do her second cruel parody. Of my embarrassed young face melting into a pathetic cartoon effusion of tragedy. In fact all in all, she successfully turned me into a human cartoon, did my wife."

"A cartoon?" I said quietly. "I see."

"Do you? Penelope trivialised my sincere distress into a farcical animated grimace. By doing which she allowed me no remnant of basic dignity, much less any simple seriousness. Whatever I said or did or was about to say or do could theoretically become the subject for an improvisatory extravagance…"

There was some of my jazz playing as we talked. I had put a

George Russell album, *At Beethoven Hall*, on the Dansette record player. That music was very far ahead of its time in 1969, and even thirty years later it sounds just as tauntingly uncompromising. Watson Holland shuddered at the meticulously sliding trumpet sequences as Don Cherry and Bertil Loewgren played together on the *Lydia Suite*. He eyed me dolorously, and said with great weariness:

"That bloody awful record that you're playing reminds me of my wife's brutal improvisations. Cold, frigid, involuted, inspissated, unintelligible. Listen, I have a proposal, Enzo Mori. Before I'm perforce obliged to retire upstairs and commit *felo de se* in the next five minutes, might we perhaps have one of your three classical discs put on instead?"

I pulled a wry face and feigned inability to lift from my chair.

"It's not much to ask seeing you've already guzzled half a pint of my priceless single malt. When you decide to puke up violently, as you surely will, it will be in all colours of the spectrum and possibly a few more. Put this beautiful Ravel string quartet on, there's a good lad. On a cheap Czechoslovak label, Supraphon, I see, but none the worse for that. By the way, it's the one thing that the humourless totalitarian scum have not yet obliterated, wouldn't you agree? Even they can't get Ravel to be anything other than Ravel and get him to say anything other than Ravel wanted to say. Thanks for being such a selfless young sport for once. Ah, listen to it, what blissfully melancholy beauty. I can feel my old soul fluttering and opening like a butterfly its delicate wings. Let's strike a second deal, shall we? If you put your Geoff Russell LP in your Ma's meat mincer before you go up to bed, I promise I'll give you a whole bottle of Glenlivet to yourself."

I looked at him sceptically. "Is that all that you have to say about your wife? She doesn't sound like a genuinely pathological monster to me."

Holland flexed his glasses on the bridge of his wide nose and pointed an admonitory finger. "You are joking! I have barely started, we are not even on the preliminary prolegomena. Listen hard to what I'm about to tell you. Outrageous mental cruelty might have been one of her versatile talents, but she was also addicted to *physical* brutality."

Boozed up as I was, I was startled, "You mean she did actual physical violence to *you*?"

"Of course I wouldn't be telling you any of this if I were sober. Say nothing, not a single bloody word, to anyone else in this house, especially not your parents, or I'll do more than steal your blinking scripture book. I've never disclosed any of this to anyone, I promise you, not even to a doctor or a priest. This is a weighty unpleasant confidence I'm bestowing on an inexperienced teenage lad. Still, it's high time you knew what unimaginable perversities certain brittle adults are capable of, young Oxford man. Ironically, no one would have credited such behaviour in my Penelope's case, as she was a strikingly beautiful, unquestionably brilliant young physics mistress at Middlesbrough Girls High. Outwardly respectable and infinitely polite when it suited her, yet she managed to practise all manner of terrifying physical aggression inside our four walls."

Suddenly I focused on the surreal vision of Penelope Holland chastising spreadeagled Captain Hornblower with a buckled belt. Terrified I'd burst out laughing, I swiftly asked him:

"What sort of aggression?"

"She would throw things at me for one thing. All manner of things. Some blunt, some sharp, some concussive, some percussive, some causing physical lacerations, others causing spiritual contusions. Plates at my head, usually the costliest ones, the wedding presents from her monied parents, the Asquiths of Whitfield Castle. She was smashing up the fragile celebratory tokens of our marriage, I suppose. Without warning, as a rule, and usually from behind. Frequently I didn't know what it was being hurled, there might be a horrible half second wondering whether it were a brick or ball bearing or something irreversibly lethal. Other assaults were more on the lines of secret police refinements as practised in the banana republics. Once, for example, we had had a fatuous, exhausting argument that I'd done nothing to provoke. As I walked away fatigued and completely disgusted, she raced after me and we struggled and wrestled by the open door. She waited until my hand was next to the sneck of the doorhandle, then reached and slammed it shut across my fingers with all the strength that she possessed. 'Possessed' is the appropriate verb, I assure you. The agony was beyond belief, as excruciating as if she'd used a sledgehammer. She laughed her demented head off, as I danced and howled and hopped around the room. The bruise it left was terrifying, I thought she'd broken every one of my phalangeal bones. Luckily as a pharmacist I could treat myself on the quiet with the proper applications. Of course in those days, ten years ago, I'd have been mortified to go and tell a doctor anything about the true state of things. You were supposed to be able to keep your little wife in check in 1959. In any event, time passed and about a month later Penelope made a kindly enquiry as to whether the hand had properly healed. Bemused, half-touched and affected by this novel most solicitous tone, I was fool enough to spread it on the table and say forgivingly, why yes. At which point, with a look of manic triumph, she produced a two-foot rolling pin out of nowhere and brought it down with all her might across the same bloody palm."

"Bloody hell, man," I said aghast. "Bloody stinking hell! Why didn't you just give her one back?"

Holland drummed his hairy old fingers and considered long. "I just couldn't manage it. I felt a terrible rage, of course, and there were occasions I sat at home waiting to confront her, ready to give her her own medicine. But as soon as she appeared before me in the flesh, I was incapable of any harsh retaliation. Not only was she extraordinarily beautiful, but Penelope also looked enormously vulnerable for much of the time. When she wasn't in an angry mood, she frequently came across as very pitifully damaged. Her upbringing was very quirky and queer, all these things have a sordid explanation of a kind. My hunch is Sir Magnus Asquith must have manhandled and dominated his only daughter in more ways than one. Some men of the old school simply cannot cope with their daughters being too strikingly attractive, if you know what I mean. He was a surly moody old dipsomaniac and his wife Lady Marion heard the voices of the dead so she claimed. Whatever the reason, I could not hit Penelope Holland. The fists would not respond to the feelings. Because, I suppose, the feelings evaporated as I looked at her, and I thought, yes, she is mad, my wife, and therefore not exactly responsible for her actions. She is crazy, my Penelope, and I am bloody well married to her for life."

After a very long silence I said in a hoarse voice, "Well. I have learnt a lot. I think I have learnt one hell of a lot."

"Oh no you haven't!" Captain Hornblower said brusquely and resentfully. And he went battering on with a dogged monotonal determination, as if resolved to purge himself, no matter what. "You have not learned all by any means. I haven't explained yet that while the beautiful young physics teacher persistently reviled me, she also liked to tantalise me sexually. No, don't blanch and look so shocked, boy, it's the kind of thing that might prepare you for the very worst yourself. You'll meet plenty of disdainful neurotic little Dostoevskyan ice-blocks down there at Oxford, believe you me. More than once mad Penelope would change from an afternoon of being vicious and abusive to an evening of being grotesquely and teasingly seductive. There is no other explanation for why I stayed married to her for five whole years. Penny Holland would throw me the agonising bait of her nakedness or her mouthwatering deshabille or her simpering suggestiveness. Sometimes she would lead me into the bedchamber and have me at a fever pitch, then clamp her legs tight and bite at my cheek or ear until the blood came. Once she varied the sadistic pattern and ran skin-naked out of the bedroom, only to bolt the door from the outside and leave me there alone, a ludicrous prisoner, all the night. I sat there like a sorrowing hermit, incarcerated, humiliated, quietly weeping like some desolate pitiful child." He snorted extremely heavily as he stared at the ends of his nicotined fingernails. "Other things that she did cannot be put into words."

I advised him brusquely, "Don't say them then. I really don't think I need to know any more."

"But someone has to know!" he snapped with an ugly, accusing face. "Someone has to be bloody well told! Why the bloody hell should I have to carry it all inside myself like some festering filthy sore? Is that all I deserve after all? You listen to me carefully, Enzo Mori, now that you've started me off on my hellish confessional. Can you seriously credit that on occasions my wife Penny, that she would pretend to respond to my embrace, then giggle insanely and jeeringly raise her manicured fingers up to my nose?"

I had no idea what the hell he was driving at. "Eh? Meaning what?"

"The index finger of this respectable middle-class physics mistress would have been daubed with something. Something disgusting, foul and evil-smelling. Something that she'd prised from her own beautiful person. Isn't it really quite incredible what certain hopeless individuals are capable of, Enzo Mori?"

I gulped and scowled at him disgusted, "I think that we should change the bloody subject, man."

He leered at me incensed. "No we bloody shouldn't! I've been changing the subject for the last ten bloody years, boy!"

"Please!"

"Not at all!" he snapped. "I have more to say yet. She would – "

But he broke off looking terrified as the door burst open and in came a very inebriated ice-cream salesman.

4

♪♪♪

Vincenzo Mori was carrying his clarinet case and a half bottle of Teachers whisky. He stood by the door smiling beatifically, then began to whistle what sounded like a recent saccharine pop song. Puzzled by his rapturous, incandescent aspect, I looked at my watch and saw it was just after one. Then I remembered that the Chompin Stompers had had an important gig that night at Cleator Moor Working Men's Club. My father, the bandleader, had earned a quarter of the standard second-string fee of thirty quid, of which another quarter had just been blown on Teachers. We all three smelt strongly of whisky, of course, but my father also reeked of eight-and-a-half pints of Hartley's real ale. Blowing a reed is a thirsty business and Vince Mori always drank copiously during his sets. Any other clarinettist would have grown tight and warbled wrong notes, but my father's virtuosity, tempered as it was within the disciplined confines of trad, rose in linear proportion to his alcohol intake.

"*Ciao*, Watson. Anchelika has told me you was teachin this boy here ow to old his drink. So's he can *centellinare* lots of Peemz an Motty Shandy wif byootiful debtante ladies, Leddy This, Leddy That, down in Osfod. Tonight I tellt everyone in Chompin Stompers band my briny son Enzo was goin to Osfod and they all buyed me a pint of Hartley's an stufft a blurry Cashtella in my clarinet." He swayed both vertically and laterally, then stumbled over a leather pouffe and cursed it roundly. "*Cattivoschifoso* fookabassardakoonta. *Scusi*. Forgiff me, Watson,

I has had a very spesal night *stanotte*. Trink, trink, trink an more trink. Also *stasera* I did two very byootful encore of *Stranger On A Course*. Also at Klitter More Workin Men's, *stanotte*, I meet a lot of very famous *celebrità*…"

He paused, rubbed his sweating nose, tried to control his rolling eyeballs, and awaited our breathless enquiries. Holland, as if by magic, had wiped away his morbid desperation and proffered his landlord a glass of malt. My father became grave, then unabashedly tearful at the gesture. To the pharmacist's horror he staggered across and kissed his hairy cheek and gave him a Calabresan bear hug. Captain Hornblower eyed me balefully over Vince's shoulder vice, as if to say, from one tale of excessive gothic cruelty to another of extravagant cosmopolitan farce.

"Inglishmens don't huck," complained Vince mournfully, after relinquishing Watson's breast.

The pharmacist misheard him and began to remonstrate loudly at the outrageous slur.

"Poppycock, man. I can assure you, Vincenzo, I for one – "

Vince hiccuped slightly, "Don't huck an don't kitz. *Per che* is this, Watson?"

"Eh? Oh I see. I see now what you're saying. Mm, cultural differences, Vincenzo. Mm ah. It's thought rather unmanly and effeminate and suggestive of homosexuality for two chaps to noisily embrace and slobber."

"*Che?*" Vince grinned lewdly. "In Roccella it was the mens who *din't not* huck an kitz was the *omosessuales*."

I sighed and attempted to steer him back to his original theme. "What celebrities? I thought you and the Stompers were the celebrities there tonight."

Far from it, grunted my old father, with a bemused if stoical expression. The Stompers had been merely a humble local warm-up band, playing for the first hour on the gigantic stage of the palatial Working Men's. It was Thursday night, meaning star band attractions, and tonight the theme was 'Pop Giants Of The Swinging Sixties'. The Stompers had been blowing their guts out to a largely indifferent audience who had only come along to listen to erstwhile superbands currently obliged to tour the lesser known northern clubs. The committee of Cleator Moor Working Men's had managed to hire for the same evening no less than four such historical megastars. The last of them, Wayne Fontana and the Mindbenders, were still busy raising the club roof. To fund such an extravagant outlay they had advertised the gargantuan musical feast widely, and coaches from as far afield as Barrow-in-Furness, Carlisle and the Scottish Borders had come to pay homage. However there had also been a superfluous and quite disgraceful enticement, a wholly disreputable mystery item, which eventually revealed its unsavoury nature as my father developed his boastful narrative.

"I talkt to Lippy Leek," he smirked enigmatically at Watson Holland. The pharmacist looked thoroughly vacant, before turning mournfully to the dying strains of Ravel's string quartet in its Czechoslovak version. My father waited patiently for his lodger's reverent adulation, but unfortunately Holland didn't know whether he was referring to a pop band, a leek show or something to do with Avon cosmetics.

"Lips and Licks?" he attempted bravely. "I see, I see, I see."

"Leapy Lee," I translated. "A pop singer who was famous a few years back. Once he toured the world as a superstar but now he tops the bill at Cleator Moor. His lyrics were about Classical Greek mythology, about Cupid and falling in love. Don't you recall his *Little Arrows that will hit you once... and hit you once again...?*"

"Extraordinary," mused Holland, "that any sane parent should christen his child Leapy."

Leapy, it transpired, had been very affable towards the respectful Stompers. He had even bought Vince a pint of Hartley's when he learnt of his son Enzo being accepted to read 'animal fizzlegy' at Osfod. Thrilled at this democratic acceptance by the metropolitan greats, Vince had knocked on the door of the Working Men's dressing room and shamelessly introduced himself to everyone inside. It was hard to credit, but apparently they were all as ecstatic as the ice-cream salesman that his son was going to Balliol in October to read about the complex inner workings of the animal body.

"Head Shoppers Omniboose," he enthused. "Great boys. Great *commediantes*. I pisht my blurry self."

"Hedgehoppers Anonymous," I whispered to Holland. "A comic parody band. Who were very very big in 1965."

"Parody," he murmured back, incredulous. "But why, I wonder, would anyone wish to ridicule what is pointlessly atrocious to start with?"

"Wong Fontana an his Moonbenders!" drooled Vince. "The Hunnikums! A bootiful *fanciulla* playin on the bloody *timpano*! She was a really bonny big-built big lash, the Hunnikum drummer."

Hypnotised by his vivid memories of that delectable female percussionist, he grabbed at an imaginary mike and began to warble ariawise the only two lines he could remember of that band's monumental Number One hit…

> *Aw gum write back!*
> *Ah just canned pear it!*
> *Ah…*

He could go no further but his smile was serenely transcendent in its depthless happiness. He looked as proudly proprietorial as if he had penned those tragic Verdiesque sentiments (*ah just canned pear it!*) himself. At last he sat down exhausted and consumed his glass of malt in a single swallow. Surveying us tenderly, Vince seemed to detect ever such a subtle Anglo-Saxon hesitation in our response to his performance. Watson Holland was a middle-class Englishman of course, very nice, *molto gentile*, but for all that he had a six-inch tungsten bolt up his arse like they all had, the English. Give 'em a manly kiss on their stiff cheeks and they generally passed water in sheer terror. Enzo on the other hand was a cocksure schoolboy who, *sfortunatamente*, was only half-Italian. He had the dour genetic endowment of Angelica who – don't be fooled by her fancy Christian name – was dockland Whitehaven bred to the bone. Clearly this muted reaction of ours to his breathtaking

Honeycomb rendition (Vince, we later learnt, had tonight blown 42/11 on their latest double LP) was responsible for the disgraceful episode that followed. Anyone else would have kept his shameful trap shut, but my father being an intoxicated South Italian could not resist a little bragging.

"Watson," he hissed with a fierce glint in his eye. "Psst! Hey Watson. *Psst!*"

It was a Reggio di Calabrian *psst!* Meaning that, as *pssts!* go, it was leering, salacious and thoroughly repulsive coming from anyone over the age of twenty. My father in 1969 was nearly fifty years old. Watson Holland stayed diplomatically silent but lifted his eyebrows with a compliant expression.

Vince Mori lit up his Castella and smirked gravely at this smartly-attired Englishman who was about his own age.

"Klitter More Workin Men's," he said gravely. "It is famoush all over Koomberlent for somefing *molto scandaloso.*"

Eyes half-shut like an 'Ndrangheta gangster, he rambled on with many lascivious winks, nods, and redundant doubles entendres. Holland, who had just been talking about something infinitely scandalous, the pathological sadism of his wife, was moderately intrigued. I, on the other hand, soon lost all patience.

"What he's trying to tell you, oh so coyly, is that Thursday night, by general agreement, is designated *wife-swapping* night at Cleator Moor Working Men's."

Watson Holland rose at least six inches in his chair. "Well, bugger me!"

I sighed at his overdone theatrical manner. "Remarkable isn't it? A remote little Irish Cumbrian community, one of the poorest towns in the country, over half of it pious third-generation Catholics. In this incongruous setting, Thursday is not only Big Group Bonanza at the local Working Men's, it is also Sodom and Gomorrah Night. That's why, you see, they have all those bloody coaches and charabancs travelling all the way from Barrow and Dumfries. Not all of them are driving up there specifically to hear a musical legend like Leapy Lee. They aren't even going to hear my Dad play two deathless encores of *Stranger*

On The Shore. Instead they're going to participate *actively* in an interesting two-hander ballet called *Stranger On The Back Seat*."

Holland said frowning, "I'm afraid you've rather lost me there. I don't really follow what the hell you are talking about."

"The ballet performed on the back seat of the Ford Zodiac or the Ford Corsair. At the end of every Thursday night, all the married couples who have been eyeing each other up, they sidle across and offer each other their car keys. With a nod and a wink they quickly agree to swap partners, and arrange to meet up at say two or three o'clock in the car park. Then these newly formed hybrid couples drive off a few miles to somewhere very quiet, and with feverish erotic impatience they take off their – "

"Yes, yes, yes," gasped Holland. "I can just about imagine what follows in this charming example of small-town pageantry. But but, dammit, one can scarcely imagine such a perverse sybaritic practice being allowed in central London or downtown New York, never mind Cleator bloody Moor. Isn't something as flagrantly bacchanalian and orgiastic technically illegal in the United Kingdom? Plus, if they are third-generation Irish, as you say, can't old Father MacGillicuddy come round in his swishing soutane and bawl and threaten to have them all excommunicated?"

My father tittered complacently as he summed it all up in one truthful sentence. *"Klitter More,"* he said wisely, *"is blurry well rotten with seksh."*

I sniffed and told him that I was delighted that I was only eighteen years old, and thus spared all this senile *News of the World* excess. So much for so-called grown adults was my implied, unspoken criticism, this back door, grubby sexual license. Watson Holland noticed that pious, superior expression of mine and could not resist the relishable irony. He leant across po-faced to about an inch from my nose and whispered just one word:

"Scripture."

Eh? Scripture? I blushed furnace red and looked to see if my grinning father had understood the reference. But the drunken clarinettist showed no signs of comprehension, nor even of wondering why his lodger was mouthing sweet nothings at his long-haired son. My father looked surpassingly vacant in his present inebriation, which was why I almost shot out of my skin at what he said next.

"I have a pair of khakis chuckt at *me* tonight…"

Khakis? *Car keys? Tonight?*

There was a remarkably noisy silence that lasted for several seconds. Then followed an intake of breath from Watson Holland. I stared at my drunken father who was grinning like the village idiot who has just won a cake-eating contest. I thought, surely to God I must have misheard him, he can't possibly have said what I thought he said.

And then he proudly repeated his preposterous boast. "It appen to me as well, the blurry khakis!"

I hissed at him viciously. "You didn't. You bloody well didn't! You wouldn't bloody well *dare*!"

"*Che?*" he said very righteously. "I blurry well did. I mean *she* blurry well tit."

I snorted, "Stop your bloody awful joking! My mother might come walking in here at any minute and it's not bloody funny."

My father wagged his head disparagingly at my puerile piety. "Anchelika is awready goned up to bed. An I am not chokin, Enzo Mori."

Not choking? He soon bloody well would be. He was smiling at me in an unctuous, baronial manner, without the faintest trace of paternal remorse.

I raised my right fist and clenched it threateningly. "Apart from anything else you had no partner with you tonight! You had no wife with you to do any bloody swap! Because your wife, my mother, has been here all bloody night with us! Not that she would ever – "

He purred away teasingly, remorselessly, "I has no patner, *certamente*. But neiffer have this woman, Chenfa. *Lei*, this Chenfa, she was sittin all alone on her blurry own all the night before she meet me."

"Eh?" I shuddered, feeling horribly dizzy. "Jennifer. Jennifer

Who? Don't be so bloody ridiculous, so utterly preposterous! God almighty, nobody in their right minds would look twice at… I don't believe a bloody word of…! You stupid, you simpering bloody old bast – "

Thirty years later I can still feel the bilious disorientation that seized me as I listened to his unrelenting villainy. His excessively Mediterranean temperament had embarrassed me plenty in its day, but nothing he'd said or done before had ever thrown me into this visceral confusion. For all his mercurial extravagance my father had always been a thoroughly conscientious husband. Twenty years earlier the diminutive Italian collier and the strapping Whitehaven factory seamstress had been solemnly married in Hensingham church. Last month they had celebrated their anniversary with a riotous hundred-invitation party at the Chase Hotel. Of course they'd had their regular bickerings and numerous heated rows and Vince had once or twice stomped out like a flouncing Rossini tenor when she'd ordered him to play less Ball and Bilk and wash more lodgers' dishes. But sexual straying, philandering? It was utterly inconceivable. It was rather more likely that Vincenzo would adopt his son's current studious reading habits and start perusing the novels of André Gide, Gustave Flaubert and Lawrence Durrell.

"Chenfa has an hoodspent on the rix," he announced momentously.

Watson Holland twitched and flinched at that baffling sentence, thinking perhaps this Jennifer had a nasty wart on her private parts.

"A husband on the oil rigs?" I scoffed. "Well I hope when he returns from the North Sea he strangles you slowly and painfully. You realise of course they're built like brick shithouses, all those buggers? But hell alive, why am I encouraging your stupid little fairytale? I don't believe a single bloody word of it."

Vince took on a tragic expression as he slurped his Teachers neat from the bottle.

"He is callt Sidney. Chenfa tell me is *un uomo brusco e brutale*. He is also a blurry cider addick, Watson. Mad, doolally, crazy and blurry apeshite wif it. He drink only draft All Tingleish cider. No trink *permesso* on the rix, of coss, but when Sidney is *in casa* in Klitter More he drink it draft up to *dodici* blurry pints every blurry night. Then he go *pazzo* an apeshite wif it, and hit poor bootful Chenfa an smash up her ouse, very nice dupple-glashed bunglow hardly any moggish left to pay off, up by Rheda. Udder times Sidney run shcreamin into *giardino* an tear up plant by rut, shrup an bettin pants an trellishish an noms and evry blurry *ornamente…*"

"Appalling," commented Holland and it was obvious he meant the oil rigger's horticultural vandalism rather than the infidelity of my father. "Absolutely bloody appalling, Vincenzo."

"This is ow it all appen wif Chenfa, Watson. I finish talkin wif Lippy Leek about alf pass ten. I say *ciao* Lippy, *arrivederci*. I walk across to say sumfink to Wilfred Fizzugly the Chumpin Shtumpin trumbunisht. *Allora*, I pass by *tavola* where Chenfa is sit right next to Ladiesh bogs, all on her own lookin very bootful an a little *malinconica*. She look up at me for juss one second and so I smile at her. I stop by table, say *ciao*, ow are you, an *who* are you?, and we is chat very easy and *affabili*. After mebbe ten, mebbe twenty minute, Chenfa suddenly look down an fish in her ant back. I fink to myself, she is lookin for a fack…"

"Good Lord," gasped Holland amazed.

"He means a fag," I glossed sourly.

"I fink she look for pack of fack. I see twenty Rickle shittin in her ant back. But slowly slowly Chenfa hand me her khaki an smile an say, I fink you is a very niesh man…"

I guffawed with a braying, demented sound.

"I fink, mister, you very nice frenly quite attractive, kind an sensitif and ave very interestin face an I these days is juss a very lonely woman…"

I snorted and thumped my clenched fist against the settee. The worldlywise pharmacist on the other hand was starting to relax and really enjoy himself. After the fearful catharsis of his own too sordid confessions, Watson Holland was more or less soothed to hear his landlord's tender little story.

"Well, I has a tate. I has a tate for a long time. But I has have a lot of Arshley's beer. I bout to say no because of coss I luff my Anchelika Mori for *venti anni*. Stop blurry shnortin Enzo, *idiota*, of coss I luff Chelika your mudder, for twenty blurry year. But *allora* Chenfa say, no, Fins, Fins Mori, is your name, eh? No for *cosi cosa* I want you tonight, but juss take me for a drife. Please, you take me for drife in your car an be *simpatico* while I tell you all my blurry trooples. Take me please some place quite an *pacifico*. I shit down obedient at her table an buy her double chin and then she tell me gradwally about Sidney an Ole Tingleish an rippin up her favourite bettin pants. Purr little Chenfa is very keen at *orticultura* so *brutale* Shidney muss tear up her owny bright and joy in blurry life…"

I couldn't contain myself. "OK. *Allora*, as you Eyeties say. Tell us then. Did you really bloody drive her somewhere? That's the only thing that really matters as far as I'm concerned. Buying her a friendly gin and tonic is one thing but – "

"Yesh," replied my father with a maudlin smile, and he belched unpleasantly in my direction. Enraged, incensed, unhinged, I lunged for his throat, whereupon Watson Holland shot up from his chair and shoved me back onto the sofa.

"You wicked bastard!" I roared, quite beyond myself, and almost tearful with anger. "Apart from anything else, you were stone drunk, weren't you? What if you'd killed someone driving your bloody car? What if you'd been stopped by the police? How would you keep your ice-cream van without a driving license? D'you think you can manage to drive around Whitehaven selling Mivvis from a horse and bloody cart?"

He sneered at me as if I were some nagging old feeble Roccella *nonna*, "Enzo, I can old any amount of blurry drink. Drifin a van all day is my blurry bishness. I can drive any blurry feekle wif my blurry eyes clost."

"You," I snorted, "can hardly stand on your feet at this moment, never mind drive. You've just been cursing an inanimate leather pouffe, you filthy old philanderer!"

"I's always cussin at that blurry puff, Enzo! *Allora*, Watson, I haff listen for long long time to Chenfa's very *triste* story. I am so terrible muffed, I decide I muss be kind to her and take her for a quiet drife. But at once I ass myself, where is shootable to go? I wreck my brines wif this problem an fink, *forse per esempio*, Wasswatter? No, too dark, *più fosco* and too blurry far. So *allora* I fink, sud we go off to blurry Moccasin Tan…?"

"Mockerkin Tarn," I threw at Holland sulkily. "Wastwater would have cost him too much petrol."

"… no Moccasin, *perche* damn road is too windy-bendy an she might be blurry shick in my car. An Anchelika haff just put new velcro cuffers on the shit, and new tartan rucks on the floor."

It was the adventitious details that did for me. Here was my father blithely, amnesically boasting to his son about his romantic liaison with the wife of a psychopathic oil rigger. Yet in between hints of the tender feelings she inspired in his painfully amorous South Italian heart, he could not omit to mention the imposing double glazing of Jennifer's bungalow, nor the new seat covers in his Anglia which his inamorata might end up soiling. I didn't know whether to laugh or cry as I was seized by a griping, paralysing fear inside my teenage stomach. I had always worked on the ballasting assumption that my parents were entirely loyal to each other, were indeed intrinsically sexless entities. To be sure, our house was currently chockful of lodgers and our two bedrooms were at opposite ends of the second floor, so unless I skulked with cupped ear by the bannisters, there was no possible confirmation of this puerile fantasy. Childishly, I assumed they'd always lain together old, chaste and incapacitated, and would have been deeply disgusted to assume anything else. I now came to the byzantine conclusion that this permanently impoverished marital state was directly responsible for my father's present fit of menopausal madness.

Before beginning his possibly risky erotic itinerary, my father's deliberations had been painstaking and lengthy. Sure enough the cost of the petrol involved had been a significant calculation. In the end he had driven Jennifer only three or four miles in the St Bees direction, and had parked up by the edge of a lonely wood. It was along the narrow Linethwaite road, nothing down that way but a couple of farms, a couple of spinneys, and a monotonous spread of undulating fields and ragged hedges. I sat there breathless and dismayed as I waited for him to explain how Jennifer took off her bra and tights and leapt upon him like a panting Cleator Moor cheetah. I also wondered how many other such assignations had accompanied his far-flung Chompin Stomper gigs. Last week for example they had been third string at a riotous Forestry Dance up at remote Kershopefoot, aka Cumbria's Ladakh, right on the Scottish border. Afterwards Vince had said his spectacularly tousled disarray was on account of being caught in a stampede to the buffet alongside a thousand North Cumbrian bucolic maniacs. But perhaps right there, a hundred yards from the border, my father had been indulging in transitional two-countries adultery. Perhaps the immoral clarinettist had a glamorous fancy woman in every single dance venue, all four hundred plus, right across rural Cumberland? How were we to know one way or the other? Presumably he had sworn the rest of the Stompers to secrecy. For that matter, probably hulking, misshapen trombonist Wilf Phizacklea, sleepy percussionist Miff Mumberson with his extremely cut-price Taiwanese toupee acquired via *Exchange and Mart*, Dave the devious trumpeter with the loose, hissing dentures, no doubt the whole bloody lot of them were two-faced philandering bloody rogues!

"It was an byootiful full moon *stasera*," said Vince in a melting, very husky voice. "*Allora, prima* me an Chenfa talk in my car about everyfink."

I turned on him witheringly. "Did you remember to tell her about me going to Oxford?"

"Of coss I tell! She was very very pleast for me. She say she has a briny nefoo Cyril does Chogfy at Hawful Pollychetnik."

I scoffed, "Cyril of Hatfield Poly eh? And did you remember to tell her about my mother as well? Did you have a good chat with Jennifer about your wife?"

"*Certamente.* She was very pleast to hear how Chelika luffs me so much. It was such a byutful perfeck summer *notte*, Watson. I say, *venga, andiamo,* Chenfa, let us leaf this car and your sad, sad farts, and let us walk by the moonlit *nella foresta*."

Hypnotised by the diminutive ice-cream Romeo, Jennifer had acquiesced of course. It doubtless made a change, this late night sylvan romping, from sad, sad thoughts of having your favourite shrubs ripped up by vengeful Old English-crazed Sidney. To wander by burning pregnant moonlight through Linethwaite Woods and see the sleeping birches frozen in a willing, tender reverie. Trees silvered by the brush of moonlight and a kind little, polite little, drunk little, comical little Eyetie clarinettist called Vince Mori. The fourpenny cornet man, the sixpenny oyster man, the ninepenny ninety-nine man, the one who talked so unintelligibly in something mesmerisingly close to Cumbrio-Mandarin Chinese.

"What happened on this walk?" I interrogated him sadistically. "Come on. Cat got your tongue has it, Vince? I don't suppose you'll have the guts to spell it all out in black and white. Never mind. Just nod your head yes or no, that'll do for now. Did you go the whole hog?"

My father blinked like a condescending old Italian count. *"Che?"*

"The whole hog. Did you go it?"

"Who is spose be this old dog, Watshon? *Enzo capisce niente.*"

"I could make a very good ribald jest, Vincenzo, but I don't think your son here would like it."

"You bastard!" I said, advancing on Vince. "Did you kiss her? Tell me, did you stop there in the moonlight and did you kiss her? Did you?"

"Che?"

"On second thoughts, don't tell me! I don't want to hear the loathsome details."

"Forse. Hic. I do not remember."

"Bastard! You bastard! You don't remember? *You don't remember?* Where do you think you are? On trial at bloody Nuremberg? Either you did kiss her, or you didn't kiss her. Very

83

well then. Did you and this woman hold hands?"

Vince yawned at me as if I were a troublesome gnat and he was a sleepy old cow.

"*Forse*," he managed at last. "Praps we tit."

"You bloody old bastard! Say yes or no or I'll kill you!"

"OK, OK, we dids. We did old ands. Why not? A mudder is allowt to old the child of the blurry and. No, *cosa contraria*, I mean the blurry and of the child! *Inoltre*, a friend may old the and of the friend. *Allora*, it is very normal. In Italy two mens will allus old and an link hams when they is good friend. But not blurry here, not in Whitey Vaughan, Koomberlent! Why not? It is a simple yumman fing to do…"

I snorted, "Not when you're married, it isn't. Not at bloody midnight in a lonely deserted wood."

"*Cosa senza senso!* She is juss an hurt woman and I is juss like a kine very dear friend to her."

"Oh really? How very touching. In that case we'll tell Angelica Mori all about it tomorrow."

"*Che?*"

"Maybe she could be a sympathetic friend for this Jennifer. Why don't we introduce them? I bet Angelica would want to kick bullying Sidney Oilrig in the bollicks for one thing." I tailed off slowly with a parting shot. "After she's finished kicking the bollicks belonging to you. If you have any, that is."

"*Briccone!*" bellowed Vince Mori, and he frothed and slavered as he lunged at me. He was hindered from disembowelling me only by an armlock from Watson Holland. "*Furfante! Va' fan culo!* Bastakoontafookabasta! I nog your fuggy blurry blog off, you longhair little basset! Say *anyfink* to my Chelika and I cut you in blurry little pishish, Enzo Mori."

"*Briccone* yourself!" I shouted back. "You bloody little hypocrite! You bloody two-faced dirty little leering, groping Eyetie!"

The pharmacist piously admonished us and ordered us to shush, lest we waken dear Mrs Mori, the finest landlady he had ever known or indeed ever would know. Her sulky old husband grunted and scowled but eventually consented to justify his equivocal legal position. On the breast of his dear dead mother, Fabrizia Ginevra Mori, he swore that he had not done anything, done *assolutamente nulla* remotely describable as 'the ole dog'. On the honour of his dear dead father, Carlo Goffredo Mori, the Roccella hamlet's long-serving gravedigger, all that had happened was a single chaste and innocent kiss with Jennifer. Understandably enough, she had seemed to want a more rewarding contact with his obviously experienced Italian mouth, but he had sadly protested his loyalty to Angelica and the lasting emotional security of this son of his who was about to start a luminous intellectual career at Oxfod.

"Thank you so much," I sneered. "That you should think so heroically of me and Mum at such a diverting time. But chew on this. You didn't have to tell us any of this in the first bloody place, did you? It could have stayed your dirty little, pointless little, grubby little secret for evermore. Instead, you couldn't resist bragging about it and polluting my mother's best parlour."

Vince Mori pursed his lips and furrowed his brow, as if to offer belated dispassionate judgement on his warm-hearted garrulity. *Forse*, I could hear him muttering witlessly inside his head. *Forse.*

"No," he said at last, exculpating himself with a confident, expansive smile. "I know I has noffin to fill any gilt about."

He went on to describe in a throaty, heavy-lidded ecstasy the beautiful mystery, the hallowed wonder of those sylvan birches and that silver moonlight. The sum of his boozy effusion was that he and Jennifer had only been five miles from a busy town like Whitehaven but they might as well have been in Avalon or Arcadia or the Garden of Eden *stasera*. The two of them, Vince and Jennifer, had held hands like awe-stricken children in a phantasmal wood. Of course those weren't his precise metaphorical terms, but his intended poetic sense was plain enough. He might have been very drunk, but he addressed us with emphatic vehemence and unashamed passion. He glanced sharply at his son throughout his tender little love story, daring him to denounce his father for having a sentient heart, and a mouth to give that heart utterance. On a once in a lifetime occasion such as this, in a beautiful wood with a handsome woman underneath a molten Linethwaite silver moon, was Vincenzo Mori supposed to act like some frightened anaemic sissy without any balls and without any soul?

They had gently held hands and imbibed the white, almost frightening vibrance emanating from the trees. They had wallowed and virtually drowned in this perfect night of impeccable, meaning sinless, romance, which was illicit and dangerous and wrong, and yet infinitely chaste and remarkably pure.

"I wunt have misst that *bella passeggiata*, my one night wif Chenfa," he concluded with a steely absolute righteousness, "for ten million blurry pound."

He clenched his powerful ex-collier's knuckles and challenged me to deny the mettle of this ineffable personal truth.

"Bas– " I began feebly.

Slowly, I turned my eyes towards the waning coalfire, well away from the defiance of my father's gaze. Having sensed, all too clearly, that I was only just a boy after all...

There came a sudden ugly growl from his direction. I looked at Vince and saw it wasn't his primitive Calabrian anger, the legacy of dire poverty, unimpeachable family honour and that ferocious Roccella sun. It was the jazz, the complex fugal syncopation of his deafening snore. My father had closed a catastrophic argument simply by falling asleep. And, yes, he looked so overwhelmingly, unbelievably innocent in his obviously untroubled dreams.

5

Those two confessionals on the same night were almost too much for me. I had listened dismayed to our exuberant lodger's pitiful history of grotesque domestic abuse, then learnt that my own father was capable not to say defiantly proud of having an extramarital affair. Those revelations had happened in surreal and rapid succession, and were so poignantly contrasting they seemed to have been intended as some preordained object lesson. But what exactly was the instructive moral, I wondered to myself, wide awake in my bedroom at half past four in the morning? More to the point, did it make any subtle difference to anything that these two shocking confessions had taken place inside the blurry mental confines of an ocean of malt whisky?

It hardly mattered that I was insomniac, because it was Saturday tomorrow. I would follow my changeless pattern and sleep until lunchtime, then sit all afternoon in Whitehaven library reading the magazines. Later, in the evening, I would go out to the cinema with my girlfriend Elizabeth. *The Thomas Crown Affair* with Steve McQueen had been on all week, and tomorrow was its final showing. That innocuous word in the title, 'affair', made me shudder, and I felt both naive and confused as I wondered whether my father would keep on seeing lonely Jennifer. Surely one night of tender, arboreal romance would only whet his Mediterranean appetite for more? Would it be wiser, after all, to tell my mother his secret? Or perhaps I should write to Sidney, care of The Rigs, Sullom Voe, Scotland, and encourage him to break Vincenzo Mori's legs before he managed to break my mother's heart.

Of course I did not tell my mother about Jennifer, nor did I mention her name again to Vince. I was far too busy with my own affairs of the heart, meaning the time that I spent with my girlfriend, Elizabeth. Elizabeth Belling was sixteen, nervous, pensive, wide-eyed and the only child of the town's longest established vet. Elizabeth also intended to be a vet, possibly even enter her father's prosperous practice, a comforting progression I found queerly irritating. Joe Belling was noted for being brilliant when it came to cows and horses, but he hated working with small animals and left all that to his youthful employees, the junior vets. Joe was an expert not only with big animals but also with big women; florid, emphatic, heavily made-up frequenters of the Cons Club and the Golf Club who were naturally teased and delighted by his money, his banter and his boyish, silver-haired charm. His wife Flora had left him when Elizabeth was eleven, and although she lived with her mother, Elizabeth was deeply attached to her errant Dad. He was immensely loyal to his only daughter, and was delighted to hear she was aiming for Edinburgh where he had also trained thirty years ago. When he discovered she was dating a young chap about to read animal physiology at Oxford, he seemed to see it as a symbolic personal vindication. No matter that he had left his bonny little daughter fatherless at a crucial stage, now she was walking steadfastly in his footsteps and even courting a young man who sounded rather like Joe Belling.

All of which flew swiftly out of the window, as soon as the two of us got to know each other over an expensive dinner in an Ennerdale restaurant. Joe Belling was footing the bill of course, and spent the first hour hectically relating farcical anecdotes of his days in the Edinburgh veterinary labs. In thirty years he seemed to have forgotten an impressive amount, and it was startling to hear him confuse the names of several important blood vessels. Even with all those sharp young assistants I wondered how he managed to do surgery on Charolais bulls and

Shetland ponies when he mixed up the brachial and the ischial veins. Perhaps large animal surgery needed the skills of a cheerful pork butcher like Joe, rather than a fussy, meticulous obsession with anatomical names and obsolete Latin. Nevertheless I was quickly won over by his artlessly confiding manner and his natural generosity. I laughed at his simple little jokes and did not correct his anatomical errors, and it was obvious he was quietly grateful. I noticed also his touchingly nervous deference in the presence of all these soft-spoken doctors, dentists and solicitors who patronised this impressively extortionate lakeside bistro.

Joe Belling was a predictably rock-hard Tory, while I was a severely Stalinist Marxist. Over the fish course this ideological disjunction became rather glaringly apparent. Apropos the exquisite salmon the teenage Stalinist was voraciously guzzling, I opined that no one should be allowed to own any private fishing rights round here, and that surely anyone should be able to fish anywhere they liked. Elizabeth scowled and kicked my feet under the table, while my host sourly informed me that his father had paid the monstrous sum of £12,000 in 1930 for exclusive salmon rights on his stretch of the River Cocker. Chiding me for my senseless egalitarianism, he pointed out that half the roughest, foulest-mouthed kids in Cockermouth came flagrantly poaching and/or throwing stones at him whenever he tried to exercise his inherited rights. In fact the poaching and the harassment were getting him down to such an extent, he was seriously thinking of selling his salmon stretch. Rather than, say, handing it on to young Elizabeth… and – surveying me morosely – whoever his daughter ended up marrying.

I felt a mad, comic sensation rising in my throat. At the incredible notion of Enzo Gianmaria Mori ten years hence dapping and trolling in waders next to a sign saying *Please Bugger Off As This Stretch Of The Cocker Is My Wife's*. But instead of sneering at my ruffled host I said he'd simply proved my point. If no one was allowed to own the salmon rights, then both he and the cheeky kids would have equal access to the fish, whereupon they would cease throwing stones at him, perhaps even treat him with a friendly respect.

"Bloody hell," gaped Joe Belling, looking worriedly at his daughter, the only female in the world who could possibly command his emotional loyalty. He scrutinised me drily. "Well you're a modest sort. Nationalise all the trout and salmon, will we? And who's going to stock the bloody river, pray? Where would all those horrible nasty kids get the income to do it? Through stripping all the lead off Cockermouth roofs and selling it to the nearest scrapyard? Who's going to sort out the bloody bailiffing and the bloody river maintenance and – ?"

I brushed all his quibbles aside, and said the state could do everything: bailiffing, fish stocking, river cleaning, the lot. The dinner had advanced as far as the *crème brûlée* and brandied peaches, just as I downed my third glass of exquisite Chablis and quoted Proudhon to the effect that 'property is theft'. I also advised Belling, who spent half his life playing golf, that all the county's golf courses should immediately be nationalised and made free to anyone who wanted to use them. In addition any rough hooligan kids from say Frizington, Rowrah, Ginns or Kells should be able to stroll into Whitehaven Golf Club's cocktail bar and enjoy as many snacks and drinks as they wanted gratis, all of this to be paid for by the state or possibly the county council. Joe Belling looked at me in cold horror, informed me that I was bloody cracked, and told Elizabeth that she should have forewarned him her boyfriend was going up to Oxford to study comedy rather than natural science. Good God, he was like one of those feverish clowns off that bloody hellish and terrifying satirical programme called – what was it? – *Monty Python's Flying Circus*. All of those sneering overgrown wastrels had been Oxford-educated as well, hadn't they?

Six months later I went up to Balliol, and Joe Belling and I never ate *crème brûlée* together again. When Elizabeth and I broke up the following summer Joe's daughter was thoroughly heartbroken, but Whitehaven's oldest vet was thoroughly delighted. He paid for her to take a year out of veterinary school and bought her first-class air tickets to the Far East and Australia.

In Brisbane she met a medical student called William Bix, ten years her senior, and they fell rapidly in love. With Joe's limitless assistance she managed to transfer to an Australian veterinary school where he doubtless calculated she'd have even less chance of meeting Enzo Mori on the rebound. But by this stage I had lost all interest in Elizabeth, and was able without any guilt or dissimulation to devote myself to a fragile musical genius called Fanny Golightly…

♩♪♫

That is, the same Fanny Golightly who even thirty years on is still the only canonised female genius of the jazz guitar. More worryingly for her, this unlikely *rara avis* has long been reckoned to be one of the greatest jazz musicians of all time. Fanny Madeleine Golightly is regularly mentioned in the same breath as that virtuoso all-male roll call of Django Reinhardt, Charlie Christian, Joe Pass, John McLaughlin, Al DiMeola, Terje Rypdal, Paco de Lucia. She had achieved this mysterious and unassailable reputation by her early twenties because, quite clearly, she had extended the guitar's vocabulary beyond all reasonable bounds.

Historic reputations aside, Fanny is still the same as I knew her inside her Cowley Road bedsit of thirty years ago. She is almost fifty now in 1999, but for me she will always be the unfading young woman of nineteen or twenty years old. Those stark LP portraits might all have disappeared, the cassettes and CDs and double CDs might have shortened her hair and widened and softened the sharpness of her facial bones. But for Enzo Gianmaria Mori, her greatest fan, her hair stays beautifully long, her face remains piquantly thin, and her eyes will always be… extraordinarily young.

Thinking of her now at the end of the twentieth century, I feel myself grow younger by at least three decades. Clearer than my own rather unattractive nose, I can still picture that bare anchorite's chamber of hers, with only a single vivid example of visual decoration daubed on its white and flaking emulsioned walls.

In the winter of 1970 in letters three feet high in broad felt tip at two a.m. one February morning, the student Fanny Golightly had inscribed a lone and desperate shout of raging indignation.

FUCK! it shrieked unforgivingly at the unfailingly uncomprehending world. Scarcely an original declaration semantically or philosophically speaking, but the distorted passion behind that interjection was real and vast enough. Those letters were at least a yard high, I have to stress. To offset the violence of that severely spartan bohemian effect, there wasn't even a puny calendar, much less a student poster or a reproduction of Edvard Munch or Vincent van Gogh…

And at twenty years old, needless to add, I was infinitely thrilled by a woman like Fanny.

We met in that very first week at Oxford, but it was almost a year before I became infatuated enough to accept her in all her intensity. The young are no different from the old in this respect and are generally disconcerted by inordinate hypersensitivity. At nineteen Fanny Golightly was solemnly beautiful as well as highly strung, a powerful and unstable combination which apparently worked in her favour. She never lacked for appreciative company and had a doting stream of admirers from the very first day she entered the cloistered sobriety of Somerville College. Almost all these young males were either tamely diffident or feebly unassertive – Enzo Gianmaria Mori being no exception – as they invariably approached in open awe of this hieratic young queen.

Fanny's hair was bountiful, long and lustrously blond. It shone and glistened not sleekly but with the vivid sheen of some strong young animal. Yet she was always remarkably pale and drawn, as if she were endlessly contemplating some absent and unidentifiable element in this new Oxonian existence. That wan and delicate Burne-Jones aura was thrown into a heightened relief by her mesmerising hair. Jarring with everything was her accent, which was rawly provincial and northern working class, and hardly common in the corridors of Somerville. This slowly waning masonic snobbery was evident in the way so few she came into contact with could place her unusual regional accent. She was variously assumed to be Newcastle, Yorkshire, Lancashire, Welsh, Scottish, even Somerset, just as I was thought to be any-thing but a Cumbrian at Balliol College. I had never of course, not even as a child, shown any vestige of Vince Mori's mind-boggling patois. However Septimus Reid, the student in the room above mine, was not only baffled by my accent, he seri-ously believed that fictive province 'Cumberland' must be a part of Scotland. Newly arrived from Eton, Reid had a closed scholarship in English and was exceedingly intelligent, yet he simply did not concern himself with the fairytale geography of the obscurest British regions.

Fanny faced the identical sociolinguistic problem. She also, and it really was a very stupefying coincidence, was from godforsaken West Cumberland. As if that weren't enough, she came from one of the three roughest council estates in an unattractive suburb of Workington. As three decades have gone by, most of the jazz world, especially the tolerant and uncritical Americans, have stopped reeling from that quixotic and touching biographical fact. But I for one will never be less than stunned by such a subversive imaginative feat on the Creator's part. When he elected to produce one of the greatest jazz guitarists of all time, he made his musical genius not only West Cumbrian, but calmly flung aside all sociological restraint and made her a West Cumbrian woman. Not satisfied with these two baroque follies and because by right-eous dispensation he has an infinitely poignant and unplumbable sense of irony, he had her grow up in a decrepit now-boarded-up little Workington council house, 37 Mungrisdale Rise, Salterbeck, Workington, Cumbria, CA14 5TU to be precise.

I was walking towards the physiology labs when I first properly noticed her. Fanny Golightly was hurrying for a philology tutorial at Keble, alone, preoccupied, and trailing a very long black trench coat. She stopped and gave me a distant but acknowledging smile. It seemed as if she definitely recognised me, perhaps from a recent party. I also thought I'd seen her somewhere else, though I had no idea where. It certainly wasn't a case of having bumped into each other in circumscribed West Cumbria. Even though they are only seven miles apart, Workington and Whitehaven exist in separate and hermetic equatorial spheres. Nor had I ever seen her swimming on Allonby beach or cavorting at Braystones dances or being drunk and incoherent at the Silloth Lido. She paused for two seconds, stared at me bemused, and made an inaudible hello. Before I could respond to the unimaginable delicacy of her hair and that sense of an infinitely significant but maddeningly transient instant, she had vanished into the hideous-looking biscuit factory that is Keble College.

We never met there again, as her philology tutorials only lasted a term. But over the next few months, usually several times a week, we found ourselves eating at that same downstairs table in George's Café. The inevitability of these first meetings was not all that miraculous. That friendly and very cheap market café wouldn't have been out of place in dowdy Workington or even drabber Maryport. It seemed to us both to have been purpose-built for two restless exiles from the north. Thanks to these idiosyncratic origins it was impossible to treat each other in any neutral or provisional manner. Fanny had a resonantly strong Workington accent and it sounded wonderfully abrasive in this calm pedagogic city. On that sunny October morning in 1969, when I first heard a whole raw Salterbeck sentence from her lips, I blinked in grave disbelief. I almost upset my vast chipped mug of evap-flavoured chicory. I leant incredulous across the table and politely challenged her to deny that she was from Workington, West Cumberland or one of its satellite villages. After she'd flushed with surprise and silently nodded, I added without irony that this, meaning she, was a turn up for the books.

"Oh?" she said quickly. She had heard just two short sentences from my lips and my glaring Whitehaven inflections left her just as puzzled. It was as if we'd been two desert Tuaregs who had somehow found themselves at the same table in downtown New York. Our unique and unglamorous provenance was more than just some picturesque coincidence.

We began to talk of common reference points. I named one or two outré Workington personalities, and she pondered and cited a half dozen Whitehaven counterparts. Then I introduced myself and sheepishly explained about my Italian father and the West Cumbrian mother with that confusingly Italian-sounding Christian name, Angelica…

She said, "It makes sense that you have such a foreign name. To be honest at first I thought you were Jewish. You have a very dark complexion, and those are very dark and piercing eyes."

"Oh?" I said blushing.

"You definitely look like a foreigner, but you don't speak like one. And I'm sure I must have seen your Dad's ice-cream van on at least one occasion. I think I bought a strawberry Mivvi or possibly an Orange Maid from him once on Parton shore. It cost me sixpence, I must have been about ten years old, so it must have been about 1960. The way he speaks, your father's English, is… really very distinctive. He's a Mister Softy isn't he?"

"Mister Whippy," I corrected. "He used to be a Mister Softy, but something happened to the franchise."

She smiled and flounced her flawless hair from side to side. Formerly a softy, now a whippy, she chuckled. It sounds like the bloody Kinsey report, like a risqué shorthand code for someone's sexual predilections. I blinked at the very confident vocabulary and wondered if I were dreaming. Surely no one with a thick Salterbeck accent was supposed to have the hair of a mournful Siennese principessa or to bandy such big words. I felt my belly tightening and twinging with a naively possessive provincial pride. Without further subtle preamble I asked my trench-coated compatriot what she made of the existential sociology of this ancient and hallowed university town at the tail end of the most culturally explosive decade of the twentieth century.

Fanny blew at the skin of her Camp and said something rather strange. She said that Oxford sometimes felt as icy as the top of Scafell Pike, and what it needed was some sort of heat... or rather, she meant warmth. It was actually a mild autumn day as she spoke, the bright sunlight was dappling my processed cheese on toast, and I was temporarily puzzled. Just as surprising was her sincere excitement when she began to describe her English student's philological fascination with Old Norse and Old Icelandic. Far from being considered recondite specialist studies, these were a major part of her literature degree, whilst hesitant entities like E.M. Forster, James Joyce and Virginia Woolf had only just scraped onto the syllabus. Like her musical talent her linguistic flair was seemingly effortless and rooted in a phenomenal memory. As several jazz histories have bemusedly pointed out, Fanny Golightly could just as easily have ended up a tenured bluestocking Somerville don. Instead of doing which, she would spend the following three decades remorselessly electrifying all those doting, idolatrous fans in Tokyo, New York, Glasgow, Montreux, the Albert Hall, Oxford Town Hall... and the Monterey Festival.

She glanced at her watch and said she must fly. But perhaps, she said considering, I would like to come for a coffee at Somerville soon? Why not next Saturday morning? I blinked, taken aback by the speed of the invitation, and she coloured dramatically. I'd love to, I said concealing my excitement, but I had an obligatory organic chemistry lecture that morning at nine. We were getting to grips with the oxalates, the citrates and the succinates. I could be round there at Somerville shortly after eleven, if that wasn't too late. Fanny nodded and smiled and opened her very faded Indian shoulder bag. On the delicate magenta and gold embroidery, I could just make out the tender scene of handsome blue-faced Krishna dancing with his wide-eyed cowherdesses. She fished out her squashed pouch of Drum *halfzware* shag, manufactured an improbably thin roll-up, then offered me her Rizlas.

"I prefer these," I said, taking out some Churchman's

Cigarellas. Their rich green and gold pack was handsomely ornate but of course smoking these seductive cheroots was like inhaling sticks of dynamite. As a physiologist I knew that forty a day of these incendiary firecrackers was little short of suicide, yet I could not do without them. They were the only things I found remotely adequate to provide a remedial existential pungence and astringence in my twentieth year. Before long the sound of Fanny Golightly's jazz guitar would provide a supplementary addiction, but at this stage I had no clairvoyant presentiment that I was in the privileged presence of a world-class musician...

Three days later I turned up at Somerville clutching a family pack of Cadbury's Fingers. I stopped and lingered awkwardly by the entrance as I realised I hadn't the faintest idea where her room was. I stepped into the gloomy porter's lodge where a stiff middle-aged woman pointed to a xeroxed list of all the staircase locations. Worriedly I inspected a remarkable quantity of preposterous double-barrelled and East European names. As in some dated American movie about dandy Oxbridge, there were even a couple of female nobles amongst them. *Lady Alethea Kempsey. Lady Janet Botting-Stobart. Maria Lukacs-Krasznahorkai. Marmara Powys. Laotitia St John-Pangbourne.* I glanced at the rigid and silent receptionist lady and thought surely this bloody roll call must be a hoax. Surely, even in late Nineteen Sixties Oxford, such a concentration of eccentric designations was impossible.

Suddenly I imagined the same woman asking me: "But what's your name, sir?"

"Oh," I would reply sheepishly. "Why it's Enzo Gianmaria Mori."

"In that case," the woman would retort, "names don't signify such an awful lot, do they?"

"I'm afraid I can't find Fanny Golightly," I said blushing.

The woman looked at me, not hostilely, but without any interest whatever. She strode across, scanned the list, and found Miss Fanny M. Golightly in two seconds.

She gave me terse directions to the staircase and tonelessly reminded me that as a gentleman visitor I must be out by eleven p.m. Which gave me, I swiftly calculated, only a modest twelve hours to come to a significant and enduring psychological accommodation with this over-intense council-house Cumbrian. Yet it was something else altogether that propelled me up that mournful ill-lit staircase with a prickling sense of visceral anticipation. Earlier that morning in my chemistry lecture a medical student called Simms had said something which had left me stunned. At weekends Simms played bass in a city rock band, and he told me that my new Somerville friend must be the same Fanny Golightly he'd listened to recently in the upstairs room of a Jericho pub. She was a very intense, very good-looking woman with remarkable blond hair, and she was also a regular pub performer. She played a very brilliant but quite incomprehensible electric guitar. Supposedly a kind of 'jazz', Simms added derisively, but of a type which even here in conceited highbrow Oxford probably less than half a dozen people would appreciate.

"Jazz?" I asked him with a queasy excitement. "Are you sure of that? You're saying that Fanny Golightly is some sort of jazz guitarist?"

"I suppose jazz is the only name for it. It was as delirious as heavy metal but it was certainly far too complex to be any sort of rock. At first I thought it might be a strung-out, bilious sort of blues, but no, it wasn't that either. Nor could you categorise it as an avant-garde dirge, though that's possibly the closest musical analogy. She had a bass and a drummer with her, two men in their thirties who both play in London clubs during the week. I was told she sometimes plays more accessible solo acoustic, if she can get a sympathetic audience. I stuck the tormented racket for about twenty minutes until I started to feel physically assaulted and then I headed for the bar. She was playing guitar chords that only lunatics try to play, the ones where you stretch your little fingers down three or four frets. To be honest I don't even know their bloody names. F 6th with an added 13th, F minor 9th? I only managed to notice that sort of detail on the rare occasions when she bothered to slow down.

Most of the time she was playing as if she wanted to set herself on fire, as if she was being chased by a bull or a tiger. Her hands were going at least twice the speed of light, it was astonishing to see it. Once every few minutes, give her her due, a trace of a tune, the ghost of a melodic line was faintly detectable. The rest of the time she seemed to be in extraterrestrial orbit and circling round the moon. Technically she's quite miraculous, if not a bloody genius. But Fanny Golightly is for the frowning cognoscenti only, the ones who are as intense and overwrought as she is. Strange really. A crying pity in my view, with all that phenomenal technique. Because if she'd only make one or two elementary concessions to – "

Simms and his famously elementary concessions. Simms and his thumpingly raucous doped-up outfit which plagiarised standards from Colosseum and the Butterfield Blues Band but sounded ineluctably like a warm-up act at Workington British Legion. I hurried through the empty quadrangle and bolted up the deserted staircase as if pursuing something impossibly elusive. After three wrong turnings I found myself panting outside Miss F.M. Golightly's chambers. Her neighbour's door was wide open and a tense, thin woman of about nineteen could be seen sweating over an essay. Her name plate identified her as Lady Janet Botting-Stobart. I could see the vivid runnels of perspiration on her worried pallid brow. I smiled at her and she grimaced back uneasily. Then I knocked on Fanny's door and waited. A long couple of minutes passed but there was no movement within. Lady Janet examined me with anxious puzzlement. No doubt, I thought dismally, Fanny has forgotten my highly insignificant visit. Or perhaps she has decided, as a light-hearted joke, to stand me up. Feeling like some sneak-thief, I gingerly pressed my ear to the door. I flinched and then frowned because I could detect an extraordinary wailing sound pullulating inside. Muffled by the thickness of the ancient wood it sounded bizarrely like a turkey gobbling.

I had a sudden hunch what it might be, and battered very loudly on the door. There was a brief pause, then tentative, almost ghostly footsteps, then a slow retreat, then Fanny's distant voice shouting a faint come in.

She was squatting on the floor in a half-lotus position and she blinked awkwardly and guiltily at her visitor. As soon as she took in that it was me, the son of the Italian ice-cream man, she smiled a sort of pained relief and picked up her smouldering roll-up. She had placed herself square in front of her record player, and the incredible 'turkey' sound was issuing loudly from its battered speakers. Far from being authentic poultry gobble, what I could hear was an extraordinarily tender but very piercing soprano sax. It was the first soprano I'd ever heard, but at this stage I was so ignorant I believed it might be the highly improbable jazz oboe. I stared at Fanny's cheap little Bush stereo which was undoubtedly a big advance on my mono Dansette though scarcely ideal equipment for a musical genius. The melamined speakers were the size of small detergent packets and she had them elevated on two old cardboard boxes. Apparently unable to endure any more of this piercing music, she shook herself and raised the armlift to pause the LP. At that moment she had the look of someone gazing up from the bottom of a very deep well. Belatedly I realised that her eyes were moist and her face was streaked, and I cleared my throat embarrassedly.

"Are you alright?" I asked her. "I mean, do you want me to go?"

"What?"

"Am I in the way? I can come another time. You look to me as if you've…"

I pointed to my own eyes. She looked uncomprehending, then winced.

"I've not been sad. I mean I've not been upset about anything specific. I've just been very affected by this particular record." She stared at me mildly bemused. "I don't suppose that *you* like jazz?"

I must have looked grotesquely mortified at that, as she in turn looked stricken.

"I love it," I told her hoarsely. "It's my favourite music. I can't play any myself and I don't understand anything about the structure or science of jazz, but I…"

She was smiling at me far too politely. With numb chagrin I saw that she could hardly square my horribly familiar accent with such a sophisticated preference. Nor come to that, could I accept that her curt Salterbeck vowels could possibly be those of a female and Anglo-Saxon Joe Pass.

"Listen to this," she said with a very sombre expression, and she carefully unclipped the record arm. Before she set it down she threw across a bright orange record sleeve. Wonderingly I examined the hazy silhouette of a man and his guitar caught in a splashing flailing flurry of orange illumination. The title of the LP was *Extrapolation*. The musician was someone in his late twenties called John McLaughlin. In those days the prodigious Yorkshireman was barely known outside of a few London jazz clubs, and I for one had never heard of him. I was blithely unaware that he was a northern working-class genius. Likewise I had no idea of the genius of Fanny Golightly. In 1969 she was just nineteen years old and had yet to make a recording. McLaughlin then was twenty-seven, and his career was just about to take off into infinity. Barely a year later he would have played on Miles Davis's *Bitches Brew* and the phonetics of modern jazz would never be the same again. They would have travelled not through a single century but through several Hindu yugas. On the cover of *Extrapolation* there was a photograph of McLaughlin wearing outsize glasses and a piquant expression. No later portrait looks anything like it, and he could easily have passed for an unremarkable English teacher from Hounslow or Dagenham. He was gazing down with tender, entranced affection at his splendid acoustic guitar. I scanned the sleeve notes and read a feverish ecstatic encomium by someone called Giorgio Gomelsky. Gomelsky was all very dazed hyperbole, but the titles of McLaughlin's tracks excited me with their oddness and extravagance. *Arjen's Bag. Binky's Beam. Two For Two.* Jazzmen, not to speak of jazzwomen, have always had an irrepressible love of demented puns and a poetic fondness for playful alliteration.

Instead of putting the stylus on the first track, Fanny took great care to hit the second. It was called *It's Funny*. Though it wasn't at all funny for Fanny Golightly. As soon as McLaughlin started his limpid gentle little hymn to what the sleeve notes oxymoronically call 'sadjoy', her eyes filled up immediately. She closed them tight and took on a look of statuesque suffering, a mask of raw anguish that in anyone else might have seemed ridiculously histrionic. Her lips began to twist and twitch as if she might be a secret epileptic, and I felt a sharp pang of unease. But any fear for her psychological welfare gradually lessened as I hastily withdrew myself to a safer mental accommodation. I stood back from the raw immediacy of the picture before me and allowed the period, the place and the historical context to assume their proper proportions. It was, after all, 1969 and we were both only nineteen years old. Unselfconsciousness, eccentricity, soft drugs, soft prescriptions, soft presentiments, they were all the rage, in fact were *de rigeur* in Sixties Oxford. Virtually no one in that indifferent city at that indifferent time was surprised or put out by anything at all...

Brian Odges's bass began to strut and cavort, but before I could savour my full quota of that, the 'turkey' began its singing. The turkey was called John Surman and he was blowing an achingly gently melancholy soprano sax. This shy Devonshire boy was already being hailed as our finest home-grown poet of the baritone sax and the bass clarinet. In fact it was John Surman rather than John McLaughlin who had Fanny Golightly crying. The tears were coursing down her baffled face in an unrelenting torrent. I stiffened my shoulders with numb embarrassment, looked down at my dusty shoes and listened hard to *It's Funny*. 'Sadjoy', the subtitle, was exactly right. I found myself wishing to erupt into something potently expressive of both joy and sadness. Such a combination was akin perhaps to the burning *saudade* of Portuguese fado. Whatever it was like, Fanny Golightly could scarcely bear it. The Devon man blew his lilting little melody, a tune so simple any child could remember it. Yet he filled it to the brim with a swelling pathos and an endless yearning sufficient to crack the very stoniest heart. The four –

or was it five? – peaked ascent, then the wilful lethal plunge into a beatitude of tender, wistful sorrow. The whole thing lasted a few short minutes but by the end of it a seeming death knell had been sounded. Meanwhile Fanny looked as if she was one of the subjects of a television documentary about Californian primal therapies. In her febrile twitching and unaffected weeping, she seemed to be struggling with the mimetic throes of birth as well as death.

It's Funny lasted for four minutes, but I awoke from a year-long reverie. I roused myself drunkenly, lifted up the stylus, then laid my arm gently on her tense, slender shoulder.

"Bloody hell," I said huskily. "I've never heard of John Surman, but I think I'd better marry him."

The quaint absurdity might have made things worse, of course. Fanny blinked through her tears and smiled reluctantly.

"Marry him?"

"So that I could listen to him playing that tune every day. So that I could listen to that single track all day every day for the rest of my life."

She said with a smileless resentment, "It's the most beautiful sound. It's so infinitely pure in its simplicity and loveliness. But its beauty sears its way inside your belly like vitriol. It ought to be bloody well banned."

I read the sleevenotes once again. "What's remarkable is that every one of them seems to be British. Is that right?"

She nodded indifferently.

"They're obvious geniuses as jazz players, yet none of them are American. What are we supposed to make of that? It's bound to take some getting used to…"

Fanny offered no opinion but remained in a state of frozen wistfulness. I hesitated for a considerable time, too cowardly to ask her if she herself was a second nascent John McLaughlin. To cope with my awkward restlessness, I offered to make some coffee. Fanny looked surprised, almost aghast, and said only very weak jasmine tea would lighten her nerves at a time like this. I set about clumsily warming the dirty teapot, scraped the mould off a seemingly pre-war lemon, then cut it into slices. As I poured the jasmine into chipped china cups, I couldn't restrain myself:

"Someone has told me you're a jazz guitarist."

Fanny flinched very visibly. I smiled at her but to no avail. She looked at me guiltily and self-consciously, as if I'd accused her of being an incurable kleptomaniac.

I stumbled on doggedly, "I mean the man who heard you, who's a hard rock philistine, he thought it must be jazz. He said that it was way above his head but that you were absolutely stunning. You were performing last week in the Dragon upstairs room."

She stared at me very strangely, pursing her mouth as if tasting something unpleasant. I found myself flushing like a foolish, errant schoolboy. After what seemed an eternity, she murmured shamefacedly:

"My music goes right over everyone's heads unfortunately. Aside from perhaps half a dozen loyal fans. I doubt very much it's getting me anywhere worth getting, the stuff that I play."

I stared at her earnestly and in my boundless ignorance I rallied her on. "Numbers don't mean anything. They really don't. The truth is probably that you're so bloody good, so incredibly original, it's going to take time for the world to catch up. I'll bet my last cent that you're a remarkable musician. This man Simms insisted that you were."

Possibly because I'd already referred to Simms as a philistine, she wrinkled her thin nose into a cynical question mark.

"You weren't sat there in the Dragon yourself? No, of course not. I'd easily have spotted you as ten per cent of my audience. Don't tell anyone Enzo, but half of those present had been pressganged."

"Can I come along?" I asked her, reddening again like an importunate six year old. I felt like some bothersome inconsequential little squirt who had no right to tag along with adults. "I'm only an amateur in the old-fashioned literal sense. I am one who loves, but is ignorant. I'm just a provincial bloody ignoramus. But I'd love to listen to you playing."

She said with a bewildered look, "Ignoramus seems a very harsh terminology. I don't think the word's particularly applicable where my music's concerned. Of course you can come along to listen. There's no law against anyone turning up if they want to. But, be warned. You may not like it one iota. You may loathe it in fact. Everyone says it's impossible to take in the first time that you hear it. My friend Lara who's reading music at St Anne's, says it's rather like Bartok and Schoenberg crossed with Cecil Taylor and Derek Bailey, all four of them blind drunk."

I said fervently and with another blush, "I bet you're a genuine artist."

She sniffed and looked a little askance at my glib testimonial. "Personally I don't think I sound anything at all like Schoenberg or Bailey. In any case, the real issue is how much I rate my own stuff. Sometimes I think I'm really original and other times I think I'm a derivative imbecile."

She was sipping her jasmine and puffing a roll-up in incongruous staccato sequence. Then she lifted up the *Extrapolation* cover and inspected it ruefully.

"Listening to this particular record – I only bought it yesterday – has given me what feels like a serious lead and a probable way forward. As a guitarist John McLaughlin is very fast, very raw, very difficult indeed when he wants to be. But he's also, when he chooses, very slow and gentle, very very gentle and beautifully tender and ever so transparent. The unique, quite extraordinary thing about him is that he's not ashamed to embrace those two extremes. He's not at all embarrassed to be both. It's that miraculous sense of reconciliation in his music that I admire so much. On that last beautiful acoustic track *Peace Piece*, I don't begin to understand how he manages to play with such terribly vulnerable tenderness. I don't know how he's capable of descending to those infinitely gentle depths without... disappearing. Without melting into nothingness and turning into sheer vapour. It's certainly a kind of dice with death this sort of music. It would be for me. But... but he seems to manage it over and over again on this extraordinary record."

6

One month later, sipping more lukewarm jasmine tea, Fanny and I first listened to the music of Toto Cebola. It was *Energetic Eels*, his debut LP, and we were as astonished as if we had been listening to the singing of whales or the nocturnal ululations of foxes. The main problem we had was in deciding whether it was electricity that was powering his instrument or whether his violin was somehow generating surplus power for the Californian electricity grid. Three years after that Fanny was spotted and signed up by CBS, and then instantly became an international name. Yet she did not meet up with the bearded, amiable Portuguese 'gypsy' until the Monterey of 1975. They played their two sets on the same afternoon and afterwards shared a table in a noisy Mexican restaurant where they'd been ferried by the festival organisers. The two awkward provincial prodigies exchanged reverent technical critiques of each other's work, whilst humbly making light of their own. Over red-hot, luscious *mole poblana* they even managed to detect a few tangential biographical parallels. Fanny Golightly had to struggle hard to describe the exact flavour of a problem-ridden Salterbeck council estate, and even harder to indicate to a former child beggar from a Fascist dictatorship why it represented deprivation. She listened intently to a few gently impressionistic anecdotes of his peculiar, almost Hans Andersen childhood. His upbringing had obviously been far harder than hers, but he showed no signs of lasting bitterness, not at any rate towards his immediate family. In any case, Cebola informed her with mock gravity, it was his circus-hand uncle, meaning his fly-by-night father, Luís Miguel de Carvalho, who was primarily responsible for his following a musical destiny.

It was spelled out in all its whimsical improbability in that 1985 interview in *Cahoots*. After he'd left the Fim do Mundo café, he had wandered home to Leonor in a worrying state of queasy exaltation. He was dazed because he had just been treated very courteously by a total of five expensively dressed foreigners. Joey Conto, the thin, restless, language-school owner with the dark glasses had shouted across the room to him as the band were taking a break. Startled out of his wits he began to bolt for the door, but the American only wanted his shoes shined. After that he had Cebola clean the fancy shoes of all four musicians as they sat sipping beer at his table. The jazzmen drank Lisbon beer but Joey Conto was flamboyantly sipping *aguardente*, the poor man's firewater. Conto ruffled his hair, teased the twelve-year-old about staying up so late, then asked him in jerky Portuguese about his circumstances. He listened attentively to Cebola, then translated the unglamorous details to the laughing, friendly Americans. The black drummer seemed a little more thoughtful than the rest. He patted Cebola's head, then held his chin musingly in his other hand. Conto fanned his mouth at his cheap hooch and told him how Wes Geffen here in the beautiful suit had scavenged on city rubbish dumps in New Jersey when he was ten years old. But take a good look at him now.

Cebola stared at Joey Conto, then answered with a very worried face, "I think he's a great musician."

The boozy, skinny American blinked at him with indulgent scepticism.

"I mean..." Cebola went on inaudibly and trancelike, "I think he was really wonderful."

Conto slowly removed his dark glasses and scrutinised this pinched and grubby boy with the mournful countenance.

"You're kidding, aren't you? You can't really have enjoyed the music they played here tonight?"

Cebola looked down anxiously at the black man's beautiful oxblood shoes. "I don't understand why I loved it. Every single bit of it, from start to finish." His voice faltered painfully, because it was such an ordeal having to talk to a rich foreigner wearing sunglasses. "I've never heard anything like this music before. But what – ?"

"What what?" Conto urged him a trifle theatrically. "Go on. Don't be so frightened."

"What kind of music is it?"

"Nothing you'll have heard in Coimbra before. It's called 'jazz'."

"'Chess'?"

"If you like. It's an American music. It started off as a type of Negro music from New Orleans. A long time ago a black man called Jelly Roll Morton took a mostly white piano music called ragtime and he freed it up into something called jazz. Jelly Roll went around boasting 'I invented jazz in 1902'. That's what he said, literally. He wasn't a modest black man at all. He also had a business card that read 'Creator of Ragtime'. Isn't that something, kid? What do you think of that?"

"I don't know," said the shoeshine. "But what is 'Chelly Rull' in Portuguese?"

"Some Europeans play it too. Quite a few in France and Germany and Britain. Barely a handful here in Portugal. Dr Salazar wouldn't like it if it really caught on outside of two Lisbon clubs. It goes all over the place, the music, did you notice that? Dr Salazar doesn't usually like things going their own sweet way."

Cebola nodded very earnestly. Then, nearly choking with the effort and his temerity, he attempted a polite contradiction.

"You're right. It does go everywhere. But it's – "

"But what? I think you must be putting me on, kid."

"I'm sorry…!"

"Take it easy. I was joking. Just relax and say what you think."

"I don't really know how to say it. I think it's very tight music as well. It's pulled in, tied up tight, it's very controlled. They, these American men who play this kind of music, they really control themselves."

"Well, well," said Joey Conto, punching his knee, as if at last he had proved to himself something extraordinarily elusive. He translated Cebola's limping, stuttered analysis and the black man guffawed and offered the intellectual shoeshine some beer. Joey swilled more *aguardente* round his tongue and addressed his brother the trumpeter prophetically. "Out of the mouths of Portuguese babes..."

"That's why I like it," Cebola added reluctantly, when they grilled him further. "It's a free sort of music but it's not really free at all. At the same time it's struggling to be both. Those two things, the looseness and the tightness, are pulling in two opposite directions. It's like an intelligent dog being controlled by its lead. If he was running wild and tearing all over the place without being tamed, he wouldn't be so nice an animal. I think maybe that's what makes this music so beautiful."

His face was so red and his expression so grave, Wes the rubbish-tip graduate began blushing in sympathy. By now he had cleaned all their shoes and no longer had any reason to talk to them. Joey Conto gave him ten times what he asked for despite his frightened protests. Instead he would have preferred to have offered his services as a gift to the kind foreigners, just to show them the depths of his humble hero worship. But before he could convince them, the interlude was over and they were shuffling back onto the stage. He watched them disappearing out of his life, assuredly for good, and his throat which was suddenly very dry, contracted miserably. Meanwhile he was shouted for by a surly little army lieutenant who had bought two tickets to impress his overweight, very irritable girlfriend. These two stern, well-heeled Coimbrans were clearly bored out of their heads by this stuff, and they sniped at each other as he polished their shoes. Even though this 'music' made him feel bloody nauseous, the lieutenant refused to leave as he didn't care to waste the price of the tickets. His wheezy girlfriend said this terrible funeral dirge made her feel quite suicidal, and asked the dirty shoeshine what the hell he had been chattering about with the Americans. Cebola flushed and said all he had told them was that he enjoyed their music. At that the lieutenant snorted loudly and said yes, precisely, exactly, it made perfect sense to him. Obviously this degenerate transatlantic cacophony appealed only to depraved intellectuals, ragged-arse shoeshines, American niggers, and other delinquent riffraff. His girlfriend who was drinking some syrupy *beirão* said, oh to hell with it, let's cut our losses and set off to catch the last of the fado in the Rua de Sota.

Cebola entered a peculiar, very uneasy atmosphere when he got home. His mother was in a sullen, pugnacious mood and barely greeted him. His Uncle Luís, who he hadn't set eyes on for three years, was ensconced with a friend from his circus and an enormous four-litre bottle of rough wine. The friend was a clown heroically called Vesúvio. That was his stage and circus name but his real name was the just as outlandish Sansão Quintanilha. He was neither a Samson nor a Vesuvius but a morose, curly-haired, shrunken individual of about forty-five. Vesúvio had a very stony and unrepentant expression which only softened when Luís Miguel began to describe the misery of his present existence. Apart from his terrible circus wages and the squalid, shitty caravan he shared with four others, there was the perennial problem of Leonor's moods. He had made the considerable effort to come and see her, but instead of showing some common gratitude she was in an almighty huff at not being given any advance notice. Notice, he sneered, why the hell did she need any of that? It wasn't as if he expected a four-course pork dinner or a set of linen napkins on the supper table. The circus was five nights in Aveiro, so Luís had got the train across this morning and would be commuting between the towns for the week. On this first visit he had brought along Vesúvio because this world-famous entertainer was his best friend, and, as he thought the world of Leonor, he wanted Sansão and her to get acquainted. Leonor grunted and yawned very rudely in the world-famous best friend's face. Moderately irritated by such forthright hostility, Vesúvio scowled at the not bad-looking washerwoman. He shrugged his shoulders as if to say, that, meaning you, senhora, is why I am invariably such a sour-looking bastard. I am sour because this world is so full of pointlessly hostile and gratuitously spiteful male and female boors exactly like yourself, Leonor.

His wordless challenge went one step further. With an expression of disdainful mystery, he ferreted in an oddly elongated knapsack at his feet. Toto watched closely as Sansão pulled out a very worn leather case. The clown unclipped the case majestically but dolefully, then fished out a battered violin. However, with regard to the young shoeshine's illustrious future career, this unveiling of a worn old fiddle was not quite as momentous as it might seem at this point. In fact Uncle Luís kept an even more battered specimen in Leonor's bedroom which he sometimes impetuously scraped at when drunk. Luís Miguel murdered execrably all but one tune, called *Porto Santo*. This engaging little melody he always rendered to a dogged perfection if without a trace of imaginative or expressive power.

Vesúvio was a horse of another colour. Snorting at stiff-necked Leonor, he picked up his bow and proceeded to play a pungent little tune from the High Alentejo. Afterwards he grunted to his startled listeners that it was called *Ao romper da Bela Aurora*. He played it with a proud, resentful expression, extremely expertly, with a quite astonishing degree of poignant feeling. All his moodiness and dolour came out unbridled and unashamed in a zestful but tempered melancholy. At one point Sansão erupted into a throaty gypsyish singing that made Toto's hair stand on end with amazement. Meanwhile Leonor Cebola was sat bolt upright and her face was relaxed into something like a long-forgotten placidity. Subsequently, her son noted, it tightened into a combative boldness. She grabbed an empty glass and filled it to the brim with the rough red wine. Leonor took a hearty fearless swallow of something that was as raw and unrelenting as this fiddle music from curly-haired Vesúvio. Luís with a foolish vaunting expression whispered reverently that Sansão Quintanilha came from a lonely village somewhere round the backside of Elvas and this must be a very old love song from those parts.

Once the morose guest had engaged the attention of the sulky washerwoman, he resorted to unabashed showing off. He drank as copiously as Luís and Leonor and gave them a comprehensive anthropological tour of the whole of Portugal. He knew a lot more than bloody Alentejo tunes, he sniffed, and he performed for them *Coro das Maçadeiras* and sang along in passable Minho dialect. Later he assumed a craggy, furtive, impassable look and transported them to the ravines of the far north east, the Trás-os-Montes, by playing them *Manolo Mio*. His itinerary was so comprehensive it even extended beyond mainland Portugal. After fiddling his way through the Ribatejo, the Beira Alta and the Beira Baixa, he lifted up his dowdy wine-soaked wings and flew his way to the distant and unimaginable Azores. *Pezinho da Vila* was his stupendous encore and finale.

"Bloody hell," blurted Leonor very graciously. "And to look at you, you'd think you'd have trouble playing a bloody comb off the market."

Vesúvio took that in the proper spirit and gave her a ghost of a grin. In return Toto's mother gave him the ghost of a wink and her son the shoeblack observed a familiar suggestive telepathy. His Uncle Luís didn't notice anything because he was examining the clown's violin, shaking it and putting his ear to it as if to work out how exactly that exquisite sound had come about. It could only be the instrument, not the player, otherwise his own frustrating limitations had no feasible explanation. For the rest of the week Luís the tent-hand was obliged to work through the day at Aveiro while Vesúvio the performer had all his afternoons to himself. The impassive little Alentejano took the Coimbra train from Aveiro station four times that week. Toto was aware of these interesting movements as he hid himself in the outside lean-to shed just in case Sansão did some more of that miraculous fiddling. The flaking walls of both house and shed were paper thin, and yes, lugubrious Quintanilha scraped and fiddled very zestfully and in both senses. A quarter of an hour of his violin music, no doubt to serenade prickly, volatile Leonor into a tender quiescence… and then the other trilling squawking furious and farcical business for an approximate half an hour…

Cebola related his mother's indiscretions to the *Cahoots* interviewer with a humorous indulgence. Clearly no puritanical monogamous *cigano*, Toto described how world-famous Vesúvio had been crudely compelled to become a temporarily contracted peripatetic music teacher. Because after that first very gratifying assignation with Leonor, Sansão Quintanilha was met at the thronging railway station (Coimbra B) by a tense little teenage ruffian who informed him without any preamble that he wanted some free violin lessons.

"You want what?" sneered the sallow-faced Don Juan from the Spanish borderlands, indolently spitting sunflower seeds onto the platform. "You seriously think I've got any time to waste on the likes of you?"

Cebola quietly repeated his preposterous demand. Vesúvio promptly recommended him to fuck off, even if he was the son, no, buggerit, he meant the honorific nephew, of Luís Miguel. That crucial genealogical slip escaped the worryingly earnest ragamuffin who came rapidly to the point. If Vesúvio did not try to teach him everything he knew in the next three afternoons, he would immediately inform Uncle Luís that his treacherous best friend was cuckolding him in his own bed. Vesúvio shuddered, then snarled and hotly denied it all. He said he was here in Coimbra today just to do some necessary shopping, to buy one or two important odds and ends you couldn't get in a one-eyed hole like Aveiro. This, despite the fact his hands were completely empty of all but his violin bag. Cebola shrugged, then related verbatim certain punctilious arrangements the two lovebirds had made. Two o'clock sharp at Leonor's back door at two o'clock this Tuesday, Thursday and Friday, to be exact. Also, her son added coolly, as a brawny circus hand used to heavy lifting and heavy loading, Uncle Luís had arm muscles bigger than Johnny Weismuller's. His best friend must surely have noticed this himself from time to time. Uncle Luís would be able to snap Sansão's pockmarked neck and/or tear out those tight curls of his by the roots without the slightest effort.

"*Ciganice*," spat the clown, in a tone of pious outrage. "What a bloody brazen little turd of a dirty gippo!"

After that it was all in the detail. They argued about the duration of these lessons, Vesúvio wishing to make them three o'clock until 3.10, Toto insisting three until five. The clown gulped and lied he had to be back at the bloody circus tent by five. But his pupil tersely quoted Luís Miguel who'd said that regular performers like Vesúvio invariably just lounged about drinking in their caravans until the evening performance. After all, it was only going to amount to six hours tuition in total. As for the venue, Toto knew a quiet little patch of rough ground on the far side of the ruins of the Convento de Santa Clara-a-Velha. None of those goggling American and British tourists infatuated with Inês de Castro's sorrowful love story ever bothered walking in that area. Oh really, Sansão said drily, poisonously humiliated at being cornered and ambushed by an obviously tone-deaf unmusical squirt. What prevented them from strolling that way if they felt like it? Oh, because there were always plenty of outsize rats scurrying about there day and night. As a matter of fact that clearing was an unofficial rubbish tip much frequented by any travelling *ciganos*.

"*Pelo amor de Deus*," grunted the stricken fiddle player.

That was how the great jazz violinist first learnt his musical notation, his chord progressions, how best to hold his instrument and even how to sing. He acquired his working knowledge courtesy of a philandering circus clown and a gypsy rubbish dump. Sansão Quintanilha might have been a better instructor if he hadn't been so extremely nervous. Of all those giant rats, that is, who seemed to be eerily charmed Pied Piper-wise by the remarkable child musician. Right away Vesúvio discerned that this kid was a remarkable natural, a possible bloody genius, a pitifully wasted talent with his skinny fingers and palms calloused by too much brushing, blacking and winter frosts. But the incongruous presence of those bizarrely attentive rodents distracted the hijacked maestro from making any sensible long-term suggestions. At the end of their three brief lessons, all Sansão could do was tell Toto Cebola that he showed real talent, quite unusual promise with the fiddle, but that given his obviously hopeless personal circumstances he should leave Uncle Luís's instrument well alone and quietly forget the whole bloody thing.

"*Até logo*," he added sarcastically, just before he leapt on the Friday night express to Aveiro. He waved disdainfully at that skinny, diminishing figure. "Though I won't be seeing you again, you ugly little gypsy bastard."

There followed a week of hollow listless inertia, a condition which got short shrift from Vesúvio-bereft Leonor. Toto stopped shining anyone's shoes and spent his days alone in the gypsy clearing with Luís's joke of a violin. He practised everything that the Elvas clown had shown him and added his own peculiar, idiosyncratic embellishments. Without thinking anything was odd about it, he played by ear improvised violin versions of what he had heard last week in the Fim do Mundo. The clown had taught him a few simple folk songs but Toto discovered he preferred to render these peasant tunes in that anomalous American code-language called 'jazz'. For example, he found that when he started off fiddling *Cantiga da Bomba* he ended up giving it what he didn't even know was an approximate Gerry Mulligan treatment of the same tune. Gerry Mulligan played the baritone sax and the Coimbran shoeshine had certainly never heard of him, yet there, in baffling retrospect, was where the frustrated novice had stood musically in 1957.

Red Conto's band, in its black-suited suavity, had performed a kind of West Coast cool, a taxonomical category which Toto Cebola was only to put into intelligible context some six months later. One cruelly cold February morning just outside the Igreja do Carmo, he bumped into an extravagantly hungover Joey Conto who amazingly was talking to himself. Conto was actually humming some Slim Gaillard scat to relieve his *aguardente* headache, but Cebola thought perhaps he had a harmless transatlantic slate loose. When the American asked him why he looked so incredibly depressed, Toto hesitated, then decided to say nothing whatever about the bad-tempered clown, the rat-strewn rubbish tip and the aborted lessons. It was only as Conto slyly pretended a cold indifference and brutally turned on his heel that Cebola broke down and managed to blurt out the bones of his story. He had to elaborate in his laughably inadequate vocabulary on Sansão's incredible versatility, then repeat the names of those Portuguese folk tunes several times, so that Conto, for whatever inscrutable reason, could write them all down. He made no mention, of course, of Leonor's unedifying seductive role in his truncated musical education.

"You don't say," Conto said, very doubtfully. "I'm tempted to believe every word you've just told me. If you didn't look so amazingly sincere, I would think you were just some screwy little deadbeat on the make. I think that you're the weirdest bloody kid I've ever met. Tell me, did you ever read a story called *Huckleberry Finn* in Portuguese?"

After a scowling, impenetrable deliberation, he eventually made Cebola a bizarre proposal. Brooding irritably he also thought to give him a plausible lie to feed his mother. That her son Toto had been given a valuable block booking and invited to come and clean the shoes of one-hundred-and-fifty English language students in one fell swoop. Otherwise, she might suspect the worst and assume that Joey Conto was a predatorial American pederast. The following Saturday the American drove the shoeshine up to his all-marble mansion near Conímbriga and allowed him to listen to half a dozen carefully selected records. For the first time ever Toto Cebola opened his ears to Dizzy Gillespie, Charlie Parker, Stuff Smith and Stéphane Grappelli. Faint and considerably frightened by all he had heard, he also played Uncle Luís's violin for this dauntingly expressionless foreigner. At the end of his curious folk-medley performance the language-school owner seemed about to clap, then abruptly changed his mind. Toto Cebola blushed and scowled at what he took to be a dismissive insult. He kept on scowling even as Conto instructed him that, as soon as it was practical, he should buy himself a cheap bus ticket and go and settle in the Portuguese capital.

"Lisbon?" he said, as alarmed as if the mad American had said Valparaiso or Lourenço Marques. "What would I do in Lisbon? How would someone as poor as – ?"

"To begin some proper musical study, kid. With an expert

teacher I mean. With a professor or some other bad-tempered old bastard who leads a violin masterclass. Look at me son, look me straight in the eye. Don't you realise that you're a bloody little musical genius?"

Cebola stared at him hostilely. "No I don't."

"No," sighed Conto. "I don't suppose that you do. How the hell could you?"

The boy looked at him woundedly. "I don't think you should mock me…"

"A budding maestro like you needs another maestro to take him in charge. You need an expert, Cebola, not some two-bit circus clown who's named after a bloody volcano."

If money was a problem, the foreigner added with bored hungover indifference, slapping his stubbly chin and wincing at the freezing cold, he and possibly a couple of wealthy jazz-loving friends in Porto and Viseu would be willing to offer him a straight no-return investment.

Cebola wiped away some freezing snot and repeated his plea. "I really don't think that you should mock me."

♪♫♪

Simms of Wadham didn't like Fanny Golightly's music because he couldn't understand its structure. In his vaunting ignorance he could not even credit that it had any meaningful artistic form. The cultural setting for that non-recognition, that disingenuous rejection of a major jazz talent by a mediocre rock guitarist, was utopian and cerebral Oxford. A year earlier in the backward provinces, perhaps with a little more justification, Vince Mori and Captain Hornblower had been equally offended by my records of the organist Jimmy Smith. To them this delinquent Smith chap seemed to be going bloody nowhere while attempting to go everywhere like a brainless maddened dog. Such a centrifugal yet centripetal, integral yet differential, nihilistic yet infinitely over-assertive music seemed all the more impudent when it originated from the fingers of a black man. Black men weren't supposed to be highbrows, existentialists, omnidirectional composers. They had enough trouble coping with their unenviable afflictions; ubiquitous police harassment, lynching and so on, without trying to imitate the crazy trajectories of the sub-atomic particles. Of course it was a waste of time trying to dissect these theoretical niceties with Vincenzo Mori, but I thought it just possible I might be able to vanquish Watson Holland in closely reasoned argument. Home from Oxford for my first Christmas vacation, as well as sporting a wispy, straggling beard and shoulder-length hair, I endeavoured to convince the clever pharmacist of the bona fide structural credentials, the seriously playful seriousness of jazz.

"Beethoven," I said to him on a chilly December evening in that same parlour where he had told me about his wife's shocking cruelty. "Just look at Ludwig Beethoven before you go any further in your arrogant denunciations."

Hornblower sipped the Montepulciano he had bought specially in a St Bees grocer's and poured me my third brimming glassful. We were enjoying our first proper dialectical battle since my return, and he was obviously savouring the merciless cut and thrust. Kelsie Mullins, the sniffy Orangewoman, had finally married Hipsley Petty and moved to a bungalow down at Waberthwaite. At the bank manager's peremptory request she had relinquished her busy teaching job and become a demure and doting housewife. Holland had no one left to needle as Angelica's only other current lodgers were a half dozen pan salesmen from South Yorkshire. They were pleasant and very friendly, he opined, these Barnsley and Rotherham johnnies, but, the pharmacist added, adopting a paradoxical J.M. Synge Oirishry, 'not killt with brains bhoy any means, me boyo'.

"By all means," he assented gustily. "Let's look at Ludwig as long as you like, my gay young cavalier."

I interrupted briefly to tell him that these days that adjective 'gay' had a novel and highly significant sociological import, viz. it referred to all those who classed themselves as homosexuals. At which point Captain Hornblower blinked and removed his glasses and rubbed his eyes wonderingly at my unamusing pleasantry.

"Ha ha. Very jocund you undoubtedly are being. It may well be the occult, masonic password on two staircases in Balliol but your charming made-up kiddies' glossary holds no sway elsewhere, I'm afraid. Queer as a nine bob note it is, and 'reet pekewleear' it shall bloody well stay for ever hereafter. Not least in the harsh industrial climes of the far north east and the far north west."

"But Wats– "

"Enough of that idiotic digression, scarcely worthy of an intelligent Balliol man. You know it's a great pity that in your meagre classical record collection you don't have *Cantata on the Death of the Emperor Joseph II*, my very favourite effusion from the godly Ludwig. Written ten years before his *Septet in E, Opus 20*, which could not be more cheerfully contrasting, and which happens to be my second favourite. My hellish wife Penelope always preferred the *Missa Solemnis* and once used my priceless 1939 recording of the *Emperor* for cutting lamb kidneys on after a row. I was subsequently tempted to use her Archiv copy of the *Eroica* as an arse-wipe, what Rabelais calls a *torche-cul* that very same evening. But I could not bring myself to stoop quite so low. In any case that corrugated old 78 would probably have scratched and seriously abraded the old bow-hind…

"The second bit, the *Emperor* recitative, is my special favourite. How about this for what I would class as no-nonsense lyrics? No Vera Lynn or 'gay' ha ha! Benjy Britten stuff for Ludwig, hein? *Ein Ungeheuer, sein Name Fanatismus, stieg aus den Tiefen der Höhe, dehnte sich zwischen Erd' und Sonne?* Know Krautish do you? No didn't think you would, Rimbaud. Even though it's an essential tool for any serious biological scientist these days. You know, you'll get short shrift if you can't read a bloody *Zeitschrift* in the original down at Balliol. But how shall I con it? *A monster, let us call it Fanaticism, climbed up from the depths of Hell, stretched itself twixt earth and sun.* That's what I call words with pith. But *Da kam Joseph mit Gottes Stärke!* Meaning,

There came Emperor Joseph with the strength of God. Beethoven, bless him, was no different from a tenured court poet when it came to calling his Emperor his God..."

This feudal sycophancy of the great composer was all news to me and I growled dismissively. "Bourgeois bloody toady. Repressive bloody tolerance! Herbert Marcuse was bloody well right. A singing parrot in a palace cage."

Hornblower wasn't listening to my virtuous Trotskyist excoriation. He said, "I suppose it might seem morbidly gothic to be so uplifted by such funereal sublimity. But what do I care? Like Kaiser Josef II, we all of us will have to face our cold and lonely death at the end of the road."

I went on just as deafly, "What I was about to say concerning Beethoven was that like all jazzmen and" – thinking painfully tenderly about Fanny Golightly – "jazzwomen, he Beethoven, was an improviser too."

"Rubbish," snorted Watson Holland with adamantine certainty.

"He bloody well was! Of course he was! He used to improvise himself when he played his own music. I've read about it in various authoritative books. Of course, these days classical performers spend their time imitating what they think is the classical canonical authenticity. But Beethoven certainly didn't see his own music as something that was set in aspic."

Holland surveyed me witheringly. "I like that word aspic, I must say. As a budding musicologist, Enzo, you would doubtless make a good bricklayer or a pastry chef. Are you seriously telling me, young iconoclast, that in the *Emperor*, when they get together to perform it in the Dresden Staatsoper or wherever, that all that assemblage of obese lady divas and waistcoated double-chinned baritones, that all two dozen of them are busy *improvising* on Ludwig's sacred original? Eh? They would be squinting and dribbling in a cachexic frenzy if they were bloody mad enough to try."

"That's a bad analogy," I answered, blushing fiercely. "That's not it at all."

"I couldn't agree more," sniffed the pharmacist. And after a second's hesitation he opened up another bottle of his

Montepulciano.

"What I meant," I went on sternly, "is that jazz music uses the same basic techniques and language as classical European music. Jazz musicians also use harmonic structures."

Hornblower leered at me like an exophthalmic Long John Silver. "That organ grinder of yours, Jakie Smith, he grinds up his harmonic structures alright. Old Smithie boy, he grinds them up to a most delightful pulp."

"No he doesn't," I said resentfully. "Like any other jazzman… or jazzwoman… he improvises on a given harmonic structure. Which is exactly what composer organists like J.S. Bach or Dietrich Buxtehude or J.J. Fux did as well. They *improvised* on the harmonies on which the original melody was based. Alternatively, they embellished the same melody. By embellishment, I mean the same as ornamentation, as it's formally identified in both jazz and classical music. Ergo, Watson Holland, there is a straight technical line that continues from the hoary composers of the Baroque all the way through to the jazzman Jimmy Smith."

"What!" bellowed Captain Hornblower, thoroughly apoplectic if not molten at my glib résumé. "It's absolutely outrageous that you dare to place my divine Buxtehude in the same artistic bag as a bohemian bloody darkie called Johnny Smi– "

"Hear me out will you?" I snorted, as I helped myself to another of Angelica's incomparable salami sandwiches. "Listen to me carefully before you continue your intolerant ranting. Jazz players I admit use a different set of tools for their kind of improvising. Blues chords, as a rule, to give a kind of provisional fluxing shape…"

Hornblower gargled his Montepulciano with a musical ornamentation of irony. "Flux alright! Fluxing bloody hellish, if you want my opinion, Sonny Jim."

I sighed. I held up my hand like an exhausted don whose anomalous tutorial student happened to be an extremely immature fifty-year-old with a handlebar moustache.

"Furthermore," I emphasised, "in the development of classical music, things like Ground Bass, Cantus Firmus and all the rest were more or less invented to help structure Baroque improvisation. Can't you see that the artistic means are just the same in both genres? What's supposed to be the difference between one lot of improvisation and another lot of improvisation?"

"A flux of a lot, in my view."

"In any case," I snorted victoriously, pointing to my recent purchase of an Indian raga album by Nikhil Banerjee, "improvisation, as you well know, is common to all kinds of music, not just to jazz and the classics. You'll find it in virtually all musical cultures and in every historical period. Hindu ragas like Ravi Shankar's or Banerjee's. Or in say French, Spanish or Portuguese folk songs."

"Portuguese folk songs eh? Okey doke. Not that I know any, but I'll bet my last escudo and the complete works of Eça de Queiróz, Fernando Pessoa and Luís Camões that those Lusitanian peasant folk songs have a *whistleable bloody tune*. They do not just go on extempora... Hell, I'm so tight I can hardly say it. Ex-temp-orar-ily."

"Of course not. But neither do they in jazz. Jazz is not about composing extemporarily, without any prior preparation. Nearly all jazz improvisation is based on a given theme..."

"You don't say? Well well. But buggerit, even if that happens to be true, Rimbaud, it's wholly irrelevant for practical purposes. The point is it *sounds* completely tuneless, aimless, discordant, dissonant, deadly. Whether or not it was produced utterly at random, or with cunning and malevolent forethought, is entirely beside the point."

I leant forward unsteadily in my chair and tried to impress Holland with my looming proximity.

"Forget about contemporary extremists like Evan Parker and Derek Bailey. Forget about historical freeformers like Ornette Coleman and Don Cherry. Aside from them, jazz *always* has an intelligible pattern, it really has I promise you. Sometimes the skeleton is the 32-bar form, A-A-B-A with eight beats to each. A being the main theme and B being the bridge. Or it can be the twelve-bar as in the twelve-bar blues..."

I didn't stop there, and when Hornblower tried to dispute my terms of reference, I battered on regardless. Fanny Golightly had given me a little modest instruction in the basics of musical structure and I parroted it triumphantly to the woozy, spluttering pharmacist. I gave him a brisk lecturette on jazz composition and told him that improvisation was essentially the overlaying of new melodic lines over the harmonies of the original song or tune. This overlaying would sometimes be as 'paraphrase', meaning embellishing or making slight alterations to the song as in many of the jazz standards. In more recent jazz it could be as a 'chorus phrase', which was to say overlaying entirely new melodic lines over the same given harmonies. Add to that the impregnable mystery of the 'once-improvised', an extemporising which endures and is quasi-standardised, but belongs exclusively to the one who created it and which cannot be borrowed by others.

"A jazz improvisation," I concluded to my ostentatiously yawning student, "is the personal expression of its improviser. Furthermore, Watson Holland – "

He interjected irritably, "Will you stop saying 'furthermore' to me you preposterous bloody pedant? Who do you think you are, C.M. Joad? Why not throw bloody 'igitur' or 'moreover' at me while you're at it...?"

"Furthermore," I repeated, savouring its timelessly authoritative resonance, "a proper jazz improviser *is simultaneously improviser, composer and interpreter* of whatever music he is playing. He – or she for that matter – is all three things at once. Chew on that as a vertiginous aesthetic and epistemological scenario, if you dare, you incorrigible old sceptic. And let me add furthermore, furthermore, Watson, doesn't it make you feel humble as you ponder the poetry and the poetic implications of that apparent three-in-oneness?"

"Eh?"

"Isn't it a remarkable triune, triadic, tripartite *phänomenologisches Urbild*, Mr H?"

"But I thought you said you didn't know any bloody Krautish, Rimbaud...?"

7

♪♪♪♫

anny began Scafell Rise Infants in 1955 and first discovered a wordless music in the sense of hovering, transient beauty in the person of Miss Sheila Black. Miss Black was young, beautiful and very gentle, whereas all the other teachers were old and ugly and impatient. Miss Black was also strangely embellished if objectively flawed by the fact of her missing two fingers. Her little finger and wedding ring finger were entirely absent and Fanny stared every time at the quaint suntanned stumps when she took out her sums or spellings for marking. Miss Black was also a misnomer because her facial colour was bright orange and she had the startling pigmentation of a South Sea islander. Fanny had no idea that the orange skin was due to inordinate exposure to an expensive Cockermouth sun bed but was aware, as much as a five year old can conceptualise such things, that if Salterbeck was her own reality then Miss Black was the other, was the diametric opposite of everything she had known to date.

It seemed to be always drizzling when she walked the half mile to the infants school which had been built in 1908 out of sombre great blocks of sandstone. The dreary, demeaning smell in the ill-lit cloakroom was of steaming gaberdines and dank rubber wellingtons. The first day at school she walked in to hang up her coat and saw that all the children's names had been printed next to the pegs. Far from being pleased, she felt overwhelmingly flustered as she was unable to spot her own in among all the soaking coats and hats. She went crying to Miss Bell who frowningly grabbed her hand and hauled her back to ferret among the gaberdines. Fanny's was the very last peg and Mary Stanwix's beret was completely obscuring her name but that cut no ice with grumbling Miss Bell. Fanny at once associated her panicked ignorance with a justifiable hostility from the powers that be. She felt enormously bleak in her tiny insides. That same day she walked home alone to the council house and passed by a straggling hedge that was full of intensely red rosehips. It was a brand new estate that had been built on farmer's fields and as well as hips there were bright, vivid haws glowing in among the briars. It was a very sunny September afternoon, an Indian summer, and the bleakness of that first day was suddenly overcome and annulled by its opposite feeling of euphoric, tender, innocent, infant joy. The words were beyond her, but it was as if the haws and rosehips contained that joy, possibly occasioned it, were perhaps the proper conduit of a joy from a special source that no one could ever know at first hand.

It was that epiphany, that hedgerow effusion, which formed the basis of umpteen painfully tender solos in Fanny the musician's acoustic repertoire. Those beautiful solos not only made half her audience fill with tears, they made the guitarist weep as well. Her tears on stage were always dry tears however, and what it amounted to was a kind of noiseless grimace of overflowing feeling. The closest parallel is the face that a woman like Fanny assumes in the throes of erotic joy, in the apparently anguished and tormented grimaces of pleasure and climax. It did not seem excessively precious or theoretical for Fanny to link aesthetically the pain and the pleasure. As she explained it, when she talked about the infant's missing coat peg, if she hadn't felt so painfully bleak at the start of the day she might never have known the acute physical joy at its end. The rosehips and the tender hawthorn bush were there to greet the unhappy worried child as she walked back to the deafening rows and the family disarray. Was it possible, she asked me one day in a dirty and disgusting Kilburn pub in the early Seventies, to experience

125

any genuine bliss in life, if you hadn't also known its genuine antithesis, meaning experienced the depths of claustrophobic wretchedness at an early age? In the jazz context, she added, witness Miles Davis's cathartic wounded infant's melancholy, or listen to Pharoah Saunders's frantic tantrum of raging anguish on a sax that can isomerise within seconds into a melting, lyrical, very childlike beauty.

Dick Golightly had worked as a signalman on the Workington to Keswick line until he was caught inside his box swigging a half bottle of Bell's while listening to a cliffhanging episode of *Mrs Dale's Diary*. He was sacked on the spot, and spent the next twenty years struggling to hold down a stupendous succession of unskilled factory jobs. Among other things, he processed buttons, trimmed wellington heels, supervised a machine that screwed together spectacle frames, stacked pallets in a malodorous meat-processing factory and, by contrast, tipped trays of different coloured sweets into a hopper which mixed them together and then shot them down for packing to the floor below. Conveyor belt factory work is certainly a hellish kind of jazz, monotonous yet dissonant, discordant yet poisonously bland, an unsavoury array of uninteresting ambiguities. None of these jobs lasted more than six months, as Golightly found their deadly brainlessness intolerable. Worse than the sickening boredom, he had to work triple shifts, in the days before twelve-hour continental shifts were commonplace, and the only alternatives were days, afternoons and nights.

Both his wife and his daughter came to dread the afternoon shift, as he rose mid-morning and spent the next three hours boozing in the Moss Bay Hotel. He kept his young family in poverty by his addiction, witlessly exculpating himself by the handouts he earned from some occasional club singing. Dick Golightly sang mournful but perfect imitations of the songs of Paul Anka, Frankie Laine, David Whitfield, Pat Boone and any other Fifties crooner whose tone was pathetically lachrymose and whose words were as pure and harmless as the driven snow. He sang in the Senhouse Street Club, in The Gunners, The

Workington Legion and in numerous dingy back-street pubs where he was often paid in kind instead of cash. Thus his spare time job increased rather than mitigated his addiction. He was a tearful boozer rather than a violent one, a disputer, a grumbler and a whiner, rather than a wife-beater or a child-beater. Nevertheless he did abuse his youngest child Fanny, though not with his fists, and he did so in the days when the strange disease was not acknowledged and the symptoms were quaintly unmentionable. Because the clinical lexicon was non-existent at the time, then the malady itself was de facto fictional. It was as late as 1987, just after that outlandish Cleveland scandal erupted, that thirty-seven-year-old Fanny, the world's finest jazz guitarist, was able to find the words to describe what her old father had done to her. At that stage, in 1987, it was as if not just Fanny but the entire sentient world could awake to what it had known in its amnesic guts all along.

The choreography of the abuse, such as it was, was pathetic, though not without imagination. By 1955, Fanny's mother had got herself an ill-paid job working permanent nights as a nursing assistant at the Whitehaven hospital. She begged a lift there and back with a ward sister called Wendy Bone who lived just outside Maryport. The overnight care of her infant daughter was left to Fanny's brothers Mark and Andy who were aged twelve and ten, and moderately sensible for their years. If he was working days or afternoons at his factory, Dick would often roll home crooning at one in the morning or later. With unfaltering regularity he would clamber like a tipsy Santa Claus into bed with his tiny daughter, claiming in a humorous whisper to be drunker than he was, more confused than he was, as he found himself in a bed he shouldn't be in. The boys were sound asleep two doors away and the infant girl was obviously very groggy, caught and pinioned between dreaming and wakefulness, swimming between nightmare and the gasping tearful sentimentality of Dick's coy paternal caresses. Fanny couldn't be cast-iron certain but she believed he'd never attempted a full penetration, rather implored her to hold something for him by way of doing him a natural, commonplace favour. The penetration that there was, was the classic pragmatic substitute most appropriate to a minute victim. Her mouth, she knew as sure as life itself, had been the imaginative replacement, and even now, aged fifty, whenever she was seized by a fit of depression, the sensation she had was of a depthless, indescribable misery that was focusedly concentrated inside her adult mouth. As if something deep inside it had exploded like an ignited match or burst fuse, bequeathing a lifeless residue of blownoutness, exhaustion, spentness... the desuetude of a dying, sickly and waterless little plant.

Fanny's notorious hurricane phase of the early Seventies, after she'd adopted the double-neck guitar in homage to McLaughlin, owed everything to those early days on the Salterbeck estate. Her phenomenal speed, intensity and volume on the eighteen strings (a conventional fretboard added to a twelve-stringed blues guitar) owed all their ferocity to the raw incendiary magma within. The relentless ascent to the heights, that determined vertiginous progress the length of both guitar necks in time signatures and chord structures of impossible complexity, those were the defiant scalings of ancient childhood panics, the racings up a nebulously threatening colossus, the renewed obsessive conquering of the two-faced, Dick-faced (dick-faced) demon lurking both within and without.

To reach such paralysing heights, she had been obliged to risk a mighty fall. It was as if she was being chased by a famished tiger or a slavering wolf as she rode her two-in-one eighteen-stringer, her appropriately phallic charger. None of her fans would ever guess the grisly fairytale origins of her exalted dramatic performance, nor of course, for artistic purposes, did it make any difference either way. The pitiless fact about art of any refinement, she told me in that same slum of a Kilburn pub, is that the historical means of its production, its subtle or gross sociological context, is wholly immaterial to the end result. Did it make any difference to anything that Fyodor Dostoevsky was suffering a suicidal gambling fever when he wrote *The Idiot*? Was it there imprinted in his text in invisible ink? Scarcely, she snorted, but looking as if she wished it had been. In any event, it was only because Fanny Golightly chose to front a group that had all the electrical apparatus of a giant rock band, that her unbending virtuosity found a transient commercial success. Leather-jacketed kids who hitherto had worshipped only deafening heavy metal decided to worship fragile Fanny Golightly instead. And why precisely was that? Because, for a short period at any rate, her band was even heavier than Black Sabbath or Hawkwind or Iron Maiden! Astoundingly it was, from 1972 to 1973, on *Blazing Siren* and *Blinding Lights*, even noisier, faster and crazier than Led Zeppelin, King Crimson or Deep Purple. It happened to be a great deal more than that, unfortunately, and the heavy metal headshakers soon lost interest when in terse unilateral style Fanny decided to change direction as she saw fit. Like the autocratic wah-wahing Miles of the same period, she moved to a startlingly peremptory on-stage orchestration, her hand raised and flagged to indicate who must take up the next solo or who should keep quiet till further notice. That sleek and arithmetical cohesion from her compliant fellow bandsmen, those much longer, much quieter, progressively more poignant solos, all sent the studded leather jackets screaming back penitently to Sabbath, Jody Grind and Blodwyn Pig.

The terror and the tenderness went together. Dick Golightly was the same father who took his young family along to the Workington Opera House in 1955 to see a proper Christmas pantomime. It was a professional production with actors from distant Manchester, not just some hit or miss affair by amiable Cumbrian amateurs. They had the best seats upstairs and the seating, she remembered clearly after thirty years, had Dick on the left, Mark next to him, then Andy, then Fanny, then her mother Doreen. The seats were plush purple velvet and the five-year-old sank into them as if sinking into heaven. Dick had bought each of his children a handsome and costly oval tin of Devon toffees. Mark's had a black tartan-collared kitten on it. Andy's had a Christmas scene of two red-cheeked Victorian schoolboys in smart tasselled caps pulling a sledge and walking past a snowcapped church. Fanny's had a brown spaniel pup with the most vulnerable large eyes she had ever seen. The spaniel looked so beautiful, and even at five Fanny knew it was the eyes and their nakedness, their creaturely harmlessness, that made that animal beauty. The little oval tin seemed like a brimming casket of enduring tenderness. She forgot about her skinny restless father and her big open-mouthed brothers and her lethargic yet twitchy mother who collectively defined themselves as a hopeless, pointless family called the Golightlys. She just sank into the heavenly purple velvet and stared at that beautiful tin.

She didn't open it until she left the opera house, and the re-emergence into wet and windy Pow Street shook away the purple dream. In the Opera House her eyes went between the spaniel pup, the Victorian Christmas scene on Andy's tin, and the stage itself where the curtains and the props were bathed in a delicate violet radiance. It was the first time she had seen stage lighting and it was a glimpse of another world. It stopped her breathing, it was so beautiful. And the boys on the oval tin with their antiquated tasselled caps and their snow-covered sledges were both smiling with happiness. Why were those two lads so eternally, so changelessly happy? That was plain enough, it was because they were *safe*, because they felt themselves protected and secure, that they smiled the smile of those who are kindly looked after. The adult Fanny understood that safety as imaginative and fictional, though even in 1999 she found it hard to accept that those happy boys and that smiling church did not somehow *exist* in some real sense. In 1955 that picture on the little tin was so comforting to look at that the five year old believed the protectedness was hers as well, or rather that by gazing at that tin she could imbibe the radiance of their tasselled festive safety. She could have stared at Andy's tenderly consolatory Christmas toffee tin for the rest of her life. The church had a plump little robin hanging on its eaves and that friendly, tubby robin too was hallowed and snug and protected by the loving spirit of Christmas.

The loving spirit? Like her template Mahavishnu John

McLaughlin, Fanny Golightly went through her extended spiritual phase. By the mid-Seventies, she was defiantly explaining the source of her music in terms of Fanny the performer being a vessel or a conduit for something 'from the beyond'. John McLaughlin doubtless saw the conquest of transcendence likewise, as his first Mahavishnu Orchestra album of 1971 was called *My Goal's Beyond*. Precious and mawkish as her aesthetic theory might have seemed to some of Fanny's admirers, it was wholly at one with the breathless infant and the oval tin and the violet other-worldly radiance of the remote provincial Opera House. However the stony British public can rarely comprehend its proletarian artists embracing anything more exotic than mandrax or benzedrine or heroin to soothe the pains of superstardom. The pursuit of oriental philosophy might have been appropriate for a questing middle-class intellectual, but the guru attachments of abrasive John Lennon or anarchic Pete Townshend were inevitably considered more perplexing. After all why should someone from a Fifties Cumbrian council estate, even though she read English at Somerville, interest herself in Hindu deities and Indian philosophy, in Vedanta and the Upanishads and the Bhagavad Gita and the Vedas? Fanny stoutly maintained that it was because Indian philosophy promised a disciplined devotee a *finished state*, an end and a goal, an accommodation to an, as it were, beckoning transcendence. The expression of her massive talent was always going to be imaginatively hazardous, if only because it demanded an orchestrated revelation of what came from very deep down inside. This in turn often felt frighteningly enormous, abyssal, unpredictable, incalculable. And above all it left her, when she was not playing her jazz guitar, unstable, uneasy and potentially self-destructive.

Likewise in the mid-Seventies, in California, the Portuguese violinist was embracing a transcendental Eastern philosophy. Fanny Golightly might never have been sent to any church or chapel in Cumberland, but from his first breath Toto Cebola had imbibed an intense devotional Catholicism. Up until the age of ten he had experienced an absolute credulity apropos holy relics, Christian signs and symbols, and the changeless efficacy of liturgical ritual. In fact I realise now that his childhood roll calls of saints' days and fasts and highly specific prayers to highly specific saints must have been much the same as Vincenzo Mori's in Roccella in the Thirties. The adult Cebola knew the names of more Portuguese saints than he cared to know, and could identify them by minute geographical region and the motley professions they protected. There was a patron saint of washerwomen, of course, but he had never discovered any patron saint of the violin, much less a patron saint of the jazz violin. Leonor Cebola might have seemed stonily fatalistic and sceptical, but with evident sincere piety she joined in all the holy festivals and made sure her little Toto did the same. The urchin shoeshine had taken daily communion before he met his American patron, the distinctly unsaintly Joey Conto, and been a minor standard bearer in successive Easter processions from the Sé Velha. His hunted, weary expression gave him a suitably penitential aspect, and besides he had strong arms from all his rubbing and polishing and could hold up a banner for a very long time without a murmur.

As for the spiritual nature of his later Californian albums, despite their embarrassing titles (*Craving Infinity Always*, *Infinite Resonance*, and the ungainly plural *Spiritual Fulcrums*) that musical spirit always seemed more progressive, mobile and Occidental than monistic, static and Oriental. To put it another way, the beauty of Cebola's music seemed as much a function of the agile movement onwards, the movement of a kicking strutting free spirit, as it did a meditative elaboration upon a static effect. Cebola on his later albums was always accompanied by a drummer, guitarist, bass and keyboards, and his keyboard player Stim Stein was a master of every rarefied electronic effect. He used dubbing and overlaying and echo to produce a massive cathedral organ resonance which (together with Cebola's violin amplification) could sound like a pulsating angel ascending the height of a cathedral. Even this radial and pulsing, as opposed to linear, progression was suggestive of the baroque Portuguese Catholic church rather than the serenely motionless Indian temple. Also, irrespective of that gigantic keyboard-cum-synthesiser and its armoury of gadgets, the overall flavour of the music was inescapably cheerful, moving always boldly and tenderly forward. It was like the poetry of a bird on the wing, or, as I've said, like a fragile butterfly flitting above the rippling Mondego. It had the buoyant unreasoned optimism of a hurtling and carefree infant who also (certainly according to Cebola's careful *Cahoots* recollections) strutted boldly and tenderly forward.

Set beside that quintessential joy, Toto's virtuoso technique was no more than a means, a contrasting complexity, intended to throw a simple and beautiful tune into heightened relief. Track 1 of *Craving Infinity*, 'Half Lotus', had 3 over 4, two chords and a mixing of time signatures and was done as a cheerful waltz tune. Track 2, 'Almost Full Lotus', had 3 over 4 with a longer progression of chords. Track 3, 'Full Lotus', had a change from 7 over 4 to 6 over 8. Those three tunes and the rest of the tracks on Side One of that 1985 LP were all in the same key. They elaborated a measured progressive variation on a theme, in the same way that every single Cebola tune is discernibly a variation on every single other.

♪♫

In the end the young Coimbran did not end up being engulfed by the size and frightening anonymity of Lisbon. Instead he spent the next five years studying the violin in the unlikely backwater of a sprawling Costa Verde seaside town. He became the only student of a grotesquely irritable Lisbon professor, Estácio Alvarenga, who was retiring to live with his unmarried sister in Póvoa do Varzim. When Conto first sounded out the gruff old gentleman over the phone, he was told Alvarenga was leaving Lisbon within the week, and also that he was retiring categorically from any private music teaching. He had definitely had enough of prima donna geniuses, as well as all the hopeless cases and the wishful thinkers; he was sick of their tantrums, their egotism, their laziness. Why, Senhor Conto, some of them even baulked when he suggested a meagre minimum of six hours' practice every day of the year, Christmas Day and Easter Day included. Póvoa, well beyond Oporto, ought to put him out of the way of most of these self-deluders. But if it didn't, he was prepared to retire to the most inaccessible hovel on the far side of Montalegre in the Trás-os-Montes. Pitões das Junias, for example, where apparently they still lived like beggarly stone-age troglodytes, that would do if need be. Joey Conto chuckled and took no offence at the biting operatic scorn in the old man's voice. As far as he was concerned it was a testimony to the teacher's reputed greatness, that splenetic, voluptuous disdain.

Cebola kept out of the way when Conto went along to inform Leonor that he was taking over her son's destiny. At this point of course she had no idea that Toto had ever held a violin in his hands. True to form Leonor did assume Joey was an overdressed American pederast, and it was only when he showed her some testimonials in calligraphic Portuguese from various eminent Coimbran authorities, university doctors, estate agents and the like, that she finally gave him the time of day. All these rich Coimbran music connoisseurs had gathered at Conímbriga to listen to Toto, and they could all vouch for his astonishing talent as well as the integrity and farsightedness of his patron Senhor Conto. Joey gave her their phone numbers and offered to take her to see any or all of them if she still doubted his honesty. He had already found Toto some excellent lodgings in Póvoa with a respectable widow called Matilde Carneiro. He had also arranged some first-class tuition with Portugal's finest violin teacher who lived with his sister a five-minute walk away. As Senhora Carneiro was a retired schoolteacher she would also be paid to give Toto remedial lessons in Portuguese and arithmetic, and possibly French and English at some stage. Aside from paying the tuition and lodging costs, he and two music-loving friends would make her son a modest weekly allowance. More to the point they were offering his mother some generous compensation. They proposed to give her roughly twice as much as her son brought in from his shoeshining, enough therefore to cut her laundry-work from sixty to only forty hours a week. Gasping inwardly but not outwardly, Leonor inquired how and where the hell had that sly dark horse Toto learned to play the violin. Joey stopped himself just as he was about to blurt all about Sansão Vesúvio and the rubbish tip. Glibly he fabricated an anodyne variant which included the gypsy rubbish dump but no circus clown called Samson. Only a deprived and half-starved washerwoman would have wished to fall for his ad hoc fairytale. Toto, he told her, had borrowed Uncle Luís's violin several times, then prac-tised brilliantly if hesitantly on some wasteland round the back of the Santa Clara-a-Velha. There he had been most fortuitously overheard by an astonished Senhor Conto who had just parked a borrowed truck bearing a broken concert piano he wanted rid of. Maybe Leonor was unaware that Toto was a regular shoe-shine at the Fim do Mondo, and had once cleaned the shoes of his American trumpeter brother Red? Red the jazzman had also heard Toto play, and like Joey believed him a nascent genius. Finally his close friend and musical authority Doctor Professor Alvarenga had stayed with him last week at Conímbriga and had been astonished at the young man's effortless if highly idiosyncratic technique. He had more or less begged the language-school proprietor to let him have Toto as his exclusive student for his retirement up north.

Cebola wasn't aware when he moved to Póvoa that there was no agreement whatever with Estácio Alvarenga. In fact Conto had eloquently campaigned for his unlikely pupil over the phone, but the proud maestro had simply guffawed as if it were all a good joke. Conto's indolent, Brazilianised Portuguese hadn't helped, nor had his crude offer to pay twice the customary tuition fees in advance in US dollars in a sealed envelope. Alvarenga informed him that he was a retired professor not a retired huckster, his set fees were his set fees, and he could not be bribed. Alvarenga had been teaching violin for fifty years and he certainly did not believe in unsung geniuses in the shape of undersize bootblacks. In any case if he really was a bootblack his hands would be calloused and useless beyond redemption. Worse still, if Alvarenga let this unwashed, unvouched-for riffraff into his sister's parlour he would probably steal all the teaspoons. Joey Conto reasonably enough assumed that Alvarenga must be a fervent Salazar man who regarded him as some sort of repugnant and incorrigible atheistic socialist.

Mrs Carneiro was a different species altogether. By the time he became her only lodger, Toto had been groomed and spruced by the joint applications of his mother and the American. Joey bought him ten pairs of smart flannels and ten English shirts from the most expensive outfitters in Coimbra. When Leonor gasped in outrage at the cost, Conto explained that the violin tutor, the professor, was of the old guard, who expected even his private pupils to doll up like concert pianists. To shut her up completely, he strolled back and bought her a Scottish lambswool sweater that made her literally howl with happiness when she held it up against herself. She wore it only on festive occasions, of course, or when resentfully welcoming Tiozinho Luís Miguel back from his circus.

Matilde Carneiro was in her late fifties and was a moving emblem of widowhood, inasmuch as her eyes were always moist with the memory of her bereavement. She was loquacious and wheezy and forever laughing at herself and forever grieving noiselessly at her irreversible loss. Her husband who had been a headteacher at Vila do Conde, had been struck by a heart attack in front of his terrified pupils, and it was the day before their twenty-second wedding anniversary. It would have been their silver wedding this year, she sighed to the American, and her tears welled up immediately. Their copiousness and her unabashed, too vulnerable sincerity made him clear his throat uncomfortably. Family, no, no family, no it was very sad but it was because of very complex gynaecological problems, occasioned by some botched surgery in Oporto just before the War. Cebola did not know the meaning of that 'gyn' word and was astonished when Conto explained it in the café later on. They dined in a place called the Café Económico which certainly lived up to its name. It was not only dirt cheap, but the set three-course meal was of such prodigious quantities that Cebola had to sweat to finish it. The steaming *grão* soup was ladled out from a vast alloy tureen, and the regular customers, mostly old men with half-buttoned flies, scowled if their huge bowls weren't filled to the brim. The main course was a full metre of *bacalhau* on an oval metal platter. There was enough salt cod to feed a family of six and the half kilo of boiled potatoes was drenched in succulent olive oil and vinegar. The dessert was a flyblown *pudim flã* as it always was in the cheapest Portuguese restaurants.

"I thought that the old senhora was making my meals," he said, pantingly replete, over a large glass of Coca Cola, only the third he had ever tasted.

"She is but not this evening. I wanted to have a little peace and quiet tonight to plan our next move. Mrs Carneiro is a lovely Portuguese lady but she gabs at you from all directions like Respighi's bloody *Fountains of Rome*. I picked the Café Económico because if ever you need a rest from her motherly attentions, you can come and eat and meditate here. No, don't ask me what meditate means. I'll explain it to you when you've grown another six inches. You want this *pudim flã*, I can't finish all this stuff? The prices in this joint are totally crazy. They can't possibly make a profit. And yet those old guys there are grousing at the massive portions, swearing that they're two millimetres less than yesterday. It confirms my pet theory, Cebola. No matter how hard it struggles human kindness can never win out against human selfishness. The more generosity you show, the more saintly you try to be, the more suspicion and rebuff you will arouse. Therefore, never be too kind to anyone, always be ready to protect your own corner. Speaking of which, this is where Estácio bloody Alvarenga comes into the equation. By the way, son. I forgot to tell you. At present the old maestro refuses to be your teacher…"

His jaws were glued up with two pudim flans but Cebola managed to gasp, "You what? He's what?"

"Take it easy. Don't choke. Don't die on me yet, please. I have this foolproof solution. There will be no problem, I assure you. This is what I shall do to get the revered old shithead to be your violin tutor…"

If Alvarenga was operatically contemptuous of most of his students, Conto was just as operatic in a different context. At seven o'clock that night when it was still stiflingly hot, the American led his stunted prodigy to the front windows of a modest Thirties villa. Estácio and his sister Emília had just been gormandising on some splendid looking *peixe agulha* garfish. They were gazing silently and temperately onto the seafront when they noticed this bizarre, asymmetrical duo. The man wore dark glasses and a trilby hat and looked like an American gangster, a James Cagney hidden by hexagonal shades. The boy was dressed respectably in flannels and a fine white shirt but looked exceedingly ill-at-ease in his pricey outfit. His face was thin and worn and irremediably that of an urban peasant, quite possibly that of a *cigano*. The villa had no protective front garden, the lawn was all to the rear, and this strange cinematic vision walked right up to the closed window and stood there completely motionless for some seconds. Emília opened her stiff, sombre mouth in amazement. She thought they might be proselytising Jehovah's Witnesses come across the border from Spain, and as a pious Catholic she rose from her chair to shoo them away. Her old brother put down his ancestral monogrammed fishknife and tugged at his meticulously barbered beard. The oddity in the sunglasses waggled a nonchalant wave and, acknowledging the sound barrier of the window, announced at excessive volume in Brazilian Portuguese.

"This is the prodigy professor. This is the young Coimbran boy. This is the phenomenally gifted student you're pretending you don't want to teach."

Emília shuddered and looked at her brother suspiciously. "Is it conceivable that you *know* these people?"

"What…" blushed the stupefied maestro. He rounded viciously and disdainfully on smirking Conto. "Are you perhaps rather raving mad, mister?"

He used the English word rather than 'senhor' and enunciated it like a vengeful Bela Lugosi.

"Mad? Only in the most laudable sense, professor. I believe in tackling impossible obstacles, and I also believe in achieving miracles. What money can't buy, sometimes audacity can win instead. I expect you'd call it Yankee effrontery or New World temerity, this standing outside your window like two Bing Crosby mummers. But enough of this rather trifling badinage. Let's get down to brass tacks. How much will it take to make you change your mind? I'll pay you three, no four, times your usual rate to tutor this boy."

Emília put down her glass of Vidago water and whispered, "Do you want me to telephone the police?"

"Eh? Don't be absurd. I can easily get rid of these pathetic buffoons myself. I don't need any sergeant reeking of garlic to help me."

Emília said flushing and affronted, "Very well. I'll go into the garden and leave you to it. Don't say I didn't warn you."

"Eh? Of what? Warn me of what? Pah, I've had enough of this ridiculous damn nonsense. Look, Senhor…"

"Conto," Joey reminded him.

"Conto?" sniffed Alvarenga, at the only Portuguese word that every foreigner knows. "Are you sure?"

"*De certo*. I'm a shameless Yankee plutocrat with a name to match. I try my honest damnedest to fritter away all the money I have, but it sticks to me like glue. One of these days I might just light an extremely expensive bonfire. Or perhaps give it all away to all the beggars in Coimbra."

"I doubt it," snapped the old man. "There are no Portuguese beggars, senhor."

Toto Cebola gasped at that remarkable statement. Joey Conto grinned very equably.

"*Por certo*, professor. They're all ham actors, every single one of them. Including some of those phony old lepers I've seen begging up in the hill villages."

"*Ao certo*. No one needs to be a beggar in this day and age. But some weak individuals are so perversely improvident they will always gravitate towards that repulsive profession. Look Mr Conto, if that's your real name, I told you over the telephone I've retired from all teaching, and I meant what I said. You could bring the youthful Paganini to my front window and I would still refuse your theatrical blandishments. This stunted ill-bred boy you have with you, you have him dressed to the nines, but I can see at a glance he is pure gypsy."

"I am not," whispered Cebola to Conto. "I am bloody well not."

"Please. Just give him a listen. Cebola, just play him the bit of the Brahms concerto we've rehearsed. He's heard it barely three times from an old record, only three times by ear. He can't read music, he can barely read a newspaper. But his Póvoa landlady, the teacher Mrs Carneiro, she's going to tutor him so that he can read the *Lusiads* by Christmas. He has a perfect audiographic memory, so it's obvious he'll have a perfect photographic memory. I'm offering you, sir, the exclusive privilege of being his first proper teacher. Cebola the shoeshine will help to keep your memory alive now that you're exiled way up north and everyone in Lisbon is ready to forget about you."

Alvarenga blazed and quivered. "You damned impertinent music hall – "

"*Desculpe*. Excuse my puerile transatlantic temerity. It's what made us so great as a nation. Or perhaps what makes us swagger with such vulgarity while others crawl and shuffle with so much style. It's true what they say, you know. Back home we have no ancient buildings or ancient literature or anything worthy of veneration. But as compensation we do have plenty of jazz. No one can take that lovely baby from us. This kid Cebola has an ear for jazz already, but he insists all he wants to play is the violin. He says he wants to be another Stuff Smith, even though great jazz fiddlers are as rare as gold. I could get him an excellent sax teacher in Lisbon just like that, but he's dug in his heels and he's only an ignorant kid. Maybe by the time he's an adult there'll be droves of violinists playing jazz. Though even by 1967 or 1977 or 2007, I doubt it. From you, senhor professor, he needs to learn some essential refinements. He needs to understand structure, notation, control, mastery of technique, advanced musical spadework in a nutshell. At present he can move his fingers in impossible ways and is capable of supersonic speeds. But he doesn't know what to do with it all. He needs someone with a huge musical brain like yourself, just to keep up with him. Just to know what the hell he's actually doing, if you know what I mean."

Alvarenga heard him out with pursed mouth and fussily folded arms. Finally he snorted:

"Just bugger off will you, you garish, vulgar imbecile! Shove off, the pair of you! Otherwise I'll take heed of my sister and ring for the pol– "

"Right," said Contro briskly. "Enough said. Play, Cebola. Go on, don't look so dumb and asinine. Play Johannes Brahms for this choleric old bast… gentleman. Let this sceptical old maestro eat his angry words."

Cebola shrugged and played the Brahms. As he played he closed his eyes and visualised Conto's boxed set of 78s turning round the turntable in his Conímbriga mansion. The revolving label on the 78s became a flawless pictorial cipher that effortlessly instructed Cebola on the emotional as well as the notational sequence. The picture on the boxed set showed a balding man covered in brilliantine wearing a dinner jacket and his face seemed rather proud and fatuous. He held his violin as if it were a pet poodle. As a matter of fact Cebola didn't particularly like Brahms's Violin Concerto, it had an over-sensuous sadness and a luxuriating grief about it that made him feel very heavy and desolate. It was that gravity and desolation, which expressed through his childike, even toylike, rendition, Estácio Alvarenga found altogether too painfully impressive. He listened to the music and looked at the midget musician and could neither believe his eyes or his ears. It might even be some sophisticated charlatan's trick? Perhaps a clandestine tape recording secreted God knows where? On the ground down below the window?

Conto raised his hand sharply for Cebola to stop. He looked at the old man magisterially.

"You have no moral choice," he informed him steadily.

"Rubbish," snorted Alvarenga. "Your insolence is utterly laughable. I have every choice in the world I assure you. The choice I have is to be left in peace. I'm not interested in this boy. I… yes… he is… he can play quite extraordinarily, I will give you that. But the colossal amount of spadework needed to match his potential talent with his present most peculiar technique. The necessary transformation would require a massive commitment on my part. I have neither the energy nor the inclination."

Conto fingered his sunglasses and grimaced sarcastically. "Are you seriously saying you are too tired? That you're too old and exhausted and beyond the challenge?"

"I am saying, senhor, that I have no wish to become involved. I simply don't like the look of the boy. Nor to be brutally candid do I like the look of you, his zealous patron. As you admit yourself you are brash, ill-mannered, and in cultural-historical terms a vulgar neonate. You are the contrary of all that is austere and classical and everything that is signified by the adjective 'Portuguese' in its noblest and most venerable cultural sense."

"You don't say? And if this kid was the son of a doctor or a general would you feel any different?"

Alvarenga shrugged. "Perhaps. Who knows? Physical inclination, attraction and abhorrence, they have a lot to do with one's feelings as a teacher."

"Such cowardice," snorted Conto on a mordantly rising note. "I mean that is the only Portuguese noun worth applying. It's an abstract noun, I suppose, but the reality itself is no abstraction. Your inescapable moral duty is to teach this unbelievably gifted kid. Apart from anything else he's taken immense trouble to spruce up and make himself palatable to an 'austere' old Portuguese Fascist."

"My duties," sighed Alvarenga indifferently, "are only to my sister, my country and to myself."

"Okey doke," snapped Conto as he drew out an improbable trump card with a smooth yet enigmatic flourish. "I think you might need to look after yourself right now, professor. By which I mean watch your heel, guard your rear, protect your flank and all those other august military metaphors. Did you know, sir, that down in Lisbon there are a vast number of British and American expats as enamoured of the cheapness and frightened submissiveness of this authoritarian country as you are?"

Alvarenga pouted irritably. "What kind of a question is that? Do you imagine I'm blind? It's impossible not to bump into you and your frenetic, arrogant countrymen at every turn. I hardly rejoice at seeing Lisbon and Estoril and Cascais and everywhere else being so crudely colonised, but there is precious little I can do about it."

"These days there's such a teeming host of them, they have their own English language newspaper, just like they do in the Algarve. In the back pages of the *Lisbon Echo*, edited by a cheerful booming upper-class Brit needless to add, you can come across small adverts for some unusual and highly unPortuguese services. You can even find an ad for such brash transatlantic novelties as a bilingual private detective agency."

"Mm?" said Alvarenga drily. "That doesn't amaze me especially."

"There's so much surplus wealth among these foreign hedonists, so many drunken parties and midnight swims and wife-swapping bacchanalia going on night after night... the net result is an inordinate amount of marital litigation. Of course the divorces, when they happen, can't take place in pious Catholic Portugal. But the keyhole espionage, the sneaky surveillance and the necessary paperwork can certainly be initiated here."

Alvarenga yawned his curled lips. "These sordid details are far from intriguing, Mr Conto. You are speaking of a wholly unintelligible world, I assure you."

"I know this one guy, a heavy boozer of an American who runs the Lavale Private Bureau just off the Rossio. He's called Dick Schnadig and he's from the Bronx. Dick hates living in Portugal but his wife is rich landowning Portuguese and she refuses to leave everything she knows and loves for New York. Anticipating our present discussion might go something like this, senhor maestro, I took a chance, and got Dick the drunk to follow your every move for the last fortnight you were living in Lisbon."

The old man started violently and with a comical and melodramatic lunge seized hold of his monogrammed fishknife. He pointed it threateningly at Conto, as if it were some potent ancestral talisman.

"You did what!"

"It was the monumental Shakespearean grouchiness over the phone that gave me the hunch. The fact that you sounded like some parody of a Portuguese King Lear. You sounded at least twice as irritable as Timon of Athens. I thought a while and then I said to myself, anyone as impossibly prickly as that guy is, he has got to be hiding *something*."

Of course Cebola could make no sense whatever of a conversation peppered with words like litigation and surveillance. But he was filled with amazement to see Estácio Alvarenga turning whiter than his beautiful Bragança tablecloth. He had never seen anyone as deathly pale. The skinny old man seemed to be having at least three simultaneous heart attacks.

"Three times in three days, bright and early, Schnadig watched you take a taxi to a rickety weird old slum joint in the Alfama. Schnadig didn't know the exact nature of that third-floor business but he soon discovered plenty that was germane to his professional calling. The first floor was an ordinary bang bang clap brothel. The second floor was for rich Lisbon fags. But the ceiling apartments up at the top where you the esteemed and dignified professor always went, they were reserved for the top of the pile or rather for the very bottom of the pile…"

Alvarenga slumped down like a burst sack and drained his glass of water like a thirsty, maddened dog. He picked up a cloth napkin and seemed to be about to stuff it into his wrinkling, stiffening mouth.

"You sure are some dark, and I mean diabolic, bloody horse. Dutiful to your fatherland you certainly are, sir. Your particular specialism is shrivelled little pubertal girls the same age as this kid here."

Alvarenga turned painfully beseeching at that cryptic denunciation. Toto squirmed uncomprehending as the old man tearfully said:

"You don't *realise*…"

"What?"

"You don't understand…"

"Really? Understand what?"

"What it *means*."

"Some even younger, believe it or not. So much for the hidebound sacred purity of your ancient Portuguese culture. I thought all that just happened in Port Said and Bombay. But no, Lisbon is a big place, an international port of call, I guess it's obliged to cater for all comers."

"You just don't understand a man like me," the maestro whispered.

"You think so? The only redeeming factor is you aren't a fag at the weekends. No little boys among them, Dick was anxious to discover. Or I'd never have let this one anywhere near you."

"But – " Alvarenga protested.

"He might be a desperate boozer but Schnadig's a very thorough private eye. He has everything that's necessary neatly filed away. Bogus hotel documentation and bogus receipts, incriminating colour shots after he'd posed there as an interested creep himself. Dick surpassed himself and even managed to take one of you grinning and drooling in your long shorts and suspenders. The whole inimitable portfolio. Don't tell me you don't believe what I'm saying?"

The old man tried to wave Joey Conto away, and began to make really unearthly coughing and sniffling noises.

"We'll be round tomorrow morning at 9.30. I'll provide you with a formal contract for the teaching hours, the fees, the frequency of payment and everything else. It'll be witnessed by a young Póvoa advogado who you'll be pleased to know is a university acquaintance of my Coimbra advogado."

Alvarenga asked terrified, "Does he... do they... know anything of... of...?"

"Nobody knows anything about you here in Póvoa do Varzim. Luckily even Toto here doesn't know what I've been talking about. I can tell by that innocent shining look on his blameless face. Let's just work it that way. Let's keep it just like that. We'll be round here at 9.30 sharp. This kid here likes Coca Cola and plenty of those little doughnut things covered with icing."

8

♪ ♫ ♫

Fanny Golightly sat beside me in the British Legion, Mirehouse, Whitehaven, holding my hand with a subtle hesitation. It was 1971, we were both turned twenty-one, and were scheduled to sit our Oxford finals in six months time. In the meantime Fanny was playing regular weekends in London jazz clubs, including The Bull at Barnes, and in less than a year would have her first North American tour. Meanwhile, with no explicit acknowledgement on her part, she had acquired a painfully devoted half-Italian boyfriend, and in the Christmas vac., at his pressing invitation, she went along obligingly to see his father's ragtime band.

On his first acquaintance, a year earlier, Vince Mori had taken to Fanny Golightly immediately, and without any intended irony he addressed her as 'Funny' for the rest of his life. As he found it all but impossible to get his mouth round 'Golightly' he invariably pronounced it 'Gelati' and thus referred to her as 'Funny Ice-Creams'. He was very impressed by her almost Italian beauty and tonight, twelve months later, assured her to her face she was like a *'magnifica scultura'*. As a mark of professional deference, she had brought the Stompers' leader the most expensive bottle of chianti she could find in the Whitehaven Cellar 5. With solemn ceremony Vince opened it during the interval, borrowed two wine glasses from the bar, and insisted she and no one else enjoy a glass with him. Then he turned to Miff Mumberson, his drummer, and said, *"È la ragazza più gentile che io conosca."* Miff was no polyglot of course, his day job was working in a Workington cigarette-tip factory. He thought my father was inviting him to quaff a celebratory gobful straight from the bottle, and reached his percussionist's paw out hopefully. Vince snorted and scowlingly turning to me, gargled Fanny's chianti reverently and whispered, "*Il migliore vino che abbia mai bevuto.*"

A year ago, when I'd informed him about the extraordinary Somerville guitarist, he'd demanded to know what kind of jazz this Salterbeck woman's band went in for. Stumped and searching for the nearest analogy, I played him one minute only of John McLaughlin's LP *Extrapolation*. In all fairness to Vince Mori, plenty of the weightiest jazz aficionados down at Oxford could make neither head nor tail of it, so it was hardly surprising that the clarinettist of the Chomping Stompers was biliously flummoxed.

"Blurry hell," he groaned at first. "You'll haff to get that blurry gramfon mendid, Enzo. You got the record revolvin on tirty-tree but the bastard is playin at seventy fuggy eight. That damn mechnism muss be blurry fookt."

I looked at him blearily. "It's supposed to sound like that, Vince."

He slapped my arm quite painfully, at the studentish pointlessness of my jest. Then when he saw I wasn't joking, he gulped with a muted outrage.

"*Ne sei sicuro?*" he leered aghast. "That is it? That ees *eet*? That ees the music *itself*? That ees the sound you pay one pound seventy-five blurry pee for?"

I nodded and began to explain a little about the technical virtuosity of *Extrapolation*.

"They're playing in 13/8, Vince, and – "

"Oh rilly? Don make me laugh in case I fuggy pish myself! In fact what they is playin, Enzo, is blurry *rifiuti! Scarti! Robaccia!* Cabbage! (He meant 'garbage'.) They is playin at blurry dog chase cat wif tins tied to tail roun and roun and roun like Micky Senate or Charly blurry Chaliapin."

"But – "

"They are blurry musical *criminale*, Enzo! This John Micky Gloveline, he is an crazy *pazzo* not a jazzman!"

148

"But – "

"Listen, I am bein very serious now! You are only young long hairt idiot schewdent, and you been blurry swindlt by a *truffatore*! Please, juss for my sake, son, you take that blurry LP, you take it back to Wooly's in Osfod, an say you want refund cos the blurry dog chewt it where that scratch on cuffer is."

"Wooly's?" I sneered. "I bought that LP at Garon Records on the High Street. It only happens to be my very favourite jazz record. I don't want any bloody refunds." Then just to bait him good and proper, I went on vauntingly. "Vince, it's worth at least a hundred pounds to me. No, I mean it's worth at least a hundred thousand pounds. That's to say, I wouldn't part with *Extrapolation* now for a king's ransom."

He scowled at my po-faced righteous tone. "*Che buffone.* You is just a fuggy blurry *pazzo* too!"

Apoplectic as a Calabrian plum tomato at my musical heresy, my reckless talk of ransoms and fortunes, Vince was also obsessed with the idea of *truffa*, of swindling. In fact there was an insidious chain of deceitfulness glaringly apparent to a shrewd little ice-cream vendor who was always alert to every commercial trick. In the first instance this Garon Records of Oxford had obviously been swindled by the glib-talking distributors of this 'Extra Pollination' album. I in turn had been duped by Garon Records who had palmed off this unplayable cacophony which no other level-headed customer would touch with a bargepole. To be sure, he conceded, I was only twenty-one, and therefore by definition a shortsighted imbecile. Deeply smitten after his first encounter with beautiful Fanny, Vince now hit on the final link in the chain. Tonight, one year later in Mirehouse Legion, he seriously proposed that it was me, Enzo Mori, who had perversely influenced poor little impressionable 'Funny' into listening to and subsequently performing that Extra Pollination din…

"She is such an intelligent little fing, Enzo. Funny Gelati is so bootiful an gentle an *sensibile*. Funny Gelati could not possible play that crazy kipper stuff wif her jass band unless you has had a blurry influence on her…"

I stared at him with a sharp suspicion. As soon as this incongruous pair had smiled and musically clinked their glasses of vintage chianti, the whole of Mirehouse Legion was able to observe him eyeing Fanny with more than just a fatherly tenderness. Of course Fanny was simply being kindly receptive to his effusiveness and effervescence, and was obviously giving him no other encouragement. Nonetheless, remembering that murky business with that tender-hearted Cleator Moor woman called 'Chenfa', I decided to keep a cautious, vigilant eye on him.

"Influence my arse," I snorted, while Fanny was safely at the bar. "You really are a credulous Calabrian peasant, aren't you? Why not say I put the evil eye on her while you're at it? For your information, it was Fanny bought Extra Pollina... *Extrapolation* first, and it was she who introduced it to me, not the other way around."

I stopped as I saw my father's oddly prescient expression, and realised I was looking and sounding far too unsure of myself. All too aware of how poignantly beautiful my new girlfriend was, how insecure and wildly possessive she frequently made me feel, I decided to stamp on my father's impertinent infatuation right at the start. I added victoriously:

"Her own stuff is twice as wild as *Extrapolation*, if you really want the truth."

But Vincenzo would not have it. Funny Gelati was his special virginal sweetheart, his unsullied platonic ideal. Perhaps, after all, Fanny herself was to blame for this peculiar fixation. If it hadn't been for her munificent gift of the vintage chianti, it would probably never have happened. Very soon I inferred that I must be the sullen and superfluous nuisance who interfered with the pristine beauty of my father's private fantasy. From then on, whenever they met on any social occasion, Vince Mori would park himself crudely and obstructively between Fanny and everyone else within a fifty-yard radius. Or, in the case of his son, would more or less grab her and tenderly lead her away to a distant corner, where he could warmly regale her with his jokes and patter to his heart's content. Clearly it was a paradigm

Oedipal situation, and Vince Mori made no attempt to disguise it with any Anglo-Saxon subtlety or sleight-of-hand. Thankfully for all concerned, my father genuinely had no physical designs on my angelic girlfriend, she was definitely his chaste troubadorial principessa. Besides, I soon discovered that Vincenzo Mori, the clandestine womaniser, had more than one case like Jennifer the oilrigger's wife on his hands. Chenfa and the tender moonlit walk together in the Linethwaite Woods turned out to be merely the tip of the ice-cream vendor's iceberg. Nor, it transpired, were all his mysterious rendezvous with lonely women quite so touchingly chaste with moonstruck adolescent poetry.

That night in the Legion, Vince surpassed himself both as impassioned musician and swaggering performer. This was glaringly apparent after the interval, once he'd canvassed Fanny's opinion and she had flattered The Stompers to the skies. Good-naturedly she had lied her head off, had sworn she adored Dixieland and wished she could play it as well as Vincenzo. In reality Funny Gelati disliked trad jazz almost as much as I did. Or rather, in Fanny's case it was something she never listened to, for as soon as it came on Radio 3's *Jazz Record Requests*, she immediately switched it off. In her opinion the art involved in trad was the same as in old-fashioned brass bands or skiffle. The devotional commitment and the skill of its practitioners were obvious and undeniable, but to anyone with any ear for subtle nuance it all sounded irremediably the same. It was jolly, jiving, jiggy, jocund, it was all of that. But as well as being crudely alliterative, it was also repetitive, flatulent and as farcical as ring-a-ring-a-roses or the hokey-cokey.

We sat side by side at a prominent front table. I was squeezing her cool thin hand as we politely tapped our toes to the bubbling showboat rhythms. I stole a sly sideways glance at her delicate and fragrant hair, and tried not to think of the cold reality. Fanny at present had two other menfriends she slept with, possibly several more for all I knew. One was a drummer called Reggie in his late thirties, married and with two small children. Reggie was an electrician from Hounslow who drove up to

Oxford to play in the band and spent the night with Fanny in her Iffley Road rooms. The other was a silver-haired painter called Edmund who lived in an ivied cottage in Iffley Village, looked at least fifty, and stammered in a shy but charismatic way. They had chatted enjoyably one freezing day by Iffley Lock, and Edmund now attended all her Oxford performances. There he would sit alone and vigilant and striking and admirably uncomplacent about his extremely youthful catch.

I ought to have been glad just to be in on the show, but like any very young man, I felt cowed and eclipsed by these mature competitors. Part of me wanted to castigate Fanny Golightly for consorting with elderly public-school men and errant working-class fathers. Had I done so, of course, the posturing moral censure would scarcely have masked the poisonous envy. The fact was I was hungry to have her all to myself, and I wondered just what I could do to win her lock, stock and barrel.

In the first half the Chompin Stompers began with a dirge-like rendering of the *St Louis Blues*. This was followed by the entire unedited A-side of the most recent Acker Bilk album. I blushed as my father actually boasted to his audience about this flagrant plagiarism and copyright *truffa*, instead of hiding the embarrassing fact. In the second half, rapturously buoyed by Fanny's insincere praises, he decided to do his flamboyant carnival party trick. This garish party piece, I reflected with a growing anxiety, was as a rule strictly reserved for Christmases, birthday celebrations and wedding receptions. Or, when so unbelievably, epically tight, the dazed clarinettist was temporarily incapable of distinguishing between horns and would doggedly try to play the wrong end of Dave Shimmins's trumpet. In front of some less exacting audience, say an Old Folks Christmas Knees Up, or a cut-price concert for the local mental hospital, he and side-kick Shimmins might have opted to do a gentle take-off of Flanagan and Allen. Tonight though, in the far more demanding hothouse of Mirehouse Legion, they chose to do their deathless parody of a jazz duo called Slim 'n' Slam.

After a minute or two Fanny looked at me in amazement.

"What the hell is that?" And she asked whether she was supposed to giggle or remain poker-faced.

"No no, laugh, fall about by all means. You haven't got much option, I'm afraid. Vince up there will be looking to make sure you're enjoying it. You're looking very mystified, I must say, for an encyclopaedic jazzwoman. Perhaps you don't realise that you're listening to an exquisite Calabrio-Cumbrian cover version of *The Flat Foot Floogie*, as sung by Slim 'n' Slam."

Funny Gelati blinked rapidly and nervously. She glared at me sternly as if I were being deliberately unintelligible.

"Slam Stewart the comic Forties scat man? Surely, like my father, you know every single one of his remastered albums?"

"Eh?" she said dubiously. "If I rack my brains, perhaps I've seen his name on the back of an old record sleeve…"

"He played with Art Tatum at one stage. A double bass man and an exemplary maestro at self-harmonising. As was Slim Gaillard, who played the piano and the guitar alongside. They went in for extravagant gibberish singing of a high artistic order, Slim 'n' Slam, whereas Dave 'n' Vince, our Mirehouse maestros, just go in for vaudeville gibberish pure and simple. To me, my Dad there sounds, and indeed looks, more like old Johnny Morris the TV chestnut seller wrinkling his whiskers and pretending to be Hammy the Hamster."

"*A sezza Fat Foot Fuggy,*" roared Vincenzo Mori. "*A sezza Fug Fat Fewty.*"

Impulsively, impressively, my fearless progenitor began to do an extravagant, eyes-closed pirouette that threatened to have him concussing himself on Miff Mumberson's shuddering cymbals. At that grotesque sight, Fanny Golightly started as if struck by a powerful barb of lightning. I meanwhile stared tensely into space and wondered why the hell I'd entered this madhouse in the first place.

As the circus performance continued, Fanny relented and decided to listen with a calm, dispassionate tolerance. Wistfully fantasising I was in the front row at a Mahavishnu Orchestra concert in somewhere nice and unCumbrian like Hemel

Hempstead or Croydon, I fidgeted miserably in my chair. My father was engaged in one of his very favourite activities; making a musical buffoon of himself in a provincial working men's club. I had precious little alternative but to sit and grin weakly at the bilious spectacle. To increase my filial distress, I was sat next to his complete antithesis, a phenomenally sensitive musical artist who, paradoxically, was tolerantly uncritical of this capering clown. It was rather as if I had been sitting next to Edward Elgar while my pantomime relative on stage was heedlessly twanging a rubber band and/or pressing a flatulent bicycle hooter.

"*I said the Flat Foot Floogie,*" bawled Dave Shimmins, servile foil to Vince's musical sovereignty. And the rattlesnake hiss in Dave's secondhand dentures was clearly audible with the 'said'.

"*A blurry Fat Foot Fuggy,*" carolled Vincenzo Mori. "*A blurry Flim Flam Flucky. A saya nowa pipple, a Flamma Flimma Flucky.*"

My father lingered long and teasingly, with many a redundant wink and smirk, over that curious noun 'flucky'. At his saucy ad hoc variant, the audience roared with unconstrained delight. At that my shameless parent started to improvise some wholly appalling, if par for the course, four-letter scat, in which the 'flucky' lost its 'l' and the adjacent vowel went through every single puerile possibility...

"*I serra fick fack focky!*" the Calabrian cornet-seller roared at the top of his exhibitionist's lungs.

Wahoo, wahoo! came hurtling back from every ecstatic Mirehouse tonsil.

"Oh my God," I groaned, and Fanny Golightly turned to me with real concern.

"*I meansa fock fick facky!*"

You bloody imbecilic old clown, I whispered soundlessly, as I stared down at a grubby little beer mat. I felt desperate enough to seriously consider enacting a fainting fit. I looked apprehensively at Fanny, but instead of seeming shocked she bore the studious anticipatory air of a field anthropologist. I glanced back at the stage only to shudder anew at the sight of my father strutting across it with a madly lurching chicken gait. At first I thought he must be parodying the toothy comedian Billy Dainty, but no, as he thrust out his hips and pouted at the appreciative Mirehouse women, it was obviously how he imagined a tuxedoed Hollywood rake would stride his bacchanalian apartment.

"Ooh yah *naughty* naughty boy," came gurgling from Mumberson as he adjusted his £10.99 toupee from *Exchange and Mart*.

"*Ah sezza fack fick ficky!*" my father screeched imploringly at his doting, hooting audience. He even had the gall to go down on his knees like a penitent, beseeching Al Jolson.

Wahoo, wahoo! hallooed his rampant Mirehouse fan club.

"Oh my God," I said as stricken, not to say traumatised as Job. "May the earth swallow me up." I turned in torment to Fanny Golightly. "Where did I go wrong, do you think? I mean it, Fanny, I'm not being rhetorical. What the hell was I doing when I chose that mad idiot for a father?"

"*I tella nowa pipple, cmon cmon cmon* (swaying of hips, thrusting of loins, squinting of eyes, drooling of tongue as obscene choreographic embellishments of that singular imperative) *a fick fick ficky!*"

Grinning, grimacing and prancing like a lewd Fellini mountebank, Vincenzo Mori was all that every Southern Eyetie was supposed to be. He was coarse, lecherous, ludicrous, vainglorious, a bloody abomination in any Indo-European language. All too aptly, this salacious, disgraceful little song made me think of the wanton cry of a Third World prostitute beseeching some drunken English sailor with a hoarse, '*You wanna do ficky-ficky?*'

I felt that I could stand it no longer. I scraped my chair brutally and hoarse with anger said:

"Fanny, did you know that Slam Stewart sang an equally famous standard called *Shut Yo Mouth*?"

She stared at me nonplussed. Profoundly exasperated by her placid incomprehension, that oh-so West Cumbrian manner of hers, I flung up my arms as expressively as any outraged operatic baritone.

"*Because I wish the hell my odious and atrocious fucking father*

155

would do just that!"

My face must have been grotesquely contorted, because she widened her eyes at the sight. The couple at the next table, observing something incendiary was brewing, began to monitor this unusual pair with a professional interest. Fanny scowled at them impatiently, then leant across to me and quietly pointed out the obvious:

"But the audience is loving it, Enzo. They're lapping it up, your father's clowning." She hesitated then said quietly, "Actually, I think he's very brave."

I sneered at her. "Brave? My father?"

"Yes. Yes he is. It takes an enormous courage to do something so uninhibited, so unselfconscious and so funny. Just look at them all. Your father is a real star for them tonight."

The fact that she was speaking the truth did not appease me one iota. His cheering spectators were so worked up by this do or die performance, they were ready to fling fivers, their retirement watches and priceless heirloom jewellery on the stage in their boundless gratitude. That cut no ice whatever with his too sensitive student son. For them he might well be a god, but for me he was more like a savage and uncontrollable totem.

"You don't say," I snorted, feeling comprehensively betrayed by her sanguine tone. "More bloody fools them! Don't you see, Fanny? Can't you see?"

"See what?"

"That they'd be just as happy to hear Vincenzo Mori in a bear outfit or a diving suit singing a perfect rendition of Franco Sinatra's, *I Did It Blurry My Way*?"

I must have been gesticulating, not to say slavering, like an inferior version of my father, like a strutting minor character out of Donizetti. I realised as much because Fanny Golightly began to blush, and told me sharply to lower my bloody voice!

Later, when *The Flat Foot Floogie* was finally at an end, she leant across and whispered in a less impatient tone:

"But he's your father, Enzo. He's maybe not another Miles Davis but he's your father and he's the only one you've got."

9

♪♩♫

Toto Cebola spent seven whole years in Póvoa do Varzim, a biblical period, or at any rate a dreamlike one. Of course Professor Alvarenga made no concessions to jazz, he tutored his unwelcome pupil in classical technique and composition, and Cebola had to continue his first love elsewhere. Joey Conto helped by bringing him a record player from Porto and providing a small but quintessential library that included Svend Asmussen, Stuff Smith, Charlie Parker, Miles Davis and John Coltrane. He also found him the only jazz club in the whole of the city, in the whole of North Portugal come to that. It was a dusty subterranean grotto on the Cais da Ribeira, which was a simple dance hall for six nights of the week and a clandestine jazz venue on Sundays when officially it wasn't supposed to have a drinks license. It was called *O Trocadero*. A dry and wiry Californian with a Scandinavian sounding name, Taf Anders, was the leader of its resident and only band. Taf played tenor sax and he gradually instructed Conto's protégé in its rudiments. The bassist was a middle-aged Frenchman called Maurice, who as well as being painfully shy had a gigantic benign cyst on his forehead. The pianist was a smileless German called Ruprecht, an art school lecturer of about thirty who spoke at least half a dozen languages. The only other Portuguese was an extremely dolorous drummer, a long and lanky waiter who faithfully lived up to his name, having been christened straight out of the Old Testament as... Job Guimarães.

Taf Anders badly needed a pianist and tried to get Cebola to learn the piano as well as the sax and violin. The sceptical little novice looked thoroughly uncomfortable and threw in the towel after a few painful attempts on the Trocadero's baby grand. Eventually, with some adamance, he explained that he only liked to play musical instruments that he could hold in his hands or his arms. Anders chewed his ragged moustache and shrugged and lent him an old tenor which Cebola carted home on the train to Póvoa every Monday morning. It was usually an ordeal to ride that rackety jolting rail line because it frequently gave him travel sickness. When he complained to Mrs Carneiro she chuckled and wheezed and said his sickness must be of his childish imagination. Only cars and buses could make you feel nauseous, it was quite impossible in the case of a good old Portuguese train. On second thoughts her lodger decided it must be the late nights and the Sunday stay-overs at Anders's flat on the Rua das Flores that were shaking up his boyish system. That and the far from credible transmogrification of his humble, entirely nondescript childhood identity. A few months ago he was virtually a Coimbran beggar, while these days he enjoyed sumptuous foursquare meals from a doting and monied old Póvoa widow. He now played jazz violin alongside sarcastic, intelligent Frenchmen and Germans, in a big though very old-fashioned city whose inhabitants had only heard the word 'jazz' mentioned in tenyear-old Yankee films.

Occasionally during the interval on sunny evenings Cebola stepped out of the Trocadero and stared at the Douro from the Cais da Ribeira. Invariably there would be a gang of noisy ragamuffin kids performing hair-raising dives from the Cais or from stationary boats. They were such brilliant little divers they ought to have been in international competitions, or so it seemed to Cebola who was only an indifferent swimmer. Tired of their diving, they would swim across to the Vila Nova side and play among the streams of outsize fish that gorged upon the streaming sewage. As Anders put it, those kids must all have cast-iron livers the size of his tenor sax. None of them ever came down with dysentery or cholera, as if magically immune. Something about the spectacle of those giant fish guzzling up all that human shit struck Cebola as piquantly poetic if not at all pleasant. Portugal was a poor country, right enough, but, as Taf Anders wisely remarked, stony old Salazar was determined to make it even poorer.

The local saying went that Braga prayed, Lisbon showed off, but Porto worked. There was plenty of hard work down on the Cais but also plenty of fruitful indolence evident in the way the stallholders would take a break to drink a *garoto* of coffee and let the stalls look after themselves. Conto gave him a weekly pocket-money allowance that permitted him to buy a few books off the quay, and in the Trocadero intervals, especially during the winter, Cebola idled his time away by reading. At Mrs Carneiro's suggestion he read boys' adventure classics by Dumas and Verne and Swift in Portuguese translation. Whenever he had time to kill, Taf Anders also read, though in English of course, and in his case it was some French existentialists called Camus and Sartre. The German Ruprecht also gulped up everything to do with *Existenzialismus*, and even Job Guimarães ploughed his dogged way through novels and treatises on *existencialismo*. Incredibly, one wet evening in 1960, when the club was completely deserted, the sax player, the drummer and the bassist were all sat around a dusty table reading *The Age of Reason* in their three respective translations. Taf Anders explained this cosmopolitan obsession to the inquisitive Coimbran kid as follows:

"Did you ever read the back of any recent album sleeves? No, they're nearly all in highbrow English, so that figures. The guys who write them, the music critics, are trying to do the impossible, so more often than not they lose all sense of proportion. The problem is, you see, they are trying to comment in a meaningful way on the absolutely inexpressible, the world of complex musical improvisation. No, put your hand down, Toto, don't interrupt to ask the meaning of big words or I'll lose my drift. Ask Job Guimarães later on and he'll explain. See how Job is listening carefully too to the old Yankee know-all. He was raised a good superstitious Portuguese Catholic like you, so part of him must be wondering why the hell it seems obligatory to read Jean-Paul Sartre in the Trocadero before he can be a jazz drummer.

"Apropos the jazz writers, these intellectual aficionados. They have two possible options. They can either ramble on painstakingly about the formal musical structure, which would soon bore the shit out any hopeful record buyer. Or they can go all solemn and turn to poetry and heavy serious literature for significant comparisons. Hence the obsession with the existentialism and the Kierkegaard and the Hermann Hesse and the Rimbaud and Baudelaire and the Flowers of Bloody Evil. Some title that last one, it sounds like a ready made jazz track, possibly by Miles. It all adds glamour and mystique, this lofty, earnest culture stuff, and it flatters both the the jazz critics and the record buyers. Jazz, you'll rapidly learn, attracts the preening show-offs as well as the sincere types. It might all have begun with impoverished black guys, but it's not any more a poor man's music. To the uninitiated, to the cloth-eared and the proud-to-be-a-redneck, jazz goes all over the place, so it frightens and repels them. Recognising that, the jazz critic feels the weight of posterity on his shoulders, and thinks maybe he is the high priest specially entrusted to explain it to a discerning minority. He gets nervous and over-protective about his elevated role and starts to act maybe as if jazz needs him more than he needs jazz. He behaves like the priestly explainer of a hermetic faith and decides to mystify instead of making plain. It's usually easier to baffle with big words than to fight clean with small ones. Then of course there is the related matter of, shhh, drugs, you'd get jailed for two hundred years in Portugal if you were mad enough to fool with them in sombre old Porto…"

Suddenly Ruprecht the art teacher decided to interrupt in a punctilious monotone. He continued to read his *Age of Reason* as he remarked in perfect Portuguese:

"The trick, in my opinion, is always to exercise an infinite discretion. And to consume that which you consume alone and behind a locked and bolted door."

Cebola widened his eyes at this extraordinary take-it-or-leave-it admission. Taf Anders hesitated, then decided not to confront such dogmatic Teutonic solemnity. He went on:

"Charlie Parker and Miles Davis and plenty more, they early on decided to stoke their imaginations with all sorts of dope. Drugs are usually accompanied by a penchant for self-examination and just as often self-destruction. The two things go together like beef and mustard or like waffles and syrup. Similarly jazz playing and a theoretical approach to fancy oriental philosophy. Frequently of the belly-button staring done in the comfort of your Greenwich apartment kind. Likewise dope and the Beat thing. *On the Road*, Kerouac, Corso, Ginsberg, all that has a natural affiliation with our airy-fairy jazz milieu. That rambling, poetic kind of frenzy seems to have a jazz all of its own."

Job Guimarães put down his copy of Sartre and remarked in a baleful voice, "I managed to read *The Subterraneans* in French translation last year. It was unobtainable in Portuguese of course, because of the bloody moronic censorship in this country. Anyway, I believe that amazing work has changed me very much as a man. After reading Senhor João Querioaque I have not been the same person since."

Anders smiled politely at the rather robotic emphasis and there was an odd unsettled silence around the table. Putting down his brandy, the sax player took out a Peter Stuyvesant and addressed the violinist:

"Take note, Cebola. Job Guimarães has been transformed by his bohemian occupation and so will you be. This peculiar world you are entering, the unusual language it uses, the night-time, secretive atmosphere of jazz, it's the very opposite of your old-fashioned Portuguese existence. Joey Conto is definitely a right-on talent spotter, you are obviously a little genius, and unless you are shooting up smack or acting baroque and drinking absinthe at nineteen, you are going to go one hell of a long way. So my advice to you at this seminal stage is, when you get a bit older and a bit more restless, Toto, by all means go in for reading weighty books and tortured poetry and epistemological philosophy and all that jazz…" He clicked his fingers dubiously, as if regretting the facile limitations of all logical explanations. "Look, see old Job smiling at my choice of words. He's noticed the interesting use of the noun 'jazz' there, a collective signification that just for once mocks its own pretensions. As for you, Toto Cebola, you can even try dabbling with esoteric religion, with the prana and the nirvana and the dhyana etcetera if that suits your style when you emigrate to the States in five years time. But make sure you keep away from heavy drugs and heavy liquor. In fact the safest thing all considered would be for you to keep on doing what you're doing now; reading *Twenty Thousand Leagues Under The Sea* and *Gulliver's Travels*. As far as I know no one ever became a junkie if they stuck to reading good old-fashioned European adventure stuff like that."

The obedient student listened gravely and then returned to the Houyhnhnms. Some five years later as a pre-performance relaxant, he was smoking joints of Red Lebanese hash in Hamburg and Paris clubs. Once and only once in Berlin he smoked some Afghan opium given him by an exiled Iranian woman called Feroozeh Zahra Shahna. As for Job Guimarães, he was drumming in Oslo and Copenhagen clubs during the flower-power psychedelic period. Whenever his and Cebola's paths chanced to cross, he was admitting to tripping on acid as a sine qua non of any live jazz performance. Job had learned to function as a heavy-lidded, dark-eyed cavernous ruin of a musician, though he was still doggedly reading *The Roads to Freedom* and still telling the numerous women in his life he could only be responsible for himself, he could not take on their existential responsibility by proxy. The one item of Anders's advice that Cebola faithfully subscribed to, was to keep on with the tenor sax as well as the fiddle, just in case he was unable to find a band who needed a violinist. His persistence with the horn meant that, when in 1966, in Paris, he surrendered exclusively to the violin, he endowed it with an extraordinarily aggressive sound the like of which had never been heard. Taf Anders's reluctant saxophonist gave his violin no vibrato, but played it

162

with a tenor be-bop phrasing and a jabbing cut and thrust that sounded like a sax as well as a violin.

Four years had gone by and it was 1961. He was learning his jazz in Porto at the Trocadero, but back in Póvoa do Varzim there was also Mrs Carneiro's jazz, not to speak of Professor Alvarenga's jazz. Even as an immature teenager, and long before he would awkwardly formulate it in interviews with foreign music journalists, Cebola was helplessly perceiving the term 'jazz' as a semantic and philosophical universal. For him 'jazz' was obviously a convincing intuitive description of nearly all aspects of human behaviour, as well as the idiosyncratic notation of a particular branch of music. Of course he didn't express it that way at fifteen, as, apart from anything else, in 1961 he wasn't even familiar with the term 'intuitive'. But, par excellence, sour old Professor Alvarenga expressed himself in a verbal jazz that improvised along set melodic lines, along timeworn fussinesses of routine and moribund social etiquette. To pluck one example at random, Professor Alvarenga's sister Emília had to deposit his *garoto* and the large *copo* of Coca (ugh!) Cola at exactly 10.45 outside the study, and was strictly forbidden to knock to signal its arrival. Frequently, of course, both teacher and pupil were so engrossed in their study that they forgot all about that imperative refreshment. Until the stricken maestro, as if belatedly noticing that his foot had caught fire, without a word shot his head out the door and angrily grabbed the silver tray. After which, observing with a massive sigh the giveaway colour of the cold *garoto*, he would begin to 'improvise' a furious lament.

"She knows how I detest cold coffee, Cebola! She knows I won't touch that disgusting frappe *galão bilge* which half of Portugal happily bebs, even if the sun is cracking the pavement outside. And yet, time after time she leaves my coffee out there to congeal, instead of making a second once it's evident that we've been so engrossed the first one must obviously have been ignored. I presume you must have heard me berating her often enough through the kitchen door? If challenged about her pathetic incompetence, my peevish sister bridles and accuses me of deliberate sadism, though to be fair that isn't the exact word she uses. Emília uses an altogether more anecdotal and imprecise term; she quaintly characterises my reproaches as 'bullying'. According to my little sister, I am just a plain old-fashioned bully. I have to confess, Cebola, I've never understood the supposed generic meaning of that word, outside of the Malthusian morass of the schoolyard, where some hulking great oaf twists the arm of some bespectacled and delicate minor. That, I can possibly agree, is a valid definition of intimidation, a proper description of an ignoble and improper use of superior force. But for someone like myself, of a disciplined artistic life and disciplined artistic mind, to urge the same virtues of punctuality and punctiliousness and calm routine upon someone who is in the inexorably dependent relationship that Emília is with me? How on earth can that be described as objectionable conduct?

"After all, Cebola, the only way that I can get you yourself to shape up, is to drill and drive you and push you to the necessary limits. Every day as you know I set you as much homework as would chill the soul of a Mandarin imperial civil servant. Recognising as I do that the only way to make a finished maestro of you, is to treat you with a benign cruelty, a kindly monstrousness. I suppose that is a questionable oxymoron, a potentially unpleasant education, but then again it is precisely the same discipline I inflict on myself, or rather what I did inflict on myself when I was your age and younger and all the way through to my recent retirement. Tell me, isn't that kind of taxing regimen precisely what you are in need of at this stage? Both in terms of your undoubted musical potential and as regards the wishes of your American benefactor, the poetically named 'Meester Conto' of the ostentatious largesse? Speaking of whom, Cebola, did you ever hear of a character called Obel Mugwish in a novel called *Great Expectations* by the celebrated English writer Carlos Dickens?"

His monologue ended so abruptly that his student started nervously.

"Last month, Professor, I tried *David Copp–* "

"Emília frequently ends up weeping and sniffing in the kitchen, protesting that her nasty old brother is simply a puerile sadist. She would sulk there for days if I let her, but instead I buy her some expensive bonbons or a posy of flowers, confident that will appease her as a pat would placate a recently chastised dog. Not that she notices, but I present them to her ironically, these petty peace offerings, as if to imply – well I know who is the puerile one now, Emília, the one who can be appeased with a few little sugared almonds! Other times I just can't be bothered to excuse her sullen silences, and I briskly point out that preparing my 10.45 *garoto* is the only job she has of any urgency in the mornings. You see, my sister makes no income whatever these days, I support her financially and have done as much for the past ten years. Before that, back in the Forties, she had quite a responsible teaching post in Chaves, one which came farcically to grief when she fell in love with the new headmaster. Unfortunately for Emília, that supine gentleman had no interest whatever in anything apart from work and blasting quail and partridge near his parents' Montalegre home. The hopelessly unilateral nature of her pointless passion was more than poor Emília could bear. No amount of philosophical or common-sensical counselling from me, or from anyone else for that matter, was of any use to her in her extremity. My sister had a protracted nervous breakdown, or at least that was what she called her fit of self-fulfilling histrionics. She took to her bed in her lodgings next to the Igreja Matriz, and began to die of unrequited love just like something out of Guilherme Shakespeare. But when it comes to it Emília is no tragic heroine, she is far too self-pitying to have any depth or enchantment as a woman, or a lover or as anything else as far as I can see. Nevertheless, she taught her geography lessons capably enough for fifteen years, and if she'd had the single-minded application of that hunting maniac, Dr Cão, the moustachioed Montalegre boor she doted on and mooned over fretfully night after night, might well have gained a headship herself by the age of forty-five. But what can one expect of a highly strung and deeply irrational individual who can't even prepare a piping hot *garoto*, Cebola?"

Anyone who knows anything about jazz and analyses this dialogue of Alvarenga, can see with what remarkable fidelity the old man talked according to its form and substance. This, despite the fact that he tersely refused to acknowledge the very existence of that 'bastardised negroid cacophony'. His perennially irritating sister is all too clearly the given melodic harmony to which the professor keeps obsessively returning. Alvarenga's 32-bar improvisation on Emília uses the *garoto* as the bridge B, and her improvidence and weak emotions as the A of the AABA. Alternatively his repetitive monologues might be peevishly orchestrated as ABAB. Obviously the old Fascist maestro didn't *have to* tell his teenage student that the teacher Dr Cão hunted *both* quail and partridge, but in doing so he instinctively used an improvisatory embellishment. Then, and on similar occasions, his ornamentation was slight and perhaps inconsequential, quail and partridge being a rather colourless semantic duplicate after all. Nevertheless his was a paradigm case of jazz 'paraphrasing'. For that matter, he didn't *have to* tell Cebola the surname of the Chaves headmaster, but as a jovial quirk Alvarenga always liked to overstress any Portuguese name that had a comical literal meaning. The fearsome Trás-os-Montes hunter was called 'Dr Dog' and Dr Dog almost made his sister pine to death because she didn't have the same attractions as the open heath or the Buçaco forest where he always went for his summer vacations. Then there was young Toto 'Onion' the ragamuffin violinist, the wayward chap who caused onion-induced tears to his furious teacher whenever he failed to listen with a scrupulous attentiveness. Mrs Carneiro was 'Mrs Mutton', the fantastically garrulous landlady of the same Coimbra urchin. It was a pity perhaps that the Professor's own surname wasn't Gato, because then Miss Emília Cat could have fallen with complete apposite tragedy for Dr Teodor Dog.

These jovial professorial improvisations were Estácio Alvarenga's and his alone. They were his 'once-improvised' jazz.

They were his signature tunes, they belonged to him exclusively and could not be borrowed by others. As for his suggestive description of 'moustachioed Trás-os-Montes boor' that was typical of the sour old teacher's completely novel melodic lines, that was therefore his 'chorus phrase', his modern as opposed to his traditional linguistic jazz. In that compressed emphatic adjectival denunciation, he painted the picture of the luxuriant hirsuteness of the single-minded backwoodsman from the precipitous mountain gorges, the remote Spanish borderlands where they came as wild as savages, and coarse and ignorant as they were (even the secondary school headmasters) they were capable of breaking the impressionable hearts of women of good Lisbon family.

♪♪♪

In 1961 Matilde Carneiro, Mrs Mutton, prepared a celebratory *rojões* for the sixteenth birthday of her surrogate son Cebola. It was not just any old *rojões*, but *rojões à moda do Minho*. The leanest pork obtainable in the quality butcher's five minutes' walk away from Mrs Carneiro's house, was chopped and then marinated in a dry white wine with onion and herbs. Then it was fried. Then it was served to a salivating Cebola with both fried potatoes and rice, a majestic redundance that was all too typical of the widow's incontinent bounty. Sure enough on the very first day they met, the senhora had industriously gleaned the details of the Coimbran boy's poverty. She had spent the last four years as it were feeding him up, building him up, letting him acquaint himself with those ineffably poetic inner states known as repletion, satiety... excess.

Mrs Carneiro attended Mass every day and was deeply religious without being at all pious. In her own naive way she saw the prime characteristic of her Creator as one of outrageously profligate excess. Her Creator had not been legally required to make the crystalline dawns and pungent sunsets quite as tenderly exquisite as they always were in the summer months in Póvoa. They could have been half or even a tenth as beautiful, and would still have been breathtaking. She instanced this divine recklessness to her Coimbran lodger when he exclaimed at the blissful copiousness of all these delicious meals. If God, she said, gave too much natural beauty by way of the sleepy young calves mooning in the Minho fields, or the snowy almond blossoms way down in the tropical Algarve, or even the beautifully brown parched wheatfields further up in the Lower Alentejo, if He was always benevolently spilling his excess to his ungrateful creation, then the least Matilde Carneiro could do was provide her young lodger with a generous groaning board. The same general principle applied to love and marriage, she added quickly with an explosive gasp and a moist little sigh. The years spent with her husband Daniel had been at least a hundred times better than she deserved, and he as a man had had more mystery, more frankness, more subtlety, more simplicity, more complexity, than any other man she'd ever met. Daniel Carneiro had always given her more than he needed to give her, that was a part of his sacred memory. He had rescued her from an attentive but domineering widowed father who had tried to discourage her from embarking on teacher training in Porto. Instead her lordly Dad had proposed suffocating accomplishments in office shorthand and dictation, with an evening regime of fine embroidery and old fashioned Minho cookery. For weekend relaxation he suggested horse riding round Penha and its pilgrimage chapel, with some bilious, pale-faced cousins on her mother's side. Her father had decreed that Matilde should work as a private secretary for him in his linen factory in Guimarães, but with the help of Daniel she had fought his stony sovereignty and insisted she wanted a dignified and meaningful profession, not a subservient and inexpressive slavery.

"I have never been able to stop talking, Toto," she said earnestly, as if her naive young lodger ought to be staggered by that revelation. "That is why teaching always seemed the most obvious profession. A good teacher not only needs her prepared notes but she also needs to be able to extemporise and elaborate and... I was going to say embroider, but no, that's not the right verb, no, one has to be able to embellish one's learning, especially history, my specialist subject, with an illustrative anecdote. I don't have a degree like my husband Daniel did, which is why he rapidly achieved a headship while I became a handy little jack-of-all-trades. I taught modern history, geography and scripture to the junior years, and ancient history to the seniors, and physical education to all years until I was fifty-five, when I began with this heart murmur, or otherwise I'd have gone on vaulting and jumping and blowing a little whistle and bawling at the children just as well as all those blousy young women teachers in their twenties.

"With regard to anecdote, Toto, as a way of making history vivid. Supposing I was talking to my kids about the Moorish invasion of our country in 711 AD. It took these invaders seven years to establish themselves as conquerors, and I would say to my twelve year olds, if you can't remember that figure seven think of the Pharaoh's dreams that the enslaved Hebrew patriarch Joseph interpreted in the Bible. Joseph of course was patiently assiduous even in slavery against seemingly impossible odds. He therefore managed to make himself indispensable to the foreign despot. Think of that as an important moral lesson while you're at it, I would tell my yawning pupils. And while we're talking about domination by foreign powers, children, by the ninth century the Portuguese Deep South was then the Al-Gharb, an independent Moorish kingdom with its capital in majestic little Silves. In Silves, I told the pupils, forgive me for sniffing, Toto, forgive me for sniffing, children, I once walked up there to the cathedral with poor Daniel my husband, it was our tenth wedding anniversary, and we had been celebrating by having a motoring tour of the south. The cathedral was built some time after 1266, on the site of a previous Moorish mosque, after Dom Peres Correa had secured the town for the Christians. On the road up to the cathedral on this lovely warm evening in

March (our anniversary is March the 17th, Toto), we passed by a cluttered narrow street where they were frying sardines out on the pavement on their little charcoal fires.

"I thought that such a touching homely thing to do, to fry tiny fish on the pavement for your supper in the company of other friendly chatting neighbours. And the fish of course was the cheapest kind, sardines in those days were something that even the poorest could afford. En route to the cathedral, which has these two great gothic towers, and looks – how can I put it without sounding irreverent? – a bit martial, a bit of a fortress itself, Daniel and I spotted this strange little shop along a shabby side street. It was a cheap stationer's purveying birthday cards and parcel tape and so on, but it also sold a few curios and knick-knacks for passing tourists. Though on this peaceful March evening we certainly seemed to be the only travellers around. The selection of souvenirs on display was far from exciting. I can still picture this primitive lacklustre paperweight which was a very ordinary oval grey stone off the beach, varnished and painted with a poor representation of Silves cathedral, plus another one painted with the ruined fortress. I can also recall a glass bottle with a little masted sailing-ship inside it such as you get by the dozen down on the Porto quay shops. But in among these nondescript objets d'art, there was visible something quite remarkable, something which common enough these days was at the time a considerable novelty. Hanging next to the incredibly dusty shop window, which seemed oddly transformed and almost, looking back, *beatified* by that gently spilling evening sun, was the most beautiful ornamental mobile I have ever seen in my life."

At this point to Cebola's consternation she burst into a flood of noisy tears. He stopped guzzling his wine-marinated pork and exclaimed.

"What's wrong senhora? I... would you like a glass of water?"

Mrs Carneiro howled anew at his kindly solicitousness. Then she dashed behind him, placed her plump, heavily freckled arm around his chin, and began to pump his left shoulder while continuing to weep into his hair.

"No, no water, no thank you, not yet at any rate. I'm so sorry, Toto to upset you with the painful intensity of my widow's recollections. It was just so terribly vivid, such a very painfully vivid picture of that beautiful little object of thirty years ago in that grubby little stationer's in that dirty little alley down in far-flung Silves. Wait though, I haven't explained myself very well. What I haven't told you is that the mobile hanging there in the dancing motes of sunlight was the most elaborate sort of sculptured aviary…"

Toto Cebola failed to picture such a baroque-sounding extravagance. "An aviary? You mean it was full of budgerigars and cockatoos?"

"Yes, yes, similar, though in fact very different altogether. On each suspension of the mobile there were four little sub-strings, and on each of these sub-strings there was a beautiful painted bird which I'm sure corresponded to no real bird unless they were all very rare exotic species from the colonies. From Cabo Verde or Macão or Mozambique perhaps, though I doubt it. The really extraordinary thing was the richness and the vehemence of the birds' colours: dark reds, cobalt blues, jet blacks, pungent ochres, a fiery palette from a profligate and full-blooded artist. That mobile had six suspensions with four birds on each sub-suspension, which meant it had twenty-four tiny birds dancing their enchanted chromatic ballet in the streaming Algarve evening sunlight. Of course I wanted to possess that mobile as soon as I saw it. And Daniel the discerning young headmaster was obviously impressed by its craftsmanship, the integrity of whichever anonymous artisan had made it with such loving and fastidious care. Without my asking for it he insisted that I have it, he could always read my transparent mind when it came to hankering after things. However the skinny old lady running the shop had been sharp enough to winkle out of us the details of our jobs, which part of Porto we lived in, and the extraordinary fact that we owned a brand new foreign car. Seeing that we were two obviously well-off teachers she demanded the earth for her aviary. We might have been very young then, Toto, but we weren't complete idiots altogether. We began to haggle with the sly old woman, and after about half an hour we had beaten her down to an almost reasonable price, probably what it was worth plus fifty per cent.

"Daniel reached into his pockets for his wallet, patted and ferretted and searched. Eventually, clicking his tongue with exasperation, he realised that he had left it in the chest of drawers in the hotel along with his cigarettes. Reasonably enough he'd assumed that a walk up to the cathedral and straight back to the residencial wouldn't require any financial outlay. We said we'd be back immediately, but she said no, no, she was shutting the shop pronto because she had to attend her great-niece's confirmation up in Silves cathedral in the next half hour. Not to worry though, she quickly reassured us, she'd be open at nine the next morning and would put it by for us in the meantime.

"Sure enough we were back there on her doorstep on the dot at ten to nine. To our surprise the shop was already opened, and at once we could see the glaringly empty space where the aviary mobile had been. It more or less screamed its absence at us. All the vivid colour had vanished from that corner, in much the same way that when a child outgrows its bedroom, when he becomes a young man and removes his toy cupboard and children's books and fills it with cigarettes and ashtrays and newspapers, all the vigorous colour seems to depart from the room along with all the childhood. Of course we assumed it wasn't there because the skinny lady had wrapped it up for us. But our sharp old woman was nowhere to be seen, her rather unpleasant looking husband was there in her place. At short notice, out of the blue, he explained, she had had to get the bus into Portimão to attend a very sick sister-in-law who'd had to be rushed into hospital. By the way, how come, Toto, that I can remember that precise detail thirty years on, the fact that it was Portimão not Lagos, and that it was a sister-in-law and not a sister or an uncle of the old proprietress that was very sick? We thought, as I say, that she had parcelled it for us the previous evening and left it with her unprepossessing husband. But the scruffy, rather smelly old man blinked, more resentful than ashamed at us two well-dressed Porto teachers, and said no, no, he had decided to open up early at eight, why waste the day and the chance of doing business, and had just sold the hanging aviary to a very fat priest from Lagos who was visiting a well-off spinster aunt in Odemira and wished to impress her with an ostentatious Algarve souvenir."

Her little lodger gasped at the Southerner's perfidy, and the landlady nodded her tearful agreement.

"Of course I couldn't believe what he was telling me. As well as being bitterly disappointed, really heartbroken, I was incensed by his rough and shameless attitude and let him know it. Just to embarrass the old rogue, I didn't bother to hide my tears of disappointment. I told him furiously about the honourable arrangement we had made with his wife, but my husband stood there impressively solemn and dignified as soon as he realised the birds and their extraordinary beauty had flown, that they were not to be ours after all. Daniel Carneiro said, ah well, Matilde, never mind, we will be sure to get another one identical some-where else. But I knew for certain without a doubt there would never be another one like that with birds looking anything like that, nowhere in the whole of Portugal or in all its colonies, even if we spent the next fifty years doing nothing but searching it out. And likewise the seedy, by now discomfited old shop owner muttered something under his garlicky oniony breath to the effect that, you'll be bloody lucky, Mr Smart Senhor from the North. My husband paid no attention to that rude old dotard's witless mutterings of course. Deep inside though I could see he was affected. Dignified he might have been, but Daniel's lips and even his moustache were quite flat and limpid with the weight of disappointment, not for himself, of course, but for me. The day before when the sunlight was illuminating those highly-coloured birds in that scruffy stationery shop, his mous-tache had been vibrant with pleasure at the sight of something perfectly crafted, something impregnably beautiful, in a world where even in the Portugal of the Nineteen Thirties patient craftsmanship had almost disappeared. It was a one-off and a once-only, you see, Toto, that exotic little bird sculpture, and sometimes when I think of it, and I still keep thinking of it from time to time now, even in 1961, I believe that maybe perhaps it was an other-worldly hallucination after all. Mad as it seems I sometimes say to myself, perhaps that skinny old woman never really existed, and the man I assumed but never confirmed was her husband was talking about something else other than our aviary mobile…"

Cebola began to blush on his landlady's behalf. "You mean a sort of… fairytale thing?"

Mrs Carneiro saw his discomfort and began to redden herself.

"No," she fluttered, chuckling nervously and resorting to her asthmatic wheeze. "I'd hardly believe something as silly and childish as that, would I? Toto, my mind has gone all blank and dizzy and vacant, and it's all your fault, I believe. You've got me away from what I was talking about, you and your boyish chatter, chatter, chatter…"

"But – "

"Anecdotes, that was what I was talking about. Anecdotes as an aide-memoire for my lazy scholars. As I was saying. Moorish architecture is still very evident today the length and breadth of Portugal. There are the remains of Arab forts and walls all over the Algarve, with a splendid example right by the Faro to Olhão railway tracks for a start. But down in the Alentejo too, in Elvas and Mertola, and in the middle in our capital, children, not to speak of those at Sintra and Alcácer do Sal. Arab forts and Moorish fortifications might be hard to picture if you haven't seen them in the flesh, but no one can fail to picture an azulejo tile. The famous and ubiquitous Portuguese tiles, almost as famous as our national emblem of the black and red Barcelos cock, the azulejos that decorate every tiny Portuguese railway station, not to speak of every landowner's mansion in the Beira Baixa, including the ones that you must have seen down in Coimbra, Toto. The Portuguese azulejos, write this down children, were brought to their apogee, to their finest ceramic heights, by the mudejars, the Moorish craftsmen, the Arab tilers, when they worked on the splendid palace at Sintra…

Cebola said dubiously, "By Arabs? Is that a fact?"

"Like you, most of my pupils could only conceive of the azulejos as pure and unsullied Portuguese. They had this strange cognitive and associative problem when it came to the mention of Arabs. To rid them of this confusion, I told them a very instructive anecdote about the time Daniel and I almost missed a train connection down at Tunes in the Algarve. This was before he had his headship and before we had a car, and we'd been to Lagos for a short Easter break, and were changing trains at Tunes to head north to visit Daniel's Uncle Arnaldo, a clockmaker in Beja. Beja by the way is a quite remarkable place that is as white and radiant as a hallucinatory dream, it is one of the most beautiful towns in Portugal. Have you ever visited the sumptuous little capital of the Lower Alentejo, Toto?"

"I – "

"We were so famished that morning that we foolishly stopped for a sandwich in the Tunes station café. The walls were exquisitely decorated with the loveliest little delicate blue azulejos. The sandwich was kid meat, this is an important detail, Toto, and it was unbelievably tender and delicious, and we were enjoying the succulent flavour so much we failed to see that our Beja connection was just about to head out on the other side of the tracks. Suddenly I cried to my husband in a soprano panic like a terrified hen, Daniel we must hurry, we'll need to run like the wind for that Evora train. Naturally I was looking for a footbridge to get over to the other side, but Daniel Carneiro saw right away there was no such thing in a poky little station like this. The only way across to the other side was to walk across the track itself. It shows how touchingly primitive the railways were in those days, but luckily we made it with all the spectators cheering and clapping and with us two young northerners panting and puffing and carefully clutching the remnants of our fantastically tasty goat sandwiches. Once I'd got my breath back, I remarked to Daniel that it was gazing at those mesmerising little azulejos in the café had distracted me so, because I was always a byword for punctuality, I'd never had to run for a train in my life. At which point, my husband said to me very thoughtfully, Matilde, those Arabs knew a thing or two in bygone days, didn't they?

"Unfortunately for me, at that stage in my teaching career, I didn't know anything about the Arab connection. I was unaware that the Arabs were such geniuses at tiles and decorative ceramics because they'd learnt it through building all those mosques. Inside a mosque, Toto, you are never allowed to make any figurative representation of God, so you put all your devout love and your humble reverence into patterns and mosaics and calligraphy. But ignoramus that I was, I thought that my brainy young husband was pulling my leg. So I bumptiously replied, Poppycock, Daniel, Portuguese azulejos are Portuguese tiles, not blinking Arab tiles! Especially in a station café in a place as old-fashioned Portuguese as Tunes! Shaking his head wisely, Daniel Carneiro looked at my righteous, wrong-headed certainty, calmly pointed at the inside of what was left of his kid sandwich, and said, *Matilde, come off it, don't be such an ignorant little* goat..."

The point being, of course, that she was called Mrs Mutton rather than Mrs Goat, and Mrs Carneiro went into jelly wobbles of hysterics as she came to her paronomastic punchline. Toto cackled heartily and aped extravagant mirthfulness when all he really wanted to do was keep on shovelling down the *rojões*. Mrs Carneiro's verbal jazz as he recalled it, was impressively arterial and branching, as ramblingly divagatory as the old Algarve rail system. Professor Alvarenga might have been capable of occasional parenthesis but on the whole his conversation was intelligently sequential and ordered and his jazz as we've seen was the jazz of extravagant ornamentation. Mrs Carneiro, by contrast, picked up a theme, developed it, remembered something else, dropped the original thread and fluttered off in pursuit of a second, a third, a fourth. Nonetheless her original melody was always there and always distantly discernible through those multiple anastomosings. The theme and the melody were the undying, painful memory of her one enduring love, the source to which she always returned. Once you understood that Daniel Carneiro was the thematic bridgehead, you were no longer flummoxed by Mrs Carneiro's remarkable parallels with the mind-boggling freeform of a saxophonist and trumpeter called Ornette Coleman...

Mrs Carneiro was also carefreely as opposed to carelessly redundant when it came to description. She had criticised the surly Silves stationer as 'an old dotard', as if to imply there might be such things as young dotards or middle-aged dotards. (The truth being, of course, that there obviously are such impossible creatures, despite the facile denials of literalists and the blindly unimaginative, there are plenty of repugnant, obstructive young men who act more senilely than the crabbiest octogenarians.) In virtually the same breath Toto's landlady had declared that 'she knew for certain without a doubt' the absolute uniqueness and irreplaceability of the aviary mobile. In the mouth of some po-faced Póvoa gossip that 'for-certain-without-a-doubt' tautology would have been painfully irritating, but in the case of chin-wobbling grief-stricken Mrs Carneiro it simply indicated the passionate heedless vehemence and certitude of one who felt all her feelings to the core.

How to put this in jazz terms? Perhaps we need to quote the English guitarist Fanny Golightly, when she railed, as she frequently did, against those jazz critics who complained that Fanny herself used too many notes, a choking struggling surfeit of them, to express what could have been more 'economically' and 'lyrically' expressed. She had begun to make her mark in 1971 (two years later than Toto Cebola), at the same time that Pharoah Sanders, John Coltrane's former tenor partner, brought out an unusually provocative album called *Tauhid*. Fanny frequently used this *Tauhid* as her polemical yardstick, with its seventeen-minute riverlapping tone poem about Egypt on the A side, and its three-minute croaking sung-counterpoint to classical Japan on the back. After that harmless aquatic sweetness and somno-lence, followed by the (according to Fanny) Lafcadio Hearn exoticism, Sanders aggressively decided to bamboozle his tran-quillised listeners. He opted in fact to go mad with a rather different orientalism. In this case, explained Fanny, the eastern locus was India and the track was called *Aum*. His first act of madness was to play alto sax instead of his tenor, and his second was to explode into an extravagant choking fit, a John Coltrane homage, no doubt of it, intended to make us jump out of our complacent and 'pisswise occidental' stupors. (Pisswise, when I think about it, was one of Fanny's favourite critical and, inci-dentally, West Cumbrian terms.)

There ensues the dense and polyphonal braying of an angry maddened turkey, which abruptly decides to howl like a hyena. The hyena is playfully contemptuous of the cheeseparing spare-ness of its musical accompanists. Henry Grimes, commented Fanny, amnesically scratches his bass as if it is an irritant itch. Warren Sharrock's guitar is all dogged, doleful mangling of an electrified rubber-band. But they are there, you understand, as the willing foils to Pharoah's vicious extravagance, his defiantly pugnacious excess. Now that your nerves are scratched raw, Enzo, and you are begging for an end of it, Sanders, like a saga-cious Zen master, smirks and pulls his ornamental oriental rug from under your feet. Now that he has led you to a peak of vis-ceral discomfort with that screaming turkey-hyena, Pharoah (as he regularly does) everts into the most rapturous melodic ten-derness. We have moved on to the next number, *Venus*, which follows without proper track separation, and therefore represents more than just a banal numerical third of the same three-part suite. With *Venus*, he is back on the tenor, serenading us with the message that out of musical breakdown and an anguished wordless dissolution comes perhaps some tenderness, some mercy, some transfixity of, what shall we call it?

Shall we call it love, Enzo? Or shall we call it Love?

Capitalised or uncapitalised, that substance wasn't on offer from Fanny Golightly. I looked at her loveliness and winced.

I followed her instructions and examined the back of the *Tauhid* LP cover. The sleevenotes by Nat Henthoff informed us that Pharoah Sanders 'believed' in all religions, provided, that is, that they acknowledged the One Creator. Whether the Shinto Buddhist Japanese or the majority of Hindus, whose sacred mantra syllable is 'Aum', would second this tolerant young Afro-American, was an altogether different matter. Had an over-hopeful thirty-year-old Pharoah Sanders perhaps got it all wrong in his head, but somehow got it all right in his sax? Had he, I asked Fanny unsurely, as if she herself were any less guilty of these inevitable confusions?

10

The traditional New Orleans sound that my father favoured was based on the interplay of three front-line instruments; the trumpet, the clarinet and the trombone. This tradition goes back to at least the start of the twentieth century, though of the first New Orleans trumpet star, Buddy Holden, there are no surviving recordings. As the early bands performed at weddings and christenings and other celebratory occasions, and as most of these were out of doors in the Louisiana sunshine, the sheer loudness of the music was more important than anything else. When it came to raw volume nothing could outdo the trumpet, which is why most bandleaders traditionally were trumpeters.

One warm July evening in the mid-Sixties the Stompers' trumpeter, Dave Shimmins, pointed this out half-jestingly, half in the spirit of a weaselly, self-seeking West Cumbrian. Vince Mori who had just received a miserable fiver for four hours' work from Kendal Legion, flinched at Shimmins before laughing him to scorn. 'Deaf Chummins' as 'a bliddy bandlidder'? Well, OK, OK, aside from the fact Deaf didn't even possess his own car and had to beg lifts off third parties, Deaf hadn't an ounce of bloody organising capacity. Nor had he Vince's salivating, emphatic telephone manner which allowed him to solicit bookings from stony club secretaries both sides of the Border. Could Deaf, week in week out, sort out gigs from Ecclefechan to Ulverston, from Creca Working Men's to the Cons Club at 'Cubby Stefan' in 'bliddy old Weshmulland'? Faced with such contemptuous dismissal, Dave assumed a wounded dignity and grumbled *sotto voce* about the so-called leadership provided by a 'furren Eyetalian'. Vincenzo Mori was genuinely amazed by this disgraceful, below-the-belt, entirely novel West Cumbrian ethnic prejudice. He flung up his arms impatiently and retorted with crushing finality:

"Deaf, you mebbe not a bliddy furriner, but when you talk on stage your bliddy dentures go siss siss, hiss hiss!"

It was the first time any of the Chompin Stompers had ever dared to ridicule the trumpeter's conspicuous speech defect. Shimmins flushed his indignation, then countered not unsheepishly, "Who shhays they bliddy do?"

"*Aiuto!* How can professnal bandlidder sound like bliddy rattlesnake when he announce next number *composhhhhhht* by Mishsha Hacker Bilk or Mishsha Cannon Ball? Ask your bliddy drummer Miff Mumpson here if you don believe me. *Per esempio*, Deaf, you don't says, Gut Even, lezzy and shenmen, like I do, what you says, Deaf, is, *Gut Even laddish and shemlingsh, tonight we shartshsh wish a number by Monty Shoonshineshhhhh...*"

Miff Mumberson broke into hectic guffaws at this too accurate parody and Dave Shimmins lunged at him incensed. Wilf Phizacklea, the trombonist, promptly inserted his huge fists between the pair of them, then addressed the susurrating Pretender to the Throne in a tough didactic manner.

"It's thee own fault, thoo bliddy Frizinton tightarse! Bliddy alf Irish scragarse eejit."

Yes, he repeated with a wagging finger, it was his own bloody fault for being so pathetically stingy. Those ill-fitting dentures, he reminded him, had been acquired at a Frizington Methodist jumble sale ten years ago for the interesting sum of fourpence-halfpenny. They'd been a remarkable bargain even by the parsimonious standards of Methodists and the prices of 1956, principally because half of the jumble had come from a dusty storeroom cache unearthed from the long derelict Whitehaven workhouse. The dentures might well be those of a 1920s pauper who died of TB or diphtheria, and there was no saying either the builder who found the cache, or the Frizington Methodists he gave them to, had bothered to give Dave's gnashers a decent wash. Despite Wilf's harangue, the Stompers' trumpeter remained stolidly unmoved. He refused to purchase a new pair of fangs on the obstinate principle that there was no point in chasing after a miraculous bargain if only ten years later you were fool enough to renounce it.

In the New Orleans tradition a trumpeter like Dave served to ornament or embellish the melody. The farting and groaning of Wilf's trad trombone provided, as it were, with punning aptitude, 'a bass foundation'. My father's favoured instrument the clarinet could be said to contribute the filigree ornamentation. Or call it instead the chasing on the silver, the icing on the cake, the chamfer on the Chippendale. In the case of that antique object known as Mori's Chompin Stompers, Vince's clarinet was not only the chamfer but the dovetail joint, the dowelling, and as a last resort the botching and the fish glue. Vince Mori held his band together against all the odds, not least in the face of the ugly mid-Sixties when the clubs really wanted only imitation Merseysound. Vince then had to convince the Cumbrian and South Scotland promoters that his traditional jazz was as timeless as these mop-haired Beatles buggers were risibly ephemeral. That, he snorted at them indignantly, was why it was called 'bliddy tradishnal'. Because it have such a great bliddy *tradizione*. Somehow his Reggio di Calabrian vehemence, the naive simplicity of his peasant eloquence, managed to do the trick. In the end the browbeaten secretaries would groan and cave in and put the Stompers on as first-string warm-up band. In the reasonable enough hope that the cheerful punters were so busy at the bar and/or catching up on the latest crack, that they wouldn't particularly notice those shambling unglamorous old buggers doing their outdated Billy Cotton antics up on stage.

♪♪♪

Fifty-year-old Vince Mori might have been washed up when it came to musical fashions, but in other significant areas he maintained a surprisingly adventurous Sixties spirit. After Jennifer the oilrigger's wife had divorced her psychopath husband and moved away to Huddersfield, Vince was briefly at an existential impasse. Faithful to his Cumbrian wife for over two decades, he suddenly decided that a menopausal explosion might be a feasible preventative against the nightmare of geriatric impotence. Frightened or at any rate rattled by my anger at his first betrayal of Angelica, he was forced to confide his conquests to his lodger Watson Holland. Watson listened to these increasingly boastful Decameron accounts with a mixture of scientific fascination and unflappable man-to-man condescension. Every time I returned from Balliol he duly filled me in on the Reggio di Calabrian rake's progress and noticed with some relief that I seemed to be showing progressively less disgust at my father's grubby nature.

It was my father's *jazz*, I said to our senior lodger cryptically, it was the predictable way that he improvised a personal history. At least it showed more imagination than his trad improvisations, and in any event, I added, I wasn't my father's keeper. Holland nodded sagely and sceptically at my twenty year old's pomposity. My mother, he said, still seemed to be in the dark about my father's affairs. As indeed, he had confirmed by some judicious public-house detective work, did everyone else in the Whitehaven area. Vince it seemed had found the perfect foolproof cover for his belated oat-sowing. What he did these days, said Holland, was to restrict his adventures to his ice-cream round, which in the last twelve months had become increasingly remotely rural. Of course he still flogged his Mivvis, 99s and Oysters all round the populous council estates at Greenbank, Mirehouse and Woodhouse, otherwise he would have been bankrupt twice over by now. But latterly, for example, he had extended his rural run beyond Gosforth to take in the furthest-flung farms and cottages up the Eskdale and Wasdale valleys. As the pharmacist decorously phrased it, he was presently liaising with a besom from Boot. Your old pater, mine Gay Cavalier

Enzo, is bunking up with a floozie in Boot.

"You what?" I said in almost a bored voice. That stark monosyllable hadn't registered at first.

"Boot-in-Eskdale," clarified Holland. "A place where the census list discloses rather more sheepdogs than human beings. And the humans, such as they are, have forgotten the English language on account of the scarcity of non-ovine and non-bovine interlocutors."

Moderately intrigued by the remote location, I asked him, "And who is this woman? She's a farmer's wife I suppose. Doesn't he feel any sense of danger or risk? Isn't he scared her husband will geld him with a pair of rusty sheep shears?"

"Not he," Holland sniffed, gargling some Bunabhain he'd purchased that day from Whitehaven's one and only off-license. "Bouf! Damn my hairy longjohns, boy! Smokey and peaty is no exaggeration. Lumme, this is the stuff to give the warring Picts and Scots as well as we Cumbrian and Northumbrian Celts. It seems to me" – holding his brackish malt up to the electric light – "the sadly neglected subjunctive mood is most appropriate at this point. In the case of this six-guinea booze, it *were* like drinking an effusion of Hebridean bog water somehow metamorphosed into classical and ambrosial nectar."

"The Bunaban?" I said dimly. "Is that what you're talking about?"

"Bunavan," he tsked and corrected. "First rate birdwatching up that way you know, round by Port Ellen on Islay. Every township up there – and by township one signifies any solitary croft occupied by a lone alcoholic postman called Murdo and his alcoholic dog called Ruaraidh Bheag – every bloody one of them has a little malt distillery. Apropos lonely rural males, your oversexed governor is not actually risking his manhood at the hands of a cuckolded farmer. Vince assures me he doesn't really like plump agricultural women with faces like WI teacakes and complexions as red as slapped backsides. In fact your pop is presently having a fling with a middle-class potter lady. She's a thirty-year-old woman called Lorna…"

I scoffed at such an idiotic fabrication. "Oh yes? She's teaching Vincenzo to use the potter's wheel, I suppose?"

"That was, I admit, my own first reaction. But it's true enough what your father says. Ring this Lorna woman up if you don't believe me. If the pre-war blow-down-the-tube exchange is operative in Boot today, that is. Your boastful Pa has shown me her calling card as well as a pretty little ashtray she made for him last week. I have the calling card on me I think."

Did he really mean 'calling card'? Wasn't that what they put in large numbers in phone boxes in Soho?

"You mean for *you* to go along as well and have your way with – ?"

"What? Doh, you unworldly young dolt! Your pa might be capable of all sorts, but even he draws the line at procuring tarts for his gentlemen lodgers. Anyway a chap of old-fashioned tastes like me would hardly be interested in some pallid, flat-chested left-wing potter girl with a name like Lorna Butterskate."

Wonderingly I scrutinised what was in fact a calligraphic business card.

"Bugger me. What a bloody handle. *Lorna Butterskate ARCA. The Hagg, Boot-in-Eskdale, Cumbria. Tel. Boot-in-Eskdale 16. Ceramic artist with postgraduate diploma from The Slade. Kiln demonstrations strictly by appointment. Glaze and slipware demonstrations strictly by prior arrangement. Showroom tours only by prearranged appointment.* She sounds almost as barmy as my father. It's more like a bloody set of bye-laws than a business card."

Holland poured more Islay malt, then tugged at a stray whisker of his handlebar moustache. He looked at me with an affectation of pitying concern.

"Vince is one of the few who needs no permit to see this anti-social potter. Every Wednesday lunchtime he parks his van cleverly out of sight behind her very remote cottage. Recognising his distinctive van engine, slowly and carefully she opens the rear French windows and pokes out her wary little bohemian nose. Her wan and etiolated artistic visage evidences a sudden blazing animal vitality, in response to this perspiring olive-skinned Italian *gelati* man. Already at the sight of your smirking pa, she is licking her lips and visibly salivating."

I glanced at him sceptically. "Those can't be his words. Vince Mori doesn't say 'etiolated' and 'salivate'. And he's definitely lying about this woman licking her lips. That's just typical Dirty Eyetie wishful thinking."

Holland absently lifted up my pack of Cigarellas before putting them down with a shudder.

"Not in this case, Enzo. She isn't licking her lips just because of brawny, handsome Vince. Madam Butterskate is actually licking her chops in anticipation of payment for services rendered."

I started, then flushed at his blandly approving tone. "You mean – "

"What do you think I mean? A sealed envelope full of five pound notes? Your father's dearest bloody *ice-creams* is what I mean!"

I stared with a moronic abstraction at our sitting-room clock. I found myself quite unable to take in what he was saying. When the penny finally dropped, I opened my mouth to scoff, but the sound refused to emerge.

"Vince in *opera buffa* style approaches his lover staggering under the weight of his costliest ice-creams. Madam Butterfly Butterskate might be a delicately neurotic flower, but she's as piggish as Bessie Bunter when it comes to tucking into all his mouthwatering gelatis…"

I glared angrily at that teasing obscurantism. "She's what?"

"As amatory quid pro quo, she insists on having your Dad's most expensive ice-creams gratis. She dallies to guzzle down two or three brimming bowlfuls before she leads him in poetic silence into her sultry potter's boudoir. Last week's hour and a half of love cost him a pretty packet for example. Three family blocks of cassata at 4/6d a carton. Two – or was it three? – triple neapolitan blocks with a special pistachio layer at 3/8d a shot. Orange Maids, Mivvis, 99s, Iced Milks, a whole cartload of the disgusting bilge. In case of getting snowbound in that Boot-in-Eskdale smallholding, Madam Butterfly has a deep freeze in her larder. If you were to break in there one night and inspect its bulging contents, you'd be quite astonished by the evidence of your father's warm-hearted largesse. Or perhaps be justifiably proud of your old man's incredible appetite for Lorna's lissom loins."

I sat there like a nodding marionette and not just because of the Bunabbhain. I was stultified to hear of the idiotic crassness of this pornographic barter system. Ice-cream of all things in return for sex, sex of all things in return for bloody ice-cream? Numbly I asked Watson Holland how on earth this incongruous pair had ever met in the first place. Eh? Oh, that was no great mystery. Lorna the potter had happened to be in Whitehaven one day for her ceramic supplies, and it being a blazing May lunchtime had done what everyone is supposed to do whenever they see my father approaching. She had stopped him and his van and had tried one.

"*Stop Me and Try One* is pasted onto his windscreen but he'd quite forgotten it was there. In fact it was the first time anyone had taken notice of that genial imperative for years. She saw him tootling and parping down Tangier Street and swiftly flung herself across his front bumper so that she could have some of her favourite food. Who should stop him and try one, but a reclusive nymphette who finds it impossible to decide whether she likes Vince's cornets more than his hornets, or his hornets more than his cornets. They blocked up the town-centre traffic as they fell into conversation about her addiction, as she called it, to yum-yum ice-cream in every shape and form. Understandably Vince pricked up his ears at such a fortuitous addiction in an attractive young female. He soon wormed out of her where she lived, her marital status, her six favourite flavours of *gelati* in ascending order. Without a blush he told her he was planning to visit a fictitious Italian chum living over the hill in Broughton-in-Furness. A week later he dropped by with her prearranged order, waived any immediate payment, and looked tellingly and insinuatingly at her open bedroom door."

I looked at our senior lodger painedly. "You mean this bartering of sex for Mivvis and Orange Maids was really my father's perverted inspiration."

"I suppose so, yes. But still, it takes two to tango, does it not? Let's face it, he wouldn't have got anywhere between the Boot girl's torrid sheets had she not been quite so desperate for a bucketful of his raspberry ripples."

I said feelingly, "It's bloody disgusting. It's so unbelievably grubby and... so debased."

For two seconds I felt almost as disgusted with myself as my brain suddenly went into imitative overdrive. Inspired by my father's crafty peasant strategy, I was trying to think of a parallel way of winning an immovable sovereignty over Fanny Golightly. At present I was one of three lovers, but I still wanted her all to myself. Maybe I could purchase exclusive rights in return for priceless vintage Coltrane or Barney Kessel LPs? Or, given her quaint obsession with Germanic philology, with the most expensive Old High Friesian dictionary printed and bound in calf's leather in Leipzig in 1869?

"This barter system you deplore, it's as old and banal as the hills. Any anthropologist could tell you as much. Even today the whole of the Hindu caste system operates on these handy exchanges, these workaday reciprocities. The outcast washerwoman launders for the outcast sweeper and the outcast tanner. In return the ritually impure tanner provides leather for the ritually impure washerwoman *undsoweiter*. There's a whole Coop-style mutual system called the *jajmani* and – "

"Watson, my father is not a Hindu! Nor is Lorna bloody Butterskate come to that."

"No," sighed Holland, "she's probably an anthroposophist or a vegan spiritualist or a Boot-in-Eskdale female shaman. But she also lives in remote Cumbrian countryside where barter is certainly a feasible way of doing without money. It definitely was in bygone days, in wretched old Boot at any rate. Just think of your father's primitive peasant heritage before you start to wag your censorious head. Imagine the direst poverty of Calabria in the Thirties and Forties when witches and spell-casters were hired to avert the evil eye or an epidemic in the cattle. Having suffered all that, why shouldn't Vince get his leg over in return for a few choc ices and tutti-fruttis? Fair exchange is no bloody robbery…"

I was irritated more than anything that Holland chose to see my father's deviancy in such neutral intellectual terms. That split between head and heart, as epitomised in this breezy but deeply vulnerable divorcee, seemed to me ludicrously misguided. After all, it only needed my mother to be found eavesdropping on this explosive conversation for our lodger's theory and the exculpation to whistle out of the window. If Watson Holland were to find his favourite landlady sobbing outside the door, he would be the first to collar her husband and thrash him to a pulp on the spot.

Meanwhile back in Oxford there was scant relief from the tyrannies of arithmetic and ideology. Fanny Golightly was still deeply embroiled with Hounslow Reggie, her genius of a drummer. Reggie was one of those inscrutable rarities capable of playing in 13/8 blindfold whilst idly daydreaming of a night in bed with his Oxford lover. If she tired of her Hounslow lad, Fanny would walk up to Iffley Village and spend two or three days in rural retreat with the fifty-year-old painter Edmund. Sometimes like a paradigm sneaky Eyetie, I wandered up there myself and observed them clandestinely from a distance. I was no stalker or Peeping Tom, but I could not tear my eyes away from the one that I loved. Edmund usually wore a broad-brimmed hat that made him look like a portly Augustus John or a whimsical Oscar Wilde. Aching with jealousy, I wavered between poisonous envy and an anachronistic, wholly unjustified class hatred. If, I muttered to myself, that ostentatious bastard ever tried walking round Whitehaven or Workington dressed like that, they would debag him and fling him in the dock before you could say Aubrey Beardsley. I seethed and fretted at the far too agreeable sound of his breathy, middle-class confidence. And at his silver-haired radiance, his gentle daguerrotype softness, his effortless maturity and that enchanting fin-de-siècle poetic splendour.

More than once I toyed with dyeing my hair the same colour

as Edmund's. By imitative magic, perhaps I could acquire the quiet painter's mesmerising aura. Maybe I should also take up painting, surprise Fanny Golightly and everyone else, and prove myself a natural and magnetic genius? On the quiet I bought a very expensive set of watercolours, then sat in my Warnborough Road garden and tried to paint the landlady's cat, William. As a rule no one bothered to sit out there, as it was strewn with rusted motorbikes and other unsavoury junk belonging to the landlady's brother. I chose this rear-garden solitude so that no one would witness my embarrassing apprentice efforts. Every day for a full fortnight I sat trying to paint not only William but a skeletal AJS motorbike, a spoutless aluminium kettle, finally in desperation an Oxford City Corporation dustbin. Watercolours are reckoned to be the toughest of artistic mediums, yet it was still a strange surprise and a wounding humiliation to see William, the AJS, the spoutless kettle, even the corporation dustbin, all looking the same identical bumblebee smudges. Painfully dispirited, I carried the hopeless watercolours inside and trudged up to my second-floor bedsit. I lit a Cigarella, flung myself on the bed, and surrendered to a stupor of abyssal dejection. I lay there moulting like a sick beast for at least an hour, perhaps two. Finally, stumblingly, incredulously, as if waking from a dream, I remembered that there was such a thing as jazz. There was such a thing as jazz and therefore such a thing as hope. Blearily I examined my two boxes of records, then pulled out an LP with a very battered cover. It was a uniquely medicinal and consolatory LP, this one. In the same way that certain tenderly written novels can be infinitely if transiently comforting, this particular record was guaranteed to raise the spirits of the damned.

When a young man is licking his love wounds, he needs to hear some music that soothes like balm or unguent. I had found such a thing not long ago in the bargain racks in Oxford's Woolworth's. It had cost me only sixty pence, this album, and it was *New View!* by the New John Handy Quintet. Even before taking it home and listening to it, I was affected by the musician's resonant name. The two words 'John Handy' sounded the epitome of honesty, fairness, integrity, simplicity. I examined his cover portrait and confirmed my suspicions. His crumpled fisherman's hat and that idle, sleepy grin immediately drew me to his side. He seemed to me like a man who would take you as calmly and considerately as he found you. Me, for example, Enzo Gianmaria Mori, he would take as a sad and lovelorn white Italo-Cumbrian working-class twenty-year-old Oxford animal physiology student.

The first track is *Naima*, a homage to John Coltrane. It was recorded in 1967 at the New York Village Gate, only three weeks before Coltrane died. It must be some of the very gentlest and kindest music ever made. Handy's alto plays like the instrument of a loving God, as it pours out a succession of wistful soothing billows which become a cumulative ocean of the tenderest sadness. Years after buying this LP, I came across some vaunting theorising by the novelist Vladimir Nabokov expatiating on his vertiginous literary aesthetics. According to the émigré master, and with due deference to Marcel Proust, the literary depiction of a profound emotion should yield that emotion in all its depth and fullness, *yet in an impersonal and undefiled aesthetic ecstasy, a miniature yet wholly blissful transcendence*. In 1977, I swapped notes with Fanny Golightly and discovered that she also knew of that proposition. By which date, just like John Handy, Fanny Golightly was a major CBS star. She had also read enough about all things Indian to know that Nabonov's absolute was not just identical with the poetic sublimity of *rasa*, but that *rasa* and the religious experience of *moksha* were more or less the same phenomenon. Handy's alto saxophone blew its healing smoking vapour across my sore and aching heart, and I yearned for an impersonal as opposed to a personal agony of hurt. I was painfully in love and to the hilt with Fanny Golightly, but Fanny was not in love to the hilt with me. At this very moment she was touring some of the London galleries with Edmund, while I was here alone and stranded and ignored by the only one I really cared for. Each tenderly whorling billow from Handy inspired a successive and dependent wave, a pulse and sequence as preordained as the susurrations of the womb or the currents of a fellside stream. That alto lambency became ever more rendingly delicate, the sympathy and the melting gentleness ever more relentlessly unselfish. There was simply no depth of wound this salve couldn't penetrate, no ugly sickness it could not face, no unspeakable, unbearable grief it could not look unblinkingly in the eye.

"Fanny," I whispered to my empty room. My eyes were brimming with my grief and for some reason I felt I was being roasted alive, "I want you here for ever beside me like my hands or my feet or my eyes or my face. I promise you I want you more than I've ever wanted anything."

The next day a long letter arrived from Watson Holland. As well as a bulky quantity of foolscap, it also contained a crisp ten pound note. Holland hoped that I would blow it on good whisky and not on 'those noisome ugly cheroots', as he referred to my Cigarellas. We weren't exactly regular correspondents, but if the pharmacist was bored and/or half-drunk he might pen me a ten-page essay on his latest socioscientific theory. Watson Holland was in fact an early conservationist, though he would have loudly scorned such a self-conscious designation. He was, for example, remarkably well-informed about such hybrid novelties as organic farming and the harnessing of natural energy sources. Holland the rigorous scientist scoffed at all religious beliefs, yet he constantly used the biblical term 'stewardship' as the appropriate description of a sound relationship between Man and Creation. After a vitriolic eight-page excursus about the deficient management capabilities of provincial technocrats apropos a recent mishap at Sellafield, he concluded his letter with a few choice remarks about a certain well-known Cumbrian ice-cream seller:

Your pa, you'll be gratified to learn, has given up those long-distance assignations with the antisocial pot-flinger from Boot. His middle-aged satyriasis no longer attempts to compete with her youthful nymphomania. However, no need to get in a concerned flap, Enzo. It wasn't that he was found out by your mother going through his overall pockets, or by a blushing Jehovah's Witness doing his Eskdale circuit, or anything as embarrassing as that. I do seem to recall that you were rather dismayed by what you saw as his mercenary approach to the business of love. You weren't at all amused by his trading the one commodity for the other. When you were informed that he offered Madame Butterfly his coffee cassata for her how's-your-father, and his tricoloured neapolitans in return for some cross-buttock, all-in Cumbrian wrestling, you weren't at all delighted...

That said, I'm sure you'd be the first to acknowledge that Vince's old-fashioned peasant cunning goes hand in hand with a hopelessly romantic nature. Which perhaps explains why the Boot affair ended quite as abruptly as it did, and with your father as bitterly critical of his potter inamorata as he was. You see, Vincenzo didn't mind swapping one type of tutti frutti *for another type of* tutti frutti, *as long as he was the only one doing this enterprising bartering. Unfortunately for Vince he was brash enough three weeks ago to drive up unannounced to Lorna's windblown Eskdale bothy. It was a freezing cold November afternoon, not the kind of weather that anyone, ice-cream addict or not, would wish to devote to* gelati *guzzling. That did not stop your lasciviously lustful father, however. As they say in Reggio di Calabria, if you have an itch you have to scratch it, and the itch that day for Vince was very powerful.*

What he saw on arrival should have given him very anxious food for thought. Instead of which it only sparked his artless curiosity. He was painfully intrigued to note Lorna's magenta Wolsey 1100 parked alongside a strikingly grubby and ramshackle old coal lorry. Instead of sneaking a cautionary look through the sitting-room window, Vince was fool enough to press the potter's doorbell. He kept on vainly pressing until his thumb was tired. As steely Mistress Butterskate obviously wasn't intending to answer her door, your pa finally turned the knob and slyly entered. (It turned out later that Lorna's bell was broken, not that that mitigated Vincenzo's horror at subsequent events.)

You can perhaps picture your father's consternation as he encountered his Bohemian paramour lying completely naked on her studio floor. I ask you, Enzo, bare-arse *naked on the stone cold flags of a freezing Eskdale cottage in the middle of November! Alas, nor was she chastely alone in her winsome cherubic nudity. Alongside her was a very odd-looking person indeed, easily old enough, in your father's memorable, ineffable diction, 'to be Lonnie Buttershite's blurry ole granfaddert, Watson!'*

Yes, the nude ceramicist was locked in the arms of an equally naked coalman from far-flung Millom. This very grimy, very sooty, extremely old gentleman, was not the proprietary coal merchant, but a moonlighting eighty-five-year-old employee called Benny. Benny might have been a very old fellow but he was still sturdy enough to fling ton bags of coke on and off the haulier's lorry. Nor, as your father noticed to his incredulous horror, was the old soul deficient in either vigour or size when it came to turgid equestrian combat with the tomato-faced potteress. Amazingly, neither half of this two-backed beast had noticed the open-mouthed Calabrian with the frozen expression stood only two yards from their fetid claspings. Vince Mori studiously observed them in flagrante *for the best part of five minutes before erupting into an incandescent Italian effusion of obscene and venomous rage. Benny the senile coalboy turns out to have an enviable record as a practised fuel embezzler and has been swindling his Millom boss and his father before him for the best part of half a century. In return for twice-monthly humpings, this Duddon Valley dotard has been providing the mercenary potter with ten tons of nutty slack and five tons of anthracite for her ever-burning kiln. As if that weren't painful enough for Vince Mori, the defiant, still starkers 'Lonnie Buttershite' refused to show the slightest token of remorse. Instead she bawled and roared at your father for turning up without* a prior and pre-arranged appointment, as he already knew was strictly enjoined on her business cards! *Understandably, your poor father grew toxically enflamed at such humourless impudence and continued in a proprietorial manner to demand that the Millom geriatric be booted out naked and forthwith. But instead of being impressed by Vince's pungent Mediterranean expression of wounded honour, the bare-arse Bohemianess grew ever more contemptuously obstinate. In fact, she employed her unpleasantly clay-smeared fingers to enumerate the various services and goods she had acquired in the last twelve months in return for sundry sexual favours. Lorna might well have been artistically exaggerating for hurtful effect, but Vince assures me that they include:*

○ *Six cartloads of weathered spruce logs from an eighty-six-year-old sawyer at Wasdale*

○ *Industrial capacity calor gas canisters from a severely rheumatic garage proprietor in Barrow-in-Furness*

○ *Top grade eco-kerosene central heating oil from the one-armed manager of a depot at Lancaster*

○ *Luxury sheep and goat organic cheeses from a hippy dairy-farmer at* outré *Ulpha called Noah, and*

○ *Last but not least, a six-month course in assertiveness therapy from a freelance practitioner called Max, a touchingly selfless gentleman more than happy to travel up all the way from Preston to offer domiciliary sessions intended to sort out old Butterskate's thorny psyche.*

Your stricken father was of course rendered speechless to hear of all this other *quid pro quo bartering…*

As for the instrument itself. Not everyone notices the obvious fact: that a beautifully moulded acoustic guitar looks very much like a handsome woman's body in all its ripeness and tender dimensions. An acoustic guitar apparently has two hips and a gently curving backside as well as a neck and a belly and an imaginatively suggested pair of breasts. Fanny Golightly's Christian name, as she herself has often pointed out, is interestingly ambiguous in this context. In Cumberland as everywhere else in the UK, 'fanny' familiarly means the female genitals. On the other side of the Atlantic, where she spends at least half her professional life, it customarily means the backside. Thus Fanny as a musician quaintly allegorises as a two-in-one, a front-and-back, both fore and aft, recto as well as verso, and like a classical Janus she faces calmly in both directions. She is by a spurious etymology the posterior foundation of her unique kind as well as the anterior seat of reproduction.

Coming out of West Cumberland, Fanny was obviously not born to jazz, but of that generation which nurtured itself on Sixties pop and even on the dog-end of Fifties rock and roll. Many of her fans are surprised to learn that her role models for the guitar included Hank Marvin of Cliff Richard's Shadows. Unfortunately the historical allegiance here was spoiled by the fact that her father Dick Golightly modelled his own stage looks on a version of Hank minus the glasses. Fanny was just turned eleven when Hank was at his apogee, when she was hypnotically humming 'Apache' and 'FBI', and when her father bought her a glorified toy guitar for the Christmas of 1961. Two years later she was studying the Beatles on 45 and 33, and taking piano lessons from fussy William Williamson, a bearded retired music teacher living in a smart new bungalow in nearby Harrington. Then in the mid-Sixties there were the euphoric eruptions of Eric Clapton and Jimi Hendrix and Jeff Beck. The last of these 'progressive' maestros steadily progressed from rock to jazz, and ten years later ended up accompanying a youthful wizard on a bass called Stanley Clarke. By the age of fourteen Fanny Golightly owned a Stratocaster given her by a publican acquaintance of her father's. The guitar's owner, his son, had been killed in a motorcycle accident the year before, and the publican wanted the boy's guitar to continue with a life of its own. Under-age Fanny was playing her Stratocaster illegally in Workington and Whitehaven clubs, passing herself off as seventeen and, not infrequently, performing on the same stage as her father. He was at first her means of entry to the local music scene, until by her late teens he was so far gone with drink that she instead became his. She would accept a gig with her rock band 'The Rawbones' in ill-lit places like The Matador, with the strict proviso that old pisshead Dick be allowed to croon away harm-lessly right at the start. She won this bizarre concession because at that hour no one was listening, or if they were they would dimly assume that the shambling old guy was a comedian apeing a hopeless drunk.

By the time she went up to Somerville from Workington Grammar School she was collecting acoustic and electric guitars as a hobby. They were pushed into a dim corner and partitioned off with a screen, just in case her scout thought she was a fence for an instrument thief. One of her prize possessions was an L-6S which Edmund had purchased at Russell Acorn's after some extraordinary luck with his Premium Bonds. He also proposed marriage to Fanny as he knelt down in public in the Somerville quad to grace her with the beautiful new Gibson. Fanny refused with a blushing, tearful gratitude, and hastily offered to return the exorbitant present. Edmund's broad-brimmed hat fell off when he made the nuptial offer, and his baldness and silvered greyness she found piquantly moving, not at all repel-lent. She almost said yes, I will, Edmund, until she momentarily hallucinated the spectral presence of Whitehaven Enzo and Hounslow Reggie in the twilit winter glory of the hallowed quadrangle. Thanks to complex and judicious swapping and trading, by her early twenties she also owned a Telecaster, a Gretsch, an Epiphone, a Rickenbacker, an Artisan Les Paul, a J45, a Gibson Acoustic and a Squier Stratocaster.

Up until the late Seventies Fanny was judged to be in the identifiable mould of Mahavishnu John McLaughlin and other lightning-fast jazz-rock players. As someone who had come from the northern pub tradition of heavy rock, it seemed with hindsight all too inevitable that her jazz should be played like the howling furies of a massive electric rock band. Like McLaughlin, it was usually performed at thundering express-train velocity, yet interspersed with poignant acoustic numbers so heartbreakingly gentle and slow, it was as if there were not one but two Fanny Golightlys. Reflex accusations of plagiarism were bolstered by the late arrival of an arch-flamboyant moog-playing pianist. Not only was he as restless and febrile as Mahavishnu's Jan Hammer, but he also happened to be an émigré Czech. He was called Jaroslav Capek, and Capek like Hammer was incapable of sitting still on stage. Capek bounced up and down battering and snorting and shouting as if he were a rebellious infant in a high chair. His moog was not an inanimate electronic gadget but his pampered favourite child, an infant that wailed like a monster accordion or a cosmic mouth organ. Capek, like Hammer, had decided to make it rant and scream with the tearing lung power of a phantasmagoric giant beast.

Even worse for the critics, Fanny acquired an electric violinist from a long defunct Nineteen Sixties rock band, The Choir. Doleful Joe Sollas looked so much like McLaughlin's Jerry Goodman, even down to the tight pony tail and the faded denims, that the jazz writers could not restrain their cynical muttering. They noted that Fanny Golightly was attracting audiences as vast as a rock star, and assumed that this dogged imitation of the Hinduised Yorkshireman was intended to win his anomalous commercial success. Like JM, FG had sold out to the crowds by a conflation of rock and decibels with a jazz of undoubted genius. She also came from the northern working class, and it was predicted in several ironic *Guardian* reviews that in six months time she would have dubbed herself 'Mahalakshmi' Fanny Golightly. Perhaps McLaughlin foresaw as much and decided to forestall it, because in 1974 and 1975 he fielded a female singer credited as Mahalakshmi on his albums *Apocalypse* and *Visions of the Emerald Beyond*...

Perhaps it was all the goading from the purist critics, the

elder statesmen of jazz (there were precious few elder states-women as Fanny regularly pointed out) that led her eventually in the polar opposite direction. One February evening in 1980 Fanny announced to me over the phone from New York that she was heartily sick of riding the electric express train. She had come to a definitive crossroads, she said, with a heavy if doleful irony. She said she'd had enough of blistering speed and her heavy-rock North English legacy. Instead, as part of a painstak-ingly hard-won emotional tranquillity, a new sense of personal stability, she'd decided to create a band that played its music 'laterally' rather than linearly. At the risk of over-zealous exposi-tion, I will have to translate carefully on behalf of a stubbornly unforthcoming thirty-year-old Fanny. In artistic terms, to proceed linearly means to go forward as if one were aiming for a conclusive terminus or goal. Alternatively, it could be described as executing a measurable journey from A to B replete with stopping places, signposts, roadside cafés or desert oases according as you will. Most occidental music and especially Western rock music inevitably proceeds thus, if only because occidentals are so remorselessly convinced of the infallible authenticity of the sequential, the temporal, the linear.

Oriental aesthetics which, as Fanny had already realised, are intricately bound up with oriental religion, suggest that linear time is best understood as a puerile hallucination of an unrefined metaphysic. Given which stark premise, it can reasonably be argued that endless 'lateral' repetition of a finite musical quantity, will result in a far more satisfying artistic richness. Self-evidently a 'classical' Indian raga, whether in its initial droning slowness or its final furious accelerations, is not walking forward to an imaginary 'end', but is radiating endlessly from a calm seden-tary focus. Likewise occidental Early Church Music, which presumably tries to mimic the transcendent effulgence of a chorus of heavenly angels, is apparently 'going' nowhere when it tries to catch itself upon the cusp of the Eternal. No longer aping a roaring locomotive, Fanny said she was trying for a 'choir' effect which would radiate like the light of a perpetually burning flame. Cryptic rather than candid in her early Eighties interviews, terrified of being held to account for any glibly pretentious musical references, she refused to make anything clear to her mystified public. But she confessed to those she trusted that really she wanted to sound more like a medieval composer than a contemporary electric jazz player. Like Tallis, Lassus or Dufay, that is, more than like 'Mwandishi' Herbie Hancock or Barbara Thompson's Paraphernalia or Chick Corea's Electric Band or John McLaughlin's Mahavishnu Orchestra...

She came to this strange conclusion via the questionable route of sophisticated electronics. Long ago as joint-smoking students, the two of us would regularly listen to an Eddie Harris LP with a brash metallic cover, entitled *Silver Cycles*. Harris in his mid-thirties was an early exponent of the electrified tenor sax, and a playful innovator with the echoplex and other precocious unSixtyish gadgetry. *Silver Cycles* was at times a vaudevillian concoction of funk and pop, but elsewhere so tenderly piercing and rarefied in those cloud-born electric echoes that one track at least always had Fanny furiously upset. Later she would be chuckling hysterically at Harris's jesting showmanship, those gimmicky trumpet tracks where the impudent sax player had substituted the mouthpiece of a sax. Those barely credible, doped-up memories resurfaced now as she told me in a worried voice from New York that she'd just splurged an absolute fortune in Broadway's biggest music shop. On umpteen electronic gadgets that would make her sound like a massed choir, one which would sing, croon, ululate, descant, and on occasions weep with both joy and sadness.

"I want to make the bloody guitar talk, Enzo. I want it to speak with its own human voice, and I don't mean that as some glib little metaphor. Can you see what I'm talking about?"

"Of course," I lied, my heart melting protectively as I listened to that brittle vehemence in her voice. This dirt-poor Salterbeck lass, who had spent so much time in the States, was starting to sound like a *West Cumbrian* New Yorker.

"Imagine me, Fanny, as an inanimate musical instrument, that's struggling to articulate a fully human and phonetic voice. I don't mean a silly Walt Disney voice, but a kind of proto-speech, a musical ghost voice. Think of it as if I were straining to get out of the guitar and reveal myself like a trapped oriental genie. Do you get it?"

"Perhaps," I said uneasily. "Though it seems rather like a nightmarish fairytale. It sounds too much like some thousand year curse."

She clicked her tongue despairingly. "I didn't mean that at all. Please, Enzo, if you refuse to understand me, no other bugger ever will! I rely on you to interpret and translate me back to myself, because I can't do the thing on my own. You don't realise, but you have an uncanny faculty of musical second sight. You have x-ray eyes, or rather x-ray ears, which can pierce through solid brick walls. You know virtually nil about the technicalities of music, but your intuition and your sense of minute nuance are absolutely infallible. You drink it all up without understanding how it's put together, but then you don't need to because you love it all willy-nilly. For you, good jazz is exactly like good food. You gobble up everything with the same voracity as if you've been through a ten-year famine. If you happen to come across an exotic, untested dish that no one else would have the courage to try, you don't give a bollocks! You just grab hold of it with a disarming smile, and merrily shovel it down with everything else."

I stayed silent for a while and stared at the mouthpiece bemused. Of course it was wonderful to be hailed as a telepathic interpreter of her ineffably inscrutable muse, but I wished that that rare devotion of mine had been given its due reward. The algebra was simple enough. If I, EM, had been her, FG, I would have rewarded my quaint devotion by focusing on me, her sole subtle interpreter, and no one else. But Fanny did not depend upon me in any sense that mattered. I could itemise it easily enough in all its glaring banality. She swore that she loved and treasured me as one of her most intimate friends; twice a week she rang me up from the States; once a month she wrote me a mile-long letter; I was her tender, kindly lover on occasion without restraint or fuss. But at the end of the day, and for evermore, she simply would not *dote* on me.

What exactly did Fanny Golightly do to make her guitar talk with a human voice? Firstly, there was her old-fashioned volume pedal. She would twist its top up to the right, from bass up to treble, the volume function working in reverse. Such was the odd toggle-like mechanism of an interesting antique which the Rawbones guitarist had used in the West Cumbrian pubs. It was Hank B. Marvin paraphernalia, and it preceded the facile sophistication of the ubiquitous wah-wah. This hoary little gadget was also able to move from treble-cut to the full tone. At first Fanny used it in tandem with the echo machine, to produce that anomalous Eighties sound which I immediately termed her Pre-natal Period. In those '80 and '81 albums *Slow Ascent* and *Steep Summit*, Fanny relentlessly explored the bizarre acoustics of the womb, or perhaps the first few wide-eyed months of the new-born. If that sounds preposterous, what else but foetal languor and uterine bliss could adequately explain that rarefied hypnotic amplification? Or its euphoric dedication to a tenderly resonant 'foetal' ecstasy? It sent many of the critics to sleep sure enough, but their cheerful philistinism (jeering accusations of 'the lost hypnotherapy tapes') didn't stop at that. One of them accused Fanny of being 'an impressively deranged Pink Floyd effects woman' rather than a serious jazz improviser. Was that just the brickwall scenario of the linear mentality in despair at the lateral aesthetic? A peevish Radio 3 presenter slated these textural juxtapositions for being 'as inclusive and unselective as an electric hoover', rather than tidily self-pruning. Fanny created an outlandish orchestral sound, employing a flat-wash technique that paid homage to an oriental 'lateralist' called Hokusai. The music (and some jazz critics protested it wasn't even that) moved 'forward', but only as echoing, resonant, hypnotic amplitudes. Music or not, it was best enjoyed lying flat one one's back, watching its susurrations fanning centripetally from the guitar's perpetual flame. Now it was no longer an ordinary musical instrument but a truly ventriloquial animal with a tantalising phonetics. Its lexicon was seemingly as impenetrable as the most baffling cuneiform. Listening to the cathedral dome orchestrations on *Steep Ascent*, the pattern appeared to be lucidity itself... but then to try and render it in words of any grace and accuracy was an impossible task. Decades later, as I was reflecting on this, it occurred to me there was an obvious explanation for a vocabulary that defied any linear analysis. If this music really was something like the imaginative 'language' of the womb or the newborn baby, then crude description would inevitably fail it. They might, babies and embryos, be able to cry or make detectable sounds, but are resolutely incapable of articulate speech. Much less that haphazard and limited makeshift called 'structured language'...

A summary catalogue of the rest of the Broadway acquisitions would include DiMarzio pickups and a Lace Sensor in the treble position. Fanny used the Marshall amps until the summer of 1984. Later, in her ECM years, she employed some unique Scandinavian Telrads produced by a self-taught craftsman. Her earliest amps were operated at a modest eighteen watts, then went up to twenty, then thirty. Fanny generally preferred, in her Oslo ECM studio, to have a master volume control (the older amps had obliged her to play far louder, less exactingly, than she wished). The signal path on e.g. *Slow Ascent* went as follows. Guitar to Marshal pedal (on *Steep Summit* it was a Boss Overdrive). Afterwards to a TC sustainer. Then to a Yamaha volume pedal (replaced by a Boss pedal on *Steep Summit*). Then a Boss Digital Delay, which Fanny Golightly used for those demiurgic 'hold' functions. The hold signified her eternally resonating creations, tightly 'held' in radiantly hypnotic suspense by their anxious creator.

After that it went into a Boss multi-effects echo machine...

Now let's give all this A Level Electronics the personal touch, and permit our wayward guitarist to have her impulsive say.

From an interview with *Guitar Canada*, March 1983

Interviewer: Fanny Golightly, as a rule do you prefer the effects-loop on the amplifier?

FG: No, Lewis, no I don't really. If I'm playing live, I go straight into two Marshalls, and use the pedals rather than the amp for overdriving the sound.

Interviewer: I see. So that...

FG: I prefer the clean channel on the amp to be a bit louder than if I was plugging the guitar in without the pedals. In which case, I need the signal only marginally boosted from a preamp.

Interviewer: Uhuh. So what about your ring modulator? Are you still using the –?

FG: Yes, the Oberheim 10-B, which has plenty of fine adjustment on it. I have it attached to the multi-effects unit, a Boss ME-8. I suppose the sound I'm aiming for is a gigantic resonant bell effect. Some British critics have unkindly described me as producing the poor man's Jan Garbarek sound, a Nordic West Cumbrian vainly struggling to be a Nordic Norwegian. You see because Jan Garbarek makes tone poems about mountains and lakes, and I live near the English Lake District, it's assumed I'm slavishly following in the Scandinavian master's footsteps. We have the same mountains and fjords of course as Jan does, but in fact they're a hell of a lot smaller.

Interviewer: Oh really? But, pardon me, do they really call them 'fjords' over in North England?

FG: To be sure. It's a straight Viking dialect usage, completely unchanged in Cumbrian place names. Any fell farmer can understand even the densest Norwegian and likewise any Norwegian can understand the very densest old fell farmer. Jan Garbarek would have no problems whatever being understood in an agricultural supply shop in Cockermouth or Keswick.

Interviewer: Ahah. Ah, someone I know, a studio engineer from Toronto, once said a ring modulator sounded like some kind of diabolic bagpipe. What do you have to say to that?

FG: Did he really say that, Lewis? Mm. Well, if used indiscriminately and unintelligently, I suppose that might be true on occasion. The ring modulator can certainly sound saturnine to the point of hellish if you don't learn to love it and get it to love you in return.

Interviewer: Saturn… yeah, OK, saturnine. Mmh. Fanny, can I ask you what part of the day you prefer to compose your music? I know at least one other jazz guitarist says his favourite time is early morning. Is that true for you?

FG: (*long pause*) I'm afraid I'm far too diurnal for that. I'm much more of a night owl than an early bird. I drink much too much cheap red wine and rough whisky, apart from anything else. To be honest I wish I drank a good deal less. Quite possibly, Lewis, I'm slowly killing myself with it…

Interviewer: Uh…

FG: No, I tend to do my best writing perched on the lavatory, as a matter of fact. After a firm bowel movement more often than not. Sometimes I sit there for hours on the bog, writing away, oblivious to everything else. It's an unsavoury detail but sometimes I even forget to wipe my bum if I'm not careful, I'm so infinitely absorbed in what I'm doing. Or maybe do I mean my 'fanny', as they call it in the States? Do they call it that in Canada as well? Or do they call it 'bum' in Canada instead?

Interviewer: Uh? 'Bum'? (*longish pause*) Oh, I guess so.

11

♪♫♫

Obviously they were destined to end up playing together.
Once that had happened, it only remained for their
guardedly receptive natures to respond courageously.
When the Portuguese and the Cumbrian first met at Monterey
they had listened to each other's musics and also to each other's
poverty-stricken histories. In the end they were brought together
by an unlikely common link, by the ironically named William
Joy. Joy was an English bass player who had migrated to New
York in 1974 and had played in almost every electric band that
mattered. As well as working with many of the splinter groups
from *Bitches Brew*, Joy owned a house in Stuttgart where he
sporadically indulged himself as a solo artist. When he recorded
his first solo bass album in 1979, his only ECM predecessor was
the German Eberhard Weber. As Weber always drily remarked
to foreign audiences in his urbane and impeccable English, only
a certain eccentric class of person has the stamina, the fastidious-
ness, the sheer foolhardiness, to listen to a performance of the
solo bass.

Joy was as gifted as Eberhard Weber but without the suavity
and the humour. Weber was strikingly blond, long-haired and
handsome, while Joy was lank, morose and physically ugly.
Nevertheless Joy provided a suitably lugubrious foil to Cebola
and Fanny in their 1990 trio 'Agog'. Half of that debut album had
Joy on acoustic double bass, the rest was on electric bass. Fanny
had apparently dropped the 'foetal' electronics and returned to

an express train's reckless velocity. But significantly now the speed of her guitar was exhilarating rather than frightening. In effect she had ceded the ethereal sound to Toto who had long been notorious for his soaring cathedral effects. Cathedral, as we've pointed out, is rather an inappropriate metaphor, given that both guitarist and violinist were already deeply embroiled in the religions and philosophies of ancient India. That said, there was no suggestion of the Hindu temple in the music of Agog, and Joy in any case was an agnostic who spent most of his leisure hours in various therapy groups, principally those allied to a Californian guru called Joachim Brahms.

The same day the Gulf War was declared, Fanny Golightly rang to inform me that she and 'beautiful Toto' were deeply and madly and truly in love. That was the message, without any pre-amble, without even saying hello, Enzo, or how are you? For a few ridiculous seconds, I thought she was talking about some new pet cat in her NY apartment, and I was about to wish her and the US moggie all the very best for their futures. Until:

"Toto and I are soul mates, Enzo. That's an idiotic cliché of course, but for once it adds up to the goods. Last night we sat in my flat by candlelight and we read the *Chandogya Upanishad* together. It was in English translation of course, but – "

I gulped. No cat alive or dead was capable of reading the *Upanishads*, either in translation or in the Sanskrit. The *Upanishads* made me think hazily and uncharitably of Schopenhauer, Christopher Isherwood, Aldous Huxley and allied minds. Massive philosophic and literary super-eminences not especially noted for their forthright worm's-eye take on life.

"Oh?" I said weakly. "And who's this Toto person, Fanny?"

As soon as I said it, I knew the answer.

"Toto Cebola of course. Who else? Tell me, aren't you pleased? You're completely addicted to his music, and always have been."

I said dazed. "Oh yes. He's my soul mate as well, I suppose. Musically speaking that is. Or at least he was until today at any rate."

After a hellish silence, "What on earth's *that* supposed to mean?"

More silence from my side of the Atlantic. "I suppose I'm shocked that's all. You're forty years old, the same age as me. As far as I know it's the first time you've ever admitted to being properly in love."

She agreed, in a moderately resentful tone. "You're right, it is the first time. That's why I'm vaguely delirious. No, not vaguely. Not at all. Absolutely, and in the vehement affirmative. In the intensative, is what I mean. I am deliriously delirious, Enzo Mori. Aren't you really very pleased for me?"

I felt leaden and mute and almost as if I were short of air. "Yes," I said feebly.

Then I clammed up like some sulking little infant. She immediately reproved me for such puerile ungenerosity. I sighed, took a deep breath, then burbled:

"You must be preparing another Agog album? You and he, Toto Cebola... and William Joy, must be spending all your time together."

"Yes we are. The album's called *Amok*. *Amok* by Agog, that is. It's due out in October on my forty-first birthday. But the way things are going, it's not going to be a bed of roses. William Joy is even less delighted by our love affair than you appear to be."

I grew very indignant. "I – "

"He tells me our passion is affecting his vibrations. It's sending them all haywire, and it's wearing him out. He's not speaking metaphorically about mental or emotional vibrations. He means the acoustic resonance of his double bloody bass."

I tried the light note. "Now there's a real artist for you. William Joy is obviously in touch with some supernatural vibrations."

With one of her confusing attacks of contrary po-facedness, she shot back, "But we're all in touch with that. All of us. Toto, me, even William Joy, though he won't admit it. I thought that you of all people would understand that."

I flushed, even though it was a freezing January evening. I could not think of a fitting response. If I played the sceptical, sardonic northerner at this point it would just seem the feeblest of sour grapes. Sniffing at my obstinate silence, Fanny informed me that, by way of illustration, she was going to quote a dedicatory verse from the cover of McLaughlin's *My Goal's Beyond*. I listened to this with some difficulty, not least because a pneumatic drill was going outside my house. The gist of this dedication was that God's chosen musical instrument was the human soul, no less. A great musician was simply someone whose soul had been fine-tuned, to make them capable of transmitting the divine sound. Furthermore the poignant message of this 'holy' music was always the same: God's endless love for his own creation, humankind.

I still had nothing to say. I waited stonily for her to do the exegesis. After all, she had a bloody Congratulatory First in English from Somerville, and she was a genius at Old Norse and Old Icelandic textual studies. I on the other hand was a West Cumbrian Eyetie with a physiology degree who taught Biology A level in a third-rate provincial Technical College. I knew absolutely fuckall really, apart from a great many heterogeneous odds and ends that could be neither marketed nor conveniently forgotten. I was a slipshod autodidact, in an age when there was no point at all in such a decadent occupation. Worse still I was permanently in thrall to a hopeless student infatuation of twenty years ago. I had been married and divorced twice since then, and I had two teenage kids, Sally and Mallie, who lived with their mothers in Switzerland and Basildon respectively. I had plenty of unassimilated past to rue and lament, if only I could take my mind off Fanny Golightly, the international jazz star.

"We're just vessels, Enzo, only conduits. We don't make the music, it plays itself through us. We just happen to be the receptive channels. Of course we're hailed as jazz geniuses and primitive wunderkinds, but really all we are is glorified mediums. No that isn't right either, that smacks of the occult, and we both hate anything to do with that. Nor are we two post-modern shamans taking orchestrated fits in 13/8. It's the endless love that McLaughlin talks about, that matters. It's the divine and sacred, as opposed to the secular quality of what is coming through us. These days Toto Cebola is making, by which I mean *transmitting*, music so tender that it almost breaks people's hearts." She paused and added disparagingly, "Sometimes I try to do it myself in my own feeble way…"

I said huskily, "You and he both? He sees it that way, the way that you describe?"

Suddenly unhingingly I recalled, of all people, the novelist Kingsley Amis. My mind drifted back hallucinatorily to a strange programme I'd heard on Radio 3 a few years back. The angry old man himself, who by that time was as fond of television soap opera as he was of the bottle, had described himself in aesthetic terms as a 'conduit' for the excellence and genius that manifested itself on his pages. He, Nabokov, Toto, Fanny from Salterbeck, they were all bloody in on it like a gang of unsmiling conspirators.

"That's part of the reason why we click, the Portuguese man and me. William Joy is very different, bless him. He sees his bass music as an infestation or an itch that he has to transmit. That's probably why he needs so much therapy. His Brooklyn shrink has informed him he'll need another twenty years at least to make the slightest headway."

To stave off my misery, I listened with undue intentness as she went on to talk about Joy's theory of music. It seemed he regarded the creative impulse as a kind of metaphysical eczema or *candida albigans* depending on whether one saw the organ of creativity as the hypersensitive skin or the genitals. If one denied one's itchlike talent or felt an impedance in its natural flow, the result would be an appropriately physical condition of asthma, dermatitis, or pruritus. Apparently, if Joy himself stopped playing his bass for more than a week he came out dramatically and disablingly with all three of those conditions: gasping breathlessness, raw and bleeding scabies of the scalp, and a maddening groin irritation that had him scratching and pulverising his crutch like a heedless chimpanzee.

I put the phone down. Shutting my eyes in freezing cold Cumbria, I struggled with the painful sensation of my musical idol Cebola having wounded me in this gratuitous, entirely uncalled-for manner. Part of the problem of course was that he didn't even know that I existed. Unless Fanny had mentioned me in passing which seemed highly unlikely, he would never have heard of Enzo Gianmaria Mori, his one and only forty-year-old West Cumbrian superfan. And now, innocently oblivious of my other great passion in life, he had gained sole possession of a musical and sentimental deity called Fanny. Toto Cebola played tunes so achingly, woundingly tender, they haunted me like the invisible hands of my own childhood, one which had known nothing at all of his poverty or deprivation. Likewise Fanny's intense guitar music was for me the liberating fever of exhilaration and absolute visceral excitement. Deep down I felt I understood her music better than anyone else in the world, and, I was tempted to add, herself included. I was her ideal fan, her irreplaceable and expert connoisseur, the indisputable but untenured Regius Professor of Modern Golightly Studies. The same went for Toto Cebola of course, because I seriously believed that his music spoke to me as it spoke to no one else in the world.

People who suffer this kind of megalomania are inevitably hoist by their own petards. In July of that year, having secured a long overdue unpaid sabbatical from the Tech, I flew to New York, drawn there by a quite irresistible force. The impulse was not a transcendent or a supernatural one, but it was fuelled by the sympathetic guardian spirit of Henri Beyle or Stendhal as he's better known. I re-read his book *Love* on that plane to New York, and I drank up every word, every last scintilla and nuance of his study of Desire, and wished in my madness that Stendhal had been sat next to me in an expert consultant capacity.

I had decided to see my male idol, Toto, in the flesh, and let him know that my female idol, Fanny, was actually mine not his. My logic in this matter might have been infantile but in its way it was impeccable. She was a council house Cumbrian, and I had been born in a Whitehaven council house. Ergo we spoke the one ineffable language, we danced to the same untranslatable rhythms and the same monotonal tune. The word 'fanny', where I was born and bred, invariably meant 'cunt'. The word fanny where Cebola had taken up permanent residence simply meant

the inglorious old arse. He, and it wasn't his fault, was an innocent bloody Portuguese, and with all due respect, he knew
nothing of what was at stake for Fanny Golightly, for himself or
for anyone else.

♪♫

Conduits? Impedance? Hydrostatic flow? Rheology? Metaphorical
barometers? On the one hand it scarcely matters two farts how,
ab origine, great music is produced, and on the other it matters
immeasurably. It matters as much as one's beliefs with regard to
the Original Creation itself. In countless aspects and in numerous religions they are intricately and inseparably linked, the artistic
and the divine creations. Added to which, so many 'artists' are so
monumentally swollen-headed and conceited, acting and playing
like petulant minor deities, there has to be some discussion of
this debatable conflation. For the bulk of them to declare themselves 'passive conduits' could either be the absolute in sincere
humility, or the contrary absolute of smirking self-delusion.

The guitarist and the violinist had their respective gurus to give
them guidance. As well as their teachers, they also had their
sacred texts. In the Rig Vedic *Purusha-Sukta* which so touched
and impressed both Fanny and Toto, the Original Man, the
Hindu Adam Cadmium is called the Purusha. From this
Purusha, it says, is created Viraj, the Female Principle, and likewise from this Viraj is Purusha created. A description so
paradoxical might have baffled many a non-Hindu, but it made
perfect sense to both Toto and Fanny. The puzzling factor was
obviously the sequential one. If the divinely creative process
was seen as linearly ordered, it made no apparent sense. But if
it could ever so dimly and meekly be conceived as something
simultaneous and perpetual...

I did not put this particular proposition to my father on his
seventieth birthday. It was held in the ballroom of the Chase

Hotel in Whitehaven, and at a conservative estimate there must have been two hundred guests in attendance. On paper Vince Mori should have been as interested as the next musician in how and where these inscrutables called 'structure' and 'improvisation' came from. Perhaps I haven't properly spelt it out, but even the woodenest of pub trad players *improvises*, however predictably and within whatever a restricted range of possibilities. Even my hidebound father cut loose on the clarinet when it suited him and would pay tribute to the following classic artists: Alphonse Picou, George Lewis, Albert Nicholas, Barney Bigard, and to resort to self-explanatory Christian names, Pee Wee, Mezz, Benny, Jimmy, Artie and Woody. Once I asked my Dad po-faced why in homage to the last four he hadn't called himself 'Vincey'. He'd scowled of course, and refused to respond to my insolence, but afterwards I formulated my own theory. I realised that the absence of a final vowel in 'Vinss' must have sounded the epitome of snakelike machismo to a Reggio di Calabrian ear. Arrived in Forties Cumberland, Vincenzo anglicised himself as Vince rather than Enzo, because 'Vinss' would have sounded all fist and fury and fearlessness, whereas 'Vincey' would have sounded more like a tittering drag artist or a stand-up Morecambe comic.

"Toneet," announced Miff Mumberson, who by now had graduated to a £199.99 toupee, a present from his doting old wife Minnie on his turning sixty-five. "Toneet we're ere to celibate Vince Mori turnin seventy year owd. And this ugly owd Eyetie bugger doesn't look a day ower sixty-nine-and-a-alf!"

A *sotto voce* cackle to Shimmins from my father. "Ee's sek a fookin koonta, yon blurry Miff! Ee's a chicky fooky laal twat, int he Deaf?"

By 1991 Deaf Shimmins was a sprightly youth of sixty who still clung doggedly to his cut-price workhouse dentures. The moulded plastic had only just begun to warp with age, so that when he grinned at you it was as if Bela Lugosi were sizing you up with a wistful purpose. Earlier he had told me that his latest dance-hall conquest, Nicole (he pronounced it, without any irony,

'Nick-All'), was only nineteen years old. What he said after that was coarse beyond belief, so I shall render it in a pallid précis. This business of turning sixty and clicking with teenagers, he explained to me, was discernibly his, Dave's, second menopause. That being the case, he couldn't even begin to express to me how keenly he was looking forward to his *third* bloody menopause, when he became a septuagenarian like Vince.

As for crucial clarinet influences, Vince said that he modelled himself on George Lewis, partly because Lewis had been a humble docker just as Vince had been a humble miner. He worshipped Lewis because of his ebullient joy and because his raw New Orleans sound had all the authenticity of wrong notes, musical rule-breaking and artless self-confidence. My father also idolised Sidney Bechet because he was a third of that tripartite constellation which included Johnny Dodds and Jimmie Noone. And, just as important, because of Sidney Bechet's slow vibrato, the epitome of Creole jazz *espressivo*. The two Italian adjectives clinched the matter decisively.

Like everyone else in this world, my father worshipped himself. He worshipped the outward projections of what he liked best in himself. Joy, artlessness, sex, vigour, vitality, racial hauteur. Fittingly some New Orleans Creoles like Jelly Roll Morton were rumoured to be even more arrogantly chauvinist than the whites. Black New Orleans music, my father opined, was more vigorous than Creole but then Creole culture was indubitably more – wassacommee? – 'kultchurt'. Vince, with a son who taught Biology in a local Tech, had an awesome respect for 'blurry big brines that make blurry big ponceshillinsanpiss, Enzo lad!' Above all he loved the New Orleans sound because it was the first example in jazz of 'hot playing'. By this was signified something akin to homely emotional *warmth*. Call Vince Mori whatever you liked (pig-headed, self-seeking, blunt, overbearing, far too South Italian) you could not accuse him of lacking emotional warmth. He was as expressive as ten fat mamas, as kind and impulsive as an old-fashioned Calabrian mayor, as angry and obstinate as a hundred black-suited patriarchs. Koombrians, he conceded, had a little more of the milk of human warmth than the rest of the *Inglesi*, a nation who, as far as he could see, had been weaned not on milk but on some sort of glacial anaemic compound left over from the First and Second World Wars.

"Urry up and finish yer speech, Miff," Dave Shimmins hissed at the drummer. "Say yer gab aboot Vince and than ah'll fuck off ter see Nick-All at Cleator Moor."

Mumberson grunted at the peremptory tone. Clearing his throat as if if were the size and width of Carlisle's Dixon's Chimney, he acceded to the oversexed, impatient trumpeter. He stood there on the floodlit ballroom stage and warmly eulogised the beaming birthday boy. First of all he extolled my father's manic energy and enterprise. He pointed out, to any unaware of it, that this seventy-year-old was still doing all the hustling for bookings, still leading the band two or three times a week, still blowing his clarinet as if his lungs were bellows or bagpipes.

"And," he confided very possessively, "if he wants ter, Vince Mori can makk byath his chicks puff oot like yon udder lezhndry gadger, Dissy Gilhespy. He can makk his fyass blow oot like a greet puff adder. Than Vince's able ter blow an blow and blow like buggery on his bliddy owld clarrynet!"

In dense Workington dialect Miff earnestly attempted to explain the subtly invisible significance of the clarinet, the way that a leader like Vince was responsible for orchestrating the overall dynamics. Their favourite New Orleans sound, as Mumberson described it, was based on the idea of 'free cunterpunt', viz. a triadic basis of trumpet/trombone/clarinet. For trumpet, he added, sometimes read cornet, but the overall principle was unchanging. On this free counterpoint system, the Stompers' clarinettist Vince more or less entwined and entangled the two brasses.

The drummer waggled his huge hand sinuously through a fog of floodlit fag smoke.

"Vinss slimes an snakes hissel aw ower laal Dave an laal Wilf…"

Shimmins and Phizacklea, who were seated on the stage with the birthday boy, nodded at this too accurate metaphor. Then with deadpan timing Phizacklea mimed a drunken horror at this nightmarish and deadly Calabrian cobra. Miff snorted and admitted that he himself functioned in the lowly subsidiary role of 'support'. He single-handed was the band's rhythm section. Over the years the Stompers had tried having a bass and a piano and a banjo player, but finally, more because of unforeseen personality clashes than economic reasons, Miff had come to render all the support single-handed.

"Yah feller," Mumberson reminisced with a poisoned expression, "Horriss Twentyman wat we hed on banjo was allus gaffin fags frae't dressin reums and blamin udders. He blamt me, he blamt Wiff, he blamt Vince, he blamt Dave. Three 'ear sen' he wass put away in Durram jail fer embezzlin frae Cummerlan Bildin Sighty where he wukkt as a coonter cluck. An a damn good bliddy thing."

"Bastard," concurred Deaf Shimmins. "He yance blamt me for pinshin his chowin terbaccy coed 'Missy Sippy Myeun'. As if I wuid chow chowin terbaccy, a dutty bliddy gippo abit…"

"*Bastardo*," echoed the birthday boy of long and unforgiving memory. "*Ladro! Impudente! Appropriazione fraudolentemente!* Deaf, back in 1976, ee pinsht two hunnert Numbing Sex facks off me, his bliddy boss! Bringt offer from bliddy Cally-Doffer by Enzo on his summer bliddy holiday."

Hearing of Twentyman's Player's Number Six larceny, reminded Miff of something even worse. His puce and addled fizzog visibly paled as he fought with the torment of inexpungibly haunting memory.

"Then there was oor yah time *penis*, Lenny."

I cocked my ears, so to speak, at this extraordinary statement.

"Let me tell youse aw aboot oor laal penis, Lenny Bigrigg. He was a varra laal feller, Lenny, vanya a bliddy midgit, in fact. He wukkt as a fitter at Wukiton steelwukks, an playt pianer fer us for six weeks in the winner of 1982. Giff laal Lenny his due, he wuss grand at vampin an gollerin at top of his voice cos he also playt pianer int Arrinton Gunners Club on Satdy neets fer drink money. He was awtergidder puffeckt as an entertainin club muzishen, grinnin and jowkin and smuckin his laal fyass at awt ugly owd wimmin an widders. But yah neet, asser, he seriously propost (the laal shotarsed bigeedit smuckin get!) an oor afoor a charty puffomens that he wantit us, the Stompers, ter play *Easy bliddy Listenin* as weel. Aye!"

Vince could not restrain himself at this point. He snorted with incandescent disgust, "*Disonore! Sporco omicciattolo* Lenny Buggery! Shotass git! *Nano impudente!*"

"Aye," commiserated Miff. "Bliddy scandless! He wantit Vinss Mori's Chompin Stompers ter lake at imitatin Chems bliddy Last an Rusk Onwy an Up bliddy Albert an Missus Mills Party bliddy Medley! Well, fwoaks, asser, we hed ter tell him, this loodmooth orrible laal dwaaaarf Lenny Bigrigg, in neah unsuttin tums, ter gah an get bliddy *fyeukt…*"

He paused to apologise for that unnecessary cursing in front of the ladies. Later he admitted to my father that he'd had to fight the temptation to continue his angry denunciations. Foremost in his mind was the hideous memory of their late Eighties bass player, Carlisle Liversedge. Liversedge's personable ex-wife Daniela was sitting here tonight at one of the front tables with her new husband Melvyn, or Miff would have felt no compunction in this belated public shaming. Carlisle Liversedge had worked twenty years for the Allerdale Water Board and had been a virtuoso in authentic New Orleans terms. Unfortunately for years he'd also had a secret existence as a diurnal washing line thief specialising in young lady's lingerie and older females' foundation garments. When finally apprehended by the police, didn't it just have to happen halfway through a Stompers' performance at a riotous fortieth-birthday party on the Scots side in the middle of Ecclefechan?! Once the Dumfriesshire locals saw old Liversedge being driven away for interrogation by the cops and discovered that the blushing bassist was a *knicker thief*, they inevitably peppered the English band with several far from imaginative insults. Worse still, that raucous lynch-posse taunting was in hellish *Oor Wully* dialect where the words all sounded like Ecclefechan butchers' terminology rather than contemptuous references to notional West Cumbrian sex offenders.

"Aware ter fuck yer puffats! Yer fleshers! Yer puddyfils! Puifs! Broon fackin hatters, gan awae wi ye! Awae ter pish, mon. Afoor we kastriti yez. Awae feck yersel hame ter bliddy Shitehaven!"

Shitehaven, no less, gasped outraged Vince, the dismal little Eccle*fuckin* chicky bastards!

That sordid business of lingerie theft had evidently worked in a subliminal way on Mumberson's subconscious. Tonight, bizarrely, it prompted him to describe himself as the all-enveloping 'foundation corsets' of the Chompin Stompers. In musical terms the Stompers' band needed its superfluous folds of fat, its belly and bum and other ungainly curves to be given some firm cosmetic support. That of course was Miff Mumberson's unglamorous job, as the solitary supporting rhythm section for the Stompers.

"Ah, Miff Mumpson, is the bliddy wassacommee, roll-on, wat lifts an supports, while flattnin an enhancin the overall figger of the Stumpers, asser."

By contrast, Vince Mori's beautiful clarinet was of a wholly different order. It was the marvel that welded and united every-thing else and acted as the four-way switch. Miff Mumberson did not use that glamorous term 'conduit', thank God. But even assuming that he had, I believe it would not have been in the portentous theological sense, but more on the workaday analogy of a circuit transformer.

"Miff!" tetched my father sternly. "*Forse è vero, certamente.* Is mebbe true wat you say about me. But you dint ave to say it fronta aw these pipple. I is very mush *imbarazzato.*"

The clarinettist was actually blushing at this delirious ovation. For the bluff old tyrant to be informed that he held the key diplomatic post in his band was precisely what he wanted to hear. Not only was he its founder-member, not only its indispensable administrative boss, not only its creative, occasionally destructive accountant, its hyperbolical PR, its illegally flyposting advertising manager, its complaining foul-mouthed tea-boy, its dionysian social club secretary, its insouciant mascot and occasional bur-

218

lesque comic turn… but he was also declared in public before two hundred of his friends to be the Stompers' subtle and invisible linch-pin and cornerstone and pivot and fulcrum and every other flattering if colourless mechanical and architectural metaphor.

I'm aware that I am using this word metaphor a lot, and I note from my reference dictionary that it comes from the Greek *metapherein*. That verb means 'to transfer', hence metaphor as substantive must derive from the noun 'transference'. In psycho-analytic terms, of course, this would more than summarise my extravagant father, who transferred and projected onto every-thing and everyone, and as if there were no such thing as keeping one's grotesque fantasies to oneself.

"In shot," Mumberson emphasised with a scowl and a jabbing finger, "Vince Mori might be a bliddy bastud ter wukk fer. But aw considert, he's a feller in a bliddy million!"

Hoots and cheers ascended to a threatening volume. Once the echoing ballroom had quietened, the two other Stompers felt duty bound to second the drunken toast master. Dave Shimmins, unable to think about anything but his appointment with Nick-All/ Nicole, grunted impatiently, "Aye, it's a bliddy fact. As true as I's bliddy sittin bliddy ere."

Dave was standing rather than sitting, but at this hour of the night no one was monitoring the trumpeter's posture.

"Aye," echoed Wilf severely. "Aye, aye, aye, aye, aye."

"Aye," chimed my father amnesically, as if he were seriously talking of someone else. "Aye, I spose that I bliddy is."

Suddenly, as if he were the best man at my father's wedding, Miff decided to tell a comic story about the extraordinary Italian. I have already related this absurd anecdote: Vince in Forties Whitehaven standing hour after hour like a tramp out of Beckett, waiting for a double-decker to Carlisle that stubbornly refused to arrive. Once Miff Mumberson had finished with the 'Karlizlee' punchline (*it blurry isn't, it bloody is, is blurry not!*) and with his audience in agonised stitches, the fussy old drummer felt obliged to adopt a solemn didactic tone. Mumberson had previously tanked himself up with a vast amount of Johnny

Walker's, so nervous he was at making this Chase Hotel laudation. In his cups, he decided he needed to say something which if not for eternity would at least be suitable and quotable for posterity. Through a fogged haze of birthday whisky, he felt duty bound to offer a short homily of general and philosophical import.

"Yah time," said the drummer, after igniting a Castella cigar and puffing away with narrowed, puckered eyes. The blinding floodlight on his £199.99 toupee, seemed particularly hallowed and refulgent at this point in his address. "Yah time, asser, there was a varra great, a varra lezhndry clarinet player wat wass cawd *Mizz Mizzra*."

The audience smiled politely, but the majority never having heard of Mezz Mezzrow, presumably thought of buzzing hornets or *miserere miserere* or anything but the legendary man himself.

"Mizz Mizzra wuzz an Amurrikan fella, yah 'ear yunger than Geordie Lewis, who wass born in 1900. He wass a white feller frae Shikaga, Amurrika. He wass a greet wild bugger an aw, wass Mizz, a real bad get at times, juss like mad Vince Mori frae Whitehebben."

The birthday boy sniffed loudly at all this heroic obsequy. There was so much unbounded love in Miff's insults it was tearfully overwhelming. This was obviously the happiest moment of my father's life to date. Once again he murmured maudlinly to the trumpeter:

"Miff is a chicky ficky koont. But I *luff* him, I luff yon blurry koont ter bits, Deaf!"

"Mizz Mizzra," continued Miff, "wuss born in 1899, an died twenty 'ear sen' back in 1972. Noo than, in a varra famous byeuk, his hortybografi, coed *Really The Blues*, Mizz Mizzra sez wat he wuid dyeuh ter makk a liffin, ter makk ends meet an stop issel bliddy starvin ter deeth. Mizz sez hoo he wuid sell dope, wassacommee, marawanga, in Arlem, Nyeuh Yokk, till aw them drug-tyannin black fellers. Noo than, Vince Mori ere, seah far as ah's aware, hess nivver sellt any drugs ter neahbody. Anyways, as we aw knaw, there's only yah laal black feller in Whitehebben an that lad, laal Sirril Hodgin frae top end ev Kells, duznt tyan drugs eider. T'only drugs Vince Mori's ivver dealt has been Horrinsh Mads an Miffis an Oysters an Nighty-Night cornets and sek like palaver. Still," puffing Castella smoke reverently incense-wise in my father's direction and addressing him with a beckoning hand, "Mizz Mizzra is yan of thy aw time eroes, int ee, Vince?"

No less oiled than the court poet after four hours of free drinks, Vince closed his eyes and tossed his head in a single dramatic gesture. As if under stage hypnosis, he informed the audience that he was vividly picturing to himself a memorable TV documentary of about ten or fifteen years ago. In this film about the growth and development of jazz in the United States, Mezz Mezzrow's angelic clarinet playing had made at least one English viewer, Vincenzo Alfredo Mori, weep with unadulterated love and envy.

"*Quale spettacolo!*" he hissed at all us muttonish West Cumbrians in the Chase Hotel ballroom.

"Speck wat?" leered Mumberson, looming over my smiling father like an overweight Workington phantasm. "Speck woh, Vince?"

Vince snorted indulgently, "Yah sek a chicky koonta, Miff! But ah luff yer enuff to giff yer a blurry big kiss!"

Mumberson might have been tight but he was not that tight. Even in the remotest English provinces, the omnivorous sexuality of the average Dago was well known. Vincenzo Mori had never shown any appetite for anything other than women, but Miff was not about to let him explore any lateral tastes in his eighth decade. He pushed my father smartly back into his seat and continued his cautionary parable concerning Mezz Mezzrow.

"This is wat Mizz Mizzra sed aboot the spirit of Noo Hawlins. Aboot the spirit, that is, of wat he was trying ter play on his clarinet. Paw, shite an onions, ah hev gone an lost me bliddy prompt! Ah writ it aw doon speshly, an bugger me ah've gan an misslate the bit ev bliddy pyaper. So ahs'll hev ter tell youse aw aboot it frae memry. Reet than. Wat Mister Mizz Mizzra said in his byeuk, *Really The Blues*, wuzz this:

"Noo Hawlins fer me, Mizz Mizzra, meant the follerin

things: Nummer yan, a celibation ev the gift ev life; nummer two, a celibation ev the fizzical act ev breathin; nummer three, a celibation of aw me mussels flexin an wukkin weel; nummer fower, a celibation of me bliddy eyes blinkin an quiverin wit natcheral ennerzhy; nummer five, a celibation of likkin me flamin chops wit, wassacommee, gusto. Meanin ev cwoarse, a bliddy celibation ev bliddy life itsbliddysel! In spite, sez Mizz, in spite ev whativver the bliddy wurld might dyeuh till thee, thee er t'udder feller! Mizz sez it wuzz like an hosanna, hosanna, till yer sweat glans, an hymn till yer achin empty guts, on the Sally Army lines ev, 'Glory be brudder. Looks ter, t'sun up above oor eeds is shinin bright!' "

My father was awestruck listening to Mezzrow's musical confessional. Even though he knew the contents of *Really The Blues* backwards, he applauded each sentiment afresh. Apropos which, I could almost see his brain clicking away self-congratulatorily with regard to those two decades of philandering with Jennifer and Lorna and all his other women. Most of them being little more than a meaningless jumble of forgettable names relayed to me by that arch-gossip and admirer of my father's amoral gusto, Watson Holland. June, Jane, Jean were three of that roll call, his mistresses of '84, '85, '86 as far as I could remember. It was as if Mezzrow's disciple, old Casanova Franco Vincenzo Harris Mori, had decided to improvise on the highly addictive j-n chord. June kept a sweetshop in Wigton, Jane kept a chipshop in Aspatria, Jean kept a fishshop on a council estate in Cockermouth. In successive years the old *adulteroso donnaoilo* had been obliged to spray himself with Brut to hide the overpowering scent of Love Hearts, Mars Bars, fish scrapings and oak-smoked kippers. All this because he had taken Mezz Mezzrow to heart too much, and listened to the flexing of his heart muscles and sundry other autonomic pulsings. He had responded to the gleam in his eye at the sight of any half-attractive woman. That ocular gleam reminded him that, while the mind might have its moments, it is the body above all that dictates how a person feels in his soul.

Nor was that all, Miff Mumberson added solemnly, showing some irritation at the drunken chattering on the floor below. Watching him swaying at the mike and fingering the knotty apex of his luxury toupee, it occurred to me that those two unusual names were not that far apart. Miff and Mizz, they were virtually interchangeable. They were both extremely passionate jazz men, even if on different sides of the Atlantic. Both surnames were alliterative as well. At which point, unfortunately, they parted company. Mezzrow was a perfect sounding surname for a jazzman. It had elan, pazzazz, a double zed, and dash. Whereas Mumberson... whereas that paradigm Cumbrian surname Mumberson, sounded rather more like the reality of Miff; viz. a pension-age Workington factory worker with a persistent history of haemorrhoids, housemaid's knee and shingles.

"Mizz Mizzra, as ah sed, wuss a white feller. Mizz sez this in his ortybografi byeuk aboot fwoaks' colour. When ee saw them black fellers playin better than issel, it madd him feel *inferyer* as a white muzishen..."

An excessive throat-clearing was heard from centre stage. "*Non ho completamente capito Mivv,*" the throat muttered, with a delicate politeness, sounding comprehensively mystified.

"Them Arlem fellers wat he sellt dope till, they gev him an infeety cumplix, yer see. So Mizz Mizzra sumtimes thowt till issel: mebbe wid aw me big ideas, ah s'll nivver be as guid as aw them black fellers!"

Shimmins and Phizacklea looked at the boozy old drummer with something like worried concern as they saw him float off into the uncanny realms of sociological abstraction. The gist of what followed, Miff's personal thesis, was that Mezz Mezzrow had put his money where his musician's mouth was in a very concrete way. Feeling grossly inferior both by race and musical tradition, Mezzrow had decided to rectify matters by an audacious absurdist paradox: viz. *by claiming that he himself was black.*

Miff peered down at us all in a superior and proprietorial manner. Almost hectoringly he exclaimed:

"Aye! Wat d'yer makk ev yon, fwoaks? Mizz Mizzra wuss as

white as me or thee. But he hed sek a rashal inferty cumplix that he allus describt issel, allus refoort till issel in public, as a *black man*. Mizz Mizzra sez till ivvrybody ee met, ah is black! Ah is as black as the next black feller doon in bliddy Arlem!"

After this monumental existential transformation (as a taxing linguistic puzzle you may imagine how that was poetically suggested rather than literally elaborated in gruff Workington dialect) Mezz Mezzrow took the final awesome step. And it was strangely reminiscent of an act of Biblical atonement, this decision by a white clarinettist to pay the ultimate price.

"Whenever ee was slung in t' Nyeuh Yokk jail fer sum miss demeaner er udder, Mizz Mizzra allus med syam demand. He insistit that he wantit ter gah in *t' black sekshun ev t' jail*! Mizz wantit ter be treatit like a black man, dispite his laal lily white fyass. Scandless eh? Them bliddy owld Amurriken jailors, they muss ave bloody ated him fer that. Aye!"

Where exactly was all this extraordinary abstract musing leading the toast master qua sociologist qua philosopher qua drum-playing cultural commentator? Sheer quantity of Johnny Walker made the ultimate teasing refinements of his argument extremely difficult to follow, but as far as I could see they amounted to this:

Just as Mezz Mezzrow put his money where his mouth was by opting to suffer alongside a suffering race, so all jazzmen and jazzwomen everywhere, *even if they did not feel naturally inclined to be so*, were obliged to be unselfconscious equals together. That at any rate, grunted Miff, was how they bloody well should be, given the poverty-stricken origins of jazz music. Looking to his own experience for concrete confirmation of his theory, Miff's eyes gradually came to rest upon my smirking father. He pointed victoriously at man-in-a-million and birthday boy Vince, then leisurely proceeded to drop an unwitting bombshell. He informed the Cumbrian clarinettist's two hundred plus guests, of the following hitherto closely guarded, highly confidential personal sacrifice. Although, he beamingly divulged to us, Vince Mori hadn't actually ever gone to jail for the sake of his jazz band, he had in fact taken out a colossal bloody great *bank loan* four years ago to purchase a complete set of new instruments and amps for his band...

The detonation of this bombshell inflicted violent shock waves upon my father. The world to all appearances came crashing round his ears. His eyes rolled up to the ballroom ceiling, he went stiffer than a corpse in his chair, and gasped in a voice gone hollow with traumatised guilt. "*Che?* Aw fook, Mivv! Fick, fick, *fick*..."

"What?" gasped my old mother, who was also up there centre stage.

"... ah mean, aw phew, ees damn ot in ere, innit, Chelika?"

"Eh?" snarled his wife, as if someone had shot her in the back.

Of course all the band members, Miff fluted on serenely, had paid back most of their sizeable sub-loans bit by bit. Even though, rather regrettably, Dave Shimmins, always the fly one and the tardy one, still had a sizeable moiety of £375.55 outstanding from 1987.

The randy trumpeter scowled, going so far as to blush. "Yer mad gobshite bastud! Didjer hev ter tell aw the bliddy wurld?"

Yes he bloody did, Miff Mumberson shot back smoothly. That was what the term 'jazz' was all about. For all those who professed this thing called 'jazz', it was all about telling the uncomprehending world. The incomparable sound of New Orleans was surely just another name for musical evangelism. It was a shout of physical and spiritual joy and a worshipping of the body and the guts and the blood and the zest for life itself. Just as Mezz Mezzrow had put it so insistently in his incomparable 'byeuk', and with how much more engaging literary eloquence than his near namesake Miff.

Angelica Mori, toffed up tonight like a silver-haired duchess, could be heard snorting, "*Bloody bank loan? What bloody bank loan?*"

My father tushed her rather too insensitively to soothe her. "*Niente*, Chelika. *Oggi* is my blurry buttday, innit? So shut yer blurry gob, please, lass."

She seized his left wrist and twisted it roughly. "I'm damned if I'll shut it. You *desperate* old bugger!"

"Is bliddy nottin, lass, honest! So true as I am shit in ear! It's bliddy nowt at all."

"It bloody is!" she rasped, and because she was so angry she resorted to an icy orthodox English. "A bank loan back in 1987? You told me it was for that brand new ice-cream van! But according to Miff Mumberson, you splurged it all on the Chompin bloody Stompers!" She pinioned him rigid by his crumpled shirt collar and demanded, "If it all went on expensive new gear for the band, who was it paid for that bloody van?"

He should have grovelled and begged for mercy at this point, but instead he opted for cowardly Calabrian evasiveness. Deplorably, he attempted to play the whimsical fool when his wife was in no mood at all for unimaginative clowning. Vince Mori grinned stupidly, before resorting to the jokey argot of the bohemian Kent Walton and his TV programme *Cool Cats*, circa 1961.

"But bebe, is my buttday!" he purred like some bizarre Italo-Cumbrian Jack Kerouac. "Don be mean chick to me, Chelika beb! Be cul to me, swit lil bebe! Not on my bloomin buffday pliz, lil leddy."

"WHO PAID FOR IT," she screamed, "YOU CRAZY OLD IDIOT?"

"But bebe pliss…"

"D'YOU WANT ME TO STRANGLE YOU PUBLICLY? OR PRIVATELY? WHO PAID FOR IT?"

"But beb…"

"WHO BLOODY WELL PAID?"

Sweating rather, as she applied a lethal tourniquet-garrotte, he gasped out, "Ees not blurry paid. I mean, it is been blurry paid! I mean, aw bugger, I is *still* blurry paying for it!"

"Eh? *Still* paying for it? Still paying for what? Why you deceitful bloody *lying*!…"

Vincenzo Alfredo Mori, five years past retirement age, was still paying for a state-of-the-art ice-cream vehicle that had been

226

sold and turned into a loss-making chip van in 1989. The transaction had been an appalling example of highway robbery, because Vince had been so foolishly desperate to buy a bargain second-hand Transit for his Stompers. In addition, the weaselly Workington chip-vendor had just finished his government-funded small-business course where he'd been advised by an equally weaselly twenty-five-year-old advisory consultant to drive a hard bargain wherever he could. Vincenzo the peasant Roccellan could normally bargain the spots off a set of dominoes, but he'd been unable to beat down Malc Messenger, a fly and ruthless twenty-two-year-old entrepreneur from Siddick just outside Workington. Angelica's deceitful old foreigner husband was thus still desperately in debt in his seventy-first year...

12

♪♪♪♫

On the flight to New York I took a large number of tape cassettes with me. For purposes of symmetry, or possibly self-torture, I took ten of Fanny Golightly's and ten of Cebola's recordings, and played one or two tracks from each. I alternated my historical samples of the two great musicians rather than overdosing on either, a ploy which did not work in my favour. The more I set Fanny Golightly against Toto Cebola, the more I realised that they had far too much in common for my liking, most obviously as they started their musical journeys through the last decade of the twentieth century.

Fanny's discography, of which I had a painstakingly nostalgic sample, extended over almost twenty years, and Cebola's for twenty-two. At first I was pleased to reflect that her restless switchings between the fevered and the dreamily hypnotic guitar had no parallel with Cebola's abrupt abandonment of the rawness of *Energetic Eels*. As a kid of twenty-four in 1969, he was sweating and angry and furious as he defiantly subjected the violin to the violence of electricity. But already by the early Seventies he had embarked on his 'cosmological' sonic effects and was never to go back to a violin playing as harsh, prickly and ferocious as in *Eels*. In a mere two years he had miraculously found himself a settled and definitive musical voice. He was not only a less anxious, less lightning-struck musician than Fanny, but, I confidently predicted, a far stabler individual in the flesh. Nonetheless, speed and technique were in themselves merely adjuncts, not the reality, not the core or irreducible essence of any kind of music. Inevitably it was the vivid evocation of mood and the measured exposure of a reality called human feeling, however subtle or concealed, that made music of any sort genuinely memorable. Listening to the pair of them side by side, back to back, and belly to belly (I was painfully aware of these anatomical and sexual correlates as I played the two of them in harness) I knew that their union was made in a heaven where the only spiritual law, as such, was one of a vulnerable fidelity to the emotions.

And which common vulnerable emotion in particular was keenest in this syzygy, this heavenly pairing? Fanny in hurtling express-train mode shouted the music of anger, molten scorn, a kind of aeronautic impersonal defiance. Fanny in her quiet tender guise spoke a rhythm of endless gentleness, of a heart which is a spiritual organ that is broken not in the name of grief, but in the name of a receptively aching love. Take that awkward and extremely embarrassing notion a little further, and you have the verb that confounds all those who are not of a romantic or a religious bent. The verb in question is 'yearn'.

Halfway through the flight I played the first track of *Sentimental Angles*. Cebola brought that album out with CBS in 1979, the year that I got married to Margaret Stern, a chain-smoking, fast-talking film producer who worked in the documentary department of the BBC. With Margaret at first it was definitely a case of yearning, even doting, on my part, with a melting calf-love for my new and beautiful if nicotiney bride. Right from the start I had to accept that at short notice she might be away filming for six weeks in Mozambique or Sarawak or Sierra Leone or the Philippines. It was not the same anguished, anachronistic emotion of yearning-in-absence as my twenty-year-old self had felt for Fanny Golightly. Yet it had the same dominant elements of tenderness, lust and reflex possessiveness, not to speak of a typically Italian and masculine self-doubt.

The first track of *Sentimental Angles* was called *Stay Beside Me* and every time I heard it I wanted to die. I don't mean that I wanted to die because I wanted to end it all. No, I wanted to die with an excess of sensuous feeling in my heart, a final testament that said Enzo Gianmaria Mori had tasted a richness sufficient to feed a man of any appetite and sensibility for fifty years at least. It had done for me good and proper, because I was fully overblown and sated. I had had enough, I had known enough, I had obtained and tasted far more than I deserved, and now I quietly wished to depart from this sphere in sheer wordless gladness of heart.

Stay Beside Me starts with a short amplified piano passage announcing the birth of an asterisk or the circumnavigation of the planets by a flight of angels. This might sound of a very grand if not terrifying order, but it is all done with minute considered modesty and in the blink of an eye, as if to say that angels and asterisks do not in this case choose to vaunt their limitless grandeur. Then there is a water-simple two-finger acoustic piano chord, repeated with slight but piquant variations perhaps half a dozen times. It is not Stim Stein at the keyboard but Cebola himself who deigns on this track to play a tiny amount of an instrument he once was scared of. Halfway through the variations he makes a gently chasmic shift in the direction of… an act of ascent. The rising up a single staircase step is done almost amnesically, but it is there like a covert humorous wink through the aether. One simple chord shift and we are talking the unspoken language of a world which we cannot name but only praise. Perhaps Mahavishnu John McLaughlin was right and the great ones, the great musical technicians, are 'mere' conduits, they really are just chosen 'vessels'. And bear witness to the fact that however ponderous or sceptical your theory of music, this finite simplicity leads to a vision of landscapes too infinite and far too beautiful to contemplate with any ordinary fluid-filled eyes.

It is piquant and it is yearning, but it is Toto on an instrument not his own. Therefore, as an illustrative preamble, it has neither the density nor the richness of what must follow. Now we have a new guitarist called Joe Zaninetti whose forte it seems is for a deep if highly necessary scarifying of the tissue of the heart.

They talk blithely of tugging the heartstrings, and Joe Zaninetti does this by making his guitar sound in part like a mournful mouth organ, in part like a bandoleon, in part like the unvoiced emotion of a painfully melancholy small child. I can see somewhere in all this, however vaguely, a little boy, a tiny good-looking boy of three or four perhaps, grimly muffled in an ugly impoverished far-from-poetic landscape against a biting northern wind. His head is swathed constrictingly in a sad, ungainly woollen balaclava, his thin hand outstretched to an oblivious parent. The hand is there reciprocally from the unidentifiable father, but absently, quite heedlessly unaware of the fragile being of his son. The small boy nurses his sore of doleful loneliness, afflicted by a generic, unpalatable sorrow he cannot put a name to. It is a very biting, very uncharitable, very icy wind from the far, far north.

Do I mean the north of England? Or the north of Portugal? From Whitehaven in the far north west? From Coimbra up in the Beira Baixa? Perhaps, given the guitarist's surname, the biographical detail is Italian-American rather than Italian-Cumbrian. Once Joe Zaninetti has had his say, the Portuguese maestro enters with due ceremony and at an appropriately 'sentimental angle'. His electric violin these days has a pedal and a custom-device rack. It takes the bandoleon melancholy of Joe Z's guitar, and subjects it to a driving pungence and an ebullient mastery. The former shoeshine has employed a drummer, Lonnie Burgos, who drives a proudly brutal rock beat. This 'jazz-rock', if that is what it must be dismissed as, gazes altogether indifferently in the faces of the worriedly scrutinising savants. Post-1971, after *Live Evil*, Miles Davis played the same teasing trick on the same thunderstruck outfit, and while they will always puzzledly lick his uncompromising boots and clamour at his feet like so many salivating spaniels, they wish somehow, in wounded retrospect, that it had been, it were, subjunctively speaking, ineluctably otherwise.

As I found myself melting over *Stay Beside Me*, I also began brooding over an extraordinary transformation in Watson Holland. My old sparring partner had apparently suffered a profound personality change. The stolid old pharmacist had recently become someone else, he was no longer the same man, and I was as confused as if Vince Mori had suddenly decided to become a reasonable human being. The image of physical elevation was very appropriate at this point. At the moment I was airborne courtesy of a Newcastle–New York jet, but also on account of the mid-period music of Toto Cebola. Meanwhile, back there in his Whitehaven lodgings, Watson Holland might be literally earthbound, but he was obviously flying ten miles high in another sense.

Watson Holland was suddenly massively, truly and deeply *in love*. It sounded like the title of a Duke Ellington tune. At long last, I realised with a shaken intuition, the spirit of jazz had conquered the jazz-loathing pharmacist. Given Holland's boastful misogyny, it had always looked as if he would stay my parents' lodger till he was carried from our house feet first. But the night before my departure, I had stayed at the family home, where I'd been informed of a historical about-turn. Boozing and arguing with Captain Hornblower in the front parlour, I noted that his eyes seemed rather more shiny than the bottle of Jamieson might have justified. He also seemed to have lost ten years and regained a resplendent middle age. His luxuriant moustache was somehow more tensile, more erectile, more suggestive of carrying the universe upon its extremities without any hint of strain or hesitation.

"You look like a dog with two tails," I said admiringly. "I was going to let you have a listen to my new CD of Rameau's *Zoroastre*. But seeing you're so outrageously smug with yourself, you can suffer some jazz instead. I've just bought this re-issue of Keith Jarrett's *Facing You*."

I put the CD on Vince's expensive new hi-fi and waited for Holland to mime the contortions of someone afflicted with terminal cachexia. It was solo piano music from 1972, of an intensely plangent and infinitely poignant kind. Sure enough, it mirrored my mood on the eve of my flight to the States, where I was going to have something out with a preposterous, tyrannically Oedipal pair called Toto and Fanny. Picture my amazement when the sniffy old chemist suddenly assumed the stupefied not to say sedated expression of a lovesick idiot in a comic opera.

"That's extraordinarily tender stuff," he purred with a fussy scrutiny as he grabbed the *Facing You* sleeve notes. "Isn't it though? The structure itself is absolutely childlike. But God the bloody feeling this whatsit Carrot/Jarrot chap injects. What's his pedigree? Classically trained no doubt, then rusticated from univ for smoking too much bhang and too much flagrant how's your father? Mm. What enormously *vulnerable* expressiveness, man. Who does this Yankee bugger suppose he is, Fauré or Schumann or Scriabin or what? Mm. You know it teeters rather dangerously this side of vulgar bathos or tinny melodrama. There's something insidiously cheapskate about it if you were guarding yourself against – what should I say? – the *nakedness* of such a music. But then, just as you are resolved to damn it on a cold clinical scale, it reaches to the very pinnacle of delicately fragile beauty. What's this particular track called? *My Lady, My Child*? It sounds almost as poignant as the Madonna and Child to me. Faw! Sniff. You hear that. *Sniff*. Faw. *Sniff*. I feel as if some chocks are loosing somewhere, Enzo. Really, it is a most extraordinary and quite worrying sensation. Bugger my timbers, if that Keith Carrot feller keeps on playing like that, I believe I shall burst into… into… tea– "

No sooner said than done. Captain Hornblower began trumpeting and weeping fit to burst. I was as shocked as if he had suddenly shit his pants. I did my best to hide it, but I felt painfully embarrassed. If it had been myself or one of my friends or even my Verdi opera father, I could have stood it. But this jovial man of steel, the jocund thespian out of an amateur drama called *The Moustachioed Chemist at Large in the Provinces*? I just didn't know where to put myself.

"Are you alright?" I asked uneasily.

"Ooh!" he groaned. "Ooh bloody *hell*!"

"Have a drink."

"Yes. Sbetter. *Ooh!* Enzo…"

"Yes," I said sharply.

"Enzo," he babbled.

"What, Watson?"

"Last time I cried like this was about 1937. I really thought I'd lost the faculty."

"Really?"

"Enzo, I'm so bloody *happy*. I'm so bloody glad to be alive."

"Are you sure?" I grunted.

"Oh!" he moaned ecstatically, and bizarrely Keith Jarrett made some of his notorious groaning noises alongside him. "Ouch! Oh! I'm bloody cracking up. Of course I'm *happy*. Too damn right I am. You're forty years old, aren't you? Can't you bloody well see when another man is happy?"

"I'm confused," I said stiffly, "because you're crying your eyes out. Don't worry though. That *Lady, Child* track does it to at least eight out of ten listeners. Fanny Golightly sobs her heart fit to break if I put it on."

The mention of her name was echoed by more of those pained soprano cries Keith Jarrett makes when most uplifted by his own sound. At that, it was all I could do to stop crying myself. The pharmacist was so exalted by his own passion he had no time or energy to notice mine. He couldn't wait to tell me about his newly found love. But before he began, he fished in his wallet and brought out a precious photograph.

"Madge," said Hornblower with absolute reverence. "This is the extraordinary lassie who has miraculously transformed my husk-dry existence."

The lassie, like the laddie who loved her, was somewhere in her early seventies. I scrutinised the little passport picture and clucked approvingly. Praising it was obviously the same as praising Holland, so I didn't restrain my admiration. In fact Madge Bimson was impressively plain, querulous and stiff-looking. She reminded me quite uncannily of a stony old infants schoolteacher I had once known in Fifties Whitehaven. The school in question had been a massive dreary sandstone monolith built by local subscription in 1889. That morose old schoolteacher, Miss Philomena Fullelove, Madge Bimson's spitting image, had been born in the very same year.

"Mm," I sighed. "She looks lovely."

"Quite, quite," he said ferociously. "You bet she bloody is. She's an incarnate blinking angel man, no point in beating about the bush. Talk about instant recognition of a unique and kindred soul. She has everything, by which I mean absolutely everything in the way of every natural gift. You might be aware perhaps that the Parsees of Bombay have an illustrious female archangel whose epithet is 'she of a thousand skills'?"

"Di–?"

"That would have been an apt soubriquet for Madgie. Her looks are as good a place as any to start. Her face is astounding, wouldn't you agree?"

"Eh? Oh yes. She… I really like her nose."

"Me too," he agreed starrily. "What is it you like most about it? Tell me what you like best about it, then I'll tell you what I like best about it."

"It's sort of statuesque," I said with a blush. "It's sort of like a certain Greek sculpture I can't just put a name to. It seems to flow… it seems as if it's flowing down her face." Gulping my whisky hurriedly. "What does she do for a living, Watson?"

"Her job? That brings me to the second of her thousand skills. Her lovely mind. Madge Bimson's brains. She has brains, I swear, nearly as big as my own."

Gratefully I seized upon our timeworn bantering tone, before it could elude us. "Some headpiece that must be. I wonder what you two great minds choose to talk about?"

He tapped his left nostril archly. "We don't spend too much

time chatting, if you know what I mean."

"No, I suppose not. But, tell me, is Madge interested in what you are interested in?"

"Of course she bloody is."

"The organochlorines?" I purred with poker face. "Citric acid? Oxalic acid? The properties of stannous and stannic oxides? The commercial synthesis of 2:4 sulphosuccinatedundecylenic-monolakylolamide?"

"Tee bloody hee," he sniffed impatiently. "But fancy you being able to parrot the formula for a shampoo ingredient. I thought in slavish imitation of a Shaivite ascetic you'd stopped washing your own hair twenty years ago. As a matter of fact we do now and again discuss organic formulae if only because Madgie used to be a senior chemistry mistress. She retired five years ago from the oldest grammar school in Durham and settled with her sister Gertrude down in Wasdale. Or at least she had settled there until recently she bumped into me at a German night class at the Gosforth comprehensive. We're getting engaged just before Christmas and we'll be married by next spring. *Frisch auf!* our German class is called, and *frisch* as plump and juicy bloody figs it is for old Madgie and old Holland. More especially when the last named is prostrate *auf das hübsche Mädchen*, Madgie. You can bet your last fifty pfennigs on that, *mein unartiger Knabe, der sogenannte Enzo Mori.*"

He was preening himself not only at his flawless German accent but at this bald intimation of his re-emergent virility.

"Everything satisfactory in the sexual sphere?" I grilled him with a laboured irony. But this euphoric and unctuous seventy-year-old had no time for any piffling nuance.

Hornblower glanced at me with avuncular patronage. "You have a nice sense of bathos I must say. If our love life were any better boy, I should be walking fifty feet in the air rather than the fifty inches I happen to levitate at present. I may as well tell you that nothing is left to chance in our exemplary relationship. That's another aspect of Madge's loveable genius, her wonder-fully methodical approach to everything under the sun. Pragmatic is her middle name, Lord bless her. Like myself she has had her painful divorce and one or two unsatisfactory flings thereafter. Various spiteful males have in the past berated her for resisting their toadishness and accused her of being insufficiently passionate. Sick to the teeth after these monotonous insults, one day she craftily decided she would approach the *ars amatoria* with some really foolproof practical preparation. On her antique bedside locker Madge Bimson keeps a range of scholarly manuals…"

"Ah," I said, far too glibly. "Alex Comfort. *The Joy of –* "

"*Joy of Sex* be blowed. If that be the best choice of verb. Neither she nor I for that matter have ever had any faith in secondary sources, nor in any coffee-table book-club DIY primers. No, the ancient east is where first Madgie and now Watson has gone for a no-nonsense scientific approach. The wise old orientals, the Indians and the Arabs, gave it all minute empirical consideration a very long time ago. They decided to treat the seemingly unfathomable business as a sensitive and delicate art like any other sensitive and delicate art. At first glance it might seem farcical to tabulate the sexual postures like so many Elizabeth David recipes. But as Madgie points out, if nobody used tried and tested recipe books to attain the highest gourmet standards the world would be full of some hideous bloody food and some ghastly bloody restaurants."

"But – "

"What it boils down to laddie is very simple indeed! Here is some gratis advice from a weathered old hand of seventy. Never forget the absolute indispensability of the hors d'oeuvres, the amatory starters, the mouthwatering mezzes. Of course Alex Comfort preaches the same thing, but it was there first in the sage maxims of Vatsyayana and Kokkoka. In a nutshell, no good plunging in with the sexual main course, the gammon and chips shall we say, before having your soup course first. Let's extend the metaphor geographically, to Greece for example, my favourite foreign destination with its wonderful cuisine. No good pouring a plateful of oily moussaka down your ladyfriend's gagging gullet if you haven't first stimulated her salivary glands with some fetching little delicate mezze titbits…"

"You reckon do you?" I murmured drily.

"Plump exquisite Kalamata olives shall we say? As plump and heavy as my Madgie's voluptuous little bow-hind. Fragrant minted tzatziki? Teasing little fricadellas of lustrous odoriferous saganaki cheese?"

I looked at my mentor with worshipful severity. "I think I get the general idea. I wonder if a marinated mess of cold and rubbery octopus salad would be a suitable starter to get her juices going?"

"What? Bah! You always have to play the bloody fool." He surveyed me sceptically, with a magisterial, whiskery and whiskified disdain. "Correct me if I'm wrong Enzo Mori, but you are now a middle-aged man, aren't you? You're also a double divorcee doing a teaching job you really hate, and you could perhaps do with a few handy hints on how to avoid a lonely and regretful old age. I know what I'm talking about boy, I spent over three decades of arid not to say arrogant bachelordom before I saw the amber light with Madgie Bimson. At the risk of repetition, Enzo Mori, the ancients got there before us, and it would be sensible to pay heed to their hard-won wisdom. In your case, before you can take another stab at any nuptial felicity you need to find yourself a suitable third female. Then if you wish to have said woman wriggling in the palm of your hand, whether she be twenty-two or eighty-two, it's all in the intelligent fiddly foreplay, you take it from me. Shish, I'm an old bloody man myself, I could have opted to retire from my pharmacy five years ago. I could have chosen to spend my twilight years piddling with mulch and seedlings in my potting shed. Well bugger that for a game of snap, says I! I may be touching seventy-one, Enzo, but like it or not I've been like a crazed Andalucian stallion since I got to know mad little Madge from Creaky Butt Crag down by Nether Wasdale."

There you had it. The wisdom of the greybeard, the seasoned, dispassionate experience of the man of many years. As luck would have it, Holland had no grey at all in his full head of hair, not even a stray wisp in his bristling and virile handlebar tash. Over thirty years his junior, I was not only balding but as grey and weathered as a senile cocker spaniel. While this youthful pharmacist had found a lasting love and a renewed fecundity, his doddery friend Enzo was embarking on something more tragic than comic. The next morning he was set to depart on a fatuously symbolic pilgrimage in pursuit of a woman who had only ever existed in his mind.

Such is the nature of addiction. Though I wasn't the only one suffering so. This dour and cynical old lodger had found himself a quite unexpected and equally demanding passion. I am not talking about his schoolboy drooling over a teacher called Bimson, that is wholly irrelevant at this point. No, once the last track of *Facing You* was ended, this jazz-hating pharmacist confounded me by demanding a complete discography of the pianist Keith Jarrett. I was roundly flabbergasted. Despite his recent tearful cascade, I assumed he was pulling my leg. Otherwise in the space of fifty minutes, courtesy of the tunes *In Front, Ritoorna, Lalene, My Lady, My Child, Landscape For Future Earth, Starbright, Vapallia* and *Semblence* ('he can play his piano like an airborne angel but he can't bloody spell, old Jarrot, can he?'), Captain Hornblower had become another bloody *jazz addict*. I pretended to be amused by his whimsical game, even though I could see he was in deadly earnest. Holland pulled out his monogrammed Sheaffer and ordered me to dictate the titles of all the available albums. Barely masking my irritation, I started with the legendary 1975 *Köln Concert*, then mentioned his earlier collaborations with the vibes player Gary Burton and the percussionist Jack de Johnette.

"Vibes?" said Holland, blinking at me like a startled old marmoset. "You know, I seem to have heard this peculiar word uttered rather frequently of late. Perhaps as some spuriously ubiquitous universal, though for the life of me I can't recall any definite context. Ah, I see, vibes as in the vibraphone. What a pretty conceit that doth sound, the concert piano and the vibraphone *zusammen*. Gary with one 'r' you say. Burton as in Weaver-to-Wearra and Hepworth. Hope his vibes 'suit' him, her, her. Hm. Title of album eponymous, *Keith Jarrett and Gary Hepworth*. Very good. What year was that? 1971? Meaning twenty years ago when little Carrot was knee-high to a stitch of potatoes, bless him. That other one you mentioned with the exotic name. The Sanskrit name, no less. *Ruta and Daitya*. Anyone like me who has read his Penguin Classic *Rig Veda* knows that that means Good and Evil. He goes for the big uns don't he, him and his drummer? Same year, you say, recorded 1971. Percussionist rejoices in the name of John de Jackette. Sorry, Jack de Johnette. Hm. You don't think 'Jackette' would have made more sense with the Burton–Hepworth connection?"

Thus Holland's jovial jazz, his *Boys' Own* love of punning. I was briefly tempted to tell him he had a namesake among the great modern bassists, one of the *Bitches Brew* apprentices, an Englishman in this case called Dave Holland. In the end I didn't, as I was worried he'd spend a fortune on acquiring a complete ECM backlist, only to find that the only album he liked was Keith Jarrett's *Facing You*. However a year later when he was married and living in Newcastle with the incomparably polymathic Madge, he wrote me a letter which entirely refuted this needless anxiety. Last Christmas, he explained, he had bought all of the available Jarrett titles as a joint present for the affianced couple. He and Madgie had been playing the exquisite stuff almost nightly ever since, sometimes (just between *Lei e mi, Enzo*) as an atmospheric preliminary to the business of *ratirahasya* (the exquisite secrets of love). Sometimes, on the other hand (best anatomical metaphor in this case?) as a tender postprandial diversion. Branching out from Jarrett and taking not a few inspired risks, my old sparring partner revealed that he'd discovered Pharaoh Saunders, Charles Lloyd, Lee Konitz, Jean-Luc Ponty, Jan Garbarek, Chick Corea, Kenny Burrell, Barbara Thompson, and, bugger him, he found that with the odd inexplicable dud on the part of each of these artists, he liked, nay loved the whole damn bloody lot. How about that for an *incredible*, one might say impossible, about-turn? As for jazz convert the new Mrs Holland, she was completely bloody incorrigible. She liked everything he liked of course, as how could she fail to wish to please her husband by sharing his every enthusiasm (Shree Pandits Vatsyayana and Kokkoka had plenty to say about that unfeminist predilection as well, bless their tradition-bound hearts)? But in addition, his fearlessly open-minded wife was now rather worryingly a slavish fan, a regular concert-attender, of the dissonant, atonal, 'experimental' jazz persuasion. She was, in her ripe and tolerant old age, an enthusiastic follower of the minority within a minority within a minority in jazz that liked to describe itself as 'free'.

There were some ink blots at this point in his letter. *Free?* Hornblower's indignant Sheaffer pen had exclaimed. Free, my hairy old bow-hind, old boy! If such was freedom, give Watson Holland the historical jazz of penal servitude, manacled bondage and lifelong slavery. Let him be enslaved by Messrs K. Jarrett, S. Rollins, C. Parker and E. Garner, rather than be 'liberated' by all those pretentious practitioners of fractured and nightmarish cacophony. Amazingly Mrs Holland loved the hideous stuff lock, stock and barrel, and was the sole and highly conspicuous septuagenarian female fan at every Newcastle-upon-Tyne and Durham free jazz recital. Evan Parker, Derek Bailey, Lol Coxhill, and various other delinquent rogues. Not forgetting alliterative Ray Russell and his Rites and his blasted Rituals. By the by, Enzo, wasn't it right, that ground-breaking album (he was quoting his atonal, experimental, thousand-skilled wife now) with its disturbing, apocalyptic cover of molten immolation, wasn't it also made in 1971? How come seemingly everything of significance was done in bloody 1971,

Enzo, how come it all happened so densely and as it were so deliberately, so fortuitously, quite eerily and uncannily, all at that particular point in time?

I arrived halfway through the recording of *Amok* by Agog. That sounds like a quote from the Pentateuch of the Old Testament and it was fitting enough that Toto Cebola had all the looks of a handsome Levantine patriarch. I don't mean I turned up literally at the Manhattan studios as the fourth of the eight tracks was being recorded. Instead I took a cab to Fanny's apartment where she and Toto and William Joy were having some makeshift supper before returning to the studio. At first, not surprisingly, she seemed stilted and ill at ease. She had after all only been given two days' notice of my arrival. It was my first ever visit to the States and when I'd rung her that evening from the deserted Tech college she'd immediately insisted I must stay with her. But I didn't need to inquire if the gentle 'gypsy' Portuguese was living with her at present in New York. Over the phone, she was so breathlessly full of her tender devotion to the impossibly gifted violinist. Hurriedly I told her I had already consulted the *Rough Guide* and booked into a small hotel nearby. I had paid a large and non-returnable deposit so there was no going back so to speak. The hotel was a brisk twenty minute walk from her apartment. Near enough, I had obsessively calculated, to feel her proximity, yet far enough away to accommodate an aggravated jealousy.

As I shook hands with Cebola, it seemed an altogether redundant emotion, an incontinent amount of wishful thinking. Being jealous of stunningly handsome Toto was rather like being envious of a figure by Michelangelo. The Somerville graduate's apartment was covered end to end with bookshelves and fittingly enough there was an entire corner devoted to Indian religion and philosophical thought. Hiriyanna's *Outlines of Indian Philosophy*, a translation of Dinnaga on *Perception*, Walpola Rahula's *What the Buddha Said*, Radhakrishnan's *The Principal Upanishads*, Mircea Eliade's *Yoga, Freedom and Immortality*. I already knew that Toto and Fanny would regularly study these difficult works together. Meaning I, Enzo Gianmaria Mori, who always floundered when it came to the cryptic intricacies of eastern thought, was gravely one down in this respect.

Cebola smiled at me with gentle warmth and friendliness. From any point of view I had every recommendation. He knew that I was one of Fanny's oldest, closest friends and that I was also a jazz nut. The first thing I thought was, does he know, has she told him, that we were once lovers of a sort at Oxford? It might have been all of twenty years ago, but in Hindu cosmology that was surely just the blink of an eye. I had seen plenty of his recent photographs, but was quite unprepared for this beautiful man in the flesh. Ironically his handsomeness was also thoroughly American, the wholesome, bronzed good looks of some West Coast surfer from the heydays of the Beach Boys. His accent was Portuguese Californian, because his home was near Sacramento and he only ever came to New York to record or perform. Over some incendiary *chili con tacos*, Fanny told me she herself was considering an imminent move to Sacramento. She and Cebola were seriously thinking of having a shared recording studio constructed near his house. Immediately I felt myself quivering hot and cold with anguished disappointment, though of course the molten tacos brilliantly disguised the fact. Fanny went on exuberantly, seemingly oblivious of my fallen, flattened face. By contrast, the smileless bassist William Joy listened to her excited monologue as if it was a radio rendition of an indifferent play. His fellow Agog members were making highly significant plans which might seriously affect his musical future, but he gave no visible sign of being moved in any direction.

"I am one third of Agog," Joy said to me soberly. He and Cebola were sipping mineral water, only Fanny and I were drinking pink zinf. "I'm very pleased to meet you."

He could have fooled me. He had the vitality and expressiveness of an undertaker's mute. As I contemplated Fanny's Californian future with a queasy anxiety, I also warily examined the phenomenon of William Joy. How could anyone as saturnine and sombre as this strange man, be a musical success? To reverse the proposition, with a creative reputation and a talent as enormous as his, why did he never crack a grin or make a moderately amiable remark? Were all outstandingly talented artists, I asked myself, required to be full-blown oddballs as well? He was staring at his plateful of Mexican food as if it were an opaque philosophical conundrum. He ate as if under obscure and gnawing sufferance. When he ground the black pepper mill over the tacos it was as if he was grinding intractable mental processes, as if trying to sift his past from his future and his present from both. All perfectly hopeless of course, his changeless expression balefully informed us. Meanwhile he had no feasible alternative but to make the best of it, to play his bass hour after hour, day after day, and brood as little as possible. Even though, all too inevitably, it was quite impossible not to brood and ponder – all to no practical avail of course – virtually every minute of his existence.

I was invited to sit in on the evening recording session, an enormous privilege, but one that I declined. I told them I was exhausted from the flight, and already very sleepy with the zinf. Plus, I didn't want to constitute even a hypothetical distraction, even if they were to plonk me outside with the sound engineer. Given that Toto and Fanny were my very favourite jazz musicians, it was a harrowing sacrifice altogether. But in every respect, I was not up to the enormous occasion. I had listened to their last Agog album at least fifty or sixty times, and drawn a definite and wounding conclusion. With no struggle at all, I could see a symmetrical intimacy between the guitar and the violin that was more than just some neatly formal symbiosis.

I use the word 'formal' in the artistic sense, meaning that pertaining to the business of structure and form. Their form was obviously flawless, but far more importantly, the guitar and the violin evidently spoke to each other as two communing souls, spirits, perhaps Upanishadic atmans. The etymology of the word 'upa-ni-shad' signifies 'sat at the foot of', implying that the spiritual learning comes through a reverent imbibing from a wiser, more grounded, more discriminating guru. With regard to the masterful electric violin and the equally masterful electric guitar, in their separate but inextricable geniuses, the teacher-pupil *guru-shishya* musical bond could be seen to operate more like Newtonian physics than on the Indian model. The two were equal and opposite, rather than hierarchical and dependent. To put it another way, sometimes Fanny's instrument took the lead in bravely evoking an abyssal poignance, with Toto following respectfully and submissively in tow. At other times, Cebola took it upon himself to establish the astronomical coordinates or targets. He then forced his violin to take atmospheric ascensions and descensions so densely and richly elaborated, one seemed to hear the instrument irritably protesting it was after all only an inanimate object, not an animate creature...

Protesting, that is, that it was just a conduit, only an empty vessel, not an original source. Who, though, I asked myself, as I thought of the infinitely refined textures of that music, who with a mundane, quotidian vision could discern, much less formulate, a source, a Source, the source, the Source? Fanny Golightly and Toto Cebola had their hard-won gnoses, their spiritual disciplines, their sacred oriental texts. Fanny was also a conspicuously heavy drinker, but then geniuses by definition can only be fired by their irreconcilable contradictions. Out of which comes fructifying, medicinal, liberating art for The Lesser Fucked-up, for all we smaller, lesser and eminently forgettable mortals. As well as jazz, I also trusted to alcohol for transcendence, a fool's prescription if ever there was. En route to my hotel, I reflected that the only thing which stopped me being an alcoholic was the helpful intervention of nausea at a critical point. I loved wine, I couldn't get enough of it, but thankfully it could always get enough of me. I hunched along the bustling sidewalks, head down as I finally concluded the glaringly obvious. This trip wasn't going to help anything at all as far as I was concerned. A gauche, uneasy stranger to this city, now and again I examined the inhabitants and studied their dress, their speech, their physiognomies. It would have been altogether eye-opening and educative, had I been in less of a hopelessly lovelorn mood. I realised my copy of Stendhal's *Love* was still in my pocket, and, dizzy with pink zinf, I was seriously tempted to open it up and start reading to an inquisitive crowd.

What after all did I know about the Americans of the late twentieth century? Principally, and to quote from another incontinent boozer, Brendan Behan, that they were open-minded, friendly and above all *curious* about anything and everything. Otherwise, Enzo Mori, obscure provincial Tech lecturer, what other choice tit-bits of reductive and racialist folklore do you happen to have to hand? Just look at them all, look at all these Americans, take a dekker, Enzo Gianmaria Mori, the forty-year-old, miserably infatuated English Eyetie. Most obviously, and most unhingingly to a man of mixed race like myself, they *look* no bloody different from us. There were more fat, far more obese folk among them, of course, as this was the world's most prosperous country. Otherwise they looked exactly like those friendly, unassuming studio audiences on the Oprah Winfrey and the Ricky Lake Shows. As motley, as sunnily homely, as the faces in a Working Men's Club in Cleator Moor, Workington or Whitehaven.

In those same remote English towns, they watch Oprah and Ricky as raptly as they do in Des Moines, Baton Rouge, Sarasota or (with Portuguese subtitles) in Porto, Coimbra or Póvoa do Varzim. Foreign and domestic audiences gazing intently at the studio audiences who are drawn addictively, they'd be the first to laugh and admit, to enjoy all these vicarious public confessionals. To hear for example about A two-timing B, or about C cuckolding D, and/or about Y sleeping covertly with the teenage daughter of Z. Then, without taking breath or even pausing to furrow the brow, they will poke their generous American oars in and give sage and/or ingenuous advice on how A, B, C, D, X, Y, Z should sort it all out between themselves. I, right enough, I,

Enzo, son of Vincenzo, ought to be paraded as a prize studio exhibit on the Oprah or the Ricky Show. Let there be me hunched and roundly interrogated, on the floodlit centre seat. Let there be also Fanny half-tight, tense but grinning, perched on the left. Let there be sober Toto Cebola shaking his fine, fair, Portuguese gypsyish, hundred-per-cent Levantine Californian hair, seated to the right. Let curious, candid, unshockable, tolerant, uncensorious America give advice on the wisest resolution of this interestingly three-pronged paradigmatic cis- and transatlantic West Cumbrio-Luso-Mediterranean heartbreak...

We had arranged, Toto, William, Fanny and I, to meet for dinner at Fanny's at the same time tomorrow. They were up to their eyes with their long-awaited album of course, while I was just a hedonistic tourist. As for any meaningful conversation, any renewed and resonant, historically significant intimacy with elusive Fanny... I realised that at this precise moment in time my mind was performing exactly like an improvisatory jazz instrument. Worse still, and more to the point, the whole of my bloody life, whether taken linearly or laterally, historically or in the eternally continuous present, *was a four-decades-long bloody jazz composition*. My jazz, the jazz suite dedicated to the undying memory of the highly formalised jazz of Samuel Beckett, entitled *Enzo Goes On Going On*, was far too frequently subject to internal modifications by way of alterations in body chemistry. One simple illustrative equation being $EM + PZ = QUEJ$. (Enzo's Mind plus Pink Zinfandel = A Qualified and Unimaginatively Enzoesque Jazz, jazz as atonally performed in a dense fog, and not on a clear, pellucid summer's day.) Once, some fifteen years ago, I had known a brilliant Norwegian freeform trombonist who had obvious designs on my Fanny (bawdy paronomastic mutterings from Hornblower about taking care of the old bowhind), who told me he invariably played his trombone under the influence of psilocybin. His name very appropriately was Bent Pedersen, and his eyes had the biggest bags I'd ever seen. He was about thirty then, in 1976, so must be at least forty-five now by 1991. In fact he might even be dead of psychotropic inanition, it was a very long time since I had last noticed his name on any ECM credits.

The next day I was about to leave a bookstore just down from the hotel when I bumped into William Joy. I had spent the morning doing a brisk *Rough Guide* itinerary of Manhattan, trying to reassure myself I was here for the enriching experience as well as for these matters of the heart. My current reading matter would not permit the illusion. At one point I had rested in a Jewish coffee shop, taken out my copy of *Love*, and perused the great master on the matter of tortured, romantic anguish. Up and down in wildly hyperbolic, never exponential arcs goes the aching heart of the overwrought lover: on the wink of an indifferent eye, on the movement of a capricious eyebrow, on the hallucinatory suggestion of a fleetingly tender smile. With a feeling of numb fatalistic desperation, I realised that the minute orchestration of these agonised nuances of acceptance and rejection, and the *apparent* acceptance and the *apparent* rejection, was like nothing so much as a teetering, fussy and minutely nuanced *jazz* ...

Joy walked across to the till where I was stood, with a faintly solicitous, almost an hospitable expression. He stopped short and scrutinised my face perhaps rather too intently, almost as if to check I had shaved and washed myself that morning. Finally he examined my bookshop purchase and gave an acquiescent shrug.

"Very interesting," he said. "Duhamel of all people. That's an extremely interesting thing."

I didn't know whether he meant the particular book, the fact it was me reading it, or their anomalous concurrence. I looked at him with sudden deference. "Do you know his works?"

"Rather too well I do. I once wrote a short undergraduate dissertation on his novels and essays. Before that I read *The*

248

Pasquier Chronicles for French A level."

"Oh," I said awkwardly. "I had no idea. That you were – "

He allowed his thin lips to crack at the corners. "That I play jazz and I'm also a brainbox graduate? But as Fanny's best friend you already know another highbrow jazzplayer. There are more of our type than you think perhaps. You remember the organist Mike Ratledge of Soft Machine? I believe he was at your Oxford college, wasn't he?"

I blushed, despite myself. "I... those Pasquier books are wonderful. I almost cried when I finished the last of them. There's nothing comparable in any language is there?"

He agreed with solemn enthusiasm. "They are addictive from the word go. An anguished saga which ought to chill, but actually delights and warms us. Even that rogue of a father's flagrant adulteries, even his unrepentant deceitfulness. He is absolutely engaging isn't he, despite that?" Suddenly he cracked a generous, wholehearted grin. "Do you remember his charming habit of telling people with big noses on public transport to do something about their disgraceful features?"

Wonderingly I focused on this interesting change in him. We chuckled noisily, then he stopped and surveyed me possibly warily.

"The *Salavin* trilogy you've just bought. Do you know it?"

"I've read it but I've never actually owned a copy till now. All his stuff is out of print back home. I had to get it on a library loan."

"It's even more remarkable than the Pasquier. D'you recall the mad scene right at the start where the pen-pusher goes and puts his finger inside his astonished boss's *ear*? Just to see what his reaction would be."

We enthused about this virtuoso exponent of twentieth-century alienation who bizarrely enough was a bustling man of affairs. Duhamel, the qualified doctor, was an army physician in the Great War. An expert in trench horror like Barbusse, yet a qualified optimist who could convey human frailty with warmth, tenderness and enormous humour. Photographs of the author in middle and old age show someone looking bizarrely like a bespectacled Sussex scout master. This gawky, gormless character, Joy opined tersely, was the undoubted forerunner and superior of Camus, Beckett and the rest. By then, we had moved across to the bookstore café and Joy was guzzling some Key Lime Pie with his bitter espresso. I was halfway through some limply improvised impressions of Manhattan when he interrupted me gruffly:

"I'm here because I'm taking a break from doing the last track of *Amok*. I've told them I'll be back at two o'clock, but they can wait." He shuffled rather roughly in his chair and squared up to me with an uncomfortably direct gaze. "OK, Enzo, we know what I'm doing. But what, I ask myself, are *you* doing here?"

I stiffened and flushed, altogether startled by his inquisitional tone. Yet I tried to discount the seeming rudeness, and pretend it was something else, as I burbled on about unearthing American imprints of out-of-print books. Joy glanced at me drily, though not altogether impatiently.

"You know I don't mean that. I mean what are you *doing* here? Here in the States in New York?"

He could see that I was crimson with guilt. "Seeing Fanny of course. Visiting a very old friend. What on earth…?"

He sighed with a stiff expression. "On a quest more like? On a matter of life and death?"

I glared at him angrily. The son of the Calabrian father came blustering to the surface. "What the fucking hell d'you mean?"

"I'm sorry," he said smilelessly. "But it's all too obvious. You're the same age as me, but you wear your heart on your sleeve like a very young boy. You are very youthful, very sensitive, and at present you're really very unhappy."

I snorted and fingered my glazed and painted coffee cup. "It's none of your bloody business what I'm doing."

He frowned with a look of archaic, ecclesiastic severity. "You are right. Absolutely not. I have no moral right whatever. It's just that you are so remarkably boyish in your… what? Your touchingly, transparently unguarded, young soul. It seems a real shame to watch you chasing after a ghost."

There was almost a minute of bruised silence as I sulked into my coffee. Eventually I croaked very throatily, "Don't you think I know it? I can see alright where her heart lies. I can see how hopeless it all bloody is. But my heart is where it is, and it can't bloody well stop wanting what it wants."

Joy corrected me carefully, in a wry, professorial manner. "You missed out an important adverb there."

I grunted. "Oh? A word that ends in 'ly', you mean. And which verb would it happen to modify?"

"You know damn well which verb. The verb is 'stop'. The adverb is 'easily'. The full sense of it, your present crisis, is that you can't *easily* stop wanting Fanny Golightly."

I mumbled at him childishly, "Is that a bloody fact? I'm so grateful you've made the proper diagnosis."

He signalled for two more coffees, then turned to confront me. "It stares you, me, and more importantly Fanny, in the face. At the moment, as you know, she's bubbling and babbling rather feverishly about her Sacramento move. It will definitely happen, there's no doubt at all about that. But because you are a dear old friend and she cares a great deal about you, under-neath the effervescence she's rather more fretful than usual. As you can see, she is very deeply in love with Cebola. You must know as well as anyone, these things only happen once."

I tore at my Duhamel receipt as if it were the love bond between Toto and Fanny. "Know it, you say? I can see it, and I can know it for a truth in this damn head on my bloody shoul-ders. It's up there alright, but it's not down there in here." He watched me angrily battering my red sweater as if trying to resuscitate myself after a cardiac seizure. "You may as well try asking me to stop eating."

Joy shook his head soberly. "Scarcely. Your twenty-year addic-tion to Fanny is profound, but it is a one-way addiction for all that. She doesn't love you, Enzo, she loves only Toto. She loves him like a lover loves a lover. And you know, before she told me all about your epic infatuation, I had already guessed the pres-ence of some invisible third party."

I flinched with astonished humiliation. "What? You mean that she's actually discussed *us*, the business of her and me. That – "

"Not lightly or flippantly, I can assure you. But she looked very anxious, very unsettled, after you rang her two days ago. She seemed as if she was coming to some point of long delayed and harrowing confrontation. She was so painfully uneasy about it, she had to talk to someone. After all, she was halfway through making an important album when you rang. It might sound banal, but she is also a businesswoman who has her professional responsibilities."

"Great! So she coolly talked about – "

"No, not at all coolly. With enormous respect, enormous tenderness, enormous care when she spoke of you. That is what you own of Fanny Golightly, all of that. A precious thing surely. All that tender, sisterly, perhaps motherly care."

"Shish," I said disgusted. "I'm fucking off. I'm bloody going now. If you don't bloody mind."

"Sit down. Please. Here's your coffee. Thank you so much. Thank you. I think you should. Go I mean, go period. Seriously. You told us last night you have an open ticket so you ought to go back to England I think. If you don't want to do that, then you could travel on to Mexico or Texas or Jamaica, or wherever the hell. I'm not saying it's for the benefit of our band, for Agog, that's altogether a secondary consideration. It's not even about Fanny's happiness, though that's important too. She has found happiness by falling in love one thousand per cent with a man who loves the same in return. She can't be shaken out of that, but of course she can be painfully upset by thinking that she is painfully upsetting you. The only one who can do anything constructive about this hopeless emotional stalemate is yourself. You want what is never to be had, Enzo Mori, and therefore you are acting in bad faith." He examined his neat fingernails minutely. "Not that it's at all easy for anyone to renounce what they crave with all their soul. But it can be done, as history proves."

I glared at him viciously, like the vengeful son of my father. "Tell me how it's done, big boy! Give me a handy fucking hint!

Not that I think you're any certified bloody expert. I've only spent a few hours in your company. But you know something…?"

I paused for effect, but Joy confronted me with an impossible, unrufflable serenity. Fidgeting with the outsize sugar bowl, I went on angrily:

"You might be another Jaco Pastorius, or another Miroslav Vitous, but you strike me as one of the most miserable, wretched buggers I've ever met! You look just as if someone went and pissed inside your mouth on the day you were born… and you haven't ever got round to spitting it out!"

Joy responded in a very patient, even fatherly fashion. "Anyone else would give identical advice. Find some distraction from your destructive addiction. Bury yourself in your work perhaps."

I found myself focusing on the very bored expression of the young Hispanic waiter's face. "But I hate my bloody work. It makes me an income, but it makes me nothing else."

Joy turned to examine the same waiter. "So change your job. Go abroad perhaps. Nobody has sent you into internal exile in West Cumbria, have they? Get another qualification if need be. Teach English in Botswana or Bangladesh or Bhutan. Why not try and help the truly needy, instead of encouraging a quite pointless emotional neediness in yourself…?"

I gulped and clenched my fists with a venomous South Italian indignation. I knew that Joy originated from Birmingham, and I could easily picture Vincenzo Mori urging me to throw the sugar plus the pepper plus the salt mill in his lugubrious bloody 'Bummygum' face.

"To hell with you and your pisswise advice! Who the fucking hell are you to lecture me from on high? You can tell me something else, while we're at it. If you're so infinitely bloody wise, how come you look so utterly bloody *dead* on the outside, Mr Joy?"

This flat, very affectless Englishman looked at me with a queer, slow-motion awakening, as if effortfully reaching up from his sombrest depths. Bizarrely, I thought of some miraculously weeping holy statue from my father's peasant homeland. Perhaps once every decade, I thought, Joy showed to the world this remarkable and embarrassing spectacle.

"Why do I look so grotesquely sad sometimes? Perhaps for most of the time? Do you really want to know?"

"Not at all," I scoffed. "I couldn't care bloody less."

He shrugged. "Very well. Maybe I'm making an error of judgement, but I'll tell you anyway. Even though you don't wish to hear it. I wonder where I should start, Enzo Mori. Like everyone else, you see, I've had my trials. *So what's new, eh?* as a New York Jew would say at this point. Show me someone who hasn't had any. In my case, it was the commonest tragedy of all, a sudden bereavement. Though with a really young child, perhaps it has been more of a lasting tragedy. I had a little son, called Samuel, only six years old, who was killed by a hit-and-run drunk."

I froze in my capacious, ornate rush chair, and stammered, "Wh – "

"It happened about ten years ago, in Birmingham, but a decade is less than nothing when it comes to your only child. This drunk, who was called Wetherby, had three previous drink-driving convictions, but amazingly he was let off with a two-year jail sentence. In fact he was out after less than a year. He can be observed, almost every day, walking around the middle of Birmingham as free as a bird. I have seen him myself there several times. That's not the end of young Samuel's story, though. My son had developed chronic leukaemia when he was only three years old. He had been through gruelling chemotherapy and bone marrow transplants for another three. Of course, three years isn't such a long period for a man, but it was half my son's brief life in effect. Samuel was enjoying a successful remission when he was run over by this drunk..."

I stared petrified at the pretty pattern of our pristine table-cloth. "God alive. I thought – "

"You thought my sombre face was just an affectation? You're not the only one to think that."

"It's enough to finish a man off. I've got two children myself. I – "

"You think so?"

His voice had maintained a dispassionate monotone, while I seemed to be twitching uncontrollably. I heard myself groaning, "God Almighty..."

Joy was concerned enough to touch my shaking hand. "Please. You don't need be so upset."

I stopped the twitching and sniffed back a grown man's tears. "Upset is the least I can bloody be. I'm so damn sorry. But if, if..."

He smiled. "If it had happened to you?"

"I think I'd have bloody killed myself! Or certainly the bastard who killed your young son."

"Hardly. Suicide achieves precisely nothing. Revenge, as a rule, achieves even less. It's all there in black and white, in the New Testament and elsewhere. Ordinary commonsense and the history of twentieth-century warfare, would suggest the same. I don't really need to go on, do I? I have my quantity of personal baggage, just like everyone else. The signs of certain indelible griefs sometimes seep out through my face I suppose. They have to go somewhere. Like the transpirations of a plant or a tree. But – "

"Yes?" I said tensely, and absurdly expectantly.

"I have my bass! I have my music. I have my jazz. I have my talent. I have myself to pour into my talent. I think my son Samuel is also there alive somehow in the playing of my bass. The sores of my bereavement have become the 'aching sweetness' of my music. I'm quoting rather whimsically from a 1988 article in *Wire* magazine. They referred to my playing as 'achingly sweet'. But," frowning and pouting comically at his expensive watch, "look I need to get back now. Fanny my businesslike Cumbrian boss will kick my Birmingham arse if I don't. And please, forget everything I said just now. Advice is cheap, and no one knows the answer to anyone else's problems. They really don't. After the death of my son I was advised to go and visit a Zen monastery in Japan, but instead I went on a trip to Patmos with my wife. I started to read the Bible while I was there on the isle of Revelations, and it definitely helped. It helped my wife too, I think. But as for Fanny and you, right enough, it's none of my business. You're a guest of hers here in New York, so of course you can do what you like."

♪♪

Joy was not exactly my lasting Nemesis, much less had he played the unlikely part of my transatlantic guardian angel. Yet he had certainly constituted a fateful 'encounter' which was definable by its absolute and disconcerting timeliness. In much the same way that in 1967 I had been rescued from my provincial stupor by a magical ingredient called 'jazz', so a quarter of a century later I was given a perfectly timed if brutal kick up the arse by a well-meaning jazz practitioner. A man, that is, whose burden of personal tragedy had not made him immune to the pettier sufferings of someone like me.

When I got back to England, the first thing I did was telephone the family home. I wanted to let my father know I was seriously considering doing a TEFL course down in London. Afterwards, I might well take a post teaching English in the remotest, most desolate reaches of my paternal homeland. The far south of Italy was still very poor in parts in 1991, and I felt as if I needed to understand the inscrutable, unarguably Moorish nature of my ancestral roots. Until now, rather anxious at what I might find, I had never once visited Italy, north or south. Bizarre as it seems, my only significant understanding of South Italy had been via the fiction of Carlo Levi and the film of his novel *Christ Stopped at Eboli*. It had featured my very favourite movie star, Gianmaria Volonte. Gaunt and handsome Gianmaria Volonte had almost the same name as me, Enzo Gianmaria Mori, and I was so proud of that startling fact. That was my provisional plan, at any rate. For all I knew it might be the Sudan or Mozambique or Guinea-Bissau or Burkina Faso where I ended up teaching the indispensable and lucrative lingua franca, *Inglese*. Did any of those places, I suddenly wondered, excepting Napoli perhaps, have any indigenous jazz bands? Or was that an insensitive, ethnocentric and absolutely idiotic bloody question?

Before I could spit out my plans over the phone, he had something he was dying to tell me. Stirred, not to say stunned, by his old buddy Holland becoming a convert and latterly a proselytiser of modern jazz, Vince Mori had decided two nights ago to give the baffling matter some serious study. Maybe in the past he had missed something, maybe he was still missing something, perhaps he could even extend his Chompin Stompers repertoire, and command more than forty pounds a set, expenses included, in 1991. He had been quite alone that momentous evening for the breathtaking experiment. My mother was staying overnight with her sister Concepta in Barrow, there was no aesthetic distraction other than the three-litre flagon of chianti he had just bought on offer from the Whitehaven Coop. By chance, there happened to be lying around half a dozen labelled tapes I'd recorded on Vince's immaculate expensive new hi-fi. Taped from the CD originals, they were the ones I hadn't been able to fit in my New York bag, so had left them at the paternal home for the time being. As far as I could remember they were recent albums by Chick Corea, John Surman, John McLaughlin, Terje Rypdal and... Keith Jarrett.

"Fust of all," he began in a laborious, discursive voice, as if we both had all the time in the world, "I played that penis feller Chip Curry..."

I experienced a vertiginous second of absolute and baffling incomprehension. "You played *what*?"

"Ship Curry. I look at CD and he have big specs an big grin, like nice feller sell taties and *cipolla* in fruit chop in Whitey Vaughan. Shick Curry Hurry. Bouncy bouncy *carnevale* shtuff. That was OK, not bad when it was cholly an lively to listen. But then Shick, he start playin blurry Moss Art shtuff, blurry great sweeps across the blurry piano like ole Rubbish and Landart pisht on blurry wishky. So I say fuggit, Shick, *mi scusi*, and turn the bugger off. Fums down like in Roman arena, tree outer blurry ten..."

"Oh yes?" I snorted. "One of the finest jazz pianists of the last twenty-five years and you'd give Chick Corea all of three out of ten? You know, you should get yourself a job hosting the 1991 Eurovision Song Contest, Vince. You speak at least one and a half languages after all."

"*Mi scusi*. Two outer ten. *Trei* was too blurry zhenrus. Next, Enzo, I try play that crazy Nodway feller, Terry Ribble. *Basta, putana*, I haff nearly blurry died wit chock."

I rasped my throat impatiently and wondered where all this ludicrous vehemence was leading. Though his disparagement of my music was par for the course, he seemed exceedingly excited about something...

"He play *chitarra, è vero*? He play gittara, but onest to *Dio*, Enzo, I taught his instumint was some blurry walrush howlin in blurry Nod Pole's aunt's attic! I taught it was blurry polo pear goin 'whoo whoo' in Souf blurry Pole or in blurry *Islanda*. Is wah-wah echo stuff, no, Ribble play? Listen lad, I giff Terry Ribble..."

I interrupted roughly, "You give Terje Rypdal two out of ten as well. Pity. I guess it would cut him to the quick if he saw you outdoing him at Bransty Legion with the Chompin Stompers."

"No. I giff him minus two! Did you know, Enzo, that in maf-muckits they haff negatif numbers, *anche*? They is less than blurry nowt these minusish. Seems crazy, but is true, Enzo."

I grimaced at my phone. "You don't say."

"As for that udder feller, Chon Summon. He play soprano sex an bass blurry clarrynet, but is like he haff *mal di dente* tuthhake an is too blurry stingy to pay a fuggy *dentista*. He also like echo-echo lektrik whoo-whoo like on Blackpull or Muckham gosht trains. Chon Summon I giff..."

"Minus two? Minus ten?"

"No," judiciously. "I giff him one and haff. One of his chuns is pretty and shimple and it make me quite happy for two minute. As for John Micky Gloveline, you know what I fink of him. Minus *cinquanta*. He go so fast, *ho la nausea*. He make me blurry traffle sick, an I only shtannin in my own blurry *casa* trinkin bitter blurry chianti! Also, why is he callt hissel 'Mamasumfin' John Micky Gloveline? *Non* blurry *capito*, Enzo."

I hesitated. Why was the world's finest-ever jazz guitarist called Mahavishnu John McLaughlin? How to explain this to my hungry-for-knowledge father.

"It's his Indian name, Vince."

"*Che?* Micky Gloveline? He is an *indiano?*"

"No. It's his religion. He's originally from West Yorkshire."

"Ah, *capito*. There is lot of Sikhs in Lids an Braffer an Pudsy an Kitley an Bitley, you know. In fack, I met one onesh in a pup in Shappeltown wif miners' darts team an *tutto il giorno* he was wore his *turbante*. He was sek a plezhunt *amichevole* feller. So your Mama Gloveline jazz feller is a Sikh from Lids?"

"No... I... Listen, forget him! Tell me instead about Keith Jarrett? Did you play that as well? Did you know that it was Keith Jarrett who was responsible for Watson Holland's musical conversion last week? I played him *Facing You* and bugger me he burst into tears of joy, and now he wants to buy everything he's ever recorded! It's as sure as shot old Watson's going to end up a serious jazz nut. So, go on, what effect did Jarrett have on you?"

There was a noisy liquid pause and I gathered that the three-litre Coop chianti must be on offer for the whole of the month.

"Yis. I listen to Watson'sh *favorito*. I play yon Kif Charrock feller, OK. An know what? Know sumfin, Enzo lad?"

"Yes?" I said, sharing his mounting excitement.

"I fort he was blurry *genio*! I rilly did, son. I fort he was fuggy sheenyush! *Dotato di potere musicale superiore al normale!*"

"A genius?" I said almost gurgling with delighted vindication. "Really? You're not kidding me, Dad? You really did?"

"I play same alpum Watson playt. *Faced Wif You.* Then I listen to very same track that old Olland luff. The track which make him gry an sop an whip, whip. *My Liddy, My Chile.* An you know what, Enzo?"

"What Dad?"

"*Voglio plangere anche!* I wish to blurry gry as well! In fack I did blurry gry. I gry fuggy blurry puckets, Enzo! To me it seem oh so *triste*, oh so *addolorata*. It was oh so blurry damn fuggy bottyful."

I felt myself almost tearful at this point.

"I'm so pleased, Dad! I really am! You know what? I'm forty years old, I'm a middle-aged man. For the first time in my life, I feel you and me, father and son, are having something like a sensible conversation. Better late than never, eh? You're a trad man and I'm a modern man, but somehow we've almost managed to gel for once! But hell, how come it's taken us so bloody long, Vince?"

"Such me, son. *Dio*, I have allus try to prick you up on strait an blurry arrow. But you haff never blurry listen to me once."

"Forget about all that!" I replied, moderately ecstatic at this new-found intimacy with my hard-boiled, unyielding old father. "So how many did you give him out of ten, Dad?"

"*Che?* Which? You my *figlio*, Enzo? How many I giff you? I giff you four, no I giff you five outer ten. Cos you're my son and I muss luff you even if you damn fuggy *idiota* always."

"No. No, not me! We're not talking about me, Dad. I know that you love me OK. But do you love Keith Jarrett, is what I need to know. How many out of ten do you give him?"

"Hic," he grunted. "I giff him ownly minush two."

"You..." I squeaked at this pitiless old critic, aghast. "You *what?*"

I was as stunned as some comic marionette. I was like another little Eyetie called Pinocchio. For God knows what reason, I felt so incredibly upset. The phone receiver almost fell from my hand...

"Eh?" I shouted angrily. "But you just told me that he made you bloody cry! You said that Jarrett's wonderful haunting music seemed so sad, so beautiful, so melancholy and so magical and so marvellous..."

An old West Cumbrian Italian snorted very derisively down his British Telecom mouthpiece. "I haff not blurry say all of blurry *that!*"

I shook the phone in a childish fury. I hissed down it angrily, "You implied it! You did! You bloody well did! If his music really did all that for you, how *dare* you give it only minus two out of ten?"

Then came the wisdom of ages, the self-protective instinct of the inscrutable and untrusting Calabrian peasant. As a result of which, by the very next day, I had already decided against teaching any English in Reggio di Calabria. A year after that, you'd have found me working for a pittance in a rundown technical college on the sweltering outskirts of Ouagadougou.

"Is very simple. Cos I was blurry *pisht* when I was listening to *Faced Wif You!*"

"No," I sighed miserably. "You can't say that. That can't poss– "

"I was cryin an owlin an whippin at my Eyefie, only cos I was fuggy well pisht wif tree litre of chianti! On next day, when I am called Stan Sober, I have play it all again. I playt all of *Faced Wif You*, an I listen *molto scrupoloso*. An you know what?"

"What?" I said in a ludicrously hollow voice.

"I dint like any of it! *Niente*. I taught it was all blurry crap. Like all modern chass, Enzo. *Putana*, I cunt blurry whishel it, an if I cannot whishel a piss of fuggy music, it int a blurry chun for me! Me, son, I fink Watson Olland is luffer of modem chass now, only because he is in blurry luff. An as for that ole *donna* of his, wassacommee?"

"Madge," I responded numbly. "Madge Bimson from Nether Wasdale."

"Match? Haff you seen her, this ole Match Plimsoll lass? She is really blurry uckly, son, she is no blurry Michelangelo. Yet luff, *amore*, you know, it make a man blind, so blind as a fuggy pat. An sumfin else while we is at it, son…"

"Yes," I growled. "What else have you got to say?"

"About Nut Yolk, Enzo?"

"What about it?" I said. "What about New York, Vince?"

"Ow is yon swit little lash called Funny Gelati?"